PRAISE FOR THE

G000122811

OFF THE E

So Tense. I have just finished *Off The Edge*. What a story, I could hardly bear to read the final chapter. The book has really alive characters who you can imagine, and vivid descriptions so you can really visualize the landscape. I can't wait to read the next. I remembered a lot about the land and wilderness, and I could just feel it as if I was there. So, so Good! *Gayle Comeau*

Really gripping. With many novels, you have to read a bit to get into them. With *Off The Edge*, the prologue kind of hits the reader...like a fish biting on a hook... All the action really sustained my interest. I also liked how the subplots intertwined and came together...This has to be a series! *Ginny McCuen*

Wow! I really got into the complexities of plot and simply couldn't put it down. Read well into the very early morning. It's an edge of your seat suspense thriller with a complex plot that unfolds with seemingly unrelated events in multiple locations. It presents unique challenges for the cast of heroes to discover and solve in order to rescue and save innocent lives that are in mortal danger. The ending appeals to even the romantic female reader, which is unusual for most plots in the thriller genre. *Jeanne Rex*

This is one of the most exciting books... I couldn't put it down. I had to know what happened next as I got caught up in the search by Jim and his buddy Brush, first to find the Pasayten Killers and then to work out how to stop the spread of the virus. I liked the parts in the wilderness. I'm not a scientist but I found I was gripped by the science. Then when we got to a wild car chase through Seattle followed by a great gun battle and helicopter chase. The end left me wanting to know what happens next. *Doug Dunlop*

I hate that Najma! *Betty Rhodes*

Intoxicating!!! Randall Perry captivates your immediate attention from the get go. That fatal day of September 11 clearly demonstrated to America that terrorists can extend their reach well beyond their borders but Dr. Perry reminds us all that terrorism can also be generated from within. The twisting plots and dual story lines are intriguing and action packed and constantly keeps you guessing. The suspense in Off The Edge keeps you 'on the edge'... *Albert Klychak*

OVER THE LINE

This book had me gripped from page one. I like the variety of characters & the ways they find of dealing with a whole host of difficulties & experiences. It's nice to meet some old friends from Off The Edge & see them change & develop but this book stands on its own. As always with RS Perry one of the most intriguing aspects of the novel is the way in which very different worlds are woven together in one exciting narrative. *Jan Good*

Having enjoyed Perry's first book *Off the Edge* in his series about the secret missions of Jim Johnson, Assistant Head of the State Department's Biological Warfare, I looked forward to reading his second *Over the Line,* knowing it would be good entertainment during the 6 hour train ride ahead of me. I was not disappointed. In his inimitable style, Perry hooked me at once with his prologue (just as he had done with his prologue in *Off the Edge*) and I read the book in one sitting, unable to put it down. I was unprepared however for the attachment I would develop to his characters. There is depth and feeling in this book as Perry carefully develops and crafts his characters. Throughout this book, Perry lets us almost live in the shoes of his characters, to involve us in his soul-searching study of good and bad and what makes people do what they do. *Catherine Fosnot*

OUT OF TIME

ISBN 978-0-9880827-2-4

OUT OF TIME

Paper back, exclusive rights, CA

Published by Penelope Ltd.

OUT

OF

TIME

RS PERRY

Acknowledgements

With grateful thanks to:
Wayne, George, Eva Lea, Loretta, Karin, Lanette and Mason,
whose hard work and friendship
made the ranch what it was.

Rosie O Twisp, Guiness, Munchkin, Tinkerbelle,
Benji, Sharifa, Pipestone, Dawn, Junior-Junior,
(the boss peacock), and all the
other wonderful animals that
made living at
Wolf Canyon Ranch such a joy.

Along with the wild animals and birds
who lived peacefully with their domestic relatives;
the people and the animals combined to make
Wolf Canyon Ranch
a special place.

With thanks to Jenny who read Out of Time
several times and wrote the first review.

I cannot praise enough the
dedication of Madeline Hopkins, for tireless editing.
No one can do without the advice of skilled,
caring, editor, especially me.

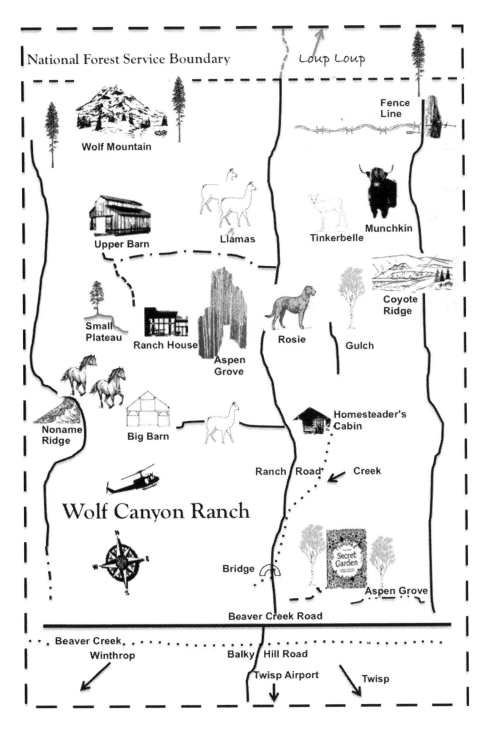

Prologue

Guantánamo Bay, US territory, Cuba, Aug 30, 2000.

S ergeant Alex Smith struggled to keep the smirk off his face as he sat at the console controlling the security gates for the CIA's new and illegal detention center. He had enlisted in the army to escape his small hometown and see the world, but it had not turned out as he'd expected. So far all he had experienced was army training camps, noisy barracks, KP duty, the white-trash mecca that was Biloxi, Mississippi, and now this holding tank for the worst of the worst. Prisoners too insidious to be tried and detained through normal channels, or so the CIA said.

Forty months of one dipshit after another riding my ass in one hellhole after another for less than minimum wage, he said to himself.

Smith knew he should have been promoted by now; he could run this place blindfolded. *Only one scrawny woman prisoner.* But the army did not agree with him. He was not rated as leadership material, and his peers just didn't like him. He had been posted to dead-end jobs because the army expected no more of him than he now did of the army. Smith's future was just as bleak as it had been after high school and he knew it.

But all that was about to change. Buck-Sergeant Alex Smith was going to secure his future with the press of button. He would even get to screw the army in the process. After a tiny, unauthorized movement, he'd pocket more money than most of his soon-to-be-ex colleagues would see in their lifetimes. Enough to finance a lifetime lounging on the beach in some third world country, maybe he'd even open a bar.

Smith glanced at the clock; it was time. Still he hesitated. Technically what they had asked him to do—what they were paying him to do—was treason, and if even half of what he'd heard about this prisoner was true, she deserved to be incarcerated. Though personally he doubted that prisoner 49C was the dangerous, cold-hard killer the CIA said she was. *So what,* he thought. *Even if she is, she won't be the only nasty woman there. The world will survive and I'll have money.*

Smith shook off his doubts and let the smirk spread across his face; none of this was his problem, and the army only had itself to blame. Without another thought, he pressed the button that opened the outer gates, allowing anyone free entry to or exit from Guantánamo Bay's top secret facility: Camp X-Ray.

The new head of the Siastra cartel had spent months repairing and rebuilding his reputation and his organization after the mysterious destruction of the cartel's headquarters and the death of its former leader. Guillermo had been driven, brutal, and focused, now remorselessly strengthening his position as the head of Mexico's most powerful cartel. As second-in-command, he had been away on business when the headquarters was destroyed, but even with all his connections, he had been unable to discover who had carried out the attack and how they had managed to succeed where so many others had failed. The Mexican government had claimed responsibility, but Guillermo saw right through that particular politically expedient fiction. They could never have pulled it off without him hearing of it first through his contacts; the Mexican government had feebly tried before. Yet his inquiries into the matter, few of them pleasant or painless for those he queried, led only to unanswered questions and dead-ends, reinforcing his determination to find the truth.

Guillermo had assembled the best team of computer experts that he could buy. They easily hacked into the Mexican government's computers. Although they were more skilled than his previous computer team—all of whom had been killed when his hacienda was attacked—they'd been unable to tell Guillermo who had done it.

Guillermo, a firm believer in the future of the electronic age, had then recruited even more computer technicians, mostly hackers, insisting that they broaden the search until eventually a small detail was found in the CIA's computers; this led to an astonishing discovery. The female assassin he had recently employed had not been killed, as he had been informed, but was incarcerated at a CIA facility in Cuba.

Guillermo had had strong contacts in the Cuban government and military before the hacienda attack dented his cartel's influence. However, with zeal, and money, he had rebuilt his influence in Cuba, with one goal in mind: to find and vanquish those who had tried to destroy his organization, his headquarters, his power, his reputation, and his future: the assassin, once free, was the only person who could tell him what had happened, who the attackers were, and what had become of his cartel men and his staff who were not executed by the Mexican government. He had to learn what had happened. He had to know. In Guillermo's business, the only way to stay on top was to avenge all attacks and eliminate all foes. His enemies feared him and consequently respected him, or they would try to kill him.

And so Guillermo had plotted and schemed and paid, and now, at long last, he would be reunited with his captured assassin. No longer would she be prisoner 49C in the CIA's purportedly impregnable, secret, new detention center. For the promise of a few million dollars, the gullible soldier was going to let her walk right out the front door.

Now Guillermo waited. Soon Najma would be here, and soon he would have his answers.

Footsteps grew louder in the dim hall behind three-stripe Buck-Sergeant Alex Smith as he waited at his console dreaming of his beach bar. The buzzer didn't startle him. He was expecting them; he'd opened the door. This was the penultimate step before his payday, the worst but most necessary part as far he was concerned. They had informed him that the Taser would shock him and knock him out but cause no lasting damage. Smith had read up on Tasers and even though he hated shocks, it seemed that the information was accurate: this would likely keep him out of prison, and it wouldn't kill him. So with a little trepidation, he had agreed to the small but necessary incapacitation. The footsteps came closer and he sensed shadows moving behind him. He gritted his teeth as he focused on the controls in front of him, steeling himself against the Taser's jolt. Any second now, he would feel the high voltage sting him into unconsciousness.

Instead, he felt nothing; his brain, communicating thoughts in milliseconds, merely questioned why electricity would make him see red—the red of his blood as it splattered on the glass monitor and console in front of him.

Chapter 1

Colonel James L. Johnson, the Biological Warfare Center's special agent, lay relaxed on his back, fingers interlaced behind his head, surrounded by blue bunchgrass that moved listlessly in a soft breeze, on the top of Coyote Ridge. This was the longest stretch of time he had spent on his eastern Washington ranch in years, and it hadn't been by choice. Jim was on an enforced rest ordered by his boss, General Will Crystal, while he recovered from the gunshot wounds he had received in Mexico, courtesy of Guillermo's assassin: Najma. Even here, he could see her obsidian eyes, so dark and penetrating that they felt like black ice, instead of living tissue.

Scattered fluffy white clouds coalesced, churning, boiling upward as he slowly erased her image by opening his eyes. His months here had been a time of contentment, increasingly tinted, however, by boredom. Jim had been careful to show no signs to Heather, who seemed to revel in his uninterrupted presence. Although he was adjusting as best he could to the easy peace and slow pace of life on the ranch, he felt an empty space inside that neither his longtime companion nor their newly adopted son could fill.

Clumps of the silver-highlighted bunchgrass cushioned his hands and hips as he basked in the sun's warmth and stared up at the blue August sky—*the color of round, blue-glass marbles,* Jim thought, willing himself to enjoy this moment. He gazed into the sky just as years ago he had looked into 'clearies'—the marbles he had loved as a child. The sky was deep and translucent in the summer heat. A charcoal tinge permeated the late afternoon air as if a fire was burning in the nearby mountains, but there was no fire, just the heat and light of late August tinting the sky. Jim imagined he was inside one of the glass marbles with its edge, the edge of the universe, far above.

His personal-Earth universe, where he lay, eyes fixed on the sky above, not the 'real' universe's edge, billions of miles away where quasars race at near the speed of light into infinity. *Or was it infinity?* He never could understand why there were not endless universes beyond ours. Billions of stars, making up billions of galaxies, making up a universe. And why not more universes in the infinity of space? Clearies, marbles, a child's universe expanded to the infinitely larger universe of the planet that he now rested on. His small planet, his solar system and galaxy, mere specks in the universe—or infinity of universes.

He looked at his boot soles, not quite six feet from his blue-gray eyes, then past them to the late-summer-tanned canyon below. Jim lay stretched out just over the top of ridge, four hundred feet above the ranch house and barns below. A small dust cloud appeared from the opposite ridge, which had no name. Several horses led by Skipper, his palomino stallion, raced past sagebrush, and then down the hillside toward the large barn.

Heather was at the barn with Pedro, putting out grain for her beloved llamas. The horses wanted their share but they would not get any of the sweet molasses-coated corn, oats, and barley mix. They didn't need it this time of year but in the mysterious way that horses think, there was no memory of a sweet-molasses-and-grain-free summer in years past, only an expectation that today they would push and jostle each other successfully for the tasty mouthfuls the llamas were now devouring.

Jim lazily scanned to his left, looking west toward the high mountains still holding last winter's snow. Oval Peak, one of his two favorite wilderness places, barely stood above the other mountains at 8,800 feet, even though it was the tallest mountain in that part of the Cascade Range.

He tilted his head and watched a lone, black cloud moving into the lower valley as if drawn into a vacuum. The small but jumpy cloud bubbled and grew as he watched it; a common sight in the late afternoon heat. Chances were that the cloud would grow large enough to produce heavy rain, but Jim could only guess where in the valley it might release its cooling drops. Every few years out of the sixteen that he and Heather had lived here, there had been a deluge over their canyon, Wolf Canyon. Sheets of rain that started as mere trickles on the ridgetops became cascading water, building strength and volume as the torrents raced lower, gouging ruts and mini-gorges from the soft, alluvial soils.

Jim watched as the cloud grew larger, darker and billowed higher, gaining size and strength. Lightning shafts rose from the ground and he saw the streaks of rain descend somewhere between Twisp and Winthrop, the two towns in the valley. Several seconds later the distant sound of low rumbling thunder resonated up the canyon to his ridge.

This has to be one of the most beautiful places on earth, he thought, as he had thought hundreds of time before. A dichotomous kaleidoscope of seasons and plants. Jim reached his hand to his right and softly caressed the shriveled remains of a balsamroot. They covered the hills in the early spring with their yellow flowers. Native Americans who had freely roamed this ridge in times past had used the balsam's tuberous root to make flour. Jim tried it once, soaking the root for days and trying to pound it into something edible; his technique failed. One day perhaps he would enlist the help of Heather and Pedro and between the three of them, they might be able to do what the Native Americans had mastered over a hundred years before.

The ranch canyon, nestled between ridges, held over twelve hundred acres, a small enclave in the hundreds of thousands of acres of state wildlife and forestland that surrounded it. Rising at the head of the canyon stood Wolf Mountain, covered in dense, large ponderosa pine, as was Coyote Ridge's north side, just below his vantage point. The trees on the ridge were smaller than on the mountain, and more scattered than at the higher elevation. The cooler, north sides of the hills were dotted with green scraggly pines, while the hot south sides were populated with scented sage and bunchgrasses dotting friable tan-brown soils. The higher elevations held thick forests of large old pines—biding their time before chainsaws and helicopters turned the mountains to slash-covered mounds, unless they burned first.

Fires, the ever-present danger in these mountains, sometimes destroyed the forests before the loggers. When the Native Americans and first settlers walked the valleys and hills, the fires rarely set the higher limbs and needles ablaze as they raged across the ground, scorching grass and low bushes. The pines' heavy bark and high branches prevented the fires from reaching the dry needles far above. Forest management, supposedly to prevent those fires, had allowed the undergrowth to flourish in recent years and when lightning or careless campers inevitably started a fire, the tall burning brush ignited the lower branches, causing unstoppable wild fires.

Jim's idyllic thoughts pushed aside that one major threat to the canyon and his home. Someday fire would come and he would do what he could to protect the animals, house and barns, but luck would have to be on his side to save the structures. As valuable to Jim as the home he had built was, he knew it was only a place, an object. Nothing compared to his family and animals. *My family,* he thought as he shook his head in wonder. Nine months and one day ago, there had been only Jim, the special-agent rancher, and

Heather, the lithe five-foot-six botanist 'llama-lady.' Days later, his immediate family had doubled. They had adopted Pedro, then five years old and, to all intents and purposes, twenty-nine-year-old Lola, a short Mexican woman who had mustered the courage to try to save Pedro from the cartel and their assassin Najma.

At the hands of the same cartel, Heather had learned that the world was not always a nice place to be. Something that Jim had known since he was eighteen in Vietnam and Lola had learned at an early age as a lowly female Yaqui Indian. Her life had always been tough but it had turned into a nightmare when the cartel killed her son and forced her to serve their whims at the Mexican hacienda where Pedro was brought after his family's slaughter by the cartel's devil woman.

Heather and Jim had been on the fence for years about having children, but in the aftermath of the hacienda's destruction, Pedro appeared and the decision had been made for them by fate. Over the past months, their initial shock had turned to fulfillment.

Jim smiled at the thought of his new family and looked down toward the barn again. Walking along the road just in front of the structure were Heather, Pedro and Rosie, their huge, tawny-tan Irish wolfhound. Pedro looked tiny next to the massive, shaggy dog. It was hard to make out the three of them over the long distance; they walked so close together that only Jim would know it was three separate beings.

He pushed himself up, stretched and set off with long strides descending the ridge on a well-worn but narrow cattle trail that traversed downward, allowing him to intercept his family just before they reached the house. While he walked with the self-assurance and efficiency of someone comfortable with mountain trails, Jim knew he needn't hurry. Heather would stop along the road to show Pedro plants and insects and, if they were lucky, they would spot something larger, a coyote or the rarer porcupine.

There was a small family of rabbits near a little grassy area they called Spooky Meadow. There were never more than a few since the small, flat field carved into the Aspen Grove was a hard place for them to survive. Coyotes and eagles quickly consumed the careless rabbits, just as they did house cats that wandered in the open.

The anxious and cautious cats and bunnies survived; the brave and bold ended up in sharper claws and bigger mouths. These were the same truths that Lola and Pedro had learned in Mexico, that both had lived by until Lola's desire to save Pedro overcame all the lessons hammered into her soul, ingrained in her mind.

Suppressed by her culture for centuries, there lurked in Lola an ancient strength that allowed her to overcome terror and fear for that one horrifying, desperate moment in time. The usual outcome of her bold break for freedom with Pedro would have been certain death at the hands of the cartel she sought to escape. In a twist of fate, she had chosen to leave the hacienda grounds on the very night that Colonel Jim Johnson and Major Brush McGuire came to capture the devil—Najma. The love that had grown between them all after the battle against Najma, their common enemy, had forged an unshakeable bond, the sort of bond that can only be built between survivors of shared strife.

Lola, freed from past oppression and fear, now spent her days taking care of her new family, slowly shedding her anxieties and learning English from Heather. Pedro absorbed words at a rapid rate, which led Heather reluctantly and Jim less so to decide he would be better off in public school come fall than home schooling under Heather. The days of their idyllic isolation were numbered.

The narrow cow trail that Jim followed vanished onto the flat bottom of the canyon. He walked through a small, steep ditch whose soil eroded through the eons by water, inexorably pulled down the canyon by gravity. There had been none for years and it was overgrown with bushes and small trees. He climbed up and out. Just as he cleared the top he was met by a running Pedro followed by a loping Rosie. Pedro jumped into Jim's arms and held him, not with the exuberance of a nearly six-year-old, but rather with a maturity of someone who knew how important it was to cling to what was precious.

Jim reached his right arm out to scratch Rosie's head and then an ear; the big dog's golden eyes sparkled and gazed back into his. Heather stood smiling, proud of her family. Pedro clung to his adopted father until Jim raised him up, holding him under tiny shoulders then setting him on the ground. He took the boy's hand and together they walked to the gravel road where Heather waited, glowing in the late afternoon sun.

She stood wearing her typical August work clothes, a baggy T-shirt, ponytail pulled through the back of an old blue baseball hat, and loose shorts that did nothing to diminish her long-legged slender shape. At five foot six, she was five inches shorter than Jim. Nonetheless, she was not without physical strength or mental determination in her hundred twenty-six pound, well-toned body. She was braless and she titillated his senses, as had everything about her since they met so many years ago. *It's a miracle to be so attracted still,* he thought, except for the fact that to his eye there was no woman more attractive in body or mind. *Amazing, yes it is—* the thought finished as she walked to him and the crinkles at the edge of her green eyes captivated him. She moved to Jim and lightly kissed him with her eyes open. He liked that about her.

Pedro had an arm wrapped around each of their legs. Rosie knew an opening when it presented itself, and with her huge tongue licked Pedro's face while he scrunched up his eyes. Pedro clearly loved the attention as much as Rosie-O-Twisp loved giving it. 'Early dinner?' asked Jim. 'Are you hungry, Pedro?'

'We're hungry,' replied Pedro, as he hugged Rosie.

'Let's go help Heather fix something then, shall we,' said Jim.

He took Pedro's hand on one side and Heather's on the other and started off to the house.

'Nope, don't want you guys in the kitchen.' Heather grinned. 'Grab something to drink and the plates and stay out on the deck.'

'Coke?' Pedro asked hopefully.

'I think you'll like the sun tea much better than a Coke,' Heather told him. Pedro could not hide his disappointment as he looked up at her.

'OK, we'll make it a Diet Coke but no more after school starts,' she added.

Pedro had a sweet tooth and Heather hoped to diminish it over time. Sugar, refined or unrefined had been a point of dispute between Heather and Jim since they had known each other. Jim argued that whatever we ate converted to sugars, lipids, and proteins and it didn't matter that much if you ate a potato that eventually became sugar. He saw no real difference in the two with one proviso, that straight sugar hit the system faster. Heather, on the other hand, argued that refined sugar was unnatural. Jim said it didn't matter if food was natural or not if it had the same molecular formula. The disagreement would probably never be resolved. It was a chemist's point of view against a naturalist's.

Pedro, at this point in his life, didn't care about either of their points, only that he liked sugar just as much as he liked Rosie and having his back scratched. They all gave him pleasure.

On the deck, Lola stood, holding a damp towel, the delectable aroma of carne asada wafting around her. 'Wipe your face, mijo, and behind your ears too. Food is on table. Pronto, la cena está lista.'

The light breeze rustled the aspen leaves near the deck. The grass trailing its way down the canyon swayed hypnotically and a hawk glided across the sky. It was warm and wonderful and the flowers next to the house bloomed bright adding soft scents. An ideal time and place. Heather turned to Jim, her eyes wide and shining with happiness. She started to reach for him just as his ringing cell phone shattered her idyllic spell.

Chapter 2

Heather tried not to jump when the phone rang, tried not think the worst. They all knew Jim had recovered enough to resume active duty and maybe this phone call was the one that would take him away from her again. Acid crept up her throat; she couldn't bear it. She hated the sound of ringing phones and this could be calling Jim away. Every day that passed made her more fearful the inevitable would happen: Jim would leave. General Crystal would call and then he would go. Just like always.

Jim smiled reassuringly as he accepted the call. 'Hey, Brush, how's it going?'

Knowing the caller was Jim's longtime friend didn't reassure Heather as Brush was also his partner in the field. He could call Jim away just as easily as General Crystal could. 'No, we're just about to eat Lola's wraps on the deck.'

Jim listened for a minute and said nothing as Heather gave a forced smile to Pedro, trying to appear calm.

'Great, we'd love a visit from you and Glenda Rose.'

Heather calmed down a little.

'Give me,' said Pedro reaching for the phone.

'Say please,' added Heather.

'Someone wants to say hi to you, Brush,' said Jim as he passed the phone around Heather to Pedro.

'Buenos,' said Pedro and then listened intently.

Pedro giggled. 'Bye sir,' and passed the phone back to Jim.

'Tomorrow, late morning. See you then,' said Jim then disconnected.

Heather let out a breath, thinking *here it comes,* and pulled her lower lip up inside her upper and then asked as calmly as she could, 'What's up with Brush? Why is he coming over?'

'He's bringing the new Enstrom over tomorrow with Glenda Rose.'

Inside, Heather's stomach knot untwined. She let out a great sigh as her immediate worry ebbed. 'Wow,' she said. 'Your replacement for Romeo Sierra.'

'Yep, I've missed Romeo Sierra and it'll be good to see Brush,' he said as he looked around the table.

'A ride please for me?' asked Pedro.

'No for me,' said Lola. 'Plane maybe OK but those things make me nervous. Little bug in the sky waiting for God to slap it. You no go either, Pedro.'

Jim paid no attention to her. 'Sure, Pedro. You, me and Brush, we'll try it out tomorrow. I know Heather won't want to come.'

Lola rolled her eyes muttering under her breath, 'Mon Dios.'

Pedro leaned forward, took a swig of his Diet Coke and, after Heather finally said OK, thought about soaring like a bird over the mountains, up in the blue sky. Jim was thinking much the same. He hadn't flown a helicopter since he had set the Enstrom down, none too softly, on Armstrong Mountain on the Canadian border. The rough landing had damaged the helicopter but it got him to Heather in time to keep her from getting shot. However, the helicopter hadn't fared as well. Jim shook his head, dismissing the memories of that time, his first encounter with Najma.

He explained to Pedro the helicopter wasn't new, just new to him. He had found it through a sales outfit in southern Oregon. A Japanese firm had maxed out the hours in Japan. By their law, it needed a complete overhaul after only a thousand hours. As was the norm, they elected to sell it and avoid the costly overhaul. It arrived in a container, partially disassembled and Jim had found a mechanic to put it together. Then he had it trailered to Payne Field, north of Seattle, where he had a new, black leather interior installed. It would be just like his old one and even had the same number on the side.

'You're not eating,' remarked Heather, looking at Jim.

'No good?' said Lola.

'It couldn't be better. I was just thinking,' responded Jim as he put his thoughts on hold and took a bite of the wrap.

Pedro giggled and slyly gave a piece of wrap to Rosie. She took it gently in her massive mouth. But the boy wasn't as stealthy as he thought. Heather scowled at him and Lola said with fake concern, 'Now I know no good, so I won't make you eat more,' as she moved the plate with the wraps away from Pedro.

'Lo siento,' said Pedro.

'We don't feed Rosie or any pets from the table. Not because we are unkind but so that they won't learn to beg for food and then make a nuisance of themselves,' said Heather. 'This is especially true out in the mountains. Are you excited to go camping? It's the nicest time of the year now. There are still flowers but the insects are mostly gone.'

Heather gave Jim a look that he could only interpret as worried.

Jim said reassuringly, 'It will be a nice trip; maybe Brush and Glenda Rose will come along.'

The look on Heather's face made Jim wonder if she was ready yet. The Pasayten Wilderness north and east of the ranch stretched for miles along the Canadian border and it had always been one of Heather's favorite places. Any wilderness in fact brought her joy in the past. Now the memories of her ill-fated camping trip to Mexico, and all that had followed, were making Heather nervous about going into the wilderness again.

Jim smiled at her and reached for her hand. 'It's time to go out, you'll be fine,' he reassured her. 'Let's just go to Oval Peak for a few days before we go on the longer trip with JT. If Brush and Glenda go, it will make five of us.'

'No, señor, I go too,' said Lola. 'You don't take no trips and leave me by myself here. The devil lady will come. I no stay by myself.'

'Najma can't harm any of you anymore. She's locked up. You don't need to worry.'

Heather said nothing. She was steeling herself for this trip. The wilderness, her treasured place of safety and refuge, had been contaminated by Najma. The dark feelings increased over time. It would take all her courage and rationality to venture out from the ranch and find again the peace and sense of unity she'd once had in the remote mountains.

Lola crossed herself, muttering in Spanish, and closed her eyes.

Chapter 3

The forklift rolled silently over the smooth, spotlessly clean, painted concrete of the hangar floor built above the Biological Warfare Center. By any standards, it was huge. It did not house jumbo jets but rather an eclectic mix of civilian and military aircraft, one being General Crystal's Huey, and the most exotic, a white Cessna Citation X. They sat quietly dwarfed in the immense, dust-free space as the yellow electric forklift moved its ten-foot tall cargo housed in a wood crate toward the back wall.

Red stencils emblazoned on all sides conveyed the delicate nature of the crate's contents—FRAGILE. A military truck had delivered it and deposited it gently, just outside the hangar. When the truck was sufficiently out of sight, an MP pushed the electric button that slowly rolled the forty-foot-tall steel door along a track separating the interior's glossy painted cement floor from the rougher outside concrete.

The delivery truck driver did not see the forklift operator, but if he had, he would have seen a tall lanky man with distinctly wild, non-military hair. The shaft of sunlight that angled across the gleaming floor was the first natural light Nusmen had seen in just under a year, since he was placed in house arrest.

To most, being shut in the Biological Warfare Center's underground facility would have been a prison sentence, but it was Nusmen's idea of heaven. There was nowhere he would rather be—which was fortunate, considering that his confinement had been mandated as punishment for his horrific and harebrained attempt to infect Seattle with a bacterium that was impervious to any treatment. Nusmen's psychologist labeled it a crime of passion, a form of reactive depression. A one-off event in her professional opinion.

The damage that the white-coated, geeky-looking biochemist caused with his engineered bacteria had originally made him the most hated person in the Biological Warfare Center's laboratories. The BWC and its laboratories were there to protect the public from terrorist-released biological weapons; a mission all its employees took very seriously, at home and wherever in the world there were threats.

Nusmen was a terrorist in the eyes of the government and the lab personnel but its director, General William Crystal, had seen things differently. His mission was to stop the spread of biological weapons, not punish people. He had taken a chance with Nusmen, hoping that he would help the lab resolve a dangerous situation— albeit one that Nusmen himself had created. The general had been right. Nusmen was brilliant, even surpassing Will Crystal's expectations. The State Department, confronted with Nusmen's undeniable genius, relented in their quest to prosecute him and instead left him in the general's care, confined to live and work in the underground laboratories.

Nusmen drove himself relentlessly, partly from his natural inter-est, and partly because of guilt. He understood what he had done and he desperately needed to undo the damage. He was certainly over the mean on the autism spectrum but being in the cloistered world of the laboratory had allowed him make social connections on a level he'd never before managed. The lab was full of intense scientists and technicians, many slightly odd to the outside world. All with one thing in common—intelligence. Nerds reigned supreme. Nusmen loved it here.

Slowly the lab workers and supervisors warmed to his eccentric behavior. Little by little, his out-of-the-box thinking, efficient work habits and his anything-but-just-plain-vanilla brilliance won them over despite what he had done. The man might have been crazy for a moment in time but now he was one of them and one of their best. The Harvard geek had finally made good and found his place in life.

When the announcement came of the arrival of the latest Scanning Transmission Electron Microscope, STEM for short, Nusmen had made it clear that no one but him could bring it into the lab. His colleagues acquiesced, knowing it was not that he thought he could treat it better than the others did. Rather it was like a newborn child to him. Excitement and pride made him demand that he and only he could drive it through the aboveground hangar and down to the bottom level of the laboratories, five stories below. The new microscope could see to atomic level and analyze chemical elements at over a million times magnification. Not an astounding advance in technology, but an advance nevertheless, and the lab always upgraded to the best and latest equipment.

Nusmen drove over the spotless gray-painted concrete to the crate. He slid the forklift blades carefully under the crate and then lifted it only a few inches off the floor, slightly tilted it back and moved slowly toward the hidden elevator.

Nusmen watched the camera as he approached the white wall, knowing there were guards monitoring. As he neared, a section of it slowly slid sideways, revealing a short corridor leading to a large elevator door with a dark glass window along one side. The guards behind the glass monitored Nusmen using several devices including infrared, keeping both Nusmen and the hangar under surveillance. Nusmen then pulled up on the forklift handbrake, climbed down to the floor and walked to a monitor containing a small red oval. He looked into a facial recognition camera and after a second, a green 'Proceed' illuminated. Nusmen, with his white lab coat half buttoned and hair looking wilder than usual, stepped to the edge of the elevator and placed both hands on glass labeled squares that identified him further by hand- and fingerprints. He made a face at the camera above and climbed back onto the forklift as the elevator slid open.

The elevator in the oversized ground-level hangar was one of two entrances to the multilevel underground BWC. On the other side of the elevator, separated by a wall from the hangar, was a one-story office building with few windows that masqueraded as a typical, dull, military structure. To the outside observer it might house dozens of office workers. Inside, however, it was empty except for a receptionist and an MP at the entrance. The office was where lab staff entered elevators similar to the cargo elevator Nusmen used now. The hangar side was for deliveries or for those arriving or leaving by plane. Jim parked his Seneca and helicopter inside when he flew to the lab. Otherwise, everyone, including the field operatives like Brush and the newest addition, Glenda Rose, entered and exited by the office side.

Even an astute observer on the military base would not notice anything unusual. Civilians and military personnel were entering an office, planes entering a hangar. But below the ordinary surface was a top-secret, secure facility, extending five stories underground and full of sophisticated equipment with seventy lab staff and trillions of the world's most dangerous bacteria and viruses. The most dangerous, the 'bad bugs,' were kept in high security level-four labs. In addition to laboratory staff, there were over one hundred support personnel: intelligence analysts, computer and communication specialists, mechanics and weapons specialists whose primary duty was to support their highly trained field operatives. These were Colonel Jim Johnson, Major Brush McGuire, Operative Glenda Rose Stuart and thirty rapid-response disease specialists along with two special C teams. Special Forces possessing highly trained combat skills along with a deep understanding of pathological organisms.

This was the organization that had taken over Nusmen's life. Military personnel posing as civilian movers had brought all Nusmen's belongings from his eastern Washington Methow Valley home, not far from Jim's Wolf Canyon ranch, to the BWC labs when his confinement sentence was authorized. Most of the small-town residents in Winthrop were glad to be rid of the man they thought of as a weirdo and few had questioned or cared about his abrupt departure. Smart aleck 'coasties' never lasted long in the valley and good riddance to the plant geek.

Under strict supervision, he had emailed his few friends that he had taken a job working on computers in Australia. Thus Nusmen had disappeared from the town of Winthrop, Washington, and even from the watchful eye of the IRS. He had become a non-resident of the US, effectively nonexistent. He lived in small quarters on the second floor of the lab. There were several of these rooms, as lab technicians frequently stayed overnight when they monitored lengthy analyses.

As Nusmen descended in the elevator, his eyes darted between the crate and the elevator numbers. He loved this place and he never wanted to leave.

As much as possible, the lab was automated. Tedious streaking of bacterial plates, cloning, separating DNA and identifying their characteristics, had been replaced by avant-garde, high-throughput automated systems. Many of the techs monitored and repaired the robotic equipment, and worked on the computer systems that controlled much of the lab's equipment, which would now include the large microscope that Nusmen carefully brought into a micros-copy room. Several white-coated techs stood ready to uncrate and help set up the new giant microscope. Nusmen waved them off. He would continue unpacking on his own, cleaning and adjusting Goliath, as they now called it, and his colleagues all knew he would not stop until he was using it, seeing what it could do. His curiosity was insatiable. He had been here nearly a year, and no thoughts of leaving had crossed his mind, no dreams of seeing his valley again. Nusmen belonged to the BWC labs body and soul—and that was fine with him.

Chapter 4

Brush slowly moved his index finger, tracing the vertebrae on Glenda's spine. She lay with her arms and legs spread-eagled, like da Vinci's Vitruvian Man, except facedown and a hell of a lot sexier.

'That feels good. I don't know why you touching my back feels so good. Sends tingles all through me.'

Glenda was well muscled under a soft layer of flesh, round bottom attached to strong legs. Full figured and, to Brush's eye, marvelously voluptuous. She also had a stunning mind that propelled her body almost as well as his own and, if he admitted the truth, maybe better, as she was more intelligent. It didn't bother Brush, he was proud to be with her and one of them had to be smarter than the other. He felt at peace with her.

'I like your back nearly as much as I like your front.'

In the past Brush had been a fan of almost any sexy-looking woman but particularly larger breasted females. Glenda Rose Stuart certainly fulfilled that desire. To him her body was flawless, including the angry welts on her abdomen and the smaller ones on her back. He thought of those scars as her badge of bravery, a decoration of the highest honor. Najma's three bullets had entered her body and two had exited Glenda's back during the gun battle at Seattle's Space Needle a year ago. The first time he had held her, she'd been bleeding profusely.

Glenda twisted her head and smiled, interrupting Brush's thoughts. 'That's not my back, mister.'

'You complaining?'

'Not for a second.'

He moved his hand to her strawberry-blond hair and arranged it along the back of her elegant neck, then he ran his fingers through it. Gently, he touched her earlobes, as she liked, and trailed his fingers along her back and legs.

'That's almost as good as stroking my back.'

'Just a second ago I wasn't stroking either.'

'I know.' She turned over, looking at him longingly.

Brush's fingers started to lightly trace her breasts, circling her nipples. He watched as they became full and hard.

'Hum. And I thought I liked to have my back rubbed,' whispered Glenda. 'My sweet Canuck, where have you been all my life?'

'Just waiting for you,' Brush whispered as he moved his fingers lower, trailing over her breasts and down toward her hips. He traced the three bullet scars on her abdomen, lingering for a moment. She had experienced the bad in the world, just as he had. Now together they were experiencing the good.

He bent toward her and softly touched his lips to hers. His hand covered the finely haired mound that he found so exciting. Glenda moaned and said to him softly, 'Don't stop, don't ever stop.'

Chapter 5

Guillermo sat, long straight legs regally crossed, on a gray-green wingback chair near an ornate fireplace, his lightweight suit pressed and immaculate. For the first time in months, he felt reasonably content with his situation. His eyes, set above his beak-shaped but elegant nose, scanned the room and he was pleased with what he saw.

His cartel's headquarters, the hacienda where he sat now, had been fully rebuilt atop the old hacienda and expanded to make it all the more secure. Only one thing was missing.

His servant walked into the room just as Guillermo stood. The male servant was a small statured Yaqui Indian. Guillermo, at over six feet, towered over the man.

'I'll have dinner on the patio.'

'Sí, señor.'

'Bring me a gin and tonic. Send for Mary; I want her to have dinner with me.' *And then after dinner, I will find out the truth from Najma,* he thought.

As he walked to the patio, Guillermo's eyes narrowed and he clamped his teeth. His daughter, Mary, instead of graduating from one of England's finest boarding schools, Maidstone Ladies' College, and marrying into a fine family as he had planned, now lived with him.

Then he smiled, feeling his power pump through his veins. Sir Peter Brandt had deserted Guillermo when he most needed him. His past defender in England had paid with his life, just like the police detective who had been insulting to his daughter.

Political officials in the Western world seemed to believe they were safe from powerful men such as Guillermo. Yet so many died in what appeared to be natural circumstances. There was no proof that he had anything to do with Sir Peter's death but several people suspected Guillermo's involvement and now gave him the deference he required.

Guillermo smiled as his daughter walked onto the patio. She didn't smile back. His smile ended. 'You will stay here as long as I say.'

'This is jail. I am seventeen years old. It's not fair,' she complained as she started to cry. Instead of compassion, Guillermo's jaw clamped shut and his eyes turned menacing.

'I'm just a possession,' screamed Mary as tears streamed down her cheeks.

'You will lower your voice when speaking to me.' Guillermo snapped his fingers and his manservant appeared. 'Have Lazaro take Mary to her room.'

'It's Maria not Mary. You're nothing but a gangster. You'll never be anything but trash to the upper class in Europe, no matter how much money you have.'

Guillermo ignored her and whisked his hand toward the door. The servant speed-dialed Lazaro and then gently put his hand on the young girl's shoulder and moved her out of the room.

Guillermo looked to the dark-blue night sky. What was it his English wife used to call it? 'Dip-dyed blue sky.' Her memory aroused no sentimental thoughts. She had died giving birth to Mary. Maria, her name for the child, not his. His thoughts turned to Najma.

He stayed seated as Najma walked into the room. It was not his custom to rise for guests. He sat elegantly in his chair and observed the once beautiful and ruthless woman who was now thin and gaunt, her once long, thick, silky dark hair, only stubble. An ugly, welted scar rose behind her right ear. She had moved like a cat that last time he saw her but now she moved slowly and deliberately toward the table where he waited. Her eyes were lackluster with no hint of the old vaporous black onyx. Clearly wounded, he wondered whether she was actually broken.

Neither said anything. She sat and they looked at each other. His former assassin, cunning and effective beyond all others, looked weak and wasted. Still, one way or another she would answer his questions.

'What can Manuel bring you, señorita?'

She glared at him, thinking of her lost child, Pedro. *I'm not a señorita but a señora,* she said to herself, and something in her eyes spat hate. Guillermo registered the flicker of life, wondering what it meant.

'Cold tea,' she said eventually.

The dark-skinned servant wearing meticulous white linen, as Guillermo required, walked away quickly. Moments later he returned with her drink then retreated to a remote corner of the room, ready to do his master's bidding. Guillermo held out his gin and tonic with ice cubes tinkling. She raised her glass.

'To freedom, Najma, and the pleasures it brings.'

She nodded and took a slow, full drink. It felt cool washing down her throat as she remembered the bad-tasting water in her prison, the nearly inedible food and solitary confinement. She would find her boy and then she would track down the men who had tortured her. But first she needed to appease Guillermo, who had engineered her freedom.

She glared at him. 'Why am I here?'

'To answer some questions for me and recover from your ordeal,' answered Guillermo in his flawless Queen's English.

'What questions?'

'I wish to know what happened at the hacienda when you were wounded and taken captive.'

Najma remembered all too well what had happened but she hesitated before replying. Her loss of Pedro might have made her sad if she had the same emotions that others felt. To her psychotic mind, Pedro belonged to her and no one else. He was something that had been stolen from her. She'd possessed him for only a few days, but those few days had changed her. She would be his mother. The thought of molding him into the sort of man she thought all men should be appealed to her.

Her only moment of pleasure had been when she'd killed Colonel Jim Johnson. Najma remembered little after that. A series of white rooms and doctors with American accents, hazy, drug induced images. And then, her cell in some unnamed hot place.

'First tell me where I was and what happened to the boy.'

'I can tell you where you were but I have no knowledge of a boy.'

'He was at the hacienda and he is my son.'

Guillermo crossed his legs, took a sip of his Bombay Sapphire gin with just a splash of tonic. Had she had lost her grasp on reality? What could she mean—her son? He stretched his thoughts back to his encounters with Najma last fall until he remembered the small boy she'd brought back from the family she had ruthlessly killed, on his orders, in Tubutama, not far from where they sat at this moment. But calling the boy her son was unexpected, if not strange, even for this woman. Still, Guillermo saw no reason to antagonize her.

'You were held by the American CIA at a detention facility in Cuba. I have no information about your son at present but I shall make the necessary inquiries, Najma,' he said smoothly. 'Obviously, my investigation will be aided by your account of that night. So tell me what happened at the hacienda.'

Najma stared unblinkingly at her onetime employer. Guillermo's brown irises were transfixed by the intensity of her black gaze but both of them knew who held the upper hand. Still she was magnetic and he admired her for that strength. Perhaps not as weak as she appeared. He knew she would tell him what he asked—she had no choice if she wanted help finding this boy she called her son.

Guillermo studied Najma, waiting for her to start the story. She said nothing so he finally said, 'Tell me what happened that day.'

She glared at him, black eyes displaying no emotion. Then, after several seconds, she spoke. 'It was the Americans. The same agents that came to Mexico and killed Raul.'

Guillermo felt anger. He knew it was the truth. 'Give me the details.'

She picked up her glass of cold tea and slowly took a drink, enjoying his obvious impatience. 'I killed the brothers as you ordered and I was returning to the airport. The pilot landed me in the desert. I saw a muzzle flash from the hill above me. It was an American sniper.' Guillermo nodded, his men had found the wrecked plane and the remains of the pilot.

'I came through the tunnel and into the courtyard. Most of your men were already dead. I shot the American colonel, then I remember nothing else.'

Guillermo continued to ask detailed questions. Her narrative lasted more than an hour and they now sat quietly, each with different thoughts. Najma's about her son and vengeance, Guillermo considering his own revenge.

Many years ago Guillermo had read all of Arthur Conan Doyle's Sherlock Holmes stories, '…when you have eliminated the impossible, whatever remains, however improbable, must be the truth.' He had never forgotten that saying. He realized now he had found no answers from the Mexican government because none existed. They had not used their special units to attack the hacienda but simply put out that story to cover up the US involvement. The

Americans had cost him much and he would make them pay.

Outwardly Guillermo looked calm, but inside a hatred for General Crystal's so-called bio terrorist group and its agents Colonel Johnson and Major McGuire swirled rancid in his brain. He did not feel like enlightening Najma that she had only wounded the colonel—at least not yet.

He stood up. 'Meet me here at noon tomorrow,' he instructed and abruptly walked away, no longer Guillermo, refined gentleman, but now El Padrino, the ruthless cartel leader.

Chapter 6

A balding man in a white lab coat walked into a hastily set up Camp X-Ray morgue. He moved quickly with his elongated nose pointed straight ahead, his eyes darting, taking in the stainless-steel worktables, dingy white painted walls and old linoleum floor. The facility was far below the standards of his office as chief medical examiner for Washington D.C. He had no idea where in the United States the morgue he stood in was located. Military Police had shown up at his home, escorted him to Andrews airbase and after a two-hour plane ride, he'd disembarked in a hot, humid military hangar. The MP's secreted him in a frigid van and drove him a short distance to where he now stood. He had seen no sign of where he was before boarding the van and it had no windows. Neither was there any indication of the location in the substandard morgue as he scrutinized it.

Two white-coated men stood near the body of an uncovered young male who lay faceup on the stainless table. Their short hair and military bearing did not surprise him. This was a military operation—albeit an obviously secret one—and he did not want to know more. He was here because of his reputation as a skilled forensic scientist and his long established contacts with the government. He would do his job, make his report, and probably be at his own facility tomorrow, hearing nothing further about this man.

No one spoke as he walked to the table, pulled the microphone lower and started his description of the early twenties, white male

Caucasian on the table, unknown to him as Sergeant Alex Smith. His two assistants were experienced and they performed the autopsy rapidly with no interesting results. The man had short hair and was in good physical condition as would be expected of a young soldier. The blood work would reveal no drug presence or chemical abnormalities. A neat hole in the back of his head and a ragged one at the front suggested a projectile that had burst through, leaving shattered bone, brains and blood in what had been a reasonably handsome head, now distorted and waxen against stainless steel.

After two uninteresting hours of careful examination and sample collecting, the conclusion was simple and obvious from purple livor mortis and the wound. The man had been shot, probably execution style, in the back of the head while sitting and had fallen forward. No one gave the chief medical officer the bullet that had been recovered. From his past experience he guessed it was probably a forty-five caliber soft-nose that had expanded while tearing through the man's brain before exiting his forehead. Death would have been instantaneous, though the doctor wondered if anything ever was actually instantaneous. From the entry and exit angle, the dead soldier had his head facing slightly down perhaps toward a desk or table.

He nodded to the two men, walked out the door and returned to DC in the same plane in which he had traveled to the naval base in Cuba. He would complete his report on the plane and arrive at his office in time for his normally busy day at the morgue with no one knowing he had missed a night's sleep. And for what purpose? Nothing had required his personal attention. Anyone could have achieved the same result.

The prison raid had been easy for Guillermo's Cuban contacts. The Navy and the CIA focused on making Camp X-Ray secure from breakouts. Break-ins had not been on their agenda. Heavy steel prevented escape, there were cameras monitoring twenty-four hours a day and sealed rooms with no windows. Sergeant Alex Smith, from his cubicle, had simply pushed a button, opened the gates, stopped the cameras and then had sat waiting for Guillermo's men to temporarily incapacitate him by Taser. The facility was not complex. He had provided Najma's Cuban liberators with a diagram that allowed them to walk in, execute him, and walk out with Najma. The rest of Guantánamo slept. There had never been an incident at the base and, while the Navy kept guard, it had become a pretense. Night guards quietly read books, played games, wrote letters home and put in their shifts. No one looked carefully at the perimeter fence. The cut section hung lazily, unnoticed. The Cubans, along with their liberated female prisoner, disappeared into the night. Hours later, Najma boarded a private jet to Mexico.

Chapter 7

Director of Central Intelligence Sorenson studied the faces of the two men and one woman assembled in the room. 'There are only four of us in this meeting. Only a handful of individuals in our employ currently know the full details of the prisoner escape from Camp X-Ray.' He paused. 'A cleanup team has removed any evidence of the shooting of the guard. Postmortem revealed nothing suspicious other than he was shot in the back of the head. Bertrand, you and Martin pick a team to work on answering how the escape happened. Find out who is responsible, and most important, where she is. I want her back before anyone finds out. No leaks. What I want are results and I want them fast. Is that understood?' he said with the emphasis required of a boss who didn't always get what he asked for.

Everyone acknowledged the director's command.

Then Sorenson looked at Deputy Director Helen Flayback and added, 'The DDCI will handle damage control.' *Shit,* he thought. *This is the excuse that the president needs to replace me. We capture our first ever terrorist and the CIA loses her on my watch.*

Sorenson was not concerned about those present at the meeting leaking information, unless it was Deputy Director Flayback, foolishly thinking she could usurp him as director by doing so. *She is arrogant enough,* he thought, *but is she that ignorant? No. She would have a rebellion from the lifers within a month.* She was not director material, not even close, or even deputy director material for that matter. He had only brought her in as he needed support from another politically savvy type like himself.

The deputy director normally focused her attention on administration and public affairs and stayed far away from Bertrand's Intelligence Directorate. The agency was staffed with lifers, employees who had been brought up through the ranks. For their part they ignored her, knowing neither she nor the current DCI would last long, or so they hoped.

Bertrand and Martin knew why Sorenson was warning them to be careful in how they handled investigations into Najma's escape: his job could be on the line if this leaked. There was little danger of the career analysts leaking to the press. They knew how to keep secrets. In general, the agency did not have a reputation for leaks but the potential always existed that sub-contractors and contacts within other governments were not as sensitive to the need for secrecy as the agency's staff.

'So...we have lost the first official foreign terrorist we were detaining at Gitmo,' said Martin Pearson, knowing he was stating the obvious but not wanting to miss a chance to gloat over the director's predicament.

Sorenson ignored the remark while feeling its sting. He was directly responsible for the decision to send Najma to Guantánamo. It was part of his long-term plan to hold other prisoners from around the world, those who were outside of the normal justice system, at Camp X-Ray. The president had always been skeptical of Sorenson's plan. Losing the first prisoner, after Sorenson's assurances that it was impossible, would effectively end the program before it even got off the ground—unless he could find her fast.

'I don't want to play games here. It's a fuckup all right, but all four of us will pay the same price if we don't get her back,' Sorenson said in a lame attempt to spread the responsibility.

'How the hell are we going to get her back when we don't know squat about what happened?' asked Helen Flayback, the thin, dark-haired DDCI.

'It's true we have little to go on. No evidence. Nothing other than the obvious from the autopsy of Sergeant Smith's body,' responded Sorenson. 'The military police have a CID team looking into the dead sergeant's background. They are officially investigating it as the off-duty murder of a soldier just outside of X-Ray's entrance. The cleanup team left some evidence to support that version. CID has nothing much to go on, nor will they. They weren't informed, of course, until after our people secured the crime scene and the body was autopsied.

'They haven't been allowed access to X-Ray to talk to any of our people and of course the other guards, like the sergeant, have no knowledge of anything inside the facility past the entrance station. What they have is a dead cut-up soldier, a sanitized site and no one to talk to.'

'Bet they are happy about that,' chided Martin.

Sorenson did his best to ignore Martin and continued, 'And so far they have found nothing suspicious about the sergeant or his friends. They've had their fun. Let's lock this down. Helen, call the admiral in charge and then tell him since his MP's are inept and can't find out anything, we'll take over the investigation.'

'What about the FBI? They will want in; it clearly falls within their scope of authority if it happened outside X-Ray,' Bertrand pointed out.

Sorenson said, 'Keep them out of it. Bertrand, you know how to play it. Flayback, when you call the base commander tell him to bring his people in and order them to keep quiet. Say it is a matter of national security.'

'I'll make the call,' she said, secretly pleased with the thought that she would be telling an admiral what to do.

Martin broke in, 'He reports to the Joint Chiefs and ultimately the president. You can't keep him quiet.' *Especially with you telling them something is going on under his command,* Martin added silently, wondering how his boss ever got appointed director in the first place.

'Quiet about what? He doesn't know anything other than one of our people was killed, but just a lowlife guard. Tell him this comes directly from the top and it is in his best interest to keep it quiet until we tell him otherwise,' instructed Sorenson.

'Hum,' said Martin, thinking, *Pretty risky, boss. If you don't get caught in this, you have more luck than I do.* They were all quiet for a few seconds.

'Sir, the fact is we don't know what happened either. We have no evidence that leads us to a conclusion, and none is likely to be found,' stated Bertrand Gupta. 'My people and Martin will press our Cuban contacts but we need to come at this from other angles as well. We need, of course, to find out everything about the dead sergeant, trace his accounts and activities and see where it leads us. If it leads nowhere, then our only way forward is with the prisoner's history. What do we know about her? Who were her associates and what was she doing before we detained her? At the moment we know only that she was captured as a terrorist in the US and passed to us by the State Department with the president's blessing. She never gave up any information when we interrogated her.'

Bertrand continued, 'Even though X-Ray was designed to deal with…atypical cases, it was, we agreed, too soon to take a prisoner in exchange for having the facilities you wanted. At the very least we should have demanded more information when she arrived,' he said, looking hard at Sorenson.

'You've made your point. Now, I need to answer questions: who had the ability to break her out? How did she communicate to anyone where she was? Who the hell helped her? Maybe we can find her then.'

'Maybe she escaped by herself,' put in DDCI Flayback.

Bertrand felt compelled to point out the obvious. 'Highly improbable. She was still weak from her wounds and our treatment of
her probably didn't improve her condition.' So as not to needlessly
embarrass his poorly informed colleague, Bertrand skipped
mentioning to Flayback that the security cameras had recorded
Najma sitting in her cell before they were turned off. She'd appeared
unaware that she was to be the object of an in-progress jailbreak. He
was astounded that Flayback had not spent any time looking at the
facts. If she were more concerned with knowing what was going on
in the agency than with politics and PR, she would already know
this.

In truth, he couldn't care less about her and what she did as long
as she stayed out of his way and didn't interfere in the directorates
or clandestine affairs.

It was not only unfortunate but highly suspicious that the entrance CCTV provided no useful information about who broke
Najma out, suggesting to Bertrand that someone inside the facility
had provided information on how to bypass their security and
monitoring. The dead sergeant was the logical choice. 'Martin, I
want a full security workup on everyone who has access to the
facility, including friends, family of employees and of any subcon-
tractors who helped design it.'

The dark skinned, five-feet-eight-inch-tall Indian was head of
the Directorate of Intelligence, and therefore one of the most
powerful people in the CIA. He was simply referred to as Bertrand
by his staff.

He was born in England. His mother, an Indian immigrant,
wanting desperately to assimilate into the social fabric of London,
had seen a book by Bertrand Russell, *A History of Western Philoso-
phy,* sitting on a table in a public library. As she'd looked at it,
wondering what would be in such a thick tome, a woman walked by

and said, 'One of the brightest Englishmen ever.' Nahla went home and decided that she would call her sixth-month-old son 'Bertrand' and not 'Shambulinga,' the Indian name she had given him at birth. Maybe he would be smart like the man who had written the book.

The slim vegetarian was indeed smart and perhaps as intelligent as the famous British philosopher. In addition, he possessed a practicality that allowed him to untangle complex issues and understand their interrelationships and significance.

Bertrand had come to the CIA directly from Oxford University and rose through its ranks on merit. By rights, he should have been the head of the world's most powerful spy agency, not just its head of intelligence. He was not concerned however, for unlike some of his colleagues he cared nothing for the political responsibility such a position entailed.

Bertrand simply did not want to be the head of the agency. He hated every morning when he was required to fill in for Sorenson and give the morning briefing to the president. DDCI Flayback should be giving briefings but she wasn't knowledgeable enough. The DDCI should also be the one to replace Sorenson if need be, and that worried Bertrand since he knew that was impossible and he could be forced into being the director for the good of the agency. It wasn't that he couldn't play the political game like her and Sorenson. He simply had no interest in it.

From Sorenson's standpoint, Bertrand was perfect. He didn't want his boss's job. And more importantly, Bertrand was good not only at his own job but also understood the operations, science and clandestine affairs. It took the burden of dealing with what he didn't understand off Sorenson, and it made him look good with the administration. Bertrand ran a tight ship and Sorenson received the benefit. Sorenson held the title of Director Central Intelligence but everyone in the company thought of Bertrand as its true head.

Sorenson, a presidential appointee, was the first ever to come from outside the agency's inner sanctum. He had been the head of the powerful SIOC, the Senate Intelligence Oversight Committee. Then he lost his fifth term re-election to the Senate and limped his way home, wealthy but without a job.

Politically, the president needed a seemingly experienced ally as head of the agency and also to deal with the committee; the SIOC and the president's advisors wanted someone the White House could control. Sorenson seemed the perfect choice.

The president's staff was right and wrong. Sorenson was a political insider. To a degree they thought alike, harboring suspicion for the agency's independence and dark operations. Even the president thought the CIA should be held more accountable to Congress. The CIA lifers well understood that doing so would castrate the agency, making it impossible for them to perform their historical function as well as bury their all too often less-than-successful endeavors.

The two groups would never see eye to eye. The politicians would never accept the agency's role; Langley would never accept what they deemed as the politicians' ignorance about how the world worked.

It was no surprise that those who had spent their life living for and within the agency's culture distrusted the new outsider and his deputy. To survive, Sorenson needed support from experienced employees but few gave more than the minimum required, biding their time until Sorenson screwed up and was given his walking papers. All, that is, except for Bertrand who did his job well regardless of who was the DCI and DDCI. Sorenson at least was savvy enough to rely on the man to formulate much of the agency's policy. Without him, Sorenson would have been doomed.

Even so, the director did not always listen to his advice. Bertrand had been vocal in his opposition to using Camp X-Ray to hold prisoners outside the laws of the United States. He had predicted it would blow back on the agency. But Bertrand was not one to dwell on I-told-you-so's. Instead, his mind continued to turn over the puzzle of Camp X-Ray's first and only prisoner, a woman who had vanished as mysteriously as she had arrived. Voicing his thoughts aloud, Bertrand continued, 'Everything centers on the woman. We get a complete picture of her and it will tell us the "how" and "why" of the escape and that will eventually lead us to where she is.'

'Bertrand, expedite this,' ordered Sorenson, repeating himself. 'No time to waste. Let's jump ahead. Say you build this story and we make assumptions about where she is. At some point, we are going to need someone in the field to collect her. This will of course bring in more people and keeping it quiet will become increasingly difficult. Helen, you start working on a cover story to protect our asses if this leaks.'

Martin Pearson nearly said, *To protect your ass, you mean.* However, on this rare occasion he managed to keep his mouth shut and not to take a jab at his boss.

Just then a knock sounded at the door and one of Bertrand's aides handed him a file as he whispered urgently in his supervisor's ear. Bertrand nodded knowingly before he continued addressing the group. 'General William Crystal authorized the prisoner's medical procedures, which is the earliest record of Najma being in the custody of the US government. So the next logical step is to ask him.'

Chapter 8

The late morning sun was bright, and just high enough to send slivers of light first through the trees on Coyote Ridge, and then filtered again by the small aspen leaves, before leaving golden dashes on the outside of the house and the octagonal deck where the family sat. The trembling leaves, with their first vestiges of fall yellow, fluttered and giggled in the morning sun rays as the warm breezes rose up the canyon. Jim, Heather, Pedro, and Lola smiled and laughed in the warmth of the dancing light.

'Just my kind of morning,' said Heather. 'I could get used to sleeping in. You too, Pedro?' She laughed, knowing the boy jumped out of bed at sunrise every day.

The distant sound of an approaching helicopter softly added its rhythm to the rustle of leaves and faint buzz of bees in the wild roses.

Jim looked at Pedro wondering when he would detect the beat of the blades slicing the morning air.

Suddenly Pedro's eyes widened. 'I hear it.'

'That's a very fine set of ears you have there,' said Jim as he reached over and ruffled Pedro's thick dark hair. 'How long before they get here? Can you guess?'

With lips pinched together and thinking hard, Pedro said, 'Maybe three minutes.'

'That is a good guess. Tell me why you think so,' prodded Jim.

'If I can hear, then not long. Three minutes not long.'

Jim couldn't help chuckling. 'Good deduction. Let's walk down and watch them land.'

'No me. Dirty dishes,' said Lola defiantly.

Before they could get up, the sound of the approaching helicopter grew louder. Pedro and Jim pushed back their chairs and suddenly it was there, just a hundred feet over them, stopped in a hover. As they looked up, two people inside waved and they all waved back in unison. Just as suddenly as it had appeared, it reversed, backed up a few dozen feet, rolled to the right and dropped lower behind the aspen grove. Pedro was running now, down the steps into the grove and through the trees on the small winding path. Jim, taking long strides, stayed close behind.

Pedro and Jim raced through the light barked trees and wild roses. The fall bushes, covered now with more red rosehips than blossoms, gave way to a flat lush sub-irrigated grassy area not more than two hundred feet from where they had been sitting. The white helicopter settled onto the long green grass just as Jim and Pedro broke from the tree grove. The blades started to slow. It wasn't only Pedro who was excited; Jim, though more stoic, was anxious to see the new red-striped and gleaming white helicopter. Pedro wanted to touch it; Jim just wanted to admire it. He couldn't explain to himself why he had liked his old chopper so much. This one was just as pretty, nearly new and better equipped, he thought. Buying it had been an extravagance on his part but some things were worth it. *Everything here is worth it,* he thought, as the blades ceased their beat.

Jim, standing behind Pedro, removed his hands from the boy's shoulders when the potentially lethal tail rotor was no longer spinning. In time, he would teach Pedro more about the helicopter, its pleasures and its dangers, but he wanted to enjoy this moment rather than instruct his son. He walked Pedro over toward the small, unblemished helicopter.

'Hey, buddy,' said Brush as he opened the door. 'Pedro, get over here, I need a big hug from you.'

Pedro rushed over. 'Ride now, Mr. Brush!'

Brush looked at Jim, who gave him a 'well, why not' look. 'We fueled up at Methow State,' said Brush, 'so plenty of juice for a ride.' Pedro could hardly contain himself.

'All right, let's go. Pedro, walk around to the other side with the major and he will get you belted in,' Jim said.

'Don't you think you better give me a little peck on the cheek first, Jim, and you too, Pedro,' said Glenda Rose as she walked around the nose with the morning sun setting her hair ablaze.

'You deserve one on each side minimum for keeping this guy in check, alive and so happy looking,' responded Jim. He meant every word. Glenda had changed the happy-go-lucky Brush into a guy who knew he had been lucky to find a woman like Glenda—a real keeper.

'Pedro, come on, you too but quickly. I don't want to keep you from your ride.'

The boy shuffled over shyly and looked up. She bent down to him and gave him a big smile and a quick kiss.

'Go with Brush, he will take good care of you,' said Glenda as Pedro impatiently ran to the Enstrom.

'Me fly?'

'You bet,' said Brush. 'First we are going to have to do a general inspection. And we need to have a good look at the tail to make sure everything is just right.' Brush was a nonchalant risk taker, but just like Jim, there were things one did not risk. If there was a weakness to Enstroms, and many other helicopters, it was the tail rotor. An engine could fail and an autorotation could get them down safely but if there was a loose bolt or damage to the tail rotor, control was nearly impossible.

'First look under the engine,' he said as they bent down. 'See any oil leaks?'

'No, Señor Brush.'

'OK. Good. Now let's look at the tail rotor.' They proceeded to circle the helicopter. Brush's experienced eye looked at everything from rivets to safety wires. To the casual observer he was just admiring the new helicopter and talking to Pedro but his practiced eye was taking in anything that might not be right with the new chopper.

'You look good, Glenda,' said Jim. 'You are going to have to tell me all about your and Brush's little Pakistan adventure. I wouldn't mind hearing a few tales from the field. In the past, I would have said Heather wouldn't want to know about it, but things might be different now. She will be glad to see you.'

Jim watched as Glenda walked up toward the house. She was a good-looking woman and a great match for Brush. Then his smile widened as he turned to the new glistening helicopter sitting on its lush patch of grass, which stayed watered all year from the overflowing spring in the aspen grove. It made him feel good to see it sitting there. No scratches in the Plexiglas yet. The same black leather interior as his old one. He slid onto the smooth new leather seat and looked at the one difference, his old Enstrom had minimal gauges. This one had a six-inch glass square to the right of the directional guide. It was the latest GPS moving map display. A mechanic had flown to Seattle from the factory in Menominee, Michigan, to add their latest turbo charger to the engine and install the new gauges. There was a digital fuel gauge now. Gauges weren't a top priority for flying them, except that is, for an accurate fuel gauge. Helicopters weren't cerebral like piloting complex planes, more like riding bicycles: once you could fly them it became second nature even after long spells on the ground. Jim ran his hand along the dash and took hold of the cyclic between his legs. If he could have anything, a thing that is, not a person or animal, he would choose this.

Brush looked in with Pedro from the opposite side and asked. 'Getting sort of warm. You wanna take the doors off, eh?'

Pedro nodded, wondering if it would take long and not really understanding what the Canadian-born Brush was saying.

'Yep, let's do it. Not windy so we can put them over there in the grass.'

A minute later Brush was buckling Pedro in the center while Jim adjusted a headset for him.

'Everyone ready?' asked Jim.

'Yes, sir,' said Pedro, wide-eyed.

Brush had an expectant look that Jim could not quite figure out.

'Pedro,' said Jim. 'I will tell you everything so you will know what to do when you learn to fly. It isn't important that you remember all of it right now though. First, we turn on the ignition and then we start the engine just like in cars. This part is different though—we wait until the engine temperature is just right, which will take only a few seconds since Brush just turned it off. Watch this gauge and when it's here you say OK.'

Jim knew that Pedro was far too young for much of what he told him. However, he thought it best to talk to and with children as equals and not condescend to them. Pedro, a precocious child, listened intently, not wanting to miss a word. Jim gave Brush a small grin as his son glued his eyes to the temperature gauge and watched where Jim pointed. 'Now, sir.'

'See this big lever, we have to pull it back very slowly and as we do, watch the rotor blades over your head.' The engine slowed a little as the blades started to move and then turned faster as the clutch became fully engaged. 'Everything looks good. You ready?'

'Sí.'

'Our feet control the tail rotor. Push the right pedal and the tail wants to move to the right. To lift off we need to push our right foot nearly all the way down.'

'Why?'

'I'll show you why later. OK? For now, watch what I do to take off so you can learn to do it. With my left hand, I twist the throttle and start to pull up on the power control. You reach over with your hand and take the cyclic along with Brush so you can feel what it does. Here we go.' Brush took Pedro's hand and gently placed it over his right hand on the co-pilot's cyclic that was between his knees.

Pedro was too excited to say anything. Brush patted Pedro's hand, loosening his fingers as at first Pedro gripped the cyclic as tight as he could. 'Light touch. Like this.'

The Enstrom lifted five feet as if pulled up by a string, steady, levitating over the blowing grass.

Jim glanced at Brush who was beaming. 'I know, buddy, ever felt anything so smooth?' said Brush.

'Who balanced the blades?'

'The new mechanic-owner who took over Bret's hangar and business. Sam.'

With no vibration, Jim checked the engine's revolution. Thirty-two hundred. He pulled up, adding a bit more power and tipped the nose slightly down. The canyon fell away as they gained speed.

'Smooth as glass, eh, partner?' said Brush. Pedro still just stared spellbound.

Jim nudged the cyclic and turned left toward Coyote Ridge. Pedro's eyes grew wide as they headed straight at the ridge, well below its top, rapidly picking up speed.

'Easy with your grip, partner, this will be fun,' said Brush reassuringly as he patted Pedro's head with his free hand. Pedro's eyes were turning to large saucers.

'Mountain,' said Pedro looking with incredulous eyes. The small white chopper picked up speed as the needle slid past the one hundred miles per hour mark. The trees seemed to be right in front of them as they headed directly at the hill. Pedro squinted his eyes but didn't close them.

Just as he was sure they would burrow into the side, Jim eased back on the cyclic and the white bird soared up as if propelled by a mighty gust of warm air—up and over the top. It was like a carnival ride. The speed seemed incredible.

'Look down now, Pedro,' said Brush. Pedro looked through the Plexiglas at his feet. Both the ridge and the hill literally disappeared as they fell away from under them. He was an eagle soaring on the up drafts. While some might have been scared, Pedro was tense but as Jim looked at him, Pedro's mouth hanging open said it all. He was thrilled but not afraid. The boy trusted Jim, an ability that he had lost for a while after the horrific deaths of his real father and mother at the hands of the cartel. Jim gave him an inexplicable feeling of safety even when they had been under fire in Tubutama.

Brush looked at Pedro, then at Jim, smiled and raised his eyebrows as if to confirm their new man was now one of them. There were thrills to be had in life but never by recklessly going over the line or off the edge. All too many of their friends had pushed to the edge, just as they were doing now, but hadn't stopped short of crossing the inviolable line between staying alive and dying. If both Jim and Brush had a knack, it was for doing just what they did, living on the edge of danger but never succumbing to reckless behavior.

'Can we do again, sir?'

'We will...son, sure,' answered Jim. He was still not used to calling the boy 'son.' 'But not today.' Pedro reached over, squeezed Jim's arm and grinned up at the man who had not only saved him but also given him a home. Something inside the small boy said, *Your life will be good and he will keep you safe.*

Chapter 9

Najma stood before Guillermo, expressionless. Her eyes moved between him and Lazaro, a trusted lieutenant who was responsible for the hacienda's security.

'Sit, please. Would you like something to drink?' asked her host.

'I want nothing.'

The two were alike in many ways and vastly different in others. He, a sociopath bordering on psychopath, cared little for others; she, a psychopath who cared for nothing other than herself. Guillermo hid his character behind a suave outer demeanor. Najma never tried to hide her true nature.

She relished the fear and control she exerted over others and was completely without morals, never showing compassion, murdering in ways that made even the most ruthless cartel members cringe. Najma killed for her own enjoyment: Guillermo the elegant gentleman killed if it brought him monetary gain, directly or indirectly. For him it was not personal: it was necessary, normally that is.

Guillermo ignored her rudeness and smiled, remembering what she had done at his behest. Beheading the brothers and placing the severed heads on their desk, eyes open to greet those who next entered.

'You have pleased me on more than one occasion, Najma; at this moment I require only information. Please go over the story again for Lazaro.' Guillermo still paid attention during her retelling of the attack, absorbing details but he also let his mind wander from time to time, sporadically considering his loss of millions in Europe where he'd planned to join the elite and live a comfortable life.

For once, his cold, analytical mind deserted him. He would have his revenge on the Americans.

'I made the foolish pilot land outside the hacienda when I spotted the attack from the sky. Found an American sniper on a ridgetop.'

'You are certain American, not Mexican?' asked Lazaro incredulously.

She scowled at Lazaro. 'Dead American. Then I entered the hacienda and tried to find my son.' Lazaro looked at Guillermo who remained expressionless. When Najma had mentioned her son in the first telling he wondered how much psychological damage the childless woman had suffered during her detainment. In the days since, she had grown physically stronger, but this fantasy of a child was still cause for concern.

'The American agents, the ones that attacked at the mine, held my son in the hacienda. There were American army helicopters outside. The next I remember, I was in a hospital bed and moved to a small room without windows. Now I am here.'

'You will avenge us and kill the American agents,' said Guillermo.

Najma stared at Guillermo. 'The colonel is dead. I killed him at the hacienda.'

'I see,' said Guillermo. 'Unfortunately he is not dead. He was wounded and he survived.'

Najma's face tightened. She glared at Guillermo. Then she got up without saying anything and left. 'Fuck,' she said when she was well out of hearing range. *Now the colonel has bested me twice.*

Guillermo summoned Vladislav and gave him a recording of Najma. 'Run the gaming scenario to fill in the gaps of the attack?'

Vladislav was silent for a minute, then said only, 'Yes.' He and his computer technicians had spent the night integrating facts and game theory to model scenarios using their newly purchased and wildly expensive Cray supercomputer. Near sunrise, they had come to the most probable scenario. During the night, Vladislav realized with great interest that the Americans must also have an elite computer group. *I will find them and then we will see how good they are,* he thought.

'There are thousands of ways the Americans or anyone with a well-trained army can defeat you here,' said Vladislav. 'The Americans used a small tactical group of Special Forces. Simply put, they had better skills and training than your men. They were aware of your escape tunnels and the location of your computer facilities.'

Guillermo sat stone-faced but inside fuming, realizing he had overestimated his defenses. He had superior weapons and men for facing another cartel or even perhaps the Mexican army. He was stunned, however, to hear that his computer technicians had been inferior.

Vladislav continued. 'You thought you had far superior intelligence gathering than they had, including penetration into the US government's computers, but you had not considered two things—the Americans had not only a better trained force, they also had personnel depth, satellites, communication, and machinery of war that you can never equal.

'Additionally, General Crystal was not afraid to violate accepted laws and crossed the border into Mexico.' Guillermo realized he had foolishly and wrongly accepted an imaginary and artificial safety net: he'd assumed that the border kept others out, that the Americans obeyed their laws. General Crystal did not fit his concept of how Americans behaved.

'Perhaps most important, they far exceeded your computer staff's abilities.'

Guillermo looked straight at Vladislav. 'Are they better than you?'

'No one is better than me,' said Vladislav without hesitation.

Guillermo sat for hours contemplating what Vladislav had told him. Owning the Mexican government and police did not make him inviolable in Mexico. He had had the edge with the likes of the DEA. They waged their foolish war on drugs, one that only enriched him. But the general not only did not play by the rules; he also had an elite force that had been better than his rabble. *I will not let that happen again.* His research found that Vladislav was one of the best in the world as was his new computer center. His men were ruthless killers and he still needed them in Mexico but they were currently no match for the highly trained Americans.

Chapter 10

Nusmen sat in a chair with bits and pieces of the new million-dollar scanning transmission electron microscope lying on the floor. The BWC's head of microscopy had almost thrown a fit when Nusmen started taking pieces out of the new machine with a schematic of its internal components in one hand and a voltage tester in the other. But everyone knew it was useless to argue with Nusmen when he fixated like this. Better to just get some sleep while he got on with it.

Nusmen had had the new STEM working in record time and for several hours was busy imaging and making elemental maps of higher weight elements. However, he quickly became frustrated that he could not image low elemental weight compounds with this new scope. He desperately wanted to view lighter elements in proteins, and the high voltage machine just didn't do that well. Then it struck him.

The problem was the high voltage. If he could change the machine to low voltage, he would gain high contrast. His problem: electronics were not something he had ever been very good at. There had been a continuous opening and closing of the door to the room where he worked. He ignored it. A head would then appear through the door and look, astonished at what he had done to the newest of their microscopes. One after another, they peered into the room as word spread through the lab that Nus sat dismantling the new STEM. Over the top even for him. The frequency of the door opening and closing slowed as fewer people were in the lab in the early morning.

'If I could get the voltage to adjust between high and low, I could use this to analyze carbon, hydrogen, nitrogen, oxygen,' Nusmen mumbled to himself sometime after four a.m. By eight a.m. a lab pool had been set up, guessing the time he would take to have the complicated machine running again. One end of the spectrum said he would never get it back together. Others, less willing to count Nusmen out when he did something that seemed to go off the deep end, said a week. The shortest time wagered was forty-six hours.

As the morning progressed, one head after another poked in the door where Nusmen toiled. Parts were still scattered here and there with a tousled Nusmen walking frantically between a lab bench and the STEM. Dr. Barbara Milton, the lab's supervisor, was aware that Nusmen had unassembled the new machine. She desperately wanted to ignore it, and clung to the hope that she would look in later and it would all be back together.

At nine-thirty she let out a breath and walked into the STEM room. Diodes and wires trailed out of the machine. 'I've seen you do some crazy things, Nusmen, but this tops all of them. I'm going to have to have a company representative fly in from God-knows-where to put this back together. Probably all the way from Holland. What possessed you to do this? Do you have any idea how much this is going to cost?' Without waiting for him to answer, she said, 'Thousands. Tens of thousands. Maybe a lot more. This thing cost over a million dollars as it is.'

Nusmen had not said a word. Intently focused, the rest of the world didn't exist for him. Barbara shook her head and walked out to change her bet in the office pool.

Guillermo's organization had been structured to survive in Mexico against an underequipped local government and other similar gangs. Understanding the world outside of Mexico allowed him to utilize international tax shelters and investments and develop a group of internet hackers that would eventually bring him wealth, control, and knowledge. For all his wealth and power, even with his own new brand of better trained 'special' forces, he understood he could never match the power and depth of large governments. He had deluded himself into thinking he was their equal last year. He would never equal the resources and capabilities of the National Security Agency, the CIA, or the Biological Warfare Center. He could, however, be more cunning, he thought.

This realization allowed Guillermo to segment his plans. He would slither amongst the large world governments, staying incognito. He would do the opposite in Mexico, remaining high profile, letting everyone understand and fear him. Then he would even the score.

He would eliminate the leaders of the Biological Warfare Center. Without General Crystal and the two special agents, they would be nothing. Guillermo smiled a little, thinking of how Najma would kill the colonel this time. In the past, she had failed but now she yearned for his death. She would slaughter Johnson so brutally the entire world would take notice. His enemies in Mexico would understand how far his power reached but those outside Mexico would not trace the killings to him.

She would be a regrettable but necessary sacrifice. As much as he admired the resourceful talents of Najma and appreciated her usefulness, he would make sure the US government blamed only her and not his cartel. He would exercise great care in helping her destroy them—no trail would lead back to him. He then summoned Najma again.

As he studied her, he noted that she was different. Before her capture, she'd had a confident nonchalance. Now she seemed morose, almost insecure. Before, she was hard inside and almost beautiful outside. Now her beauty had a hard edge.

'I am in the process of gathering the necessary information that will allow you to destroy our enemies. In the meantime, I have a job for you here. Are you recovered enough?' he asked, sounding his usual polite self. The colonel's death was too important to leave anything to chance. He needed to test her first to see if she was up to the task he envisioned for her in America. This job would give him the opportunity to see if she retained her skills, her composure.

'Give me the details,' responded Najma. She had been captive and impotent far too long. Now she hungered to see the look in a dying man's eyes again, to hear someone plead for their life. She would willingly kill whomever Guillermo wished, even knowing her benefactor was not to be trusted. That was irrelevant; Najma would do whatever she had to in order to kill Colonel Jim Johnson. Then she would deal with Guillermo if or when she needed to.

She would enjoy something to take her mind away from her failure with the gringos. If she could hate, she hated men, starting with her father and his sick friends who had brutalized her mind repeatedly, just as they had her body—male bastards. *If I could kill them all I would,* she thought. Then she thought of the colonel. She despised him yet he was a worthy adversary, different from other men.

Brad Spinkto thought Nusmen was the smartest person he had ever met. That's why he'd bet that Nusmen would finish reassembling the machine in less than forty-eight hours, the shortest time in the pool. He wanted to win the pool. The pot had grown to several hundred dollars but it had been almost two days. Brad looked nervously at his watch, then at Nusmen, unshaved, hair gone totally wild, waiting for a bird to nest in his wizard's hair.

It was eleven in the evening. Nusmen lay with his head on the worktable in front of the tall electron microscope. Two lone parts lay on the floor. Suddenly he realized there was an image on the STEM screen.

Brad clasped his hands together tightly, mouthed 'yeah,' and jumped out through the door. Outside he ran down the hall and grabbed the first three people he bumped in to. 'You gotta see Nusmen. He's a fucking magician.'

The two women and one man followed Brad into the room. Nusmen had not moved. He sat slumped. Shirt untucked, head on his hands making little burbling noises.

A woman tech said, 'He doesn't have it back together,' as she pointed at the two electronic parts on the floor. The other woman, an experienced microscopist, walked over and looked at the screen. The sharpest, highest contrast image that she had ever seen showed on the screen. 'Oh wow.'

'What is it?' asked Brad.

'I don't know, but it's some sort of biological tissue. The machine's in transmission mode.'

'What?' Brad knew nothing about the microscopes. He worked on gene cloning.

'He's using it to transmit light, Transmission Electron Microscopy.'

She touched Nusmen on his shoulder. He didn't stir. So she hit him a good blow on his arm. He raised his head and with blurry eyes said, 'Huh?'

'What's on the screen, Nusmen?'

'Oh, ah, it's a bit of biofilm,' and then added, 'from my mouth.'

'You are weird all right. Why is it so clear?'

Nusmen's Adam's apple bobbed as he swallowed, looked around at the group. 'I changed the electron voltage down from ninety kilovolts to four kilovolts. The voltage is now adjustable. So you can see images better and detect light elements.'

The other woman said, 'What are those parts for?' as she pointed to the floor.

'I don't know, didn't need them.'

Chapter 11

Sheilla had spent several relatively peaceful months learning her new job as BWC's lead technical analyst. She was not bored, but the highlight had been when Brush and Glenda had gone to Pakistan on a mission. She'd been their lifeline back at the lab and had loved every sleepless moment of it. Sheilla wondered whether she was getting hooked on action. Everything seemed slightly bland in the office since the attack on Seattle and the events in Mexico.

She reasoned that the general had used the relatively undemanding mission in Pakistan to test Glenda Rose's and Brush's effectiveness working together in the field. She hoped they were ready for something more challenging. Or Colonel Johnson was ready to return. He had a way of making things exciting.

A resonant voice, much softer than normal, penetrated her thoughts as the general said, 'Sheilla, your mind is somewhere else.'

'Yes, sorry, General.' For a second she struggled to remember what they were talking about. 'How long will they be in the mountains?'

'Jim said the camping trip would be a few days, maybe more.'

'I want to go sometime and see why they think it's so special out there. I'm just not sure about the llamas.'

'You don't need to worry about anything if you go out with that crew. Heather is a diehard naturalist and Jim and Brush are comfortable just about anywhere. Me,' said the general, 'I'm happy to be close to good restaurants and military bases. I've had enough remote places for one lifetime. Maybe because someone is always trying to shoot me when I'm out there.'

'Do you think Heather would mind if I asked to come along sometime? Though it worries me a bit, being so far from civilization and safety.'

'Ah, I'm sure she would be delighted. They're planning a reunion in a few weeks with JT, Ralphy, Misha, Vidya, and the two other kid hackers at Huachuca. They're all going to the ranch first. I think Heather will want to get back out in the mountains more before the snow sticks.

People make civilization dangerous, Sheilla, not the wilderness. You should join them; it is safe out in their mountains. Not many people.'

Sheilla lowered her eyebrows, thinking, *But it's not. Only last August the terrorists killed the cowboys out in the Pasayten. The general nearly died and still hasn't completely regained his old swagger. And how could he forget what happened to Heather and her group of scientists camping in Mexico? What is it with this man if he can wipe such horrific events from his memory?*

'Mexico and Horseshoe Basin won't happen again, and not where they are going anyway,' said the general as if he were reading her thoughts. 'That was a one-off event, the terrorists killing the cowboys and they got lucky nearly killing me.'

'Um, huh.'

'Try to imagine the most dangerous place in the world and consider that wherever that is, you would be safe with Jim and Brush. That was not the first time they saved my old bones.'

'Sounds a bit wild out there to me; it feels nice and cozy here underground, even with our untamed lab types.'

'That reminds me, our resident exotic, William Edgar Nusmen, has been here for a year. This morning they found him sleeping on the new electron microscope. I thought I was saving him from prosecution and it would be a punishment to stay here under house arrest, but I was obviously wrong. He thinks he is in heaven, not jail. He has never said one word about leaving, works harder than anyone and accomplishes more than I would expect from even our best lab techs. And, well, geniuses are often problematic and unstable. He needs a breather, everyone does. Without one I'm afraid he'll lose touch with the world and eventually his own sanity.'

Sheilla was fiddling with her long, dark auburn hair, worn today in one long braid, and barely listening to the general. Despite everything he'd done in the past, and as crazy as he seemed sometimes, she liked Nusmen and she thought he liked her, though he never did anything to show it. Perhaps they should meet for a coffee or meal outside of the lab, and they could talk on a more personal level—if he ever left the lab, that is.

'He's a very intelligent person,' she said pensively while unconsciously twisting her braid back and forth between her fingers.

'We have a lot of those in the lab, including you, Sheilla.'

She blushed a rosy pink that complemented her brown-red eyebrows.

'You're no slouch in that department, General.'

'Enough of the mutual admiration,' he declared, embarrassed but liking it nonetheless, especially from Sheilla.

Effective, efficient people. It's what makes being in this place fun, he thought. He couldn't be happier with Sheilla. He had come to depend on her advice, and she'd never let him down. He had been lucky to recruit both her and Glenda Rose Stuart from the FBI. That organization of egotistical men had overlooked and underrated two unique redheads. General Crystal would never make that mistake.

'Enough,' he boomed, resuming his usual outsized tone of

voice. 'You get Heather to take you into the mountains and I'll personally fly you there.'

'Well, thanks. But I'll think on it some, before jumping out with all those bugs and crawly things.'

Chapter 12

Bertrand Gupta sat at a desk that looked as though it was in total disarray. It was not his usual style but even in the chaotic mess, he knew where everything was.

Martin Pearson walked in without knocking. Bertrand scowled instantly; he couldn't help himself. He hated being interrupted.

'Cleaning out your files, Bertrand?'

Martin's humor wore thin at times. However, out of the people in the CIA's upper level who were working on Najma's escape, Martin was the most capable. Sorenson lacked imagination and understanding of the agency's role. Flayback was very bright but too ambitious, understanding even less than her boss and too focused on advancing her career. On top of her other unappealing attributes, she was often self-centered and egotistical.

'I found out a little something that I think might be interesting to you, Bertrand. I mean you probably already have this but...'

'I'm waiting, Martin.'

'We don't know anything about how Najma was captured, right? All we know is that she was part of the terrorist attack during the Seattle Bumbershoot fandango. And the Bio Warfare Labs...'

"BWC, Martin, Biological Warfare Center.' Bertrand was always precise and it annoyed him when others were not. 'The administration renamed them more in line with what they do. They never were just laboratories.'

'Yeah, OK,' Martin continued. 'The BW-whatever tracked her, shot her up, and the general along with the State Department dropped her in our lap.'

'Get to the point, Martin, I don't need a summary.'

'Jesus, Bertie, I am!'

Bertrand's scowl deepened. He hated being called, "Bertie" and Martin knew it.

'OK, I'll continue,' he said, adding a mumbled, 'if I may.'

Bertrand shook his head and was about to tell Martin to get out and come back later when Martin said, 'We don't know anything about where they captured her. I always assumed it was in the US.'

Bertrand sat a little straighter. Martin had his full attention now. 'An old buddy of mine in the DEA told me he'd heard a rumor through a mole in the Siastra cartel, something about a Mexican woman who's now apparently disappeared. She was new to them as an amateur informant; the cartel had killed her son and she was getting even spying on them.'

Bertrand rolled his eyes at this lengthy digression.

Martin hurried to continue, knowing he'd pushed Bertrand as far as was wise. 'Before this lady vanished she passed some information about a woman assassin who was at the cartel's headquarters; she referred to her as the "she-devil," and what details and description she was able to share sounded a helluva lot like Najma.'

Bertrand nearly jumped out of his chair. 'Martin, I must say sometimes you earn your pay. What else?' Then before Martin could answer, Bertrand fired more questions. 'How did the general's group get our terrorist lady if she was with the cartel? Unless she was on another mission back in the US. They wouldn't have violated Mexico's sovereignty…would they?'

'DEA hasn't been able to figure out lots of things with the Siastra cartel. The Mex gov said they raided them and captured their leader. It appears the cartel lost a bunch of people all right and have been reorganizing, and recently they rebuilt their old headquarters, which is just south of the US border near a small town called Tubutama. DEA says it doesn't add up. The government was too corrupt and it never made sense that they had the ability to raid a large cartel without the cartel hearing about it first. Basically, Bertrand, we have a woman that fits Najma's description seen with the cartel at the same time that it took some sort of hit, and then Najma was handed to us shortly after.'

'Jesus, Martin, great piece of work. If Najma was caught in the raid on the Siastra cartel, a lot of things start to make sense—including all the mystery surrounding her.'

'Yeah, OK. It is plausible, isn't it? Someone, maybe BWL, shit, BWC, went over the line, waged a small war with the cartel and nabbed her. Illegal as hell but not outside the realm of possibility. One more little tidbit. It seems Colonel Johnson was injured just about that time.'

'So if the US government took her from Mexico and put her in Camp X-Ray, then it stands to reason the cartel broke her out. Find out about the cartel and see how they are connected in Cuba. Drugs, maybe. That might confirm the hypothesis. But first, see if you can verify that Najma was actually with the cartel and what she was doing with them. The "she-devil," as you say.'

'OK, Bertrand. Glad I could add something,' said Martin knowing this was the reason Bertrand put up with his jokes. *Sometimes I deliver the goods,* he thought. 'I'll get some more feelers out.' Almost adding "Bertie" and glad that he didn't.

Bertrand hesitated and then said, 'Hell of a good job, Martin.'

Sheilla turned to her computer monitor and pulled up an NSA tracking program the computer gang in Huachuca had given her. She shouldn't possess it and she had only looked at it infrequently after Najma's capture. But discussing the cartel and Mexico had renewed her curiosity, something more than camping had bothered her about that case. An hour later, she picked up the phone.

'General, something important. Need to talk again. When can we?'

'Now is good.'

'Be right there.'

Moments later Sheilla was in the general's office, ready to share her information.

'I was just going to have some coffee. You want some?' said the general, softer than usual. Sheilla had long ago come to terms with his outsized voice and now it only made her laugh when he turned the volume up. She noticed his voice was softer than normal again and wondered why. He didn't usually offer refreshments either, preferring his team to get in and out of his office.

'Coffee's good for me, uh, sir.'

At that moment, the general's secretary brought in a tray with two cups and coffee and moved toward the desk with her usual efficiency. As far as Sheilla could tell, he hadn't ordered coffee for her. Marsha saw Sheilla's expression.

'New shortcut. Normally I can hear him from my office and know what he wants, but this time I didn't hear him, so I just assumed you would join him for coffee,' Marsha explained as she set the coffee tray down.

'Of course,' said Sheilla, feeling slightly embarrassed for not realizing the obvious: Marsha knew Sheilla liked coffee. 'Thanks, Marsha.'

'Some advantages to everything.' The general winked. 'No intercom needed.' Then noticing that Sheilla seemed distracted, he added, 'What's on your mind?'

Sheilla started talking in her usual contemplative manner. 'Immediately after our Mexico adventure, we monitored key words at NSA and other agencies, if you remember, to see if they tumbled to us being in Mexico illegally. One of the obvious words we tracked was "Najma." '

The general raised one eyebrow. 'I thought you stopped monitoring them, no need to with her in detention at X-Ray.'

'We did officially, sort of, but monitoring's not much trouble or time consuming. I just read a short report, every once in a while.'

He waited for her to continue.

'In the last couple of days Najma's name has come across several times in communications, mostly from the CIA but also DEA. It seems someone high up is asking about her. If you approve, I'll put someone on it full-time, step up the monitoring and expand the key word search. It may not mean a thing but it seems worth checking up on why they are suddenly interested and asking questions about her. There hasn't been a peep for months—until now.'

The general continued speaking softly. 'Are you certain you can keep them from finding out you are snooping on them? I don't want any surprises, Sheilla. Make no mistake, I'm glad you did this and I want to pursue it. But we sure don't want to get caught poking around in their communications.'

'Then I had better check with the Wolf Pack, first. Just to be sure,' she replied.

'Crazy lot, those four. I like them. Computers and their uses are evolving by the minute, particularly with the CIA and NSA changing and improving their systems almost every day. You are correct: we need them. Call the Wolf Pack in right away, before you monitor more. They'll be able to check things out and advise you if either the snooping kings at NSA or the other agency can detect you.'

Sheilla was still getting used to his sometimes calling the CIA the "other agency," 'Fred occasionally talks to a guy he met during the Mexico operation. I think Fred likes being associated with the Wolf Pack but he is also a little intimidated by the lieutenant and the sergeant. They're way above his abilities.'

'I thought the two professor types gave both those upstart hacker kids a run for their money,' responded the general.

'You are right about that, General. I think the two kids started out thinking they were the top computer guns and Misa and Vidya have taught them a few lessons about who is first and second best.'

'You think there is any chance we could entice those two up here? If there is a place we are weak, it's computer abilities.'

'I'll feel them out when I can but my take is that the four of them are happy as clams together. With the synergy between the Wolf Pack and our background with them, I think they would do anything we asked. It's almost as good as having them here.'

'You are probably right. The army keeps them busier than we could and I think they like us just as much as we do them. We couldn't have done what we did in Mexico without them. Don't push them then, but you never know if one or both might want to leave, so drop a hint if you can.'

Chapter 13

After a forty-five-minute drive along the winding blacktop River Road, Heather drove over a narrow bridge onto Buttermilk Creek Trail, then carefully up a steep rutted road, climbing slowly; the truck lazily rolled from side to side as it approached the small trailhead.

The unloading area, notched out of large old pines and firs in the dense low-mountain forest, felt cool and fresh. *The trailhead is empty,* she thought. No other cars, they would have the trail and the camping to themselves. It was late morning but even in the shade, the air was warm, swirling with the scent of pine needles and moss. Heather expertly backed the white and red truck against the log-loading ramp.

'Peaceful trip up,' said Heather.

No Shasta, mused Jim silently, but he did not want to remind her that her favorite llama caused all the trouble in the truck, kicking and spitting at the other llamas. She continued to be distraught about the limping Shasta who couldn't go on this trip.

Heather had saved Shasta from certain death as a baby. His mother had milk but insufficient colostrum. The baby received few immunoglobulins, leaving him with a dysfunctional immune system to counter bacteria. At two days old, weak and runny eyed, Shasta was only minutes away from death when Heather desperately took a liter of whole blood from his mother and injected it directly into the dying baby's jugular vein. Luck was on her side, the blood type matched and within hours, Shasta, with the protection of his mother's blood immunity, was prancing around the field like any other healthy baby.

The problem now was with all the baby handling by Heather, the llama imprinted, which meant as an adult he was apt to spit equally at any llama or person that invaded his space. The imprinting on people reduced his fear of humans but there was something more, something ingrained in his personality, probably bad attitude genes inherited from his mother, who was an ornery animal. What she raised was a llama that was bad tempered toward humans and llamas alike. Still, he behaved better around Heather, rarely spit at her, and she loved him almost like a son.

Jim didn't miss him, though, and he was certain the other llamas were much happier without him. Nevertheless, he was unhappy when Heather was and so would even put up with the bossy Shasta if it made her happy.

Lola and Heather had made short work preparing and packing the food. Heather, sometimes on the slow side, increased her pace to match the speed and efficiency of Lola. Meanwhile Jim, Brush, and Pedro loaded the eight llamas in the truck for the drive to Oval Lakes trailhead. Pipestone had been the first in the white truck with its red painted wood stakes, and immediately laid down forward. Pipey, as everyone called him, rose to the top of everyone's affection list. Of all the llamas, he was unique. Affectionate, cute, and the only llama that they trusted not to be tied up at campsites.

Jim gently pushed between the llamas and started attaching lead lines to their halters. He passed Meteor's and Cinnabar's leads to Heather, then attached lead lines to Black Star and Cosmos, finally arriving at a recumbent Pipestone: the only llama without a halter. The brown and white llama casually stood as Jim moved toward him, holding out his head as Jim held his halter just in front of his nose. Pipey pushed his nose into the halter and held still while Jim gently fastened the halter strap.

'How old is Pipestone?' asked Glenda as she poked her head in the back door.

'Eleven, or thereabouts.'

'How long will he be able to pack?'

'Hard to say,' said Jim. 'Heather loads him light these days. He gets the coolers going in and they are empty except for trash coming out. So far we haven't had any llamas that are too old to pack. But I'm betting even when the old guy can't carry a pack Heather will still let him come on trips, as long as he wants to.'

Brush, never far from Glenda, also poked his head around the corner. 'He'll probably outlive us!'

'I hope so for Heather's sake,' said Jim, laughing.

'Not funny, buster. You two had better live a long time for both Heather's sake and mine,' Glenda replied, only half joking.

Brush watched her walk away, raised an eyebrow at Jim, shook his head and said, 'She is something.'

'Yep, looks like you've finally met your match. Let's get the rest unloaded.'

'You guys talking about women or just plain talking instead of unloading?' Heather asked before they could start again. 'We can't waste too much time or we won't make Oval Lakes before dark. Tie the rest up over on the left, Brush,' Heather instructed as she rubbed Pipestone's neck. She put her head forward but he pulled away and wouldn't touch noses with her. 'No kisses. I guess he wants to get going too.' She laughed. No one understood what llamas were thinking, but they always acted excited while being loaded for a trip.

'Even so I can't understand why any living thing wouldn't want a kiss from you.'

Heather looked at her partner seriously. 'You really are nice to me, Jim. I know you meant that and weren't just kidding around.'

'I meant every word. So why do you think the llamas get excited about going to the mountains? Change of scenery?'

'I think it's the sedges and other grasses as much as anything.'

'Like dessert for them?' asked Brush as he returned for the next group of animals. 'Thought we were in a bit of a hurry, Heather.'

'OK, OK. Let's get a move on then. I miss Shasta,' said Heather as she moved off.

'Well, I don't miss him and nobody else does either,' said Brush. 'One of these guys would be covered in his green slimy spit by now.'

Nusmen stumbled up to his room and collapsed on the bed. He slept for seven hours, waking up tussled and blurry eyed as Dr. Milton shook him. He hadn't shaved in days nor changed his clothes. He had almost forgotten about his bacteria-toxin experiment while he'd worked on the STEM but as his head cleared he realized they needed immediate attention.

'A little ripe aren't you, William Edgar?'

'Huh.'

'See you downstairs.' Dr. Milton walked out the door, musing, *Just think, I used to really despise him. But now...I almost like him despite that terrible smell.*

Nusmen rolled out of bed, splashed cold water on his face and, without drying, set off to his lab bench.

He was so focused that he didn't even notice the mob of people near the stairs. As he walked down with his mind consumed with images of bacteria toxins and how to neutralize them, the clapping penetrated through his thoughts. With mouth hanging open he looked around wondering what was going on.

Brad stepped up to him. 'Nusmen, you smart ass. I knew you could do it, and I bet on you and won the pool.'

'Huh?'

Of all the people Nusmen worked with, Brad was the one he bumped shoulders with more than the others. Mainly because they worked in the same area much of the time.

Nusmen stared at the people, not understanding why they were here and uncomfortable as they clapped and looked at him.

Dr. Milton walked to him and said, 'You seem perplexed. Did you know there was an office pool as to if or how fast you would get the STEM back together?'

'Um, no.'

'You know what you did?'

Nusmen just looked at her, clearly wishing he were back in his lab area. 'The company has a representative on their way here now. You've made them their first low voltage electron microscope. Fetvev Inc has been trying to make one work for ages.'

'Ah...I was just wanted to see some proteins.'

Everyone shook their heads and laughed. Their very own legend. Some said Nusmen looked like Ichabod Crane, tall and skinny, protruding Adam's apple, racing manically through the lab late at night. 'Hip hip hooray,' Brad yelled, looking at Nus and holding his winnings.

Nusmen turned away but Barbara Milton saw the tear that he brushed from his cheek. She looked at him, considered his hygiene, and then reluctantly put her arm around him, saying, 'Glad you are part of our family,' which brought a few cheers and shouted agreements from the crowd and caused another tear to wind its way through four-day-old fuzzy whiskers.

Only Barbara noticed, thinking maybe he was not as much of a people phobic as he pretended.

With the llamas tied out of the truck, all that was left was to unload the over the cab rack. *This will go fast,* Jim thought. The roads weren't bumpy getting to the trailhead so he had minimally secured the panniers and saddles in the overhead stock rack. Heather normally tied them all down with so many ropes that it took forever to undo them. She wasn't worried about them being damaged but did not want them falling out on the llamas, and as she said, they had never come undone proving her point. However, in Jim's efficiency-controlled mind, the fewer knots tied, the less to untie. Jim and Brush had secured them the minimum they thought was actually needed. He was already putting the packs and saddles by the back door when Heather came back and looked at Brush.

'Take this red saddle over by Cinnabar. I'll start to put the coolers on Pipey.'

'I want to help with Pipey,' yelled Pedro as he ran over to Heather, followed closely by Rosie-O-Twisp. Pedro weighed just over forty pounds, while Rosie weighed in at nearly one hundred and thirty pounds.

'Okie dokie. First, go get the dog pack from the Suburban. I'll wait for you and we can saddle Pipey together. You need to get Rosie loaded and where's your pack? Bring it too. I want to see how heavy it is.'

Heather had Meteor's packsaddle on by the time Pedro got back. She lifted Rosie's small pack. 'Sort of light, huh. Let me see your pack.'

Pedro sheepishly handed it to her.

'Sort of heavy.' She raised an eyebrow looking at him. 'Rosie weighs three times more than you do and can carry a little more weight, don't you think?'

'I don't want her to get hurt,' said Pedro.

'She'll be just fine. Take some of the dog kibble out of your pack and put it in hers. We'll weigh it to make sure but it will only be about seven pounds per side. Rosie will carry how much then?'

Pedro counted in his head, 'Fourteen.'

'Hum…your math is getting to be very good!' Pedro beamed. 'OK, let's get her loaded and start on Pipey.'

'OK, Mama.'

Heather instantly choked up. It was the first time he had called her 'mama.' She turned away and pretended to work so he wouldn't see; the boy had seen so much sadness she didn't want him to misunderstand her tears.

Chapter 14

Thunder rumbled up a dusty border-town street. Najma sat on a low bench against an adobe wall, sheltered from the glare of the early afternoon sun but not its oppressive heat. Ominous dark clouds moved closer, accompanied by lightning flashes and thunder rumbling up the street. She could feel the air popping with static, much like the thrill rising in her blood.

She looked up at the restaurant on the first floor just as waves of rain struck buildings and awnings. Red dust splashed into the air from the heavy drops as she mounted the first step. Halfway up, she looked back as the torrents of water began flooding the street below.

She entered the rustic restaurant with its wooden tables, red linen napkins, and sombreros hanging on the walls. A table was available near a window and she ordered the first thing her finger touched on the menu with no intention of eating any of it. It was a perfect vantage point from which to observe the target, just forty yards down the street.

Killing these Mexicans was not much different from her last assignment for Guillermo, the two brothers in Cabo San Lucas she had taken care of for him nine months ago. A glimmer of a smile crossed her face, as she remembered.

The story of what she'd done had passed by word of mouth, cementing her reputation as the she-devil, which had begun with her sadistic annihilation of Pedro's family in the small village near the cartel's headquarters in Tubutama. She was now a woman feared by the cartel's thugs, who had never felt fear for a woman before.

It wasn't only the anomaly of being both a woman and a killer that caused the fear she inspired in the cartel. It was the way she killed, like a predator toying with its prey: needlessly cruel, ruthlessly thorough. She became an evil demon in cartel lore, a being to be feared. '*Todo el mundo temen a la diabla. The devil is feared by everyone,*' they said while crossing themselves.

Her job was to eliminate a small gang of drug dealers that had offended Guillermo. She didn't know why nor did she care. Three of the men sat at a table outside a small and dingy bar as she watched from her vantage point. Clearly, the shabby little bar did not cater to the Nogales tourist crowd. It was open to the street with only two small rickety wooden tables inside along the walls and a rough wooden bar in back. Not much of a challenge if the men were no more sophisticated than this hole-in-the-wall bar. Nonetheless, Najma never underestimated her adversaries. She had never lost to an opponent, with the exception of the American agent. That memory made her angry as she sat staring down the street through curtains of rain. Then she pushed it out of her thoughts, replacing it with the task ahead. She would take out her anger on these small-time hoods in the bar; she needed to feel alive again.

The rain continued to pummel the red mud river that only moments before had been a street. The level was rising close to the top of the high curb. She scanned the street for police, old people, kids, anyone who might be a lookout for the gang. People standing on the walkway above the curb were nervously looking for some place higher to get above the rising waters. She ended her scan at the small bar and watched a man carrying a woman on his shoulders splash through the water and into the bar. It was the gang leader. She recognized him from the photograph Guillermo's lieutenant, Lazaro, had given her. The rain had plastered his long black hair to his misshapen, pig-like face.

The muddy water swelled over the curb and lapped against the floor of the bar. The three men, the bartender and the two new arrivals, moved inside and toward the back, away from the advancing flood. The sidewalk was now under water and empty of people.

Najma had been in no hurry but she sensed an opportunity. She was incapable of anxieties or worries but had an innate gift for seizing her moments. She laid down enough money to cover the meal and walked swiftly from the restaurant, carrying her large shoulder bag. She waded across the street, now a red-brown river, pushing against the flow, climbed the curb, and stepped into the bar. The heavy drops of water continued to pound down, enveloping the open bar in a curtain of rain. Lightning flashes crackled upward and were immediately followed by a rumble that shook the ground and building.

She took a quick glance behind her; no one else had braved walking against the rushing torrent. The sidewalks swirled with muddy water, the heavy drops pushed sideways by the wind hitting the buildings. There were no people in sight and she could not see the restaurant where she had sat just moments before through the slashing rain. The pounding rain and the thunder provided a continuous din in the background. The five men and the woman were sitting on the edge of the bar facing the street. The ugly leader was the second from the left, laughing with the woman, her thin but shapely legs next to his dirty jeans, which were tucked into silver-toed boots. Najma's water-soaked shoes sloshed onto the bar's floor just as lightning lit up the interior with a blue-white flash.

The gang members sat transfixed by the female apparition in front of them, never for an instant suspecting impending death. An ugly, grinning face highlighted a gold-capped tooth reflecting yellow in the flash of light. Darkness and then another blue flash. Suddenly the meaning of her presence shocked them to attention; the apparition was holding a silenced automatic weapon pointed straight at them. The alien sight of this dark-haired woman holding a gun, in this storm, in this place, rendered them motionless. She waited. They stared. Then, coolly and efficiently, without hurry, Najma squeezed the trigger, hitting the gold-toothed man in the stomach. In quick succession, she placed a single round in the center of each man, just like shooting metallic figures in a carnival game.

The woman with them sat frozen, traumatized, while the five men clutched themselves in pain, groaning and cursing. The leader looked at Najma. 'Pinche culero, fucken asshole woman. Messing with me, you're dead.'

Najma looked at him with cold eyes, lowered her gaze, and shot him just above the testicles. 'Greetings, señor, you now have a new asshole in the front, compliments of Guillermo,' she said evenly. His mouth dropped at the mention of Guillermo and his mind tried to push his body toward her but it would not move.

Two of the men remained draped at odd angles over the bar counter, illuminated with lightning flashes; the other three were now flailing on the wet wood floor. Najma walked closer to the woman, staying just out of reach of the men, constantly flicking her eyes from one to the other, making sure none pulled a weapon. She looked into the woman's dark brown eyes. She was only a girl, perhaps thirteen or fourteen years old. Pretty, wearing a low-cut blouse showing the tops of her small breasts. The girl started to shake. 'Por favor,' she uttered so softly that it melted into the sound of the rain.

Najma wanted to prolong this, her greatest pleasure too long denied, but the storm could stop at any time and she had selected the moment, obscured by the torrent, to kill Guillermo's offenders. It was good to have a weapon in her hands again, and to see fear in the girl's eyes. This was what she lived for; the power to control fear, to watch it rise and be momentarily replaced by hope, and then to see the confusion and terror as her victims realized she was not a creature of mercy but a bringer of death. Najma would have liked to play with the girl a bit more, she was irritated at having to end this so quickly.

Najma smiled at the young girl, and her fear visibly diminished. People always believed a woman would show mercy, particularly to the young. Najma found this a strange assumption. The fear dissipated in Rosanna's eyes as this woman seemed to say she would be OK, she would grow and blossom into a full woman.

She watched the fear recede and then fired one round directly into the shallow valley between the girl's breasts. The girl looked uncomprehendingly down at the red spot marring her youthful skin then slowly sank backward; her young body slumped spread-eagled, pathetically and unglamorously on top of the bar as she rasped her last breath.

'Mon de Dios,' gasped the leader, now lying still on the floor.

'Are you uncomfortable, señor?' Najma asked. Without missing a beat, she turned and shot the two men still on the bar and then looked at the three floundering in the rising water on the floor. One looked near death, and she shot him in the head. She quickly changed the rotary clip. The other man was making small moans and trying to get up; she shot him in the groin then with a pause, watching him, watching his eyes comprehend, she shot him in the head. She turned and smiled at the leader while she replaced the clip in her gun.

He crossed himself, staring with a mixture of resignation, hate, and disbelief. His bravado disappeared as she shot him first six more times in the abdomen, watching the pain devour him, his beady eyes go dim in his pig-face as death rapidly approached, and finally she shot him in the head.

Najma felt comforted by the killings, regaining some of her confidence. This was what she knew, what she did. She took a last moment to appreciate the scene, like the finale of a stage-tragedy.

Bodies were sprawled over the bar and on the floor. Blood mixed with the water on the floor, the remnants of lightning turning it rose colored. She turned and splashed out across the sidewalk, stepping into the deep water now raging down the street. A lone figure disappearing into its flow.

Chapter 15

'I can't wait to get on the trail. It is so beautiful here,' said Heather.

'Woods are spooking,' said Lola to no one in particular.

'Spooky, Lola, but they aren't. They are peaceful safe havens from a crazy world.' *Normally at least,* Heather thought as she remembered the ill-fated camping trip in Mexico.

'Make me shiver. I afraid for my niño.'

'Pedro, come here for a minute.'

'In a minute, Mama. I'm helping Mr. Brush.'

'As soon as you are finished then.'

Heather fussed over the llama packs, pushing them, checking the straps were snug but not too tight. Cinnabar gave her a look that could only be construed as saying 'quit messing with me and let's get this show on the trail.' The packs were all fine for weight and balance but, as was her way, she double-checked then triple-checked, out of maternal protectiveness for the llamas.

'Sí, Mama. Vámonos?'

'Sí, hijo, we are leaving soon. Are you happy in the woods?'

'Sí, muy bonita.'

Heather was happy for him to speak Spanish as much as he wanted. He would have all the English training he would need soon at school. She didn't want him to lose touch with his origins.

'Yes, it is very pretty and serene,' said Heather.

'Sareen?'

'Se…rene. It means peaceful. It is green and lush and someday we will spend a day in the woods looking at the mosses and lichens. I always feel serene in the deep woods.'

'Very serene,' he said. 'Can we go now?'

'Yes, sweetheart. Let's get on the trail. It is a long way and the llamas will have to eat along the way.'

'No doubt about it now, General,' said Sheilla. 'The CIA is asking about drug cartels in Mexico and Najma. From what I gather, they are trying to see if there is a connection between her and the cartel. Also a couple mentions of us.'

'Not welcome news. I hoped that any interest in how she was captured had died down. Why do you think they are asking? Do you think she told them we captured her in Mexico and not in the US?' The question was more directed at himself than Sheilla.

'I can't even guess. I need more details. I just wanted to apprise you that it seems the inquiries are increasing. Is it really so important that they don't find out about us crossing the border? The Mexican president did give us his OK.'

'We sidestepped drug enforcement, disabled their border plane's reconnaissance systems. We didn't inform the FBI and some other agencies. It wasn't legal per se; going over international borders is in our mandate, but for the intended purpose of chasing bad bugs and bio weapons, not just bad people. But then the Mex government wanted it covert so they could take the credit. It suited their purposes to have a success in their war against the drug cartels and it suited our purposes to stay silent. It's potentially a big can of worms. The president and secretary of state don't want it to become public. Besides messing with the DEA, and the border patrol, we never advised the CIA.'

Sheilla looked at the general. She already knew this but it sounded like it could be worse than she thought. Politics were not her thing.

As if reading her thoughts, the general added, 'Step up our monitoring. High priority. Don't worry about anything else, just nail down what the CIA is after as soon as you can. Let me know about anything, no matter how trivial. Use your instinct. I always want to know what you think, not just what you know.'

Chapter 16

'Holy cow, look at that,' exclaimed Glenda Rose as she pointed at an enormous rock-covered hillside. 'I always forget how awesome that talus slope is,' said Heather.

The side of the rocky ridge, traversed by the trail, appeared to be nothing more than a piece of a mile-long thread, angling up the massive gray-blocky slope.

'Es muy grande,' said Pedro with his lower lip dropping open and his brown eyes transfixed.

'We climb there. Look dangerous. Goes up and up and long way,' said Lola as she let out a long breath. 'But I no want to stay here so close to the woods.'

Heather looked around near the base of the slope and then over into the thinning woods at a tiny green spot. 'Over in that meadow is a good place to camp,' said Heather. 'What do you think, Jim?'

'We won't have much time to set up before dark if we climb to the top of the ridge, but we can handle it, if you think that is a better idea.'

'I would just as soon plunk down here,' said Brush. 'Looks fine to me. We can climb up tomorrow and not have to set up in the dark tonight.' He was thinking more about being in the tent with Glenda earlier than he was worried about setting up in the dark.

Jim nodded agreement. Brush smiled to himself.

'Malo, muy malo,' muttered Lola.

'Stop it, Lola. We'll be fine here.'

'More bears lower down, though. Lots of huckleberries above the meadow,' added Brush with a wry smile.

'Stop it, buster,' said Heather, exasperated. 'Don't scare her or Pedro either.'

'I no scared, Mama.'

'Bears, big bears! Dios mio,' said Lola as she crossed herself twice.

Jim was already walking toward the meadow with Pipestone. Heather had to follow with the string of seven as they started to fidget when Jim and Pipey began walking away without them. Jim turned and smiled, slowed a little and Heather smiled back, moving up behind him. She knew he was just getting on with it, cutting the nonsense with Lola's worries short.

'Rosie and I will protect you, Lo,' said Pedro. He put his arm around her stocky body and started walking, trying to catch up with Heather. 'No hay muchos áborles. It looks very serene.'

'What that mean, mijo? What that last English word mean?'

'It means safe and peaceful,' said Pedro with more than just a little bit of pride after using his new word. 'You protect me before and now I protect you. I am older and stronger now.'

Guillermo, one leg lazily draped over the other, was sipping wine from a fine crystal goblet with a small round polished stone set between the base and the stem. He'd had the glasses made in Europe; the smooth stones were from the village where he grew up. It was not a sentimental reminder of his birthplace. He thought of it as how his life had evolved and would end. From dirt and pebbles to fine European wine and crystal.

'Mas vino tinto, señor?'

Guillermo said nothing but gave a slight nod while daydreaming about wine and Europe. Without being aware of what he was saying added, 'please.'

The diminutive Felix, dressed in immaculate white linen, tried hard to display no emotion around his boss. His was a privileged position but one that still terrified the small, dark-skinned, northern Mexico Indian. His predecessor and former boss had simply disappeared after working as Guillermo's headman for a year. Felix had been promoted, and now he faithfully but nervously served Guillermo.

Guillermo adding 'please' to the end of any request was not normal and it made Felix even more edgy than usual. Guillermo held up his glass and Felix concentrated hard not to spill a drop as he poured and then retreated to just outside the living room door, letting out a long, nearly silent sigh.

While Felix was anxious, Guillermo was feeling very pleased. He had men in Nogales watching Najma's targets. They had reported the grisly scene immediately to Guillermo. He now wished he had had them take pictures. From his men's description, the scene sounded like art. *Yes,* he thought, *I will get pictures and then perhaps commission a painting,* as he visualized an old rough wood bar, red blood swirling in the rising water, his former associates draped incongruously on the bar and below on the floor.

He pushed the number one on his cell phone and ordered Lazaro to have the men get pictures before the police disrupted the scene. 'I want pictures from the road looking straight into the bar and close-ups.' He hung up without waiting for Lazaro to respond.

He set the phone down on the polished wood side table. 'Send Najma in.' Felix immediately walked as softly as he could through the room and out a carved double-door on the far side. Standing and facing directly toward the door with eyes fixed on Felix was the only person who terrified him even more than Guillermo.

The dark-haired, olive-complexioned woman wore black with a red belt, reminding him of the spiders that lived in dark places in the villa. He thought of her as a shiny poisonous thing not a human person. *Yes,* he thought. Like the female spider with the wineglass symbol on her belly, this thing in front of him would kill any male that was foolish enough to breed with her.

With his eyes looking at her chin, he said, 'Por favor, entrar.' He slightly twisted his body and with his left arm making a sweeping motion, pointed toward the carved door without moving his head. For several seconds she remained perfectly still looking at Felix's downcast eyes. He felt her eyes pulling his own up to hers. Yet he didn't dare move and remained frozen. He started to tremble slightly as her power consumed him.

Then to his relief she moved past him, soundlessly like a cat, no longer a spider or a devil but a panther. The door slowly vacillated after she passed through, and it stilled before he regained control of his mind. He closed his eyes and then quickly walked through the doors across the sitting room and to his station, waiting for Guillermo's orders.

Heather loved setting up camp and directed everyone like a master sergeant. She told Jim where to pitch their tent. She wanted Lola and Pedro's tent close to theirs and away from the kitchen. 'There could be bears or cougars here so I want all the llamas staked close to our tents,' she told him.

'There hasn't been any bear sign. You don't want to bother hanging the food do you?' asked Jim, hoping they would not go to that extra effort.

'No, no, it's cougars that are making me nervous now. That business with Pipestone and the cougar last year still haunts me.'

Jim knew she was always a little over cautious and it would not accomplish anything to try to convince her otherwise. It was a small price to pay, trading what he saw as a bit of nonsense worry for her peace of mind. Cougars rarely bothered them, although one could decide that a llama looked like a snack.

'Lo, let's both set up the kitchen and we'll get dinner started,' said Heather.

'What you want me to do? What is cougar?'

Heather ignored the second question. 'Unload that red pannier sitting by the rock. It has the stove and we'll put it here.' She marked a spot on the grass. 'Jim, after you take the packsaddles off, you and Brush can put up the tents. After that, could you stretch the nylon tarp over the kitchen?'

'Sometimes she reminds me of our DI in basic training, partner,' said Brush as they walked off with panniers and tents.

'Truth is, I love an assertive, efficient woman, when what they say is right. I have to put up our tent close to the llamas but that little grove of trees looks like a good spot for you and Glenda.'

'Far enough apart, eh.'

'We're all set to start cooking, Lo. I'm going to check on the llamas. You come with me while Jim and Brush put up the tarp.'

'Better I stay here and start food.' She looked at Jim.

'Not a problem. Let her stay and start cooking, we will stay out of her way,' said Jim as he and Pedro inspected the trees next to the kitchen.

'Tent up and we take all the llama saddles off and llamas are eating,' said Pedro happily.

'Where is Brush anyway? I thought he was going to help with the tarp,' asked Heather

'Best help there is, standing right here,' Jim told her as he placed his hand on Pedro's shoulder giving it a squeeze.

'Oh, oh...no Glenda either. I see.' She shook her long straight chestnut-brown hair while she looked at the lush meadow. 'Can you and Pedro handle that big tarp?' asked Heather as she winked at Jim.

Pedro looked up at his new dad and received a slight nod. 'Sure we can, Mama,' he told her.

When Heather returned, Jim and Pedro were sitting just outside the kitchen with Jim showing Pedro how to tie a bowline knot.

'That was fast,' said Heather as she looked at the tarp. 'Nice job on the tarp, guys. Maybe the best job of tarp stretching I've ever seen!' Then she looked at Pedro.

'Did I miss helping?' asked Brush as he and Glenda walked up holding hands and looking rather pleased with themselves and each other. Heather noted an unmistakable look of contentment on the slightly flushed face of Glenda Rose Stuart. *She...no, they, look very happy,* Heather thought. *Maybe Jim and I should be here alone.* But it wasn't possible now with Pedro, and that thought, instead of making her sad, made her happy.

'I don't think you missed anything, Major McGuire. Could you uncork a couple bottles of wine while we finish getting dinner ready? I put them in the stream by that big boulder,' Heather said mock-sternly. 'You want to set up the table, Jim?'

'Me too, help.'

'After we set up the table, Pedro, practice the knot and then show me your best bowline.'

Jim and Pedro quickly set up the lightweight three-foot-square camp table. It was reasonably sturdy, made of one-inch by three-inch wood slats sealed inside blue vinyl: it rolled open sitting atop screw-on aluminum legs. That done, Pedro and Jim sat down in nylon-covered rigid foam chairs with no legs. It was Jim's favorite type of camp chair.

'Anyone tell me where the wineglasses are?' asked Glenda.

'Me no know,' said Lola.

Jim stood up and started rummaging through the panniers until he found the right one, packed with utensils and the plastic wine-glasses.

'They plastic. No good, you tell me that,' said Lola, sounding confused and looking defiantly at Heather.

'It sure isn't but it's a time-usage issue,' Jim replied.

Lola made a face. 'What that mean?'

'We don't use them often,' said Heather before Jim could continue.

Brush and Glenda grabbed two of Heather's favorite frayed canvas over foam chairs and sat down with Jim and Pedro, their chair-backs now against the lined up rows of panniers that Heather had set in a semicircle surrounding the wilderness kitchen. The kitchen backed up to a large rock on one side, with a few scrubby trees standing behind the boulder and protected on the other side by the line of panniers. The tarp, strung high up over her cooking area sloped backward toward the scrubby trees. There was no sign of rain but there would be a lot of dew this time of year. Brush prodded the small fire they had started while Heather and Lola worked on the cooking as the sky darkened into night, Lola muttering about the no good kitchen, her short stocky body sitting crossed-legs in front of the green cookstove.

'Pour me some wine, you guys. I'll be over in a minute,' yelled Heather.

'Who wants red wine?' asked Brush.

'I will,' 'Me too,' said Glenda and Jim.

'Heather, what do you want?'

'White,' she yelled back.

'Which for you, Pedro?'

Pedro looked around, not having really expected Brush to ask him. He didn't know what to say and wondered whether Brush was teasing him. His new mother was having white and his new father red.

Brush recognized his indecision and said, 'I'll pour you a very small red wine with a little water.' Brush handed him a couple of sips in a plastic cup saying, 'Here's to friends and family.' Then he poured one for Glenda and said looking straight at her, 'To the beautiful wild...erness.'

Glenda teasingly elbowed him but with a look that was unmistakably full of the feelings she had for him.

Jim reached over and clicked Pedro's glass as did everyone. The glass-like plastic sparkled tiny light-prisms in the firelight. Pedro, feeling proud, took a sip of his wine, and was not sure why anyone liked it but he drank the rest, pleased that he was an adult and feeling *serene* under the first kernels of stars.

Chapter 17

The general sat in his chair pondering what Sheilla had told him. Najma was the subject of chatter. Why? Maybe they should run a mission to Guantánamo. Just a little looking around on a US base. *I need to see if Captain Kramer can work in the field,* he thought. *Yes, this was a mission that required the legal investigation that Glenda was trained for and perhaps Kramer could learn something.*

He would like to send Glenda and Brush but Kramer needed field experience. An intelligent intelligence officer with no suntan. Besides, he knew that one or two missions would not prove that Glenda and Brush could take on a difficult task. He had never had a male-female team before, and in the case of Glenda and Brush, ones that were also partners at home. Being in Pakistan together for a short mission had worked out well. Still, long-term the general didn't want Brush and Glenda together. He wanted Jim back to work as Brush's partner or running the BWC.

Jim's wounds were fully healed months ago. The general hadn't called him back as there was nothing requiring Jim's field skills and there was his newly adopted son. On the other hand, he'd been hoping Jim would come back of his own accord and replace him as the head of the BWC. *Asinine thought. Neither of us are ready to cash it in yet; Jim and his field missions or me retiring.*

General Crystal looked up as a tapping penetrated his thoughts. A tall man with wild hair stood outside his door, Nusmen. He waved him in.

'Sir, I am sorry to bother you but I thought you would want to know that we have a new antibiotic that disrupts the DNA of the resistant staph.'

'You tested it?' asked the general thinking they must have just produced it and not really tested it thoroughly or he would have heard about it already in the daily reports.

'Sort of. I've just produced it...I did set up several tests last night. It's a combination of synthetic antibiotic and a phage.'

'Phage?' said the general in surprise.

'Yes, sir. I have been following some new research using phages. I thought it would be nice to know the mechanism of exactly how phages attacked bacteria. I worked that out and it gave me...er, us, the idea of using an antibiotic that we were developing to enhance the phage's entry into the bacteria. It kills it and what may be even more interesting is that the bacteria will be able to build a resistance like they normally do with antibiotics. I want to work on this one hundred percent of my time and with every tech I can have, so we can test it and get it out to the people that need it. I think I can get some great images in the new STEM too, if you need them for a publication. It will be really cool to have a three-dimensional image at over a million magnification and, er, high contrast...definition...with elemental mapping of light elements.' He trailed off as he was not sure if the general knew he had taken the new STEM apart.

The general studied Nusmen. He knew Nusmen was working to overcome his guilt, and he had a lot to atone for where staph infections were concerned. Still the testing would take a long time before they could consider providing it to the public. 'I heard about your taking our new machine apart and putting it back together minus a few parts.'

'They weren't needed...' Nusmen stopped as he knew the general didn't care about that sort of detail.

'Well then, good news, Nusmen, and just at the right time. You have been here a year. You have not been outside once other than to the hangar door.' General Crystal opened his desk and handed a paper to Nusmen. 'It's a full pardon.' He had obtained it three weeks ago and had been waiting for the right moment to give it to Nusmen.

Nusmen stared at the form. 'But, General, does this mean I have to go? I don't want to leave. I want to stay here.'

Will Crystal could not help smiling this time. 'When you come back you will be a GS12 employee here and Dr. Milton's second in command of the lab.'

Nusmen did not seem to care about the extraordinary pardon and the even more extraordinary promotion. 'I don't know if I even want to go outside the lab. I need to keep working on the new STEM. It is phenomenal and the staph needs more testing. I—can't I just take a vacation later?'

'I want you out!' the general boomed. 'That's an order and stay out for two weeks. Everyone needs a break.'

'I, ah, haven't been out for a year and it...scares me. I lost it out there; I feel safe and valuable here.'

'If I have to I will have the MP's escort you out. I want you back here ready for work in two weeks, not a moment sooner.'

'What about the phages? I need to see it through.'

'Explain it to Dr. Milton and she will take care of it. I don't want to see you here tomorrow morning. Got it?' the general thundered.

'Yes, sir,' said a sulking Nusmen as he shuffled toward the door trying to hold back tears. He stopped and turned. The general had had enough and was about to tell him to beat it or else, but before he could say anything, Nusmen with his head down said softly, 'Thank you, sir, thank you for everything you have done for me.'

The general just nodded as Nusmen walked out and closed the door. Maybe he was not as stupid or single-minded as he sometimes appeared. Maybe he had a heart after all.

With Nusmen gone the general's thoughts turned back to Najma and the CIA. He picked up his phone and punched the intercom. 'Have Sheilla come in as soon as she can.'

Moments later, there was a soft knock on his door. 'Come.'

'You wanted me, General?'

'Sit. I want you to do some prelim planning for a mission to Guantánamo.'

'Najma?'

'Yes. Put together a mission packet on Guantánamo and X-Ray. I'm sending Glenda and Captain Kramer to see what they can dig up about Najma.'

'Kramer!' said Sheilla, looking astonished. 'I mean, is it safe for Glenda?'

'Kramer needs to get his feet out from under a desk. Intelligence officers are only half as valuable without some field experience. Glenda can handle him for something like this. Don't worry. I need to get Jim up off his home-body ass and we'll send Brush, too, to back them up. That's between us, don't tell Glenda and Kramer they have backup.'

Sheilla didn't say anything. She sat quietly, biting her lip, thinking that doing something at last sounded exciting, even if something with Kramer could not be too exciting.

'Get Kramer started on gathering intel.'

'OK,' she said without a lot of enthusiasm. Then she shook her head wondering again how it was that she had gotten hooked on excitement even if experienced vicariously at her computer.

'You and the Huachuca computer whizzes see what you can find out without letting anyone know. I have an old friend at Guantánamo. I'll contact him and see what he has to say. We'll evaluate and decide on a plan.'

'It's gorgeous, just look at those stars,' said Heather to Meteor as she moved the llamas close to the campfire for the night. The thrill of being in the mountains had completely replaced her earlier trepidations about venturing into the wilderness after what happened in Mexico. She hadn't said anything, but she'd been worried that she'd lose her nerve, overcome by memories of the horror she'd endured on her last camping trip. But the sheer clarity of the skies awed her tonight. It was all so special; Pedro's first mountain trip and llama hike, Jim long recovered from his wounds and being here together in the late summer. The past atrocities moved to the back of her mind. Her finger involuntarily touched a hairline scar on her cheek where Najma's knife had so easily sliced her previously unblemished skin. Her mind stayed on the present though; she felt at peace once again in her beloved mountains; she had a family, Jim, plenty of food, and her llamas.

Then a dark thought drifted across her mind. A vague misty thought like a dream, an image of dead women with mice sitting on them. Heather shook her head and forced it from her consciousness. Jim had had similar thoughts that haunted him, a nightmare memory of two girls and their mother that he felt he had betrayed in Vietnam. Saving Pedro and Lola, finally, after twenty years, pushed those thoughts far enough from his consciousness so that his flashbacks seemed to be gone. The boy Pedro—his boy, his personal exorcist—had been the catalyst necessary to banish the nightmarish images from his thoughts.

Heather never completely comprehended how Jim's bad memories could continue for so long. She'd led a charmed and happy life, lost in academia and research, never witnessing the dark side of humanity. Through their years together, his and her thoughts juxtaposed, coexisted, but never fully melded. He had seen and done things she could not even conceive of. That is until now. Her understanding only blossomed as the dark memories from his mind manifested themselves in hers. Different as they were, nevertheless her understanding was now edging forward. Nightmares and flashbacks of Najma in Mexico. The senseless rape and torture of her beautiful friends, as Najma forced her to watch.

Then Jim saving her and the rest of the survivors from the Mexican cartel men and the dark-haired psycho woman. Heather had never seen anyone killed before, especially not murdered and tortured only feet from her. She had seen them kill her friends and then watched Jim kill them. She continued to look through the eye of her memory as the vision melded into a blur of death.

Seeing a different world with its cruel side came with a penalty, the pain brought by her own nightmares. She had not been the cause of the deaths in Mexico but she was a part of it. She had talked the university researchers into going: she was more to blame than anyone. The images caused her pain whenever they rose in her conscious mind, even though good things had come out of the terror of Najma and the cartel: Pedro, Lola, and her new friendship with Glenda. A friendship born from shared traumatic times that was deeper and with more understanding than she had known with another woman.

Then there was Jim. Their lives partitioned between their personal life together and his work, his missions. She had always known generally what his job was, but now she had seen him at work. Her personal involvement, watching him dispatch men with seemingly no compassion as he rescued her and the others in the Mexican desert, brought a harsh reality.

Her past world of simple pleasures and escapes now seemed trivialized. Jim would say: there was evil in the world, evil people just as there were good. The evil consumed the good if there were not people to combat it. The hairy, pockmarked, cruel Raul and his type had to be removed so kind people could exist in peace.

Her experiences and the new explanations represented an improvement in her understanding; she had been in a dark place for a while after Mexico. Pedro had helped; motherhood had helped. She,

Jim, Lola, and even Pedro had witnessed and endured things no one ever should. And yet she wanted her boy to look for the good in people, to be gentle and kind himself, just as her parents had raised her. And she would hope the nightmares that still plagued them all would recede over time.

Still, it was the antithesis of everything she had believed previously. Her father had taught her that to be gentle and kind is the way to improve the world. He had quit a successful accountancy-management career to become a small town minister. He didn't preach an eye for an eye. Everyone, in his mind, had some good in them if you only looked. Forgiveness was the way forward. Where was the 'good' in Najma? She had killed Heather's friends, good decent people.

Glenda Rose had tried to help her understand that it did not make Jim less good. He was not like the Najma's or the pockmarked Raul's of the world who felt nothing and made people suffer. Heather had tried to talk to Jim about it but he couldn't or wouldn't explain his feelings to her—at least not in a way she could comprehend. If she had known Guillermo or Hitler, she would be confused again. Hitler loved his dog. Guillermo loved his daughter but killed or had killed the daughters of others with no guilt. Was Jim like them?

Heather's mind reeled under the confused thoughts. *No, Jim, Brush, and Glenda are not like that...stop, stop, stop!* She shook her head. She wished Jim would open up to her, help her understand.

'Mama, you are not answering.'

'Oh, sorry, little one.'

'I not so little.'

'I am not so little,' she corrected. ' "Little one" means that I am very fond of you, not that you aren't a big strong boy.' Pedro hugged her. Tears welled up in her eyes. She battled them away. *I'm too emotional about everything right now.*

'He want to know what big star is,' stated Lola, 'but I come to get you to help me bring food over. It ready now.'

'You sit tight, Heather, I'll help Lola,' said Jim.

'No…I'll go.' Jim cringed slightly at the word 'no,' a word he hated.

Chapter 18

Points of light were beginning to prick the darkening skies. The campfire glowed warm red. Jim lit two candles on the table. There was not enough breeze to blow them out. The temperature was dropping but the warmth from lower down the mountain would rise and they would be comfortable for another hour.

'It is incredible out here, isn't it,' said Glenda to no one in particular. 'Come on, Pedro, let's get some food. Did you like your wine?'

'I like it OK, but Coke better.'

'Coke it is,' said Glenda.

'Cokes are in the stream, Pedro,' said Heather as she set two plates full of food on the table. 'Jim, go with him, would you, but hurry back before the burgers get cold.' Lola handed her two more plates, one with corn on the cob wrapped in foil and another with lettuce and cold vegetables.

'I bring the rest,' said Lola.

Jim picked up Pedro and put him on his shoulders and walked off at a fast pace.

'Not exactly low calorie,' said Glenda, eying the plate of hamburgers. She was the only one of the group that watched her weight. A few extra pounds would be easy for her to add and she didn't want to be 'fat' rather than 'voluptuous.'

'With the hiking and altitude we can use all the fat we can get,' said Heather. 'The hard part is when we get back down. We can drink and eat like crazy up here and not gain a pound but when we are back to low-land, it is a temptation to continue eating the same way.'

'Still, I was hoping to lose a little,' Glenda whispered.

Heather eyed her and said, 'I think Brush likes you just as you are. I think any man would.'

'I've heard that before from men but actually it irritates the hell out of me that they look at my boobs and not my brain. That's all they see.'

'Not Brush,' said Heather.

'Brush is different. Sure, he likes these, but it isn't the same as the oglers. I know he likes me for who I am and that seems to be all of me, body and mind. It puts a better slant on life. Still I don't want to ever get fat.'

'Nice to be lucky, isn't it? We both are.'

'Come on, you two beauties. I think I heard my name,' said Brush. 'What are you two whispering about?'

'Wouldn't you like to know,' said Glenda. 'You expecting me to bring you a plate while you sit there drinking wine?'

'Kind of hoping,' said Brush.

'OK, this one time, but you owe me.'

'Owing you sounds good.'

'Well, buster,' she said as she handed him his plate loaded with a hamburger, corn, and potato salad, 'I was thinking along the lines that I would sit against a tree and watch you load our stuff in the morning.'

'My pleasure.' He turned his head and gave her a soft kiss that seemed incongruous to his brawn.

'Mama.' Heather looked toward Pedro. She was getting pleasantly used to her new name after hearing him use it for the first time just hours ago. 'I asked what the big star is up there.'

'Jim will tell you. He's the astrobiologist.'

Pedro looked at Jim. 'It is big. That's a good observation. Can you say more about it?'

'It big and bright and out sooner than other stars.'

'Exciting that you noticed that. Do you see anything else?'

'It clearer maybe. You know answer, you tell me.'

'You just told me exactly what a scientist would. It doesn't twinkle the same as all of the others, clearer you said: because it isn't a star. It's a planet, just like the one we are sitting on.'

Pedro looked perplexed. 'Why it with other stars?'

'The stars are very far away. Can you guess which planet it is?' asked Jim.

'Mars.'

'That's a very good guess.' Pedro nodded and looked pleased.

'Could it be any other planet?

'No se.'

'Well, just so we can eat, Mars was a very good guess but it's Jupiter.'

'How you know?' asked Pedro, hoping Jim might be wrong.

'Enough for now,' said Heather. 'Time to eat, both of you.'

Felix carefully placed a filet mignon in front of Guillermo. Then from the serving tray, he offered steaming vegetables, small red potatoes, and a variety of sauces. Guillermo liked to add sauces depending on his mood. Najma only wanted meat. Her food tastes had changed in Guantánamo. Her captors had quickly found out what she liked and didn't like, then all meat had been withheld from her. She had never liked vegetables particularly and after months of nothing but her least favorite vegetables, she now craved only rare meat.

Guillermo lifted his wineglass. 'To a true artist.' Najma nodded but his approval was meaningless to her. Killing the pig face and his troop had felt good, revived her.

'Perhaps I will have another need for your talents while we are preparing for you to terminate the Americans. The major of Mexicali is becoming a nuisance. But for now, let's talk about the Americans. It will be difficult and complex. The Americans are well trained and dangerous. As you remember, the colonel, by himself, killed my top lieutenant and enforcer, Raul, and six of his men.' Guillermo avoided saying that Najma had been there and failed to stop the colonel. Instead, he said, 'And he has eluded you.' Then, while watching her black eyes, carefully added, 'This time you will have the advantage. You will be the hunter and he the game. I have thought carefully about this plan. My computer team has run many scenarios. I have recruited one or two special people who I will introduce to you in due course.'

Najma didn't like the sound of this. 'I don't work with others. I work alone.'

'So you shall but you have to cross the border and move without anyone knowing you are there. That requires assistance. Besides Colonel Johnson there is also the general. I want to terminate them all. You will need assistance. You will be in charge, of course. Their headquarters and the colonel's ranch and the general's Fort Lewis house are both under surveillance. Vladislav is monitoring their communications. Finding them and deciding where best to kill them will require much effort.'

'I have crossed the border before on my own. I work alone.'

Glenda put her hand on Brush's knee and wondered if the years would diminish what they felt now. She doubted it.

'What that noise?' asked Lola, sounding frightened.

'Just deer walking. They know we are here and are looking for salt and minerals.'

'We bring some for them?'

'Yes and no. If you don't want to be up listening to them pounding their hooves around all night, make sure you pee where I showed you.'

'Oh my, they eat my—'

'They are interested in your urine,' Heather cut her off.

'Lo, forget about that. What about the other thing?' Heather tilted her head toward the kitchen.

Lola rolled her eyes, and walked away mumbling 'food, bathroom no go together,' as she walked the few feet to the kitchen, lifted a plastic lid and brought back a chocolate-brown cake with creamy icing.

'Wow,' said Pedro.

'What is it?' asked Jim already having a pretty good idea. It was a specialty of Heather's.

'I think you already know that: a carrot cake. Anybody doesn't like carrot cake saddles the llamas in the morning,'·said Heather, trying to look serious. 'Glenda, can you cut it? I don't want Jim or Brush doing it. They're both just as bad as the other about sweets and will start sneaking licks of the frosting.'

'Thought you said we could eat what we wanted on this trip,' said Jim.

'I'm not thinking of your tummy, sweetie, I just want the others to get their share.'

'OK, guys, who wants to dry dishes?' asked Heather.

'How about I wash and you dry,' volunteered Jim.

'You know why he's volunteering to wash, Pedro?'

'Why, Mama?'

'Because it's the best job out here. A good way to really get your hands clean.'

Pedro looked at his hands in the starlight and said, 'OK, I wash for you.'

Jim winked at Heather as he said to Pedro, 'You got the job.'

Guillermo carefully chose a honey-mustard sauce for his asparagus, sliced a piece of the tender steak and dipped it in the same mustard sauce, just to see if it enhanced the meat's flavor. He nodded his head slightly and looked across the table at Najma. She lifted her dark eyes from her plate and met his eyes.

'But first, there is this business to attend to here. I believe this will bring you pleasure, Najma. I have two targets I wish to have you eliminate. Both important enemies. One is a young army general, Ramos, and the other the mayor of Mexicali, Juan Diaz Silva. This newly promoted general, I am informed, is a naive fellow, and he has convinced the mayor to aid him in stopping our drug operations passing through Mexicali into California. Vladislav will give you a map of the army garrison they have set up outside Mexicali and the mayor's villa and offices along with a file with pictures and information. Then talk to Vega if you need anything else.'

The next morning the aroma of coffee percolating on the stove drifted into the tents. After Heather, Pedro was the next out of his tent. He caught his foot getting out and tripped, falling onto the outer edge of the tent and soaking his jacket with the night's heavy dew.

'What you do out there?' shouted Lola.

Heather laughed. 'Don't worry, Pedro, it will dry. It's going to be a beautiful day. I am going to cook you a special treat this morning.'

Pedro walked toward the kitchen, trying to brush the dew from his coat. His mind was not on the dampness, however. 'Carrot cake?'

'Not for breakfast. I am going to cook you fry bread. You go wash up in the stream but don't drink any of the water, just wash.'

'Yes, Mama.'

Chapter 19

Guillermo was pleased with Najma's progress. He reflected on her first mission since arriving. She had dispatched the small gang and left a very colorful scene, a postcard message. The locals and the police knew that Guillermo's cartel was responsible, which was Guillermo's point. There was always someone thinking they could do their business outside him, line their own pockets. More importantly, he now felt confident that Najma would be able to handle the Americans.

Killing the mayor and the general should be a good lead-up for her as well. Next the Notre Americanos. His game plan had started, the pawns moved across the border first. Fort Lewis was under surveillance and his soldiers had begun assembling in Washington State.

He sat evaluating his position. His new computer people were the best money could buy and they could do almost anything the American giant could. Although his few employees did not have the breadth to run multiple operations at the same time, in a focused, head-to-head encounter, he was confident that they were better than the Americans.

In the ruins of the old hacienda, Vladislav found a nearly destroyed computer and salvaged its hard drive. It contained valuable information for the back doors Guillermo's previous computer group had left in the US government's computers, allowing him to penetrate into the CIA's and NSA's most secure computers.

Vladislav then developed a new program for monitoring key

words, similar to those the National Security Agency used, many of them in fact stolen from the NSA. Where they had failed to find anything useful was with the general's secret center at Fort Lewis. Vladislav's expert team easily hacked the BWC's computers but found no documents or files about any past operation. There was nothing about an invasion and destruction of Guillermo's headquarters.

Vladislav had told Guillermo that Sheilla's team was monitoring nearly the same key words as he was. The CIA was making inquiries about his cartel and Najma, along with other queries about her past. However, there was nothing about her escape or Guillermo's part in it. After much thought, Guillermo concluded the BWC didn't know anything at all, and the CIA was concealing his her escape. It was the only conclusion. He could make no sense of why they did so.

He had assumed that news of Najma's escape would be widely circulated. In fact, he had counted on that and devised a plan. He had spent a great deal of time and effort finding a stand-in for Najma, a double he planned to kill in a way that would get the attention of the colonel and the general.

Assuming Najma was dead, they would drop their guard and become easy targets when he sent her to destroy them. However, it was not working. The Biological Warfare Center seemed unaware of Najma's escape. He was hopeful the high profile killings he was dispatching her on might draw their attention and he could still make use of the Najma double.

Guillermo had been pleased to find someone as good as Vladislav so quickly after the demise of his last computer professional. The Russian's no-nonsense approach suited Guillermo, as did his past deep involvement in internet crime. When Vladislav got on the wrong side of the Russian government, Guillermo had quickly offered him safety and a job. Then it had taken several months for Vladislav to recruit and train experts he deemed good enough, but now the computer group was a thing of beauty.

Guillermo spared no expense in buying the latest equipment or paying top-dollar for the best people obtainable. All the while his previous experience, etched firmly in his mind, told him his new group, as sophisticated as they were, would be no match for large governments and their large staffs. His group would be surgical. However, they could never match the brute force of the United States or other big governments. This understanding, which he had lost sight of before, would give him an edge.

'Why, Vladislav, would General Crystal not know what the CIA knows?'

The Russian said nothing in response since he never speculated. Data and facts were all he dealt with.

'Run a simulation. I want the results by six tonight.' Guillermo was especially pleased that he had been able to obtain a sophisticated computer simulation game that could formulate possible answers to just this sort of problem.

Vladislav nodded and left without saying anything. The tall Russian related to computers not people, not even Guillermo. He had no interest in anything social. He was tall, six feet four inches, with light brown hair, violet eyes, and always dressed in jeans and old black T-shirts. His rugged features and piercing gaze befitted his abrupt manner. He appeared to show no deference to Guillermo and this made some cautious around him. However, the only valid reason for fearing the man was because of what he was capable of doing to people with his computer.

Sheilla twirled in her chair, her long auburn hair almost lifting off her slender shoulders. Mulling and twirling, as she so often did. The CIA had Najma incarcerated in Guantánamo Bay. The only plausible implications from the increased mentions of her were that either she had not talked and they were investigating her, or that she had talked and they were attempting to verify what she had told them. Or...?

She wondered if Najma were dead and they were trying to piece together information about her past or associates for some reason. But why would they care? Nothing quite added up, and Sheilla never yielded to a mystery without solving it. She kept spinning, round and round. The turns became a mantra for her, allowing her to concentrate.

Chapter 20

'I'm stuffed and I may not be able to get up if I eat any more of Heather's fry bread,' Glenda announced, polishing off the last of her coffee. She stood up. 'I'm going to start packing up our gear.'

Brush got up too and turned to Heather. 'If you make this every day for breakfast and carrot cake for dinner you'll get no complaints from me.'

Heather smiled and stood too.

One by one they got up, saddled the llamas, packed up their tents. The rainflies still wet with dew, were shaken and then packed too. Heather would rather wait until there was enough sun to dry them but they would dry later today when they made their campground up by Oval Lake. Her fear of the wilderness dissipated, she couldn't wait to revisit her sanctuary.

The dark room glowed from dozens of computer screens. Misa had two monitors, each attached to a different computer while the others had three screens forming semi-circles on the top of their desks. Colonel Jake Montgomery, a kid of twenty-two years, headed their unit. His proficiency with computers had jump-started his military career; his military supervisors recognized, just as Guillermo did, the importance of the internet in modern warfare.

Outside the door to the room hung a sign saying 'Wolf Pack.' The group had adopted the name nine months ago after Guillermo's failed attempt to kill Colonel Johnson in the Mexican desert. Two brilliant and arrogant kids, Jake and Jason Lyle, thrown together with two mid-thirties academics, Vidya and Misa, had become a cohesive and unstoppable unit under pressure. When the incident had ended, they'd stayed together by choice and mutual respect.

'Whatcha got, Jason?' asked Jake.

'I'm mirroring NSA search programs. So far I don't see anything interesting. They picked up the killer lady's name from the CIA.'

'We already knew that, Jas,' interjected Misa, her bobbed blond hair flying as she turned her button nose away from the screen. 'The question is, what is their interest? Our friends up north want to know why the interest in Najma.' The two older and the two younger members of the team were constantly battling to establish who was the best, the self-taught youngsters or the university-educated elder. Despite their ages, all four had started with computing while it was in its infancy, Jake and Jason as early hackers, eventually breaking into government computers, while Vidya and Misa had started programming on flip-lever computers and communicating with mainframes with punch cards. Their first computing machines were housed in huge buildings and less powerful than their current phones.

Jason started to defend himself but Vidya cut him off. 'She's right. New programs are interesting but not what we should be doing. Let's search and see who gets some answers first.'

Sergeant First Class Jason Lyle felt a little chagrined but said, 'I'll beat all of your asses any day. Losers buy Krispy Kremes tomorrow.' Misa rolled her eyes at the skinny twenty-year-old who ate so much junk food that he should be a Jack Black look alike. Instead, he remained skinny as a rail, just short of five feet nine inches, sandy brown hair, worn far too shaggy for the army, and dark brown eyes. His face was so smooth complexioned that Misa doubted he had ever shaved.

Then she glanced at the newly promoted kid-colonel, Jake. Just a few months ago, he was a lieutenant, then a major. The rapid rise had nothing to do with an earned promotion or time in service. The army needed top-notch computer people just as much as the BWC and Guillermo did.

Jason and Jake were not so long ago two teenagers busted by the FBI for breaking into sensitive government files. The government had agreed not to press charges in exchange for their 'voluntary' enlistment. They'd promised them computer positions that came with a mandatory three years in the army for Jake and five years for Jason. The two had proven so valuable that the army kept increasing their pay in order to tempt them to stay—but the only way the military could pay them more was to promote them. Jason's pay was less than Jake's because he'd made the mistake of signing a confession instead of getting a lawyer. The army had him dead to rights. By military standards, he was promoted faster than normal but still only to the level of master sergeant. He never wore a uniform and the word 'sir' never crossed his lips. A twenty-year-old master sergeant was the subject of stares of disbelief by the other crusty older sergeants. But none of them could do what he did with a computer.

Colonel Jake Montgomery, on the other hand, was coming close to his required term of service and the army would do just about anything within reason to keep him. They couldn't make him the first twenty-two-year-old general. The only option was to keep him happy now and offer him a sweet civilian deal when his required service ended in seven months.

The thirty-eight-year-old, Oxford trained Misa carefully worked her ergonomic keyboard, while Jake danced over his with flying fingers, constantly breaking to crack his knuckles and then resume typing with a flourish.

Vidya looked admiringly at his colleagues while he thought of how best to start solving their problem. He loved this group and the camaraderie they all felt. He thought back, as he often did, to Mexico where the cartel men had raped his girlfriend and beaten her to death under the watchful eye of Najma. At first a thirst for revenge had propelled him into the day-and-night fight to hack into the cartel's computers along with Misa, Jake, and Jason. Their history together, buried in Stratcom's underground rooms at Fort Huachuca, Arizona, had now forged unshakable bonds.

Vidya stopped his remembrances and got to work trying to answer what Sheilla and the general had requested. The game was to put answers together as they searched through the government's computers including those of the BWC. Little did he know that soon they would once again be back attempting to break into Guillermo's computers. This time with a more dangerous cyber opponent, a legendary maestro with more skills than anyone they had encountered previously.

Brush sighed. 'I'm getting pretty used to this easy life. I doubt it will last much longer.'

''Spect you're right. Probabilities are against it. Not unless the world suddenly becomes peaceful.'

'Fat chance, unless everyone goes on Prozac. How will Heather take it when you leave, Jim?'

'Don't know.'

Brush nodded his head and raised an eyebrow, clearly conveying to Jim that of course he knew how she would take it.

'You're right. Probably should talk to her before the general flies in with a mission. I can feel it coming too.'

'He wants you taking on more of the admin; maybe he will send you off to Washington instead of the field.'

'He knows I'm not ready for the office chair.'

'Has a habit of being right.'

Jim thought for a second. 'Likely Heather knows that too. Wouldn't be surprised if Will had Katarina build a profile to see how both of us will react.'

'Things have changed for me.'

'I'd say for the better too. About time you settled down.'

'Not planning on that. Just not going to chase after skirts anymore. It's a temptation for me to stay close to Glenda, but I'm not ready to give up our adventures either, eh.' Brush paused. 'I've never missed anyone before.'

'I heard you and Glenda did well together in Pakistan,' said Jim. 'You saying you didn't miss me?'

'With Glenda next to me, afraid not, buddy,' Brush deadpanned.

'Can't say I blame you one little bit. You've got the right woman this time,' Jim said sincerely.

'Yeah, you got that right and I won't say having her along didn't have its advantages.' He paused while he thought back. 'I'm glad we had the chance to see if we could work together. Made me respect her even more but it adds an extra layer of pressure feeling responsible for her. Probably for her too. With your attraction to bullets I always expect to lose you, but I have to admit it would be hard for me to lose her.'

Jim didn't feel like saying anything cute back. His mind had turned to Heather and how he had almost lost her in Mexico. Then he thought of Brush's gift for avoiding flying pieces of lead. He said, kidding Brush back, 'I just always get in the way of the bullets meant for you, buddy.'

Brush chuckled good-naturedly.

Jim added, 'I know how you feel about being responsible. When Najma kidnapped Heather, it clouded my thinking.' Jim grinned and switched to the joking tone he and his long-term partner habitually used to speak of serious matters. 'Just because

I was always taking the bullets in the past, you better watch yourself now. Probabilities, you know: one of those little projectiles might find you yet.'

'Uh-huh, it's not like that, buddy. Some luck for sure, but you gotta have the skill too. All about the way you move and at the right time, eh.'

'You're turning American. What's with not saying, "aboot"?'

'Good question, maybe I have only ever used it because Americans think it's cute and up north we don't like to be pestered by Americans aboot it.'

'Yeah, you Canucks do have a belligerent side.' They both laughed.

'Makes me a better thinker about risk, keeps my skill levels up.'

It was true; that's how the two partners had stayed alive through so much. Skill, judgment and outside the box thinking throughout their long experience together. Nevertheless, luck played a big part. Jim was fond of saying, *Remember the probabilities: expose yourself enough and your luck will run out.*

'I guess I better talk to Heather in the next couple of days. Should be opportunities at the lakes and I know this trip has helped her conquer some of her worries. Best to see how she feels about me returning to work while it's still hypothetical and she's in a good place.'

'Glenda says Heather's plenty scared inside. She's just not letting it out. After what she went through, I don't blame her. She saw things I hoped she could avoid in life.'

'Anything happening?' Sheilla immediately asked when Misa answered at the Fort Huachuca computer center.

'The young one's eyes are getting raster burn but nothing yet to go on. Sorry, we'll get something soon.'

Having talked to Misa on and off for the better part of a year, Sheilla had grown intrigued by the small but never-ending differences between American and British English; she loved the other woman's idioms.

'You OK up there in the northland?' asked Misa.

'Yep, just fine, the general just got a lot more money to expand his field operations but now we just need something to do. No weird bugs out in the world causing trouble,' *or Najma's,* she added silently.

Sheilla heard voices in the background. 'Gotta run,' said Misa. 'Talk again soon.'

Chapter 21

Bertrand Gupta was closing in on his objective. He didn't have all the lines filled in and probably never would, but the story could now be told with some level of confidence. Najma was a terrorist. She had worked as a mercenary and escaped capture after the attack on the Seattle Center. What he didn't know was where Najma had disappeared to after the attack. Their assumption had always been that she had been hiding somewhere in the United States and was captured there by the general's group. Bertrand realized that this was where he had been wrong.

He knew, or at least the evidence suggested, that she had gone to Mexico, taken up with the cartel, and become one of their enforcers. He had no tangible evidence but he strongly suspected she had been captured in Mexico. But then how had she gotten to a US hospital before X-Ray? A secret operation run by the general—an illegal operation? Had she been captured at the hacienda? It had allegedly been attacked by the Mexican government but that, he reasoned now, was unlikely. The Mexican government was either impotent or in bed with the cartel and it mattered little which of the two it was. He did not think they would have attacked the cartel headquarters.

Now he concluded it was likely a secret US operation, probably headed and run by General Crystal. No one else had his field operation capabilities. He had either worked with the Mexican government or used them to cover his trail by giving them the glory. The aging head of the cartel had eventually been hanged in Mexico

City with much fanfare, but the de facto leader, referred to as El
Padrino, a nasty character named Guillermo Vasquez, was now its
head.

He'd assumed complete control of the cartel after the attack and,
according to Martin Pearson's source in the DEA, he rebuilt and
expanded the original hacienda headquarters. Bertrand wondered
whether this Vasquez could have been working with the Americans
to overthrow the old cartel leader. It was certainly something the
agency would have done. Would the BWC? Maybe this El Padrino
was now a high-level source for someone in the American government, if so the Drug Enforcement Administration would be the most
likely possibility. But how did Najma figure in?

Bertrand could feel someone maneuvering behind all this. All
Sorenson and Flayback wanted was to cover their own asses after
Najma's escape; they were bureaucrats not puppet masters. But
someone was pulling the strings. He ran over a few scenarios in his
head.

As a rule, Bertrand stayed as far away from politics as he could
manage but this might be an opportunity to replace Sorenson with a
capable director. The company was floundering under Sorenson and
it needed someone from within to take the reins, someone with field
experience and strength who could move them away from politics
and back to being an effective organization. They needed to be at
their best to wage the new war on terrorism he visualized in the
future. The world was changing and the CIA needed to be ahead of
the changes, both within and without.

Bertrand couldn't care less about whether it had been an illegal
operation or any of the rest of it. In fact, he had always thought
General Crystal was good at what he did but if he'd pulled that off,
he might even be better—or at least trickier—than Bertrand had
previously thought.

A knock on the door brought him back to the present. Martin

looked in cautiously. 'Step in, Martin. Since when have you been so timid about walking into my office?' Bertrand asked.

'Since Sorenson...'

'Forget that right now. You find out anything else useful?'

'Not one fucking thing. Very weird, I'd say.'

'The whole thing seems to revolve around General Crystal's biological anti-terrorist group.'

'Agreed, but that doesn't help us much. Nobody knows dick about them, including us and the FBI, except they have a big secret laboratory operation that nobody, including us, seems to know much about; an enormous budget; connections to the top; and field agents so good that everyone borrows them for sensitive operations.' Pearson could sometimes be just as crude as he was sarcastic.

'Come on, Martin. We should be able to find all we want about them. What about our contacts in the FBI? It's their area stateside. Surely they have someone in Crystal's organization. What about our computer experts getting into their files?' suggested Bertrand.

'We've snooped their computers but we haven't found a damn thing worthwhile. I'm not so keen on talking to the FBI. They might have something we could use but you know they like to trade, not just give up info. They'll start wondering why we are asking.'

'I'm not that worried about them. See what you can find out from them. Give them something inconsequential if you must. Meantime I want a complete update on the general and his two hotshot agents. Eventually we'll figure this out and get Sorenson his get-out-of-jail free card.'

'You really want to give him that card, Bertrand?' Martin sighed, 'Alrighty, I'll keep digging,' said Martin, looking at Bertrand as if to say, *Notice I didn't call you Bertie.*

Bertrand already had a thick file on many of the past exploits of Jim and Brush. The two operatives had often worked on operations for the CIA. He knew they worked either as a pair or with their own small group of Special Forces. He thought they were smart not to trust agencies such as his own. The CIA had a bad habit of sacrificing men like them when some desk-jockey thought it served the greater good.

Sheilla heard a soft ping and swiveled toward her computer screen. In the lower right corner, a flashing pale green message from Fred: 'CIA queries shifting to us.' She eased back in her chair and sat motionless.

Vladislav and the Wolf Pack had also picked up the queries that Pearson's department was making. The focus seemed to be shifting from Najma and the Siastra cartel to the BWC.

Sheilla immediately headed to Will Crystal's office, wondering why they were zeroing in on them—was it just blowback from the Mexico raid or something else.

'General, the CIA's now sending out queries about us, the BWC, and you personally,' she told him without preamble. 'Something's up.'

Sheilla's cell phone rang. 'Excuse me, General. It's from Fort Huachuca.'

'We need to talk,' said Misa as soon as Sheilla answered.

'I'm with the general, tell us.' Sheilla hit speakerphone without missing a beat.

'What we've found out is someone else is snooping around in the the gov's computers just like we are.' Sheilla heard a whoop in the background and then someone saying, 'Fucker's smart!'

'Who?' asked Sheilla.

'No idea yet, but I wanted to let you know. The juvenile delinquents are all excited. It's a big game to those two.'

'Hang on a second.' In the background, Sheilla recognized Jake's voice saying, 'About time for a nap there, old-timer.'

Sheilla laughed. Misa said, 'They can't think of anything derogatory to say to Vidya and myself about our skills, so they tease us about being old and we give it back to them about being upstart teenagers! It doesn't help that I have some gray hairs starting; at least they mix in with the dishwater light brown hair and don't show up too much.'

Then Vidya came on the phone. 'Hi up there. While Misa was nattering on we found a back door into NSA's computer system. Looks like it might lead back to our old amigos. Jason just found out a company owned by Guillermo years ago did some programming for NSA. Go figure—a Mexican cartel leader owns a company contracting work with the US government's secret computers. We'll call you back as soon as we've got more. Gotta go.' The line went dead.

The general let out a sigh. 'Shoot, I can feel our little excursion is about to be known to the CIA...Do you think the cartel has rebuilt their computer capabilities? I thought we had put them out of business.'

'Maybe we did and this is another cartel or maybe even another government or a hacker.'

'Or maybe the cartel isn't as defunct as we thought. We didn't get Guillermo. Have Fred research what happened to him. Or have you already done that?'

'After the raid we had no interest in him or the cartel,' said Sheilla, feeling as though she had made a mistake.

The general noticed her hang her head a little. 'Sheilla, you are so far ahead at guessing what the future brings...this is one time no one could have foreseen we might be dealing with the cartel again and maybe we aren't dealing with them. Let's find out.'

Sheilla bit her upper lip and said, 'OK, I'll get right on it.'

'I've been postponing going to Washington about some routine things but now I better get those over with and advise Art Willis at State about this new interest the CIA has in Najma. A personal appearance might just shake something loose on the DC grapevine. Keep in touch with Misa. You can bring me up to date on everything. Let Mark cover that ten o'clock HR meeting and anything else I was supposed to do. You're on this and only this. Roger that?'

Sheilla nodded, and, obviously pleased with her assignment, hurried back to her desk, making a mental to-do list and running through all the avenues she needed to explore.

As Sheilla went out the door, Marsha passed her and said, 'I guess I'll be making some travel arrangements. It's always so quiet around here when he's gone. Bless that big mouth of his. General, you want me to start setting up your transport to DC?'

Chapter 22

General Crystal picked up the secure phone in the Citation X and called the assistant secretary of state. 'Art. Will Crystal.'

Operation over the line...shit, Deputy Secretary of State Arthur Willis, thought. 'I hoped that was history, Will. You want to tell me what you heard?'

'I'm in the air, ETA fifteen hundred. Get a silent room for sixteen hundred. I'll brief you then.'

The general's plane landed and he said a quick goodbye to his two hitchhikers, a senator and the governor of Washington, then he jumped into a waiting helicopter.

'I don't get it,' said Governor Liz Montgomery, watching him go. 'Why the heck does he get this kind of jet and then ride a chopper to wherever he is going?' she said.

'I don't know, nothing to do with my finance committees,' responded Senator Luke Graven. 'But for the moment, I'm not complaining. This is the third time I have hitched a ride with him and count myself lucky. We were waiting for a less fancy military plane, and we got here a might faster. Nope, no complaints from me.'

'Nice ride, but a big freaking waste of taxpayers' money, if you ask me,' she said in a disgusted voice. The senator turned away from her. This new breed of macho women was not to his taste.

The climb up to the lakes had left Lola's legs sore. She crawled out of her tent and stood up, rubbing her thighs and looking around in the early morning light. She spotted Heather in what she had called the kitchen and hobbled over making far too much of a fuss over her legs. 'I no like this, señora. I need go toilet now.'

Heather just shook her head and reached into a pannier. 'This is all you need, Lola,' she said as she tossed her a roll of toilet paper.

'Where I go? I afraid of bugs and serpents.'

'None here, so you don't need to worry. It is not the same here as Mexico, different environment. Besides snakes aren't so bad.'

'Ugh! But where?'

'Go back down the hill a little and into the woods over...oh come on, I'll go with you.'

Lola made a face. 'I no need help going!'

'Hum, not what I had in mind,' said Heather. 'We just walk together, nothing else. I'm just going to show you where the bathroom is. Then you're on your own.'

'This good, why you no tell me before? Why government make nice toilet and hide it in the woods?'

Heather just smiled and said, 'The government owns these woods so I guess they can do what they want.'

Jim and Pedro were sitting in the kitchen when she returned, Jim with a cup of coffee streaming vapor trails into the cool morning air. Pedro had a glass of cranberry juice. They looked happy and relaxed.

'It nice here. Serene,' said Pedro with a big grin.

'Very serene, isn't it,' said Heather, 'and very good choice of words. You two want some eggs and bacon or French toast and bacon?'

Pedro made a face and squirmed in his chair.

Heather pointed in another direction from where Lola was. 'He's all yours, lover. I just showed Lola the facilities. I'll start breakfast. Could you two check the llamas on your way?'

'Sure. Let's go, Pedro.'

Chapter 23

The general walked briskly down the State Department's labyrinthine hallway, his straight back belying his short stature, wearing a colorful blaze of medals on his traditional green army uniform. The deputy head of the State Department was having a hard time keeping up with him. Close behind, however, his adjutant, Captain Malone, strolled easily on long legs next to an overweight woman with short dark hair and an interesting name, Maeve.

She had been with Arthur Willis for thirty years and, like her boss, was also having a hard time walking this fast. The general remembered that even just a few years ago she had been very slim. Something had happened and Maeve had put on a lot of extra weight, but her keen mind made her as attractive as ever. Art Willis trusted her and relied on her. She was his personal assistant and as is often the case with PA's, shared and even influenced her boss's decisions more than he cared to admit.

Maeve is special and I would add her to my staff in an instant, thought Will, as they continued down the bland government hallway. At least he had the ability to give Sheilla a title befitting her abilities, something Maeve would never have. They neared the door to the secure conference room. Sweeping the room for recording devices before every meeting protected confidential discussions from eavesdropping, along with metal walls and low energy magnetic fields.

'I know this isn't going to be good news, with you jumping on your fast plane for a face-to-face,' said Art Willis.

'Maybe, maybe not. It's too soon to tell. The CIA seems interested in finding out about how Najma was captured.'

'That sounds like the usual card-playing the CIA and FBI do. Get some data and use it to their advantage if possible. Sorenson is looking for bargaining chips.'

'Since we went into Mexico, there's been no mention of Najma's name for over eight months. Then the last two weeks there is lots.'

'You monitoring CIA?'

Will continued without answering, 'My guess is that someone got information from her and is investigating...no matter, not good for us if they find it was our operation across the border, and we left everyone out and, worse, disabled the border recon planes. It's the sort of thing CIA does every day but the president's enemies in Congress might push for investigations and then hearings.'

'Your charter isn't restricted by borders, Will. The problem is that we cut out DEA, CIA, and everyone else that should have been in on it as a joint operation. Plus, we gave away the credit, which is never a popular decision in DC. Stupid question here, why is she still alive and why did we give her to Gitmo and the CIA in the first place?'

'I see your point but we haven't become executioners. The CIA agreed to act as jailers and Sorenson was keen on his new off-our-soil jail.'

'Something they seem to want around the world. In a way I sympathize with them, some of our overzealous liberals are always at odds with the agency's methods. It's somewhat understandable that they want out of Dodge where they can function outside our laws.'

Maeve started laughing. 'For all your experience, I think I hear you saying you trust the CIA.' Maeve did not say it as a question.

'The only reason you gave them Najma was to keep the secret operation out of the press and politics.'

'You're right of course, Maeve.' The general looked at her and asked, 'What do you suggest?' The general valued her opinion and he wasn't interested in past mistakes, only solutions to what might become a future problem.

'Sorry, General,' said Maeve, putting on a serious face that belied her intuitive sense of irony. She was a linear thinker who went straight from A to Z with detached accuracy. 'To start with, we, the State Department, are in this with you and not much either of us could do to separate ourselves. It's both our problem. It seems obvious that what we need are facts, not guesses. Find out what Sorenson knows and who is mining information: what is Najma's status? Why is she suddenly back on the radar? Have the secretary of state or the VEEP call in Sorenson. One of them tells him that there has been some rumor about Najma and he or she wants to know what is going on. She might not get much truth from the man, too much the politician, but he will have to give up something.'

There was silence at the table. General Crystal and Deputy Director Arthur Willis silently contemplated what she had said. It was nothing startling, typical, simple logic.

The general's mind wandered to what he perceived as his biggest weakness: the lack of high-end computer staff. He needed the skills of the Huachuca Wolf Pack working for him in the BWC. *I need to figure out a way to entice them,* he thought once again. 'OK. Then who brings Sorenson in for a discussion, Art?' he asked.

'Myself, the vice president, and the secretary of state. Overcome him with numbers and titles to pressure him,' said Art Willis. 'Ganging up on Sorenson will suggest we know more than we do and he might tell us something useful.'

'That might be a mistake,' said Maeve. 'It will suggest that it is too important. It would be better to keep it lower key. Secretary of state will be enough of a power play. Sorenson will have to trade something. He can't just stonewall her.'

'It's worth a try,' said Will Crystal, thinking that it was still a man's world but without the Sheilla's and Maeve's of the world, it might all come crumbling down around their macho male edifice.

Chapter 24

Glenda strolled over to the kitchen looking relaxed and content in the crisp mountain air. 'Good morning,' said Heather. 'Coffee? French Roast Starbucks, or do you wanna try some of this really great, local 'Bluestar' coffee. A friend of mine has been trying to come up with something to compete with Starbucks.'

'You bet. Sounds great. You already know I can't live without my morning java.'

'Two cups of strong coffee coming up. We're alike in so many ways and so different in others,' said Heather.

'There is a lot we know and a lot we don't. Here's a silly question, what was your birth weight?'

'Seven pounds two ounces, I think,' said Heather. 'Funny thing to ask. I've never heard anyone ask that before. I don't even know Jim's.'

'Just curious. I've been thinking more about babies lately—not that I really want one now if ever but...especially seeing what a perfect child Pedro is...Mine was seven point four,' said Glenda.

'Plus or minus standard deviation and that makes us about the same. Pedro had a shock watching his family killed. Everything is new to him. I doubt being so perfect will last much longer.'

'I didn't think about the shock not wearing off yet. You think he will have problems like post-traumatic stress syndrome?'

'I really don't know. Only time will answer that and I'm trying to take it as it comes. Where were you born? I don't know your birthday or how old you are either,' added Heather.

'Feb second, sixty-three, near Mystic, Connecticut. You?'

'Shit, you're younger than I am. March sixth, sixty-one.'

'And born where?'

'I was born in Hood River, Oregon, which is a pretty cool place but I loved that movie, *Mystic,* what was it? *Mystic?* Who starred in it? Was it Cher?'

'*Mystic River?* No, I think you mean another one, *Mystic Pizza,* and it was Julia Roberts not Cher. We ate at that pizza place when I was growing up.'

'Oh yeah, I remember her in it—it was a fun flick. Is it really as neat of a town as in the movie? It would be fun to see it again sometime.'

'Yeah, it's a quaint town and it was a nice part of the world to grow up in. West of the river is a bit posh. We lived on the east side. I'd love to show you around.'

'You want to go skiing sometime? Jim told me that Brush mentioned you skied. I love Whistler. Ever been there? Or anyplace in Canada?'

Glenda laughed. She had grown used to Heather's way of speaking and asking numerous questions all running back to back. She rubbed the corner of her eye, wondering what the first question had been. 'I like skiing when I've gone and we had some pretty OK skiing in New England, even Connecticut, not like the West, though. Then at the University of Miami, not a lot of snow around.'

'How did you end up in Miami?'

Glenda quickly responded before Heather could add more questions, 'Even though I was from the working side of Mystic, tennis was a big thing in the area. I got an athletic scholarship. Since college, I've been too busy for sports, law degree, then Bureau at Quantico. I think Brush is probably a very good skier. It might be the first thing he'll be certain he can do better than me. I like things equal but suppose I can allow him that one bit of superiority.'

Heather laughed. 'Ha, men are always like that but we know better. You and me then, we'll go to Whistler or Banff since they open early and we can practice up. With your hand-eye coordination, I'll bet you'll be great in no time. We don't want our guys thinking they are superior in anything.'

'I doubt that, Heather, I really wasn't ever very good, but it sounds like a nice time to me. Just us two.'

Senior Chief Gould, who really worked for the CIA, lifted up his hat and ran a red cloth bandana over his glistening dark brown, hairless head. 'I am going to be glad to be rid of this mother of a place. Nobody tells me zip but after that idiot enlisted man got shot inside X-Ray, people have been moving in and out left and right.'

Dougal, a senior petty officer, sat with his shirt off outside a gray painted wood building facing a chain-link fence. 'Suits me, bro, I'm tired of this place too. Never want to come back.'

'I wish you'd knock off the bro talk. You a marshmallow, you not a brother.'

'Not all of us can be unlucky.'

'One of these days I'm going to kick your ass, Dougal.'

'Never happen. Have a go whenever. Sounds like a nice break.'

'Not really hot here, not like it was in Yemen, and a little exercise would do me good, maybe I should teach you some humility.'

'What you doing in Yemen?'

'Usual,' said Gould. 'Worked with a real prick. Had a ton of money trying to buy off some of the Houthis.'

'They're Shi'ites?'

'Yep, you would think the desk jockeys that dream up these plans at the agency would learn something. Not my job to complain; there's always a little extra green to go around.'

The two CIA operatives had been friends for a long time and

occasionally engaged in banter. In Guantánamo their mission, however, was one they took seriously. The CIA thought the best way to keep Camp X-Ray secure was to have some of their own people integrated into the base. They listened to the talk in bars, clubs, and mess halls.

'What you think the inspectors are going to do here?'

'Hell if I know.'

'Heather, I'm not sure I should bring this up...although it's probably going through your thoughts anyway. You know Brush and I went to northern Pakistan. It was good. We work great together but there are risks and it's not ideal for us. Truthfully we were probably not as focused on the job as we should've been. He was always distracting me. Happily, I might add. But even a split-second loss of concentration at the wrong time is dangerous. Brush has always worked with Jim before with no distractions. That's probably why they're both alive. They're a team and they stay focused. It's all about the mission, nothing else.'

Heather let out a breath with her cheeks puffed out. 'Phew. I know, I know. And I can tell Jim misses it, whatever "it" is. I just...I haven't wanted to think about him going away again. I've tried to ignore it but I know it's coming. He simply isn't ready for the office yet and maybe not me full-time—much as I wish he were.'

'Sorry to bring it up.'

Heather smiled seeing Jim and Pedro walking across the meadow. 'Maybe we can find time to talk more later. It's not your fault, Glenda, and I appreciate your honesty. It's just that after Mexico. I know more now about what he does, I've seen what he is capable of, and what others are capable of doing to him. It scares the hell out of me.'

Chapter 25

The heavy door opened into the large dark-wood paneled office befitting the highest ranking cabinet member and the fourth person in succession to the presidency. The office was meant to intimidate but it had no effect on Sorenson. Secretary of state was an appointed position that had started with Thomas Jefferson in 1789. Expansion in all agencies of the US government was an evolutionary process, State Department was no different and its size and scope had expanded worldwide to over twelve thousand Foreign Service employees.

The secretary held a great deal of influence with the president and she influenced the future of world affairs. On a daily basis, she was involved with intrigue that sometimes rivaled the CIA. Sorenson, however, viewed the woman and her two predecessors as amateurs playing his game. In truth, he did play at a different level. Nonetheless, the power he thought he had was misconceived, derived from a Napoleonic attitude that he had first acquired as the head of the Senate Intelligence Committee and now, as the head of what he perceived to be the world's most powerful intelligence agency. He envisioned his importance to the CIA as equal to what J. Edgar Hoover had been to the FBI.

Nevertheless, he tempered his misconceived lack of respect with his acceptance that while he ruled the CIA, support from the secretary of state was useful. Still, he wouldn't allow her to give him any grief.

'Good morning, Mona.'

'Good morning, Sorenson.'

He knew she was no pushover. He had showed his lack of deference calling her by her first name and she threw it right back at him,
calling him by his last. He let her win the greeting game. 'What can
I do for you, Madam Secretary?'

She held his gaze and answered him in her own good time. 'I
want the truth about the woman you are detaining in Guantánamo
Bay.'

'What truth?' Sorenson's tone remained impassive but the secretary sensed a slight twitch in his eye that told her she had taken him
off guard.

'Knock it off, Director. You know exactly what I mean.'

She was a skilled politician and wanted to draw him out.

Sorenson, still nonplussed, regrouped. He guessed she was fishing. 'What do you want to know about her?'

She let out a breath and decided he wasn't going to give up
anything unless he had to. She would be straight, as straight as she
needed to be. 'Why the sudden interest in looking for information
about her? She is supposed to be in your care, a nonentity at a prison
that doesn't exist; yet you're drawing attention to yourself and the
facility. I want to know why you need to know more about her.'

Sorensen became a little concerned. Was the State Department
or the executive branch monitoring the CIA? She couldn't know of
the escape, could she? He decided to be careful. She could be setting
him up. 'No idea, probably just something routine or connected to
another issue. I'll look into it,' he parried and stood up to leave,
saying, 'Is that all?'

'Our agreement was there would be no leaks. Putting her name
out for any reason violates our agreement. I want an answer.'

He walked out without saying anything further. *Impertinent
bastard,* she thought.

'Mona says Sorenson gave her nothing, but her gut tells her he's hiding something and either way she would like to see the bastard fired,' said Art Willis.

'Not surprising,' said Maeve. 'He's lasted longer in the job than I thought he would. He's no political pushover and full of himself, but he's not a good director. Good thing he is not a hands on director or he would wreck the agency, What's the next move?'

'I could call the base commander in Cuba,' said Art. 'They're separate from X-Ray but he might know something.'

'Who is it?' asked Will Crystal.

'Admiral Cameron.'

'I don't know him,' said Will.

'Won't hurt to call him,' said Maeve, 'just be nice.'

The deputy director of State nodded as he pushed an intercom button.

After a brief conversation Art said, 'No help at all. He says Camp X-Ray is completely off-limits to his people; he doesn't like it being on his base.'

'Where did that directive setting X-Ray up come from? You're going to have to change that nonsense immediately,' said Will in a voice that made everyone cringe.

'Cameron says it's direct from the White House.'

'All right then, who in the White House? I don't accept this. The CIA is always slipping these things in and it reflects badly on the military. Call the White House chief of staff and see what he says.'

Art pushed his intercom again. 'I'm going to ask the director to call. She's out for two hours in a subcommittee meeting. Get some lunch and check back with me.'

'Maeve, I don't need lunch but I need to use a conference room,' said Will.

The general dialed the BWC and just as he asked for Sheilla, Maeve opened the door to the conference room next to her office and said, 'Art managed to already talk to the chief of staff. They called him about you. Since you are in town, the VP would like a meeting at noon.'

The general looked at his watch. That was twenty minutes away. 'Didn't say what it was about?'

'Not a word, but you'll find out soon enough; our driver can get you there in sixteen minutes. He's waiting in the garage.'

Chapter 26

'General, have a seat. You look healthy. I would ask you about the family but you never seem to have had one.'

'It might be one of those things I am starting to regret, Mr. Vice President.'

'Never too late,' replied the other man amiably.

They studied each other for a moment. The general waited, wondering what the vice president wanted.

'I assume then that your Colonel Johnson has recovered?'

'He's recovered.'

The vice president walked over to his desk and pushed a button. 'Supposed to record everything, posterity and all that, but I don't like it so had this little device installed that interferes with the recording device. Is Colonel Johnson fully recovered from Mexico?'

'He is.'

'He has been valuable with the hard missions but I find I don't know that much about him. Eventually he will be your replacement, I imagine. You met in Vietnam?'

The general wondered what this was all about. He was also certain the VP had a full brief on Colonel Johnson's history. Before he could respond the vice president said, 'And I hear you have a woman agent now?'

'The colonel and I did meet in Vietnam. The woman came over from the FBI after getting shot up in Seattle.'

'She's the one, huh. The redhead. I remember hearing about

her.' The general didn't like where this line of questions was leading.

After a pause the general said, 'Tom, we've got a potential problem with Guantánamo and the CIA.'

The vice president was waiting for the general to open this line of conversation. 'I don't hate that place as much as some but I've never been comfortable with Sorenson. He's a pain in the ass and he's a political dinosaur. I would really like to see someone new that could work both in the agency and with us. Gupta might make a good director. He's definitely clever enough and pretty civil. He recognizes the value of technology.'

'Won't it look odd, appointing a new director in the president's second term?'

'We are looking at all the appointments. There might be changes that will improve our second term and build for the future.' It was no secret the VP longed for a chance at the big office.

'My impression is that Gupta would never take it. He is an analyst, a thinker at heart. You need someone who has been on the ground,' said Will. 'Someone the rest of the agency employees respect. They are in a tough place, running something that is outside of most of our laws but that we depend so heavily on. You have a couple of good candidates. Most experienced and capable is John Watson, operations director. He would be my choice.'

'He has the right reputation all right, but I don't know that much about him personally. What I do know, he is an insider and he wouldn't work with us. Your name has been brought up a few times.' Tom watched the general closely.

Shoot, so that's it, thought the general none too happily.

The vice president detected nothing in Will's expression, however the general quickly responded, 'I'm honored, sir, but I have no interest in the position. You have plenty of good choices. People that have put out for this country. I belong where I am. I like my team and mission directive. We're more efficient than CIA and less publicly accountable.'

'That's the answer I rather expected.'

The general changed the subject. 'Whose idea was it to make Camp X-Ray off-limits to the military?'

The vice president knew it was not a good time to try and change the general's mind, so he went along with the topic change. 'If the military was overseeing it, there would be more potential for leaks. The CIA, to their credit, does know how to keep their mouth shut. It isn't clear what the legalities will be but one thing is for certain. It could be a PR issue if it gets out we are holding people without due process.'

'It seems pretty clear to me what the illegalities are. My immediate concern is that the CIA is asking questions about the woman detainee and I want to find out why,' said Will Crystal. 'I've got a very bright analyst that puts two and two together better than anyone. I was just about to check with her when you called me over.'

'Call her now. Use the sofa phone. That phone is secure and the recorder is still not doing its intended job,' he said, sounding pleased with his interference device.

The general moved over to a dark forest-green, satin sofa and picked up the phone.

'Sheilla. I'm here with Vice President Thompson.'

'Hi, sir.'

'Anything new?'

'All the queries from the CIA have stopped abruptly. That bothers me.'

'Go on.'

'The last intercept was a message sent back to the CIA. Someone in the Mexican government said that it was not the Mexicans who pulled off the cartel raid in Tubutama.'

'It won't take the CIA long to figure it out, if that is what they're looking for,' said the general with resignation in his voice.

'They don't have any proof.'

'They don't need proof. The assumption is enough. When Sorenson's people put two and two together, he can turn it to his advantage against the president. We excluded the CIA. We went around the FBI and put the DEA's and Border Patrol's surveillance planes out of business. Not to mention we tricked them into moving border security to a different location. None of that will make any of them happy. The president wants to replace him but Sorenson will use this to keep his job secure or there will be a leak letting the press know what happened.'

'You think he would blackmail the president?'

'He'd say something like, it would be tricky if this ever got to the press, sir.'

'OK then, stalemate,' said Sheilla, silently thankful she didn't work in DC.

'Most times, nothing wrong with that,' said the general.

'One more thing. We picked up a report of a killing in Nogales, Mexico. Underling drug group of Vasquez's—executed. It could be your normal cartel hit but it appeared to be one person doing the killing, a woman. The profile fits Najma, as does the description. Maybe she has a sister, or the cartel has a copycat.'

'Jesus, Sheilla, Najma?'

'Maybe, maybe not,' said Sheilla, knowing that something wasn't right, but she couldn't put her finger on it. 'Maybe the cartel is keeping her legend alive with a copycat?'

What the hell? thought the general. He sat there mulling over the realization that Sheilla could be right. *Back in Mexico,* he thought. Sheilla sat still and quiet thinking her own thoughts. After a few minutes the general burst into Sheilla's thoughts and barked, 'I need to talk to Milton.'

He put the phone on speaker and sat thinking while he waited. Dr. Milton would be out in the lab. It would take her several seconds to get to the phone. Sheilla's instincts were one of the reasons he had recruited her. She wouldn't think twice about the cartel killings, except that it had Najma's signature. The CIA had a sudden interest in Najma and her past. It could be that they were just gathering information or...? It added up to Najma having escaped—or had they released her? For a second Will Crystal wondered if the CIA might be trying to use Najma as an assassin for some insane reason. *Nonsense,* he said to himself. *Flights of fancy should be in my chopper not in my head.*

Through his thoughts, a voice was talking.

'General. Are you there. Hello?'

'Sorry, Barbara. Is the new antibiotic for the *Staphlococcus* testing OK?'

'Small problems. It isn't getting through the cell wall as effectively as we would like. Nusmen said that might be the case and made a suggestion before he left. We're working on testing his hypothesis.'

'That answered my next question.'

'He's gone. He left sulking, grumbling that you had ordered him out.'

Chapter 27

'I am going to get fat eating this way,' said Glenda, reaching for another cookie.

'Don't worry about it. I told you, you'll never gain an ounce up here,' said Heather.

'That's what you keep saying but I'm going to get used to it, and I won't want to stop eating when we leave.'

'Can be a problem,' added Jim.

You all too skinny, need fattening up, thought Lola with more than a little pride. *They now my family. No good here in woods though I train them, eat, get fat, and stay home.* She grinned and whistled to herself. Brush raised an eyebrow and looked at Glenda. She wondered if he was thinking she would get fat and then she knew that was not what he was thinking at all. Her eyes glistened, thinking how lucky she was and wondering how she could have lived without feeling this way.

'Okie dokie smokey,' said Heather.

'Okie dokie smokey,' repeated Pedro, giggling.

'What is your pleasure today, Pedro? Hike in the high ridges, go swimming, climb some rocks?' said Heather, winking at Jim.

'Fishing. I want catch daddy fish.' Heather grinned at the boy's name for the huge fish who'd taunted her from the lake in the past. Pedro had loved the story of her many failed attempts to capture him.

'All rightie. Well, we have to wait a little. He's probably still sleeping. Lola and I'll get things cleaned up and we'll go in a while.'

'No, we go now.' Pedro stamped his foot.

Heather was taken back and momentarily speechless.

'We're going to walk up that ridge, Pedro. You want to go?' asked Brush as he pointed to his right.

Pedro gave Heather a disappointed look. 'You've got time before fishing, Pedro, go ahead and go. I have to check the llamas after the dishes and then we'll fix a picnic lunch. Then we go fishing.' Pedro walked off, looking back at Heather with a pout.

'I'm trying to remember,' said Jim, 'what having no patience was like at his age. I'll go move the llamas for you.'

'Do it quickly, I want to talk to you before Pedro gets back,' said Heather with a serious look.

'Let's talk now. Lola can finish up while you and I go check the llamas.'

'You OK, Lo?' asked Heather.

'Sí, sí, no problema,' she said waving them off. 'Do all dishes and everything by self,' she said, genuinely happy to be useful and treated with respect, away from the cartel and the things she had been made to do for the cartel men. They'd beat her, raped her, and would force her to drink alcohol and do awful things when they were drunk. She shook her head to get rid of the memories.

Heather wrapped her arm around Jim's waist and they walked out into the still damp meadow. The sun refracted in the millions of dewdrops sitting on the short meadow plants that resisted the drying warmth that would come as the minutes passed. Pipestone grazed far down the meadow, eating the sedges that he liked above all else.

Heather walked up to Meteor. The llama lay on the ground with his head straight up. He didn't move and continued working his jaw back and forth, grinding what had once been green plants, his dark-brown back was covered with a surface layer of matted dead wool saturated with the dampness.

Heather bent down over him. He folded his ears back slightly as if to say, *Don't mess with me while I am feeding myself.*

'Always amazing, isn't it. He looks soaked but this old wool mixed with all the lanolin keeps the water completely off his undercoat,' she said with the awe that was always in her voice when she did this. 'They're perfectly adapted to the wet even though they're from the high dry mountains in South America.'

Jim indulged her. He refrained from letting her know she had said this dozens of times. She never stopped marveling about the llamas or the wilderness. To her, llamas represented the perfect evolutionary result of camels fleeing the Ice Age for warmer South American climates. 'I grant that they're exceptional but there is always room to become better adapted. People could, for instance, have an eye in the back of their heads to see what's behind them.'

'You would like to have that third eye, wouldn't you? Llamas, though, have exceptional peripheral vision and don't need rear vision. We are the ones lacking. Let's continue this later, Jim. Right now, I want to talk about something.' Heather raised her gaze from Meteor and looked straight at Jim, her eyes serious and questioning.

'Let's walk over to that rock under the tree. It should be dry and we can sit.'

They walked over and sat as the scent of pine drifted down, joining the wet plant smells. 'Jim, I'm getting nervous. When are you going to be called back to work in the field? Have you heard anything you haven't told me? Couldn't you work at the BWC and not go out? What do you want to do anyway? I can see you're getting a bit bored staying on the ranch twenty-four seven. But why won't you explain why you want to go away from me on these missions, knowing there's a chance of you being killed? You have responsibilities now. Pedro needs a father.' She looked him straight in the eye, a thousand more questions ready to erupt.

The sun blazed hot off the adobe walls of Mexicali. The ground was warming, befitting the city's nickname, 'Warm Land': the city that captured the sun. Najma, indifferent to the morning heat, strolled through the town dressed in a scruffy Mexican skirt, her short black hair under a white woven, small brimmed hat. With her olive complexion and dark eyes, she blended into the crowds of people heading to the street markets.

She knew precisely where she was going but as was her way of doing things, she walked in ever widening circles around one of her targets, wanting to fully understand the lay of the land. The mayor's office building was not large but had an ornate façade hosting the national flag of Mexico alongside the state of Baja flag and an unknown third, swaying lightly in the warm breeze, mostly yellow with some blue and red. Najma assumed it was the city of Mexicali flag, and all three flags attested to the importance of the mayor's office to the townspeople.

Earlier she had walked through a Chinese area and been surprised there was one. If she had looked carefully at the bundle of papers Vladislav had given her she would have seen a description of Mexicali's Chinatown: she'd only glanced at them. She would figure out the city's layout with her own eyes.

What she cared about was the target, Mayor Juan Diaz Silva. He was short and overweight, described as being pompous and taken with his own self-importance. Najma's lips curled up slightly, imagining how she would enjoy puncturing his fat stomach and seeing his beady eyes widen in disbelief.

She felt good. She was happy to be on the hunt.

Najma entered her hotel. With her hat removed, she revealed inch long hair, the stubble gone; she looked less like a local and

more like a tourist. Her no frills, dull, white cement block hotel was
ineptly named the Fiesta Hotel, but Najma was oblivious to the
irony. It was large enough and filled with low-end tourists, no one
noticed her. She walked across the nondescript tan tile floor to a
display cabinet, using the reflection to observe people behind her.
Seeing nothing out of the ordinary, she went to the two small,
white painted, metal elevator doors and pushed the up button.

She rode to the floor above her own and walked down the
long corridor on wavy, brown-stained carpet to the stairs. She
stepped silently down the dingy cement stairs to floor two. She
listened, and hearing nothing suspicious, she looked at the door
hinge, judging whether it would make any noise when she opened
it. Slowly she cracked the door and peered down a hall identical
to the floor above. The hall was empty and she quickly entered
her room next to the stairs.

The room had been booked by one of Vega's men per her
instructions. The man also booked another room directly across
the hall. She wanted to have a quick escape route. From her room
she would also be able to tell if anyone entered the hall from the
fire escape door. And she could easily, if necessary, drop the ten
feet from her balcony to the ground. She received a call on the
bulky cell phone that Guillermo had given her. Two men would
bring her luggage containing the supplies and weapons she had
instructed Vega she wanted.

The two men first approached the room cleaners down the
hall from Najma and gave them each a thousand pesos and a stern
warning not to enter or disturb their sister's room at the end of
the hall. Desperately poor, the cleaners willingly took the money,
but they would have done as instructed without any pesos. They
knew better than to cross men like these. They both watched the
men walk away toward the elevators and looked beyond them,
down the long corridor toward Najma's room. Both crossed

themselves wishing they had not come to work today.

Jim sat, not knowing which of Heather's many questions to answer or if he could answer any of them except that, 'The general has given me no indication of any missions. You are right, perhaps someday soon…you don't need to worry.'

'After Mexico, I understand things about you and what you do that I never did before. You're very capable of defending yourself and shooting people when you need to, Jim, but now I also realize how dangerous what you do is. I was there and saw how evil those men and that woman were. And for you to say I don't need to worry…do you call getting shot at the hacienda, careful? You could have been killed just as easily as wounded. You always tell me, skill is only one part of anything, luck is the other component. How long will you be lucky?'

Jim pulled her to him. With his arms holding her close, he whispered, 'As long as you are here waiting for me, and now Pedro too, I'll stay lucky.'

She hugged him hard, knowing there was nothing she could do other than believe in what he said. Heather leaned back, tears glistening in her green eyes, refracting grains of light. Then she moved back and held his shoulders with her hands, looking into his blue-gray eyes only a few inches above hers. She said nothing and then, tight-lipped, moved her head up once and then down, knowing this was all he would offer her.

Vega scanned Vladislav's compilation of General Ramos's schedule, collected over weeks of observation by cartel men in Mexicali. He'd distributed his men throughout Mexicali, instructing them to never follow or interfere with Najma. They were told to report her whereabouts but only if she walked past them. The young general did not vary his daily routines. He never left the compound without several guards. Then they would often drive to the market and Ramos would walk through the stalls, picking up whatever he wanted and waving as though he were a celebrity. Once he even took a picture with a tourist.

Dressed meticulously in tan uniform adorned by braids and medals, General Ramos did look more like a Hollywood star playing a parody of a general than an actual military man. His demeanor and clothes were distinct from the Indians and the Chinese that maintained stalls and the hundreds of migrants waiting to cross the border into the US, milling with those who had just been deported to Mexicali by US border authorities.

Vega guessed that walking through the market would be the prim general's weakness. Four lax bodyguards provided no protection from Najma. It was crowded and escape would be easy for her.

The mountain forest and meadows continued shedding the night-cooled air as the sun's warmth penetrated the morning sky. Heather still felt edgy after talking to Jim, but tried not to let it show. She hoped her worries would dissipate, knowing she couldn't live with this knot in her stomach forever. Heather started getting the lunches ready, watching Jim still out in the meadow, sitting on top of a house-sized round glacial boulder, desperately wanting to know his thoughts.

Jim sat thinking about Heather's response in Mexico to the grim reality of a world she had not encountered before. Under pressure, she had risen to the challenge, fought her way out and kept her emotions in check even after all she had witnessed and endured. But now, back in the cocoon of the ranch, with a young son to raise, and his future to provide for, her attitude had changed. She had always been concerned when Jim went out on a mission but now that she had firsthand experience, everything was different. No longer did she just worry that he might not return or be incapacitated, now she worried at the ease with which he could kill, at the frequency with which it was necessary. She worried about their new son not having a father; she worried that his conscience might be compromised. Even after explanations from him, Brush, and particularly Glenda, Heather still found it difficult to reconcile how a person could cross over the line from wholesome partner to killer and then back again, over and over. What if one day the killer wasn't there when Jim needed him? What if one day the partner wasn't there when she needed him? She had told Jim all of this when they first came back from Mexico, explained it so well that he didn't know what to say. So he'd said, *Trust me.* He hoped for both their sakes that would be enough.

'Here they come. That was fast,' said Heather.

Brush and Glenda each had hold of an arm and were swinging Pedro in the air as they walked across the meadow.

Pedro let go with a squeal and ran up to Heather then looked around for his dad. Jim climbed down, meeting Pedro in the meadow as Heather watched from afar. He scooped him up and twirled him around. 'What are you so excited about?'

'Going fishing with Mama.'

'Has she been telling you about that big fish that she never quite catches?' said Jim, knowing that she had.

'I catch him.' Father and son were laughing as the group rejoined Heather.

'Heather, we're going up on top of the ridge to that little lake you told us about,' said Glenda.

'You'll love it up there. It sits right on top of the ridge—feels like the top of the world. It's like an oversized swimming pool. Maybe we can go up later too. Pedro, you ready? Let's get the fishing gear. Won't you go with us?' she asked as she looked at Jim.

'I'll walk down with you but I think I'll walk up to that scree slope. There was some slip and slide opal near the top where there was a small fault line.'

'I remember it. Bring some back for us.'

'Sure.' He looked happily at her, glad that things seemed easy between them.

Glenda looked at Brush. 'Slip and slide?'

'I'll explain it on the way,' he whispered as he put his arm around her. 'See you later, guys,' Brush called over his shoulder as they walked off.

'Madre Dios,' exclaimed Lola shaking her head.

Heather smiled and said, 'High mountain air, Lo.'

Major Brush McGuire and Glenda Rose Stuart felt their desire grow with every step up the hillside to the lake. Their love had not abated during the months they had been together. Neither was it mature in the way of Jim and Heather's, but they shared their minds and thoughts easily. Something Jim and Heather had never been able to do.

It was still impossible to distinguish between love and lust for them. They both felt like teenagers and lost themselves to their feelings. Underneath, an acceptance existed, perhaps partly based on respect for each other's abilities both in and out of bed. This was the longest relationship in Brush's dizzying past. Too many women to count and none that captivated him and held him enthralled as Glenda did. He knew this was the 'real' thing. How he had always imagined it would be with all the women he had adored before; he knew now he had never really loved before Glenda Rose Stuart.

Whenever he stopped to wonder if they would last, if there were someone better for him, more capable, the thought hung for seconds as if on the edge of a cliff and then it tipped to the side of certainty.

Glenda had not been in many relationships, just a few casual romances over the last few years. She had been too busy studying law and then FBI training and she had never met anyone that made her feel even close to the way Brush did. In the past, she had been generally leery of men, particularly her colleagues. She wanted respect for her abilities. She had overheard a degrading comment once at the FBI, 'the redhead with the big boobs.' She had never forgotten that comment or the way it made her feel, and she was determined to move ahead based on her ability and intelligence. She accepted who she was in both mind and body. The girl with ability and smarts, a great figure, comely face and ginger hair. The men could go screw themselves; she had pride and, more importantly, better things to do than worry about their lewd behavior.

The FBI used her as an undercover agent on several occasions, although at first blush it seemed to violate the principal of being incognito. Brush remembered well his first thought—it was absurd for a voluptuous redhead to be undercover, the antithesis of being undercover. Jim had pointed out to him perhaps she was so obvious that she was ignored as a threat.

Chapter 28

Sheilla spent most of the night rehashing the information she'd gathered. The CIA was asking questions about Najma. Why? Why would they risk revealing their off-the-radar detention center to find background on a prisoner they'd held for months? She considered dozens of scenarios but every hypothesis ended up falling apart as she found reasons to disprove one after the other. She had to focus in on what she knew but what was that exactly?

She picked up a yellow pencil and started to write in a lined lab book. First she wrote, *CIA asking about Najma.* Second, *Nasty execution near the Mexican border.* This had Najma written all over it.

She moved away from her desk and started twirling in her chair. She thought best like this, spinning late at night.

Her thoughts took the form of a conversation with herself, question and answer, probing toward a plausible explanation. The Mexican police has no useful information about the killings in Nogales other than that the group killed was associated with Guillermo's cartel and there might have been some friction between them. *So what. There's always friction. Did Najma train an apprentice? No. The best conclusion: Najma is in Mexico, not being held by the CIA.* Or a lesser possibility, the cartel wanted to keep her image alive. Useful, to have a phantom assassin.

We need to know what is going on in Camp X-Ray and the cartel's hacienda. The Wolf Pack is the best hope. Fred, the BWC computer specialist, is good, but not anywhere near as good as the two civilian academics and the two ex-hackers at Fort Huachuca. Nonetheless, I'll try to nudge him to find Najma in Tubutama. Having a way forward brought Sheilla's spinning to an abrupt stop.

Chapter 29

Pedro skipped and ran as the lake came into view. 'Hurry! Come on, Rosie, Mama. We catch big fish.' But he needn't have said anything. Jim and Heather walked almost as fast as he ran and Rosie would follow him whether he called her or not.

'It is big lake,' said Pedro.

'It is also very cold and very deep. Let's walk to the far end, down by those rocks.'

They skirted the dark lake still shaded by trees on a deer trail. Little ripples appeared on the lake's still surface.

'Looks like plenty of fish,' said Jim.

'Not many insects so they might just be hungry. What do you think? Our favorite little red and white spoon for Pedro?'

'Easiest thing to try first.'

'Let's see if Pedro can catch the first one and then you can fish if you want,' said Heather.

'I'm happy just being here with you two. I'll sit back and watch for a while,' said Jim. 'You can kill the fish, and I suspect it won't take long before he'll catch one.'

Heather had never thought much about it before, his distaste for killing animals, fish, and even insects. But now it seemed abnormal to her. Jim killed people and, as she had observed, without noticeably caring. She wondered if she would ever understand it. Understand him. One thing she did know and understand: Jim never aspired to be normal.

When Jim was a boy, he had loved going hunting and fishing with his grandfather. They had gone out on the lake in front of the cottage, or hunted pheasants and deer, which they only rarely actually managed to shoot. His grandfather had one glass eye as a reminder from the army. Jim liked going out into the woods. He liked shooting, but he knew now he had never really wanted to kill the animals.

It didn't bother him that a cougar killed a deer. It was the natural way and he knew he would not hold it against a cougar if one were to kill him. Everyone gave lip service to the Earth's most dangerous predator being man, but he wondered if many really believed its veracity. Animals did have different personalities, he felt certain: some loving like Pipestone, others like Shasta seemed bad-tempered by comparison, but Jim questioned whether they had the same mean streak that some people seemed to have ingrained in their souls. He concluded that they probably did.

He had seen men kill ruthlessly in battle and with no qualms even when there was no battle. He had seen children kill with no more thought than most gave to swatting a mosquito. Women were no different. Some people, given the opportunity, immediately embraced the power they could have over the life and death of others.

Yet there were still people everywhere who were kind and gentle and wanted nothing more than to help those who needed it. Others preyed on the good and kind people of the world with sociopathic lust, destroying families and communities without compassion. He despised this human tendency. It was true he felt nothing when he terminated them. Ridding the world of the bad people even gave him satisfaction.

Heather, on the other hand, had little compunction about breaking a fish's neck. Just food to her and, both of them agreed, good food too, especially out in the mountains. He doubted whether she could or would kill a person, even someone like Najma. Fish and animals were one thing, but Heather walked carefully around delicate plants, saying they shouldn't be damaged and, befitting her name, always complained when anyone stepped on the mountain heathers.

There was never a satisfactory answer to these questions. If Heather searched for that answer now, she would come away with no more understanding than he had. Jim lay back on soft moss in front of a pine tree and watched his newly adopted son and Heather enjoy the morning, thinking it was amazing that Pedro seemed so normal after watching Najma kill his family only months ago.

'I catch one,' yelled Pedro.

'Quick, give a small jerk to set the hook,' said Heather. 'Now reel him in.'

'You think he papa fish?' yelled Pedro in glee as he pulled and tugged on the bent pole. 'It big I can tell.'

Heather stopped herself from correcting his English since she knew he was about to be disappointed. The lightweight flexible rod that they fished with in the mountains bent and quivered even with small fish.

'He's coming out of water. He small, he no big fish,' said a disappointed Pedro.

'It's not the big fish, Pedro. It looks very nice though, and it will taste good tonight,' Heather said as she grabbed his line and unhooked it. 'You are a very good little fisherman.'

Pedro was too excited to inform her that he wasn't little, but he was startled as Heather put her thumb in the fish's mouth and bent its head backward snapping the brown trout's neck.

Pedro stood there with his mouth open. Heather thought that maybe she should have killed the fish out of his sight but instead said, 'It's kinder to not let them suffer.' Pedro looked over at Jim who gave him a thumbs-up and a look that seemed to say, *I understand how you feel but she's right.*

'Throw your line in again and maybe you'll catch a big one; I'll start cleaning this one,' Heather told him.

The excitement of chasing the big fish took over and Pedro soon lost all thoughts of what had happened to that fish. He'd seen far worse.

Pedro was proud as he walked back into camp later that afternoon. Lola sat huddled in the kitchen. She jumped up as they walked across the meadow. 'I afraid to leave kitchen.'

'Someone had to stay to guard the llamas,' said Heather.

'Funny big blue bird keep landing in kitchen and making noise. Too much like a person. Not afraid. I think he a spirit, no bird.'

'Camp jay,' said Heather. 'They are pretty but can be a nuisance. It won't hurt you and it certainly is nothing more than a bird. It's hungry is all and not afraid of us.'

'Why you gone so long? Why make me stay here? Nobody here. Llamas no care. Others no come back.' She didn't really expect an answer as Heather had told her why before they left and again a few moments ago.

'You catch fish?'

Pedro opened the heavy bag and held it out to Lola. 'I catch mucho.'

Heather patted his head and said, 'Better get to work and get these ready for dinner. They're gutted, you want heads on or off?'

Jim said quickly, 'Heads off for me.'

'Me too,' added Pedro.

Chapter 30

The pudgy Mexicali mayor was nearly half as wide again as his five-foot six-inch height. His dossier said he was actually three inches shorter and wore elevator shoes to achieve that height. His neatly pressed, oversized, white suit coat was too full. Instead of letting his bulk push and strain against the material, he chose to hide his girth in the tent-like coat. The ruby red tie drew attention away from his rotund body, as did the sparkling glass pinky ring. He worked his way down the building steps to a waiting vintage yellow Cadillac. The car pulled slowly away. Najma, dressed in blue jeans, one size too large, and a faded gray shirt, walked slowly along the street in the direction that the mayor's car and driver faced.

The yellow Cadillac, with a number one on its license plate, drove with a soft patter over paving stones, passing Najma and turning left at the first corner. Najma followed without hurry. The mayor's car drove two blocks and stopped in front of a bar. She watched him disappear through a brown wooden door.

She walked past the open window of the bar. She could see him sitting with two men and a woman dressed in a full blue skirt and matching top. They talked animatedly while drinking from small shot glasses. Juan Diaz Silva pushed himself up and placed a stubby hand on the bare-shouldered woman. She smiled up at him and then as he turned away, the smile faded as she looked at the two men.

Glenda put her arm around Brush's back as they walked across the flat meadow toward the higher lake. He took her hand as they came to a winding trail through the woods, then released his grasp with a squeeze as the trail narrowed and started to climb up the ridge behind their camp. 'We just follow this trail and it will get us to the swimming lake, according to Heather,' said Glenda.

'None too soon. Who needs a lake anyway?'

'Keep calm, buster, we'll be there soon enough.'

'Glenda, if there is one thing in this world that is impossible for me to do, it is to keep calm when standing next to you.'

She looked at him playfully. 'Then we'll just have to do something about that,' she said and then added, 'at the lake!'

'What are we standing here for? Let's get a move on it,' said Brush as he headed up the trail at a fast walk.

Glenda Rose grinned and loped after him. 'Slow down some. It won't do you any good to get there without me.'

Brush slowed down with a small groan.

The lake, topped with a white, gentle, mid-morning light, sat peacefully on a ridge high above Lake Chelan. It had been smoothed out of hard black basalt by ancient glaciers, leaving a mountaintop infinity pool. A few short conifers grew on an outcrop to the left. It felt like the top of the world. Nothing but blue sky in all directions and distant snowcapped mountains to the west separated by the fifty-mile long Lake Chelan.

Brush dropped his pack, pulled out a towel, and stripped naked, his muscular frame planted on the smooth rock at the edge of the lake. He looked at Glenda as if to say, 'What are you still wearing clothes for?' and then dove into the cold mountain lake. He came up sputtering. 'Jeez, man this is cold. A guy could shrivel up to nothing in here. We should have waited. Maybe it will warm up later.'

Glenda stood, creamy translucent parchment skin, light red hair just touching her shoulders, her full figure still taut at thirty-seven years. Light red pubic hair nestled below the only mar on her flawless body, three welted red scars, a memento of the undercover assignment in Seattle where she had first met Brush.

Will this ever change? Brush wondered. *Is there anyone else in the world that could have this effect on me?* Despite the cold water, he could feel himself responding to her.

Glenda stepped daintily into the lake up to her knees and splashed water over herself, sat down and quickly stood up, climbing out onto a wide flat-topped rock at the lake's edge. She unrolled the sleeping pad, threw her towel on top and laid down, sprawled open to the sun and sky.

Brush moved through the shallow lake and out, stout legs propelling him like a robot. He moved directly over top of her and looked down.

'Where did you get that smile from, mister? You wear it well.'

'If I have a smile in my life it is because of you. You are the most beautiful woman in the universe.'

'Dry off and get down here. I want to make love everywhere with you but right now, out here in the open with all this to ourselves, looking up at you—what was that you said about cold water…'

'Fish good, you catch plenty.'

Pedro felt proud as he watched everyone eating his fish. Lola studied Pedro. He did look happy. She was certain he was. She had hoped for a short while in Mexico that he would replace her dead son. Then they had nearly both died while trying to escape the cartel, and she realized she would never be able to protect him in that place. Fortunately the Americans came and saved them both.

Pedro had been drawn to Jim, a small dark-skinned boy taken with a tall white man streaming red blood on the hacienda floor.

Why? Lola would always wonder, *Why did he go to this man?* Minutes later they were put on a helicopter. She went from imminent death to safety, and then everything happened so fast—interrogations, flying in planes, and talking to Heather and Jim, who were kind to her, doctors and then papers and more papers to sign. Another plane ride near the sea, out of the rain and up over white peaked mountains into a valley.

She had quickly realized that Pedro had first clung to Jim for some inexplicable reason, and later Heather; she would not replace her lost son with Pedro or become his new mother.

Lola, for a short time had been upset by the loss of Pedro as 'her' son, then the feeling of safety and security and a home in America had brought her to her senses. She not only had a boy to watch out for but she would care for the whole family. Nursing Jim back to health left her feeling just as responsible for him. Heather was always kind but it took Lola weeks to warm up to her. Suddenly the happiness welled from her body as she shook off the ugliness of her past life. She now loved Heather like the big sister she had never had, and for the first time in her life Lola felt at peace.

Sounds, voices began penetrating her thoughts. She heard some strange words directed at her and then her name, 'Lo, Lo, are you OK?' She had been staring, mouth open, sitting motionless. She shook her head and looked around the faces lit by the orange glow of their campfire: Jim, Pedro, Heather, Brush, and Glenda. Almost overcome by tears, her dark round face then broke into a glowing smile big enough to crack her cheeks. She beamed at her new family. No one spoke. They were all transfixed by the sudden change in her expression.

Heather put her arm around Lola and held her in a hug.

After several seconds Lola broke the silence, 'Good fish, you good fishman, Pedro.'

Jim sat wondering what had just happened. An epiphany?

Something had changed, they'd all felt it and would never know what it was.

Najma walked several blocks to a store no bigger than a closet. She purchased chips and jerky and walked back toward the market. She sat at a small metal table outside a bar and ordered black coffee.

It didn't take long to spot the general and his bodyguards. He smiled as he took an apple, not paying for it.

After several minutes he walked down a side street, entering a door that climbed to a rooftop cafe.

'Pedro, what do you think about sleeping out under the stars tonight?' asked Jim.

'Yes, please, all of us?'

'No me,' said Lola, still clinging to Heather. 'I sleep inside where safe.'

Brush looked at Glenda and she looked back. 'Inside,' they said almost together, then laughed.

'Come on then, Pedro. Let's get our bed made up.'

'You sleep next to my tent,' said Lola. 'I feel safer you close outside.'

The campfire burned to ruby-and-lace black coals. Lola, Heather, and Glenda finished cleaning up and doing the dishes with Brush drying. One by one, they disappeared into the darkness.

Najma looked for a place to sit where she could observe the rooftop restaurant. The best she could do was to sit at a small lunch stand where she could see the exit door at the bottom of the steps. She waited for two hours. Normally she could wait for hours thinking ahead to the pleasure of killing. This time something didn't feel right. She gambled and climbed the stairs to the rooftop restaurant. It was empty.

She felt too exposed looking for another way out from the patio, the way they must have departed. Outside she circled the block and the building. She saw no other exit that they could have used. A car approached from behind her. She stood off the narrow street partially hidden in a recessed doorway. The yellow Cadillac softly purred past within two feet of her. It stopped by the same stairs the general and his men had used earlier.

Heather and Jim snuggled into the big tarp-covered sleeping bag they had brought. Two bags zipped together made it almost queen sized. Pedro, wearing his clothes, cuddled in between them as they lay looking up at the stars.

Rosie lay down on the ground with a thud, at the top near Pedro's head.

'Many stars same like Mexico,' said Pedro as he scooted up, putting his head on Rosie's wide chest.

'Always beautiful. It takes my breath away. When you and your dad climbed the talus slope, after lunch at the lake, did you find some slip and slide opal?' *I forgot to ask Glenda what Brush said,* Heather remembered.

'We did, Mama.' He proudly reached in his pocket and pulled out a large piece of opal.

'It's pretty too, just like the stars, isn't it?'

'Very shiny, I like.' His dark hand still holding the white crystalline stone drifted onto Rosie's chest.

Chapter 31

Najma waited for the Cadillac to move down the narrow lane. Its chubby passenger, breathing hard, ascended the stairs to the patio. She silently climbed the stairs behind him when he disappeared around the patio corner. A door closed. She walked onto the empty patio and quietly opened the door. Under an inner door she could see light. Then a shadow crossed the light from under the door and she quickly moved back. She could hear the door opening and she retreated to the stairway.

Then she heard a lighter snap shut and could smell smoke drifting into the still oppressive late morning air. If she had been armed this might have been her opportunity. All she had was her small two-sided knife. She quietly pulled it from her pocket. The man moved. She could tell from his shadow that he was large. One of the general's guards.

The man moved toward the stairs. She held her position breathing slowly, deeply, and quietly. She couldn't retreat. So she stepped down two steps and said, 'Hello, hello,' as if she was a lost tourist. Then, making a show of stepping up the stairs, she moved noisily toward the patio.

She could feel herself falling into darkness. Without hesitation, the bodyguard threw a heavy punch hitting her right ear. He hadn't held back and had put his oversized body behind the blow.

As her knife danced across the tiles, he knew he had made the right decision. Blood flowed from her ear. The man's knuckles had split the top of it as it sent her brain crashing against the inside of her skull knocking her out.

The big guard opened the door. 'Dracul. Aqui pronto. See what I caught.'

The smallest of the guards opened the door and looked at the woman. 'Muy bonita.' He bent over and felt her breasts and then looked in her empty pockets. 'What was she doing?'

'Nada. A stupid tourista.'

'Why did you hit her, Romero?'

The big man shrugged. 'She was lurking on the stairs and see, she had a knife,' pointing at Najma's small double-bladed knife lying on the red patio tiles.

Dracul removed a small vial from his pocket. He grabbed Najma's cheeks and squeezed hard, forcing her mouth open. He tapped powder in near the back of her throat and as a second thought he placed a small amount in her nostril and held her mouth closed, then blew in her nose sending some of the powder on its way to her lungs.

'What is that?'

'A present from my Colombian amigo. Good for women in bars. She will remember nothing when she wakes up. This woman very sexy, no.'

General Crystal went straight from his plane to his office. He called Mark and Sheilla, instructing them to report to his office ten minutes apart. Mark had just finished debriefing the general when Sheilla dragged into his office, dark circles evident under both eyes. She acknowledged Mark and sat down.

'Sheilla, are you OK? You look exhausted.'

'More like discouraged. I'm not finding out anything and what I can conclude I don't like. I love puzzles but...'

'Any news about the CIA?'

'Nothing really to go on so far.'

'It's always that way until we find something that leaps us forward.'

'The only thing different is the lack of any traffic about Najma. It stopped completely. I could use more computer staff.' Sheilla did not have to say that she needed better help accessing CIA's computers. She knew the general would understand what she was asking.

The general's PA placed a coffee next to Sheilla.

'Thanks, Marsha.'

'When was the last time you talked to the Wolf Pack?'

'A few hours ago.'

'Let's call them. It won't hurt having me involved and they can do a lot in a few hours. Kramer, after the call, find out who their boss is.'

The general pushed the intercom and said, 'See if you can get a Lt. Montgomery, first name Jake, on the line.'

Sheilla corrected, 'Colonel Montgomery.'

The general just looked at her and then said, 'At that speed he will outrank me before I get him on the phone.'

'I have him on the line,' said Marsha.

'Hello, Colonel, this is General Crystal.'

Before he could say another word, he heard 'Neat' and more faintly 'Guys, Will Crystal's on the line.'

The general laughed. Jake, nothing more than a kid, was now officially a white-hat hacker, a colonel who talked anything but military. *A new age.* 'You're on speaker with Sheilla and Captain Kramer,' he told him as he depressed the speaker button.

'We're all cool, General. The unit is official now but we haven't really been put to the test since you helped get us together. We often talk about the Tubutama operation. What happened to Misa and Vidya was, to say the least, a disaster in Mexico, but we all feel somewhat vindicated with what we were able to help you do against the cartel. If they're back in business, we'll all work our asses off to help you in any way possible.'

Just what the general wanted to hear. He couldn't help but chuckle though. A few years ago a junior officer using words like 'cool' and calling a general by his first name would have received an article fifteen court martial and been thrown out of the army.

Jake then said, 'Hi, Sheilla.'

'Hi yourself.' In the background they heard a chorus of 'hi guys.'

'You two name it and we'll do it.'

'Who is that I hear?' asked the general.

'Same old guys, Jason, now a warrant four, Misa and Vidya. We don't want or need anyone else in our group. The two professors are having more fun here with us and decided to stay on as private contractors. General Whitcuff offered them the position before he retired and now no one wants them to leave.' *Except me,* Will thought. *I want them here in my group.*

'It adds a mature outlook,' said a female voice with a crisp English accent—Misa. 'And we are headed your way to Jim and Heather's ranch in a few weeks.'

'Jake, Misa, Jason, Vidya. Anyone else with you?'

'Nope, just us four.'

'This has to be an unofficial request.'

'What else is new? That's our usual modus operandi.'

'Good. I don't know your new base commander and even if I did we couldn't fill him in on our old exploits and how this might be connected to them. This is an off-the-record request. No chain of command.'

'Yeah we get it. Fortunately no big army internet war goings-on for us so we're putting in full-time for you. Jason's monitoring the CIA's and NSA's computers. For the moment there's no traffic about the woman.'

'Our incursion into Mexico is still privileged information as are the terrorists captured there. The CIA doesn't know about it, at least not yet. The president, your group, the Special Forces team and the secretary of state and his deputy are the only ones that know, but that adds up to a lot of people. It's a good testament that none of us seem to have leaks.

'Logic says the woman is not at Guantánamo,' interjected Jake.

'Sheilla agrees.'

'She either escaped or for some convoluted reason, the agency might have turned her loose,' added the general. 'Any comments, Sheilla?'

'The sooner we figure it out the better. The woman is a killer and needs to be permanently stopped.'

The general looked at Sheilla surprised to hear her talk about terminating someone.

'OK, dudes, back at you as soon as.'

A chorus of 'byes' rang out in the background.

'Good thing I'm not a stick up my ass type of general.' Crystal smiled.

'I don't think they would even talk to you if you were and they certainly wouldn't do us any favors. Besides, I think you proved very well who you are when you went over the line into Mexico.'

Chapter 32

The knife-edge of the setting sun cut across Najma's face. White circles danced in her blurry eyes. She couldn't focus her eyes on the outside world any more than she could focus her mind: fragmented, foggy apparitions moved around in the dark recesses of her mind. Male faces, rough beards, stinking breath. She reached down and felt her pubic hair. Not soft, fine hairs, but crusty and glued together. Her anus felt raw and crusted. Her thoughts turned red with rage, still remembering nothing but now knowing that she had been beaten and raped.

For a moment she could see herself as if looking down from above. Clothes ripped, olive skin bruised and baked from the sun, her lips and her ear crusted with blood. Raw skin. Dirt sticking to her thighs. Her body was damaged and worse, no memories appeared. She vaguely remembered following the fat fuck mayor up some stairs.

She tried to get up and fell back to the desert ground. Ants paraded across her legs. Flies buzzed on and off but she felt nothing but anger, remembered nothing to assuage it.

Nusmen was given a government car, valid driver's license, and two weeks to kill before the general would let him get back to work. He had no idea what to do and felt lost outside the lab; he didn't even have an apartment anymore. This was no longer his world and the realization both frightened him and left him feeling despondent. Without any plans, he decided to drive. He had never been a good driver and now, if his anxiety level was any measure, he was a terrible driver. He would head away from people, toward the wilderness.

The guard at the west entrance to Fort Lewis waved the car through but what he saw inside made him shake his head. A long-necked geeky guy, with way too much uncombed, wild hair gripping the steering wheel with both hands. He looked so crazy the guard considered stopping him but he decided it wasn't worth it.

Nusmen went the way his instinct told him to, north toward Canada, north toward his old home in the Methow Valley. He eased up a little on his grip and settled into the slow lane of the freeway heading north toward Seattle. He was certain he had no friends left. He'd never had many. Heather was perhaps the one person he liked and that was probably only because she too was interested in plants. They had had some nice times working on botany programs for the Forest Service.

Once, in the lab, shortly after he had been incarcerated, he had asked Jim how she was, and had received what did not seem like a very friendly reply, just that she was fine. It didn't surprise him since he had always thought Jim did not like his working relation-ship with Heather, as it meant going camping for days at a time in the wilderness. It was unfair of Johnson as they had only been friends, but Nusmen always seemed to rub people the wrong way.

It was true that Jim didn't like Nusmen much—then or now. Jim understood that Nusmen had fallen over a mental cliff and acted irrationally. But Jim was slow to forgive anyone who had caused harm to people, and differing from the general, he thought Nusmen was a danger to have around. Jim certainly wouldn't be pleased to know he was back out in the real world.

Nusmen passed Tacoma and its entertainment dome without even noticing. He was surprised to be so close to Seattle. The increased size of the sprawling Southcenter Mall shocked him, followed by Boeing Field and the lights of the city. Nusmen left the BWC the day he was told to, but he had lingered, procrastinating well into the afternoon, going over and over the proper procedures with the lab techs and Dr. Milton. To them, Nusmen was a nut, but a brilliant nut; they respected him, or at least his abilities, so they just rolled their eyes and put up with his picayune overexuberance.

The city was just coming into view and he knew that soon, down to his right, from his vantage point high up on the freeway, he would see the University of Washington. The Udub, home to his ex-girlfriend, Professor Gabriella Pinski. He tried not to think of her, of what he had done, but he knew he would never forget. She had brought out that unhinged, hostile side of him. Nevertheless he knew that spreading the bacteria was his own fault, his own choice. She had dumped him, however he alone had caused irreparable harm to others, spreading the antibiotic-resistant bacteria. He stared straight ahead, avoiding looking down at the campus. The university exit sign registered in his mind but he tried to pretend he didn't see it.

Nusmen felt there was no one he could talk to outside the lab. He didn't want to. His only friend besides Heather had been his college buddy Wally Banks, now at MIT, and he was not sure Wally would even talk to him anymore.

He continued to head north and as if drawn by a force he could not control he turned off the exit for the North Cascade highway. The last time he had driven this route was when he'd had the bacteria sitting by his side on his way to Seattle, not away from it. The traffic was light and for long stretches, there were no cars at all, typical of midweek going over the mountains. The curving road was perhaps one of the most beautiful in the world, travelling through towering peaks before descending to the drier pine valleys on the east side of the range.

The sight of the mountains made him decide what to do. Probably not the social normalization plan the general wanted him to indulge in but Nusmen had had enough of people and wanted solitude.

The general looked at his watch. Twenty-one hundred. No sunrise or sunset in the underground center. Even so, the labs ran on a diurnal cycle as many of the technicians had normal lives outside. Consequently, the night staff had far fewer personnel. The general decided to walk through the labs. He spent more time on paperwork and politics and the operations side than the real reason this place existed: exploring killer microbes, stopping their spread, and inventing new ones then finding ways to kill them.

His first love, the reason he was here, was medical science. It had been years since he saw anyone in a clinical setting. Will Crystal consoled himself that the deadly microbes, viruses, prions, and weird parasites the lab, his lab, worked with had profound effects on human and animal health and as biological weapons. He had been the catalyst in setting up the laboratory after convincing politicians of its value. A potential always exists for a new kind of war using microbes. The 1918 influenza pandemic killed nearly eighty million people. Genetically engineered bugs had the potential to do much worse.

Microbes had killed millions of people in the last few thousand years, far more than any natural disasters or wars. It was a balance of survival. The bugs needed their hosts to survive long term but often their presence caused the death of the host. Humans fared poorly when new strains infected them. With the advances in genetics, the general was convinced that viruses like the N1H1, 1918 Spanish flu variants would be manufactured by someone or government, with the sole purpose to kill.

He thought of the four hundred thousand US citizens killed in World War II; there had been two thousand times more deaths from the 1918 virus. Of course there were more casualties from that war in other parts of the world, ten million in Russia, maybe forty million worldwide. Still the influenza killed more than all the wars then and after. *Why was it that only war between governments was commemorated, not the fight for survival against deadly viruses?*

The first mission of the then Bio Warfare Laboratory had been to form a line of defense for terrorists' biological weapons. The public was unaware of many attempts to infect Americans; but General Crystal knew every detail of every attempt. The labs quickly evolved beyond defense to engineering and experimenting on dangerous microbes. The idea was to stay one step ahead of both the natural and the human-engineered bugs and the perpetrators.

The development of highly infectious and deadly organisms, however, took time. The special reactions teams from the now newly named Biological Warfare Center were always on alert but did not have to deal with threats day in and day out. When the microbial world seemed calm, the general selectively loaned out his field agents and, less frequently, their backup teams to other agencies. He had one firm rule that he never violated, he would never allow a third party to dictate what his men did. He and Jim decided exactly how they would run a mission and who with. They worked the missions themselves. His people, like Sheilla and her team, were instrumental in the survival of Jim and Brush and the BWC's other specialized personnel.

With his oversized budget, General Crystal had to employ all the political prowess he possessed to keep his facility afloat. The government would spend billions on tanks and ships but they were loath to spend money on microscopic bugs they could not see or understand. He had to fight hard for the funds for his lab and operations. Fortunately, enough senators and congressmen understood the lab's value and enough knew that his team had gotten the government out of several tight places in the past. *Maybe one day this place will save more lives than any of the armed services,* he pondered.

Nusmen, a discombobulated lone wolf, had been a reminder to

everyone. The Nusbug he had created long ago at Harvard was resistant to all antibiotics. Fortunately, but sadly, it only infected immune-suppressed people, making it the opposite of the N1H1, which killed mostly middle-aged healthy individuals by overstimulating their immune systems.

The general walked through the labs among machines with jiggling vials on automated shaking tables and small test tubes moving down automated lines. He peered through the outer door window to the high security labs, thinking this was where he should spend more time, when his pager buzzed. His night clerk said, 'Tom Grant is holding for you on the secure line.'

'Nice surprise, Tom.'

'I'm returning your call, old buddy. You called me remember?'

'I did; how's life?'

'Not bad. My thirty's coming up and I'm out of here. What you need, Will?'

'How's your connection with X-Ray?'

There was a silence. 'Shit, how do you even know about that place? I hoped you were going to ask me something easy but looks like that's off the table. I know quite a bit about it. I helped design the security. But I have a feeling you already know that.'

Nusmen felt more relaxed after his decision to go to the mountains. The absence of traffic, especially in the evening, also put him at ease about driving again. Every fifteen minutes or so he would do battle with an approaching car, to see who would turn their bright lights off last. It was an old game on country roads. He didn't have any camping gear but thought he could maybe get something at the gas station store in Darrington.

He pulled in front of the store. It was bigger than he remembered. He parked at the one lone pump and filled up the tank of the Chevrolet sedan then went into the store. There was lots of junk food, which suited him, and he started to fill a basket with chips and candy bars. He seized on some Milkman powdered milk, not something he expected to find here. He couldn't carry liquids into the mountains as they were too heavy but he would get what he could find; he was now determined to head into the wilderness, even if he carried supplies in a plastic store bag and slept under leaves. Then, to his delight, in an alcove he found fishing supplies, a camp stove, sleeping mat, and an inexpensive sleeping bag.

'Do you have tarps?' he asked.

'Bottom shelf in the back.'

He knew he could survive now. He returned to the counter with his goods, hoping the credit card that Marsha had given him worked. 'You don't happen to have any backpacks hidden around?' he asked the counter clerk.

'Not that kind of store,' said the young woman behind the counter.

'Why not?'

The young woman was clearly a little nervous of this crazy-looking guy. Yet he looked just too weird to be dangerous. 'You just get out of the pokey or something?' *Or maybe the asylum,* she wondered.

'Just the opposite,' mumbled Nusmen.

She decided not to pursue it and started ringing up his items. It was a good sale to start the day with.

'You didn't say why a store in the middle of the woods doesn't have more hiking stuff?'

'Hikers come through here all the time but they don't look to buy that kind of stuff. They're all fitted out in Recreational Equipment clothes.'

Wish an REI was here now, Nusmen thought. Besides his new home at the lab, REI was heaven to him and they would have everything he needed.

'They get gas and food,' she continued, 'and drive right on over the mountains. What we have here are loggers and they have no use for that stuff.'

Nusmen wanted to get going. He gave her the card. She swiped it and handed him a slip to sign. He walked out, mumbling his thanks and was relieved to get in his car. He was excited now but also getting tired. He decided to pull in to the national park. If he left early in the morning, he wouldn't have to pay, then he could get to the Mazama store early for muffins.

He was really starting to like this plan but his nervousness at being out in the world had taken a toll on his mind and he was suddenly very tired. He spotted a new picnic area near Marblemount, pulled in, got in the backseat and into his new sleeping bag, and drifted off almost immediately.

He didn't mean to sleep late but through a dream filled with microbes rushing through arteries, he heard a pounding. It was just getting light and a maintenance man was knocking on his window.

'You can't sleep here. The sign says no use between eleven at night and seven in the morning.'

'But I was tired,' Nusmen protested. 'I saw another sign on the road that said "pull over and take a break, falling asleep driving kills." '

'Yeah, yeah, move it.'

Fucking police state even out here in the middle of nowhere,' mumbled Nusmen as he climbed out of his sleeping bag.

Only a two-minute drive east on Highway 20 and his spirits soared, the encounter with the man forgotten. Just the other side of the small company town of Newhalem and its dam, the road climbed out of the Skagit River valley and into the mountains. He had forgotten how beautiful it was here. Nusmen sent out his thanks to the overzealous trash guy for waking him up. It was great and the sun was not shining directly in his eyes. He should be able to get to

Washington Pass before it crested the mountaintops.

He drove on, climbing into more and more spectacular scenery and decided to stop at the pass, mostly just to breathe the air and feel the mountains close around him. He got out of the car and took a lungful of clear, intoxicating pure mountain air.

Maybe the general was right. I did need to get out. I love it here, Nusmen thought and then a pang entered his brain. *They will mess up the staph antibiotic without me. I have to get back.* But he knew he couldn't. 'Damn, damn, and double damn,' he muttered as he kicked a chunk of granite along the highway. And then, in a lightning change of mood,

'Muffins!' he yelled. 'Mazama muffins. Here I come.' And he jumped back in the car for the long downhill grade with its big sweeping turns into the Methow Valley.

Chapter 33

Nusmen was soon in the one-building town of Mazama heading straight for the country store that everyone for miles around knew had the best fresh baked muffins in eastern Washington.

The western rustic store looked just the same as he remembered. Three pickup trucks were parked outside. He hoped it was not someone he knew. He peeked in the window. Three men sat at the counter, two baseball caps and one cowboy hat. He couldn't see their faces but they did not look familiar. Nusmen opened the door. A bell tinkled above the door and the three men turned and looked at him.

They turned back to their coffee. 'Another early morning hippy from the coast,' one of them muttered.

'No one uses "hippy" anymore, Frank.'

'Yeah, I do. It rhymes with yippie when I pound on their skinny asses.'

'This guy looks like a nut all right. Crazy hair.'

'Skinny too. Looks like a plant eater.'

Nusmen made it just around the first shelves heading for the muffins when the bell chimed behind him. He looked back. Three people dressed in new hiking clothes and boots stepped inside. He could see a black BMW parked outside.

At the counter the cowboy said, 'Gotta go, Rufus. Place is going to hell.'

'Nothing new in that anymore,' replied the red baseball cap.

'It has been like this since the highway was built and the coasties started their invasion.'

Everyone overheard that comment including the woman behind the counter.

She shook her head and said, 'You three are a dying breed, couldn't happen to nicer folks either. You think you three big spenders keep this place open?'

Frank got up and started out. He scowled at Nusmen, tipped his cowboy hat to the yuppie hikers with their zip-off nylon pants and UV-safe shirts and said, 'Morning, ma'am,' to the woman with them, then turned and said to no one in particular, 'If you didn't make such dern good muffins I wouldn't come in at all. Sure as hell not for that fancy coffee you brew.' The other two followed him out grinning as if they had gotten the best of everyone.

'Sorry about that, folks. The loggers and cowboys who are left around here used to think they ruled this part of the world and now they just grumble along trying to pretend that the trees and grazing will last forever.'

Nusmen ducked behind a shelf and stopped short. There was a whole row of backpacks lined up on the wall. He picked one out, tried it on and then scurried around looking for more food. He considered getting some real food in town. Instead, he grabbed peanut butter, several freeze-dried pouches, and a plastic water bottle. Then he added a bottle of wine. Not to carry, but to drink at the trailhead.

He thought of turning back to Washington Pass and heading out from up there but then he realized he wanted to see his old valley, so he drove into Winthrop with its western style wood buildings. Nothing was open outside of a few restaurants. He drove on down the valley toward Twisp and decided that he would turn up the Twisp River Road. There were lots of good trailheads heading back up into the high peaks.

Sorenson sat scowling. He was in a foul mood. 'I thought you would have your story by now, Bertrand. We're nowhere. We're the Central Intelligence Agency. We have resources that no one has even thought about and we can't find one little scumbag woman.'

'Pretty good summary, boss,' added Pearson.

'Pearson, you joke with me today and you'll find yourself in some godforsaken backwater for life.'

'I thought that was where I was, Director.'

'I'm warning you, test me again...!' Turning away from Pearson, he said, Bertrand? How can we crack this? We can't keep the escape quiet forever.'

'We've no place else to go. No forensic data, no satellite data. Nothing suspicious leaving or coming into Cuba. We've checked with sources in the Mexican government, the FBI, the DEA. Everyone. Not one shred of data.'

'It has to be Cubans. Is she still on the island?' asked Helen Flayback. Always the politician she never offered anything that could get her in a tight place.

'I agree the Cubans have to be involved. Unless,' offered Martin not joking, 'unless it was one of our own...'

'What are you implying?' asked Sorenson before Martin Pearson could finish.

Before Martin could answer Bertrand said, 'I think he is implying that a government agency broke her out.'

'Is that even possible? And why?' asked Sorenson, sounding frustrated.

'Let's suppose she wasn't even a terrorist. We had orders not to use any extreme methods. We were told to soft-pedal any interrogation. Why? Maybe it was all a setup to embarrass you,' said Pearson.

'General Crystal and State?' asked Sorenson.

'Maybe someone is sitting out there laughing at us. Letting you as director cook yourself.'

'So I didn't report it. Either way, if she is a plant or if we lost the first real terrorist in captivity, I'm about to be confronted with this by the president and told to resign.'

'Sounds like a good plan,' said Martin. 'Ingenious actually.'

'Our only defense is to catch them in the middle of their plan and reverse it,' said Helen.

'Blast it all anyway. I have a committee meeting. Have your people work on this and get me some answers. Immediately.'

Bertrand added, 'My money is still on the Cubans. I know we have no evidence. But first I think we better find a way to see if General Crystal was behind this, on his own or maybe with State or the president.'

'Other choice is to admit we lost her and let the story shake out. Maybe you can let it slip that we're investigating someone in the US, possibly the US government. If they are in on it, that should give them pause,' added Helen.

'Find me something, anything,' Sorenson commanded as he rushed out the door.

His muffin craving sated, Nusmen started up the Twisp River Road and decided to take the Oval Lake trail. It was not a hard choice since it was the best trail into the mountains from the river valley. Because it was popular, he decided he would park below the trailhead and walk up to see if there were any cars there. Cars meant hikers and he didn't want to bump into any.

Nusmen parked the car and started walking. He was disappointed when he saw a flash of white through the trees. Pouting he turned around to walk back and then decided to walk up and take a better look.

To his surprise, he immediately recognized Heather's white and red Ford stake truck. He knew she was not close since there was no sign of llamas and she wouldn't go more than a few yards away from them. She was protective that way. He wondered whether it was a pleasure trip or whether she was doing some work for the Forest Service. He wondered if Jim was with her.

Nusmen walked up to the truck and looked inside the cab. Locked. He then walked around to the back. There was a plywood board covering the back opening. There would be nothing except llama droppings. He looked around and there was no sign of anyone so he put his foot on the back outer tire and pulled himself up.

He looked directly into a pair of eyes staring up into his. 'Damn, shit, what the hell,' he yelled then looked around wishing he hadn't shouted so loudly. 'Who the fuck are you?' The dirty apparition just stared back but his eyes got wider. 'Who the hell are you and what are you doing in this truck?'

'Not your truck,' said the dirt encrusted man.

'Not yours either, but I know whose it is,' said Nusmen.

'Me too. Llama lady,' said the old man.

'No shit, Sherlock. You're lying on top of llama poops.'

'So.'

'You a vagrant?' The man didn't answer. 'You homeless?'

'This my home. You go away.'

'Look. I'm an old friend of the owner of this truck and I'm not letting you treat it like it's your home. You'll probably start a fire in the back if it gets cold or something. No way. Get out or I'll drag you out.'

The old man scooted back to the opposite wall with fear now showing through a smudged face that looked like he hadn't washed for weeks. Nusmen saw the old man's fear and immediately felt sorry for the dirty old guy.

'OK, OK. Take it easy. You want a candy bar?' Nusmen dug in

his pocket and pulled out a Mars bar. The old man just looked and started to shake a little. 'Come on, old guy. I won't hurt you. I was just worried about my friend Heather.' He tossed the Mars bar over. It hit the floor and the old man didn't move. 'Go on, It's yours. If you don't want it, throw it back to me.'

'You can't make me with candy,' said the ragged old man.

'Make you what? I don't want to make you anything. Just being friendly.'

'I don't want no friends.'

Nusmen gave up, jumped to the ground, and started to untie the wood board. There was no way he was going to touch him and no way to get him out over the top without touching him so he would have to coax him through the door. Before he could get it untied, he heard a thud as the old man landed outside the truck. He looked around the corner and saw the old greasy jumble of rags get to its feet and start to move off in a hunched-over run. 'Good riddance,' shouted Nusmen.

The old man stopped and came back a few feet. 'You leaving the truck, huh?'

'Maybe, maybe not. What's it to you?'

'Stuff in back.'

Nusmen shook his head and started to untie the plywood. It had holes drilled every six inches and, as was typical of Heather, each hole had a cord tied with at least four knots. *What a bother,* he thought. *Maybe Heather is at the lakes by herself. Jim wouldn't tie it this way. Mr. Efficiency. More knots tied meant more to untie.* This was one time he agreed with Jim.

'Heather's work all right,' he muttered.

'What about her? She a nice lady.'

'Don't get any closer; you really stink, you know that?'

Nusmen looked in the back of the truck and saw some tattered camping equipment.

'You live here, in the woods?' he asked incredulously. Then Nusmen looked closer at the old man. 'I know you. You're the old guy that used to hang out in the summer up on the Canada border,' he said.

'You goen to tell?'

'Tell who, what? You didn't used to look this bad. Maybe a little rough before, but you're filthy now.'

'Wilderness guards throwed me out and I lost my stuff. Came here weeks ago. Don't tell. I've got nowhere else.'

'Old Man Shuksin, no just Shuskin. Right?' asked Nusmen.

The old man just stared. 'Look, old man, we met before. I used to spend a lot of time in the Pasayten Wilderness and you were always lurking about.'

'Plant man?'

'Yeah, I guess that's me alright.' Nusmen jumped up in the truck and picked up his candy bar. The wrapper was intact. 'You want this or not?'

'OK.' The old man grinned showing disgusting stained and missing teeth. 'Jesus, old man. You sure you can eat this thing?' Nusmen jumped down. He was going to pass Shuskin's things down but he didn't want to touch them after thinking about it. 'You want to get your stuff? Not really worth getting, is it? I've got a suggestion.

'You won't do this but it would be to your benefit. I am going to town and going to get you some stuff, otherwise you're going to die out here. Don't ask me why I'm doing it: probably because I'm nuts just like you. You wait here and I'll be back inside of two hours. OK?'

The old man didn't say anything. Nusmen thought that at the worst the government would waste some money doing what it should be doing anyway, taking care of indigents like Shuskin. He'd buy some stuff, food, maybe a better coat and a tent for the old man using the credit card he'd been given. Get some more things for himself too. If the old fool was gone, then he would take what he could use and leave the rest in Heather's truck.

'You sending Kramer on his own?' asked Sheilla.

'He would be way out of his depth. He's had no field experience.'

'Too bad as he is fluent in Spanish and might be able to pass for a Cuban,' said Sheilla. 'Jim then?'

'Not Jim. It's time Kramer got some field experience. Should be easy and relatively safe on a base. Let's go where we should have in the first place. Marsha!' yelled the general.

'Yes, sir.'

'Get Kramer in here and get a plane for two to Guantánamo Bay.'

Sheilla raised her eyebrows, as Kramer hurried into the general's office.

'Sit, Captain. I've got a mission for you.

Kramer looked stunned. 'A what, sir?'

Nusmen hesitated at the door to Twisp Feed Store. He didn't want to run into anyone he knew and through the door he could see Nancy. She walked from behind the counter holding some papers while talking to a man. Then they walked out the front door. He had read while surfing the net about his old home area that she and her father had purchased the feed store. They were Quakers and hard workers. *It would take that to make it a success,* he thought. The small local store had always struggled financially.

Nusmen let out a breath and stepped inside, glad he had entered from the feed-storage side door. They wouldn't have anything all that special for the old man but they had work clothes and a few camping supplies and to his delight some better fishing equipment.

He quickly gathered up an insulated cotton duck coat then some more snack food. *The government can afford it, and they threw him off public land, so why not,* he thought and grabbed a cart quickly filling it to overflowing.

A dozen times on the way back up the river road, he told himself how great this place was. As he neared the trailhead, he wondered if the old coot would still be there. He would leave the stuff for him in any event. There wasn't any 'real' food but the guy looked like he needed calories and Nusmen had bought plenty. The granola bars were likely the most nutritious.

This time he pulled in a few feet from the truck. The old man was gone.

Chapter 34

Sheilla sat at her desk, twirling round and round. *Think, think, think,* she told herself. As the soft ringing of her encrypted phone penetrated her thoughts.

'Maccarrick,' she answered, feeling like she was waking up from a deep sleep.

'Hi, Sheilla. I thought I would save you from the uber cool young pups and call you myself.'

'I would rather talk to you anyway, Misa,' said Sheilla. 'You still liking it down there in southern AZee?'

'Actually yes and no. I love the job. Though I don't like the climate or being this close to Mexico, so I pretty much hang here, inside with the computers.

I could use a little dose of English weather.

'Where are you from, Sheilla? I feel like we are friends but I hardly know anything about you.'

'I was born in New Haven, Connecticut. Not much to tell but I'm with you about staying inside. Really, how do you like it there with those two adolescents?'

'Truthfully, I've never had so much fun. Vidya and I tussle with them some but they're good guys and as skilled as anyone, I've ever seen. Which is what I'm calling you for. To quote our very own Colonel Jake, he's getting raw fingertips and his brain is oozing pleasure being inside the CIA's computers. Nothing on Najma yet but the CIA is hacking into your computers as we speak.'

'What!'

'That's why I called. I wanted to warn you to be careful. They're pretty sophisticated. But no match for our kid hackers. Jason is inside your computers now too. We're trying to trail them and see what they're looking for.'

'Jeez, Misa. What the heck is going on?'

'Get back to you as soon as we figure it out. Make sure none of your staff or Fred communicates with us using your computers. Only use encrypted phones to call us until I tell you otherwise.'

Sheilla immediately dialed Fred. 'Don't use your computer to communicate with Fort Huachuca. Be in my office with Katarina and Mark in thirty minutes and I'll explain.' Sheilla sat thinking and spinning in her chair. She wanted to think for another minute before she told the general what Misa said.

Nusmen walked up the trail around a bend and then stopped. He wondered whether the old reprobate had taken off or was lurking around, waiting for him to leave. Hikers used to talk about a phantom in the Pasayten but the locals who spent time up in the wilderness, eventually figured out it was Old Man Shuskin, staying out of sight while he watched unwanted trekkers entering his 'home territory.'

Nusmen moved off the trail, and as quietly as he could, worked his way back until he could see the truck. Everything was quiet. He sat down with his back against a fallen tree and decided to wait for a few minutes.

He hadn't been thinking for more than a minute when the bushes parted and the old man slowly walked up to the white truck. None too gracefully, he pulled himself up inside and put the bare plywood over the door opening. Nusmen could hear stuff being moved around.

Old Man Shuskin could hardly believe what Nusmen had put in the back of the truck. He had been cold and hungry since his eviction from the Pasayten Wilderness and he would never see the supplies again that he had collected from campers' leftovers that he had scrounged and hidden in his secret places over several seasons. In all his years, he had only done one good deed and that was returning the lost llama to the llama lady. In all that time, no one had ever done a good deed for him. Until now that is, and he never would have expected the lunatic plant man to be the one.

The truth was that Nusmen's personality had changed after what he had done a year ago. He had never been mean. Narcissistic and oblivious to others, yes, but never with harmful intentions; and now that he had been forced to confront that side of himself, he wanted to mitigate that part of his personality. The old man might be nuts but despite Nusmen's bitching to himself, it made him feel good now to help someone.

The old man was so busy putting candy bars in one pile while feeling warm in his new coat that he did not notice the truck move, ever so slightly, as Nusmen stood on the tire. Nusmen was tall enough to see over the top slat. He watched Old Man Shuskin for a few seconds and then scratched softly on one of the red slats so as not to frighten him too much. The grimy face looked up and Nusmen smiled at him. The old man stared and then held up a candy bar.

'Thanks, Shuskin, but they're for you. I've got enough of my own.' Shuskin continued to hold it and Nusmen put his feet on the lower board, lifted himself up, reached over and took it. 'Thank you. I don't think Heather would mind you staying in her truck for the night, if you left it clean. But she might come out today.'

'She went two days ago. Had a big load. Not back soon.'

'You know where she went? How many people?' Nusmen was hoping she was alone.

'Lots of 'em…little one.'

'You think she's guiding?' She might be taking a paying group in. She used to do that a long time ago.

'Same people, all same 'cept Indian lady and brown boy.'

Nusmen decided that meant Jim was with her but was confused by the rest. He remembered someone saying something about a boy at the lab but he had paid no attention. Shuskin went back to going through his new treasure pile. He moved carefully, picking each item up and looking at it and then organizing it into a group, all on top of the round llama pellets, in piles that would only make sense to him. He picked up a bar of soap.

'You could use that, you know. You definitely look a bit better with that coat on. Why not put the hat on too? I'm going to sit out here and have my lunch before I set off.'

Nusmen went a few steps away and then, picked up his new pack and settled with his back to the stock loading platform and started to think about whether or not he should hike up to the lakes. He heard the old man drop to the ground and then watched him walk toward him, clutching a big bag of Fritos and a can of Vienna sausage. To Nusmen's surprise, he sat down a few feet away and started to eat.

Najma pushed herself up onto an elbow. Her brain clearer; her body still aching. Her memory remained nothing but vaporous dust. She looked at the brilliant stars. In the direction the sun had set was a bright spot. A planet, Venus. At least she knew the direction for west. That didn't help her a bit. Mexicali could be in any direction. If she was even close to Mexicali. Her confusion made her angry, and the knowledge that she had been raped made her furious. She worked on trying to fix her clothes. As she sat up, she could feel pain both inside and out, which made her angrier still.

After a few moments, she stood and searched in all directions. To the north she saw a small amount of light as twilight passed to darkness. That made sense. Whoever had dumped her in the desert couldn't take her north over the US border and both east and west of Mexicali was too populated. She must be south.

Anger settled into resolve. Vague memory fragments darted in and out through the mental fog as she walked over the starlit desert pavement and, around cacti, through small arroyos toward the increasing luminosity on the horizon.

'Why would the CIA be interested in our computers? Stupid question—Mexico.'

'Misa said she would call as soon as they found out anything.'

'Irks me but I'm not surprised. What surprises me is they've been caught at it.'

'Misa said their group is tracking them in our computers.' The general just shook his head, thinking it was a new world. 'When you talk to Misa, ask her to keep proof.'

'What I want to figure out,' said Sheilla, 'is what this means. Why the interest in us?'

'Do we have files they can access that will tell them about Najma and capturing her in Mexico?' asked the general.

'They no can do,' said Sheilla, looking pleased. 'Files are offline and can't be accessed.' She said this with more than just a little bit of pride. She and Fred had developed this idea of a safe place to store all the files. Their computers could be broken into but with the files moved into offline servers, no one could get to them. Only when they brought the servers with the files online could they be hacked. Even then, they had data on several different servers and their plan was that no one could start up more than one at one time. The only way was for someone to steal the physical servers, something that would be difficult, if not impossible, as they were stored in the basement of their secure labs on a well-guarded military base.

The general interrupted her thoughts at top volume. 'Sitting around in the office is getting us nowhere. That settles it. I want a team in Cuba ASAP. I want to know what is going on.'

Sheilla tucked her lower lip under her upper teeth and scrunched up her nose.

'I want some answers and there is no way I am going to send Glenda out with Kramer without good backup. Time for everybody to get into gear.'

'I thought your old buddy was there?'

'He is and a stroke of luck too. He needs to stay incognito. Jim needs to get his ass back doing something and so does Brush. Get on the horn and find out where Neilly and his crew are. We are going to make something happen and I want everyone ready to go.'

'So Glenda and Kramer go in openly, then Brush, Jim, and Neilly's crew stand by to back them up,' she mused. Then, 'You're going to fly over to the mountains and bring them all back?'

'Not just me, you're going to fly over with me.'

'What!'

'You think you're going to come up with answers twirling in your chair? I don't think so; you don't have enough data. Maybe a change of scenery and my sort of twirling will snap something into your head. The Wolf Pack can keep us informed and you can help me get Jim up to speed on the trip back. As you said, only secure phones. Enough talking and speculating, Sheilla, it's time to move out.

'If you need some mountain clothes, ask Sergeant Mason to get you some and whatever else he thinks you need for a trip to the mountains. We'll leave eleven-hundred tomorrow. We have a lot to do. Drop the CIA. Let Misa and those computer whizzes deal with them. Besides we don't want them catching us talking about them.'

Sheilla sat dumbfounded. The general was disgusted with slow to no progress and did the thing he knew how to do best—get into action doing something, anything, to jump-start his brain, take a ride in his helicopter and some answers would shake loose. Sheilla, a few minutes ago, had felt frustrated; now she was irritated. She wanted to figure out what the CIA was up to. Sitting in the chair in her office was the way for her to solve it but the general did not seem to be giving her any choice.

'Don't just sit there. Get a move on. It'll be fun.'

Chapter 35

It was nearly dawn when Najma reached the outskirts of Mexicali. She walked to her hotel avoiding the looks of the bell captain and the registration desk. On the walk back she remembered there had been a large shadow at the top of the stairs. It must have been one of the general's guards. The big bodyguard. He would tell her exactly what happened when she got hold of him.

The fat man had trudged up those steps where the prissy young general and his four bodyguards had walked. She knew what had happened to her but only through logical deduction and the physical pain she felt. Najma wanted all the facts so she would know exactly whom she was going to make pay the most.

One thing was clear: the mayor and the Mexican general met next to that patio for some reason. The chances were they would again. That would be her opportunity and revenge.

Pedro snuggled between his new parents in their zipped-together, queen-size sleeping bag, and then lifted his head looking for Rosie. She slept next to Jim and lazily lifted her head, with golden eyes lit by stars. Pedro made a soft 'pssst.' For an instant Rosie lifted her head higher and then let it drop languidly down. *I know she smiling. She happy like me,* he thought. He felt safe now snuggled here. Not so distant memories flitted, with lessening frequency, through his mind: of his family and his old mutt, Rojiso, in Mexico. New data flowed relentlessly into his six-year-old mind, pushing old traumas back into the remoter recesses of his brain. One memory overshadowed all others and stubbornly refused to extinguish itself— the dark-haired woman with the raised scar behind her ear. He had looked at that scar as she lay dying. It was branded in his young mind: Najma.

She killed his family and his dog. The memory of what she had done made him shiver and go tight inside. It would still take lots of good to displace the images from the night he and the gecko had watched Najma murder his mother, father, sisters, and brothers. *I hate her,* he thought.

'You awake, sweetheart?' asked Heather as she ran her fingers lightly over his cheek dispelling the ugliness with a soft touch. The sky was turning from charcoal to pearl. 'You want to come with me and make some coffee or stay snuggled up here?'

'I go with you, Mama,' as he hugged her in a fierce grip with his small hands.

Heather briefly choked up, overcome by the emotions of having a son that loved her and laid next to her now, hugging her with all his might.

'Okie dokie, then,' she managed to get out.

'Okie dokie smokie,' said Pedro, happy again, with a rapid shift in mood that only to children are capable of.

Jim rolled over and said, 'I'll stay here for a couple of minutes and then take care of our bedding. Beautiful, isn't it?'

Heather and Pedro pulled on coats against the morning's coolness and walked lightly over the meadow.

Heather could never reconcile the active Jim with the laid-back Jim in the mountains. *Same problem as the killer and the lover,* she thought.

The Huey sat on the tarmac looking big and army olive drab. It would have seemed uninspiring to Sheilla if it were not for the spectacular blue August sky shrouding the fourteen thousand foot, white-topped Mount Rainier looming into the sky to their east.

'We're loaded, let's hit it. I want to get up there with lots of daylight left.'

'General, then why didn't we leave earlier than eleven?'

'I can't stand to fly directly into the sun, in this case the morning sun, when there is a choice, and there were things I needed to do this morning.'

They lifted off straight up but only to ten feet. Then the general turned one-hundred-eighty degrees, exactly centered over an invisible point on the ground. Staying level at ten feet, he then flew backward across the tarmac away from the hangar. 'On the right side of your headset you can turn the volume up if you need to,' he said casually as if flying backward took little attention.

'Oh my god! I didn't know you could go backward.'

The general then started to rotate, 'twirling,' as he continued to back up. Then he stopped motionless at precisely the same ten feet above the ground and started forward turning full circles. He smiled. 'I love helicopters and this old UH1.'

'Wow, wow, wow.'

'Fun, huh.'

'I had no idea you could this. I've never seen helicopters do this.'

'It's just something I like to do for control practice,' said the general, enjoying the compliment and her excitement.

'This is fantastic; we're two peas in different pods: me in my office chair and you in your twirly bird.'

'Tower, Six Centaur, northeast departure.'

'What's Six Centaur?'

'My call sign from way back.'

Nusmen started up the long talus slope with Old Man Shuskin working hard to keep up with his long strides. He was a grizzled and tough old mountain vagrant but with age came bad knees and a painful hip.

Nusmen looked back, shaking his head, still shocked that the old goat was following him. 'You OK, Shuskin?'

'Hip hurts.' Shuskin was not used to walking fast. He had no reason to. One place in the mountains was nearly the same as another.

'You should get it looked at. The old doc will do it for you.'

Shuskin didn't say anything. Doctors were outside his realm of thinking.

'We don't have too far to go but it's all uphill, and there are some pretty steep switchbacks ahead.'

'I know about them lakes,' said Shuskin, wondering why he wanted to stay with Nusmen. He just did. He didn't contemplate much even with all the time he spent alone. Cities had not been kind to the old man. Arrests, beatings, begging had made the wilderness an escape. The snow and cold eventually forced him out of the mountains in the winter. He stayed as long as he could. He was lost in society and cities. In civilization, people tolerated him no more than a stray dog. Less even. No one went to the shelter where he stayed to adopt him like they adopted dogs. The church missions weren't kind, just tolerant. They bartered his soul for crumbs and cots.

'You want to take it slower and catch up with me later?'

'Stay with you.'

Nusmen wondered what Old Man Shuskin was doing. As far as Nusmen knew, he shunned people in the wilderness. They walked along and Nusmen started to wonder what he was going to do with the old mongrel. It was not what he had in mind when coming to the mountains.

If Shuskin were an animal, the first thing he would do is dunk him in a stream and soap him up. He probably had fleas. There was no telling what bacteria he was harboring in those old creases. He would have loads of *Staphylococcus aureus,* probably even lots of other staph species. *Strep of course,* and he wondered if bacteria sitting on him for so long had evolved any new sub-species. *Get some cultures,* maybe. Nusmen's thoughts wandered—how were the antibiotic tests doing. He wanted to be in his lab, not out with this deranged old man. Damn General Crystal anyway. Then he sighed. The general had saved his ass and given him more than he could imagine. The lab was now his home, his love.

'We'll be at the lakes a little after two. No hurry,' said Nusmen, looking exasperated but trying not to show it in his voice.

'Llama lady there,' mumbled Shuskin.

'Another reason for leaving later is this, Sheilla.' The general pointed at the snow peaked mountains, green meadows, and lakes that reflected cerulean blue with the sun overhead.

'It is beautiful and there's so much of it,' said Sheilla.

'The Methow Valley is just over a hundred air miles from the BWC. Most of that distance is wilderness.'

'Oh god!' exclaimed Sheilla. Mount Rainier towered above a sea of low clouds forming around its base. Then she looked north. 'Is that a fire or smoke on top of that mountain?'

'Mount Baker fumarole,' said Will.

'It's active? I didn't know they were active volcanoes.'

'Some are and that one is. Rainer is too but for the time being just sits there quietly. Ask Jim if you're interested. He's the geology expert.'

'How long now? How do you know where they're camping?'

'I don't; thirty, forty minutes more depending on how fast we find them. We need to pretty fast, so we don't run out of fuel.'

'Out of fuel?'

'I mean on the way back. I carry extra, otherwise it would be impossible to fly over and back. Jim said Oval Lakes area, so we'll cruise up the Columbia River and then up Lake Chelan and over the north ridge to Oval Lake. If we don't see them we'll fly to the trailheads. We should see their red and white stake truck at one. Then we just follow the trail until we find them.'

Sheilla puffed out her cheeks and expelled the air. 'I guess this is not a bad way to get into the wilderness. It saves a lot of walking.'

'A helicopter is quicker and more fun than walking, that's for sure.' General Crystal smiled, meaning every word.

At the top of the rise above the big talus slope, the two antisocial men paused for a snack. Nusmen was stopping more for the old man than himself. He could see Shuskin struggling behind him but the old guy never let Nusmen get more than ten feet in front of him. An invisible cord held him precisely at that distance. *What do I do with him? Right on my heels. He acts like he likes me. Now how am I going to get rid of him? Shit. I want to be alone,* he thought. He had wanted to see Heather, but no one else—especially not this raunchy, oil-matted old fart. The struggling Shuskin walked hunched over with stained teeth and black nails, filthy except for his new canvas gold-brown coat and red stocking hat. He was a sad sight and blemish on the pristine wilderness. Nusmen sighed.

The Huey beat the wind as it ghosted up the languid flow of the wide Columbia River, only feet below its belly. Patches of houses dotted the river's sides mixed with hundreds of acres of apple trees. The general gained some altitude and headed to the left. A long dark blue lake, held back by a dam, angled its way back up into the mountains to their north; its end was out of sight, fifty miles up and four thousand feet below the llama camp.

The general sat with upturned lips, in black polar fleece coat and gray nylon hiking pants. Under his light-green David Clark headphones he wore a baseball cap with a small yellow helicopter emblem.

'I'm always happy flying. You look like you're enjoying it too.'

'It's very pretty. I don't think I look so pretty in these clothes that the sergeant gave me, though.'

'You look just great. The green army coat looks good with your hair. And they are plenty roomy enough so you're comfortable.'

'Exactly. I could fit another half of me in them. Not very becoming.'

The general didn't know what to say to her. He thought she was probably the prettiest woman he had ever flown with but she was also his subordinate. He sat uncomfortably until Sheilla said, 'It really is much drier over here on this side of the mountains. Seems odd to see all this water and snowcapped mountains when it's still summer.'

'There's always lots of snow up here. It feeds the lake but it doesn't snow, except rarely, down in the river valley. And it hardly freezes. If there are frosts, the orchardists hire helicopters to beat the air over the orchards to keep the fruit from freezing.'

'Learn something new every day,' said Sheilla, really warming up to this new adventure as she stared out the window.

'Chelan state, helicopter one-one-eight, two thousand two hundred, heading three-one-zero, two miles southeast.'

'That wasn't what you called yourself before, General?'

'We don't use military designations on civilian frequencies.'

The slow steady beat propelled them over the dark lake with ridges rising taller on their sides in the U-shaped valley. Eventually, the lake ended with a river emptying over a wide gravel bar into its head. The general lifted the Huey up the steep-sided ridge. The forested slopes changed to glacier scoured rocks. As they crested the top of the ridge, a small lake set in dark stone sat peacefully on the very top.

'Eyes peeled, Sheilla, they might be swimming.'

'Wow and double WOW. That is beautiful,' exclaimed Sheilla.
Maybe we can go swimming?'

'Sorry, General. Your sergeant gave me a duffel full of clothes but a swimsuit was not one of the things included.'

The kitchen, overhung by pine trees, looked over the edge of the sunlit mountain meadow but was hidden from the air. Llamas grazed near the far fringes where the meadow sloped downhill on three sides, rising only to the west where Glenda and Brush walked toward the ridge-top lake before dropping steeply to the north end of the lake that the general and Sheilla had just flown over.

Lola and Heather were busy making sandwiches and coffee. 'Guess we'd better get some chocolate bars out of the dessert pannier before everyone gets over here. Otherwise Jim and Pedro will be sneaking more than their share,' Heather said.

'They come soon.'

'We agreed around noon. They'll be here in a few minutes. And here they are.' Heather spotted Pedro, closely followed by Rosie, running down from the ridgetop.

'Hello, Mama,' he shouted and ran up to her and wrapped his arms around her legs. 'Come,' said Pedro, wanting Heather to go with him to greet the others.

They walked out of the kitchen and met the others as they walked up. Heather gave Jim a kiss.

Pedro looked at his mother and mimed pee pee.

Heather turned to Jim and said, 'We're going to walk down the trail to the woods for a bit. I need to stretch my legs. You guys can get cleaned up. The sandwiches will be ready soon.'

'Now, Mama. Go. Pronto please.'

'Shake a leg then, guy.' Rosie pushed herself back up with her long body following as they walked the same trail they had arrived on the day before. 'Let's walk a little farther down.'

'I go now. Have to pee now.'

'Well, sweet stuff, just go over there behind that tree if that's all you have to do. Then we can walk a little.' Pedro barely heard her as he ran twenty feet before he stopped.

'I hungry,' he announced as soon as he came back.

'I am hungry,' she corrected automatically. 'We'll walk just for a few minutes more, not for long. I have to go too. I need you to protect me.'

'Okie dokie. I take good care of you.'

They walked for a few minutes into the cool woods. When they reached a huge glacial erratic she said, 'You stay here and I'll be back in a few seconds.'

A minute later she emerged from behind the rock that had been carried from somewhere far away on a glacier and then deposited in her wilderness. She walked quietly up behind Pedro. She couldn't help herself. She grabbed him just under the arms and started to tickle him.

Pedro yelled, then giggled while he struggled to get out of her grasp. He fell on the ground, laughing and pleading for her to stop. She kneeled over him and continued. He laughed so hard tears ran down his cheeks.

'We're close to them lakes,' said Shuskin. 'Who's laughin'?'

'I heard. I'll go ahead and see who it is.'

'You'll come back.'

'Of course I'll come back.'

'Don't like no folks. 'Cepting llama lady and you, maybes.'

'Huh...don't worry. Go behind that big rock.' Shuskin didn't and followed even closer behind Nusmen.

'Mama. Someone talking.'

Rosie started a deep low growl.

'Maybe they're hikers. Let's go see.' Heather patted Rosie's head. 'It's all right, girl, only nice people up here.'

They stepped around another big rock dropped by the retreating glacier as it melted its way north. Heather stopped short. Pedro ducked behind her holding her leg.

'Nus!'

Nusmen jerked his head around and Shuskin started to tremble.

'Sorry, we didn't mean to startle you.'

'We?' asked Nusmen. 'Oh, the dog.'

'And...' Heather coaxed Pedro around from behind her as she said, 'What in the heck are you doing here and with the phantom of the mountains too? How did you find us? Who let you out?'

'Yeah, um, I was told to take a vacation. I wasn't trying to find you, exactly.'

'But Jim told me you weren't allowed to leave the labs.' Heather looked around wondering if she should be saying secret information out loud and in front of the old transient. She had only seen the old man this close once before. He was usually nothing more than a shadow in the woods.

Shuskin just stared, wanting to hide. He pulled at Nusmen's sleeve.

'Shuskin. Don't touch me.' Nusmen pulled his arm away. 'You're OK. Heather is a friend,' he said and then looked at Heather as if to verify that she was.

'Thassa mean big dog.'

'That's just Rosie. She won't hurt you,' Nusmen reassured him, as Rosie, not feeling the same repulsion as Nusmen, walked over sniffing and started to lick the old man's pants.

'We're friends, Nus, but sometimes I wonder why. What possessed you to turn that bacteria loose?'

Nusmen looked down at the ground, knowing he could never

defend what he had done.

'Mama, we go. I...I am hungry.'

'Mama?' said Nusmen. 'How did that happen?'

'Seems there are lots of stories,' she said as she walked over closer and stood in front of Shuskin.

He shrank back a little and closer to Nusmen, then raised his head and looked at Heather quizzically.

'We need to get back. Come on, let's go. We're camped just up ahead.'

Old Man Shuskin didn't move and then looking upset, half limped, half walked behind Nusmen up the trail to confront his worst fear—more people. A day ago he would have gone the other way as fast as he could. A month ago in the Pasayten Wilderness he had been warm and had food. Here he had nothing until Nusmen came along and was nice to him.

Heather moved back with the old man.

'Why are you here and not in the Pasayten? When was the last time you had a bath? Let me have that rucksack. Come on, give to me.' Shuskin just shook his head and said, 'Mine.'

'You're limping. I just wanted to carry it for you.'

Shuskin wasn't sure if he believed her so he moved a little closer to Nusmen and received a scowl in return.

'She won't hurt you, old man,' Nusmen told him. 'You said you liked her.' Shuskin still saw no reason to pass over the only belongings he had in the world.

'OK, OK. You keep the pack. But we need to get you looking decent. I don't know what we can do to get you cleaned up. I don't want you in our camp looking so dirty. The fish lake is too cold, maybe the upper lake after lunch,' Heather said.

Shuskin started shaking his head. The idea of a bath, something he had long abandoned, scared him almost more than losing his new belongings. His chaotic mind told him to run but his body didn't obey. He scooted closer to Nusmen, only to receive another disgusted look and be shooed away.

Jim stood up as Nusmen and Shuskin walked across the meadow toward the kitchen. He was surprised to see Nusmen but not as much as Heather had been. The general had discussed his plan to get Nusmen a pardon and Jim had reluctantly approved. Even so, he was surprised to see that the general had turned him back into society already. The bigger question: what was William Edgar Nusmen doing here and with the old codger?

'Chingadera!'

'Watch it, Lola. Not around Pedro and not a nice thing to say,' said Heather.

'Lo siento, señora. That'—she pointed at Shuskin—'that old thing can't come in kitchen. He too dirty.'

'Where is your generosity of spirit, Lo? Well...OK. I see your point.' *And I agree.* 'He has no reason to be in the kitchen. We'll eat out here.' Lola just shook her head, thinking, *What next?* She didn't like the look of this old greasy man any more than the tall thin one. They would mean more work for her. Then she mellowed. More work but good work after the things she had been ordered to do in Mexico, bad things. No one here knew the things she had been made to do and she would never tell anyone.

They sat down with Shuskin staying behind Nusmen and a little away from the group. Lola brought him a plate with a big sandwich but set it down a few feet away and gave him a look that told him to 'watch it' with her.

'Nusmen. Time to start telling us what you are doing here and how you seemed to have adopted the old phantom of the woods,' said Jim as he looked steadily at Nusmen.

Even though Nusmen had had little contact with Colonel Johnson, he knew he was the second in command behind the general. He also knew his reputation and was a little frightened by him. Jim was usually away when he and Heather did field botany together and he had never been invited to the ranch. The colonel had not been in the lab more than a few times since Nusmen's arrival months ago.

'I...I...' he started to say, but everyone looked back over the meadow as the unmistakable whump, whump, whump, of a Huey beating the air grew louder.

'Shit,' said Heather. 'I knew this was going to happen. What's he doing here?'

Chapter 36

Bertrand opened the director's door and walked onto the dark red oriental rug. Sorenson moved to a brown leather sofa and poured himself a cup of coffee from a silver pot. He motioned to a second white china cup.

'No thanks,' said Bertrand. 'We have a location on Najma. She is in Mexico, not far from the US border at a Siastra cartel headquarters. She seems to be a favorite of its leader, Guillermo Vasquez.'

'It's about time we found her.'

'Pearson has been instrumental in figuring this out,' said Bertrand, ignoring his boss's comment.

'You going to be able to tell me, I hope, how she escaped and got to Mexico?'

'Yes. The cartel. Vasquez is connected in Cuba. We have a Cuban source that said a group of Cuban military, like our Special Forces, were engaged to break her out. Then she was flown on a Cuban diplomatic plane to Mexico.'

'Why the bother? What do they want her for?'

'That I don't know, but we found how they entered X-Ray. The dead sergeant that controlled the gate had fifty thousand deposited in a Cayman account. We know the plane landed near Tubutama. Then a few days later there was an assassination of a small band of drug dealers in Nogales. DEA says it was a splinter group of Vasquez's cartel. There is word of a woman who fits her description in a restaurant across from where the drug dealers were executed in their bar hangout. A police source says there is a woman they have heard called the devil lady at the cartel's hacienda headquarters. There is little doubt—it's her.'

'Go on. I suspect you are now just getting to a more interesting part, such as how we can get her back.'

'Maybe, but first I would consider it prudent to inject some more information into this story. Just before she was handed to us by State there was a lot of activity at Fort Huachuca, southern Arizona. General Crystal was there and the DEA said they were chasing ghosts on the border and their surveillance was mysteriously out. The timing is more than coincidental. The hacienda was partially destroyed and suddenly we were presented with her, injured as if she'd survived an attack.'

Sorenson couldn't help but smile. 'We don't even need to get her back. General Crystal and someone high up in State, probably the man himself at the White House, sanctioned a raid into Mexico—an illegal raid. A Senate Committee will crucify them. They can't touch me.'

'True in one sense. The president won't fire you or demand your resignation. Although it may not have been all that illegal. General Crystal's mandate is worldwide, just like ours.

'But it's also true that the first serious terrorist in America has been lost under our watch at a new, test detainment facility. You'll keep your job for now but lose X-Ray, and the first excuse they find, you'll be history. And I don't want your job and I sure am not going to work for Flayback.'

'Bertrand, I can assure you that if I leave, Flayback will be out of here too. So your idea is to get the woman back and then I use the information about the illegal raid in Mexico to my advantage. No reason for the White House to know she escaped,' said Sorenson.

'Maybe we can keep it quiet. It would be a media fiasco if it ever got out; illegal capture and then illegal detention, then the CIA lets her escape from Camp X-Ray, a detention center which some will say violates the law and probably the constitution, and then she goes on to kill for a cartel. Great press for some and bad press for the agency.'

'What do you have in mind?' asked Sorenson feeling better than he had in days.

'We observe the cartel's headquarters, have an insertion team ready close by, and extract her back to Guantánamo.'

Sorenson sat for a minute, sipped his coffee, and then said, 'Do it.'

Chapter 37

The general stole a look at Sheilla as she smiled and waved at the campers below. *She is a fine-looking woman,* he thought. It was not the first time he had thought that about her but he quickly dismissed such things from his mind. He had no time in his life for foolishness and less reason to think that Sheilla liked him in that way. He also doubted he had the slightest idea what romance was. He had spent his career avoiding obligations, complications, and women. In the last two years, however, he'd had thoughts about the possibility of a relationship when he retired. He remembered finding Misa attractive when they were in Arizona.

He had recruited Sheilla for her abilities, then found himself rereading her file several times, not ready to admit why he wanted to reread it. She was eleven years younger. A negative; she was too young, similar to Misa. He wobbled the helicopter, momentarily not fully focused on his flying. Only Jim and Brush noted the slight lapse of concentration in his usually steady handling of his helicopter.

Sheilla looked at him. 'This is fun, General. I think I like helicopters almost as much as my chair,' she said as she smiled broadly at him.

'I'm glad. We could go anytime. I don't get to fly enough to suit me.' He immediately regretted sounding forward. Sheilla, oblivious to his thoughts, said, 'I'd like that.'

The helicopter settled to the ground. Dried grass, small stones, fading flowers, the loose debris of the meadow, swirled under its blades' force and blew as far as each of the differing masses would allow. Pedro was up and running, shouting, 'Chopper.' With long strides, Jim easily caught up with him, concerned that he might forget about the dangers of the tail rotor.

Only Heather did not move toward the landing helicopter. Grief consumed her face, and her fears boiled inside her head. The confirmation that Jim would leave her again left her limp. She sagged to the ground on her knees. Old Man Shuskin momentarily forgot his own fear as he looked at Heather. He felt an emotion that was the opposite to the one he had felt last year when he returned her lost llama. He hadn't really understood his act of kindness then but it had made him feel good. Now he felt sad.

Jim looked back toward the camp, toward Heather. He waved at Brush to come over. 'Keep an eye on Pedro.' Then he swiftly walked to her. He dropped to his knees beside her and took her shoulders in both hands. Seeing her wild eyes, he pulled her to him. At first, she resisted and as quickly relented grabbing him, holding him.

Nusmen got up and walked toward the Huey, smiling as he turned and looked at the bewildered Shuskin, hunched on the ground. The general had come to get him. They needed him in the lab. Heather would take care of the old man. *On my way home,* he thought, overjoyed at his good fortune. He hadn't noticed Heather's anguish.

'Ride now, Mr. Brush?' shouted Pedro.

'Kind of doubt it, little man. Maybe later, eh.'

The general told Sheilla to take off her headset and shoulder harness. 'You can get out now if you want. The blades are too far above to hurt you. I need to shut down and no use in you sitting here.'

Sheilla fumbled with the door, looked appreciatively at the general then stepped onto the meadow and into the crisp mountain air.

'Major, it is probably as much a surprise for me being here, as it is for you, seeing us in the middle of your camp,' she said.

Brush grinned. 'I'm used to seeing the general fly into stranger places than this but I can't remember ever seeing him fly a lady before.'

Sheilla didn't know what to say and then looked down at Pedro and raised her eyebrows.

'Pedro, meet Sheilla.'

'I'm pleased to meet you, Pedro,' she said as she stooped and took his hand.

Pedro looked up at Brush expectantly. 'We can't go now,' responded Brush. 'The helicopter is being shut down and it isn't ours. It's the general's.'

'He take me?'

'We'll ask him later.' Brush put his arm around Pedro and walked him back toward the group at the kitchen, wondering whether he would want to be a father and whether Glenda and he could be parents. He liked this little guy, but...

'Where's Jim?' asked General Crystal, emerging from the Huey.

Glenda looked at Brush who looked at the general. 'Let's just say that your unexpected arrival overwhelmed Heather a little.'

'She very bad,' added Lola.

Glenda gave her a look.

'OK, OK, I cook, no say nothing.'

'Nice to see you, General,' said Nusmen, all smiles.

'Big surprise seeing you here,' responded the general.

'I thought you knew I was here,' said Nusmen, still assuming he was going back and looking at General Crystal with a mixture of incomprehension coupled with hope.

'Our arrival shake up Heather?' asked the general, knowing the answer.

'Maybe all of us,' said Glenda. 'Don't get me wrong. It is nice to see you. Maybe you could tell us what this unexpected visit is for?'

Sheilla felt the tension. What had been a fun trip with the general had morphed into this strained atmosphere. They all sat silent, waiting.

'Tell us,' asked Heather, who, together with Jim, had appeared behind the general.

No one spoke, waiting. Recognizing the stress he was causing but not one to avoid a conflict, the general said, 'We need help with some problems. Ones that can't be avoided longer.'

'You're taking Jim.' Heather said it more as a statement than a question. She knew the answer. This day was the one she feared and knew would happen.

'I need more help than just Jim.'

Nusmen smiled and sat down cross-legged with his new protégé hidden behind.

'Little curious here. Who is that behind you, Nusmen?'

Nusmen glanced back. 'It's just Shuskin. How are my experiments?'

'I'm not here for that,' stated the general.

Nusmen sagged. 'Then why, sir?' he said dejectedly, not really curious at all but feeling more depressed than he had all day.

'General, I want to know too. What are you here for?' asked Heather.

Jim put his arm around her shoulders. 'Let's sit down and he'll fill us in.'

'Nothing dangerous or complicated. Glenda is going to the Caribbean for an investigation. I want Jim and Brush for something else.'

Heather sat silent, despondent. She had known this would happen. He was taking Jim from her, and she knew Jim would go willingly.

Glenda squeezed Brush's hand; this was their life. Maybe not always but for now. Nusmen sat staring at his lap.

'Different mission.' The general looked around. Heather still had her security clearance from a year ago. Not that it meant much in reality. 'Who is that behind you, Nusmen?' he boomed again.

'Like I said, that's Old Man Shuskin.' Nusmen swiveled his head at Shuskin. 'Meet General Crystal, old man.' Shuskin didn't answer and shimmied closer to Nusmen and hid his head.

'You told me his name, not who he is.'

'He's a vagrant, sort of nuts.'

The general looked straight at Nusmen, who looked up with his eyes, not moving his head. He couldn't hold the general's stare and looked back at his lap.

The general then looked again at the old man. 'Can you send him to do something so I can talk freely?'

'He isn't going to move two feet from Nusmen from what I have seen,' said Heather. 'He is not all there, so please, spit it out. Just ignore him.'

Jim looked at Nusmen. 'Nusmen, take Lola, Pedro, and Old Man Shuskin and make sure the llamas have enough to eat.'

'Huh,' said Nusmen.

'No understand,' said Lola.

'What's to understand? Move it, Nusmen, and you too please, Lola, right now,' said Heather as a reluctant Nusmen followed by an even more reluctant Lola, followed immediately by, in lockstep with Nusmen, the old phantom of the woods. The short, plump, dark-skinned Lola, Pedro, the tall pasty-white Nusmen, and the unbathed, bowed-over Shuskin, walked and limped out into the meadow.

After a moment's pause the general spoke. 'I need Glenda in Cuba. She's going with Kramer.'

'Huh?' exclaimed Brush.

The general gave Brush a look that said, *Mind your own business; she works for me.* 'I'll give you a full briefing on the way back.'

Heather held on to Jim, there was nothing else she could do. Her anxieties were now realities. The shock left her feeling weak.

'Kramer's an idiot…'

Before Brush could say more Jim cut in, 'Let's leave it until we are in the air.'

Heather looked at Lo standing in the meadow with a disgusted look and waved for her to come back.

'What a sight,' said Brush, shaking his head, as the crazy-looking Nusmen, the diminutive Yaqui Indian holding on to Pedro, and the old dirt-encrusted vagrant, wearing probably the first new coat he had owned in years topped with a red stocking cap, walked back to the kitchen.

'General, please, I want to go back,' said Nusmen loudly as he approached.

'Not a chance. You take your full vacation; return a minute sooner and you'll be out of the lab for a month. What's the old man's story? We don't have all day, spit it out,' commanded the general.

'I don't know, I don't know. He hangs out in the mountains and they threw him out of his usual place in the Pasayten and he was hiding in Heather's truck.'

'So?'

'I got him some food and clothes, that's all.'

'Very generous and kind of you, Nusmen,' said Glenda. 'What are you going to do with him now?'

'What do you mean, now?'

'I found a dog once and gave him some food and took him home. He went nuts whenever I left. It looks to me like you have the old man for life.'

Nusmen sat there with his mouth open, then looked behind him again and scowled, looking disgusted. 'No fucking way!'

They all laughed. Nusmen really did have a heart after all. 'Come on, Nusmen, get him a bath and take him home with you,' prodded Brush.

'Don't talk about him like he isn't here,' said Heather, regaining some composure.

'Sheilla, would you like to stay here for a few days with

Heather?' asked the general. He would rather have her ride back with him but then maybe he could come back and fly back with her alone. Stupid crazy ideas. He had a job to do. So did she. What was he even thinking?

'No way,' said Sheilla rather weakly. 'I want to go back now. I need to be in the office.' She knew the general rarely said something and then changed his mind.

'I think it would be good for you to stay. I'll keep in touch with the new computer whizzes. Stay here and get to know Heather. Keep Nusmen on the straight and narrow. I'll pick you up tomorrow.'

'OK.' A concession of one day was all she was going to get from him.

It sounded more like an order than a request and Sheilla wondered if he had a reason. 'But I don't know anything about being out here,' she protested.

'Heather and Nusmen are experienced and I'm sure that Heather could use your company. It's a plan then. I'll fly back tomorrow afternoon. Maybe we can hike up to that lake we saw flying in and then we'll go back and solve our problem.'

Heather's throat was dry. Her mind a kaleidoscope of thoughts. Jim leaving, Pedro, Nusmen and Shuskin, Pipestone. She said nothing.

'It's a good idea, Sheilla. You'll enjoy yourself,' said Jim. Sheilla apprehensively looked around and then at Heather. She obviously needed someone with her. Lola, Pedro, and Shuskin would be no real help, and Nusmen looked useless.

'I take care of my mama,' said Pedro.

Jim smiled at Pedro. 'I leave you in charge then. You have lots of people that need your help,' said Jim. Pedro was no less proud of Jim's faith in him than Jim was of his new son.

'You no leave me here! You take all back to ranch! Madre Dios!' exclaimed Lola. 'No leave us with loco hombres. No place for women alone.'

'I'll take care of you too,' said Pedro.

'You three get your gear. West sun will be in our faces soon,' ordered General Crystal.

Jim looked at Heather and said to the general, 'Will, there's nearly a full moon tonight.'

'Good idea. We'll head back when the sun is behind the mountains. Sunset and then moonlit mountains.'

Everyone stared at General Crystal. No one had ever heard him say anything that sounded the least bit romantic.

Glenda broke the silence. 'Moonlit mountains has a nice sound to it.'

The general said, 'Full moon, so we can see the terrain.'

Jim leaned close to Heather and whispered, 'I'll always come back to you.' Then a realization struck Jim. He wanted to leave. He felt drawn back to his life with Brush, to be in some faraway place, on the move. He had been sitting idle for too long.

Chapter 38

Najma stood in a steaming shower. The water did little to erase her anger. The right side of her face and ear rebelled against the hot sting of the water on her raw flesh. Memories of her abusive father and his friends flooded her thoughts. However, nothing but ghosts of memories from the previous day appeared.

She reconstructed the events again trying to force a memory into her consciousness. She had followed the waddling general and his guards to a rooftop and its closed café. Then they had disappeared. There her memory dried up. Had she walk up the stairs? She vaguely remembered being on them.

The only explanation: she had walked into a trap. The general's bodyguards had...what? Why hadn't they killed her? The answer: they didn't know who she was. Just a woman, another piece of meat. They had raped her and tossed her aside. Amnesia? Hit on the head? She reached up and felt her ear. *Is that why I can't remember?*

She tried to tell herself that it didn't matter. What mattered was that it was the wimpy general's men, maybe even him or the fat fuck mayor. Had they wanted her dead? No. They reasoned she was a nobody. Just a piece of entertainment and they didn't care if she survived or died.

She stepped out of the shower and went to the closet naked. The case with the weapons the cartel men had delivered earlier sat there looking like any locked suitcase. She tossed it on the bed and opened it with her key. She closed the case and dressed, ignoring the pain; replacing it with the thought of revenge.

She dressed in dark clothes, grabbed the suitcase and left the hotel by the fire escape. She didn't care if it was alarmed or not as she walked fast down an alley and into a street. She still couldn't remember details. Nevertheless, she continued to reconstruct the story as she walked at a brisk pace toward the café terrace.

Over and over she tried to remember. Somehow, she had been caught unaware, hit on the head, causing her to lose her memory. They had raped her in the desert. Or had they raped her at the unused café and then dumped her?

She passed a small store and quickly purchased three bottles of water and several burritos, replacing her pain with thoughts of the pleasures awaiting her when she caught her rapists.

She thought of the men her father had let molest her for a price. Those men were dead and she had only been a girl then. Her anger grew with every step. She found the street and then the stairs. She stood for several minutes, listening. A distant memory made her conscious that the air held no cigarette smoke. She removed a twenty-two caliber pistol with a silencer from her pocket.

She moved to the stairs and watched, listening. Calm and focus flooded her, no longer did she dwell on the past. Hunting pleased her. She would kill the men responsible if she had to kill every male in this town. After several minutes, satisfied that no one was there, she silently crept up the stairs. She suddenly froze. A shadow crossed the red tile patio. She raised her pistol and the shadow disappeared. Her mind was not functioning as it should, Najma realized. She remembered the shadow of the big man and the smell of smoke. It was a memory of a shadow. No one was above on the terrace.

She silently stepped off the stairs, then listened at the door leading off the terrace; satisfied, she slowly twisted the handle and walked into a dark hall, lit only by outside lights, which passed through the door's small rectangular windowpanes. No one was in the building. She could feel the undisturbed air and quiet. As her eyes adjusted, the dim gray became clearer. She could see a door in the hall. Inside, the large room filled with tables seemed familiar. She knew they would come back to this place. Her instincts told her they would. The last vestiges of sun painted the dark wood floor orange as she sat waiting and listening.

Clouds drifted by the office window as Bertrand watched their filmy edges curl and turn. He had his story. Pearson supplied the important pieces. Bertrand knew that underneath the sarcastic remarks Martin had a fine mind and was a good analyst. He had field experience, admittedly a long time ago. Still, it was a crazy idea having Martin head this operation. But he would be in the background coordinating, nothing more. He nodded his head making a final decision.

'How you doing, B?'

Bertrand ignored this. 'I want you in Mexico to head up the capture of the escapee. Review all the intel you need. Draft up a plan ASAP. Get an insertion team ready. And bring Najma back without any fuss.'

Martin froze, for once speechless. Bertrand was placing a lot of trust in him. *Why me?* he wondered. Then he saw it as an opportunity.

'I'll bring her back so quietly that no one will know, Bertrand,' Martin said, trying to sound confident. He hadn't been in the field for a long time and then not much at all. He had been pulled in and given a desk job after making a complete mess of his last mission many years ago. Maybe he could do it right this time. A second chance. *Why the trust?* If it was anyone other than Bertrand, Martin would think he was being set up.

'This isn't Sorenson's idea is it?'

'No. One more thing. Make damn sure that none of your team knows her real identity. Our guys can keep a secret but there will be some contractors and informants involved. Use Eduardo Freeman to be in charge of the capture. Listen to him and you'll be OK. You're just going to be my link. Don't forget: don't give them the full story. They don't need to know.'

'Sure. Thank you, Bertrand. I mean that.'

'Don't thank me yet. Do this wrong and you won't have a career left. Do it right and then I'll thank you and so will the director.'

'Maybe with luck it won't be Sorenson thanking me.'

If Martin botched this, they would have a new director sooner rather than later. If not, they would have Najma back in Guantána-mo. In a way it was a no-lose situation. The agency would be embarrassed if Martin failed but Sorenson and probably Flayback would take the fall, and with luck, they would get a more capable director from within the agency, someone with experience.

Within the last few days Bertrand had come to accept that, re-gardless of Martin's success or failure, Sorenson needed to be replaced. Flayback needed to go as well. The agency had been Bertrand's life and love. The president had realized his error in having a politician head the venerable agency. Who would be the best person to replace Sorenson from within? One immediately stood out in his mind. A thirty-year veteran, Eric Sands, had the experience and presence of mind to take the agency forward. He had been one of their most successful field operatives and had extensive experience in intelligence. He understood the important function the CIA performed and he was smooth enough to handle the politics that came with the job. The cold war was becoming a technological war. It would be a difficult transition for anyone to make. Sands had all the right skills.

The meadow became quiet as the Huey disappeared over the

ridge to the west of the camp. A plane would be ready for Glenda and Kramer at twenty-two hundred. After getting the news by satellite phone, the general had decided to leave immediately rather than wait until after sunset.

Pedro was proud to be in charge but disappointed that he didn't get a helicopter ride. Nusmen was acting surly. Sheilla was not sure she would survive the night in the wilderness and started staying close to Heather, bombarding her with questions about bears and poison ivy. Lola couldn't believe that the only men around were the gangly, weird-looking, sulking half-man with the bobbing Adam's apple and the stinky old man. She kept crossing herself as she stared at the protrusion in his throat moving incessantly up and down. Then she looked at Shuskin, thinking that he would be no help to anyone. She couldn't have been more wrong on both counts. Nusmen was experienced in the mountains and Old Man Shuskin had spent years surviving there.

Heather moved in a trance. She barely answered Sheilla's questions. 'No bears. No, no poison ivy. Yes, I have been out lots by myself before.' Sheilla felt for Heather but didn't know what to do around the camp.

'Can I help you do anything?'

The only answer she received was, 'No.'

'Maybe I'll go see how Nusmen is doing then.'

Nothing from Heather, so she decided that Nusmen would be better company.

'Nusmen. Have you been here before?' asked Sheilla.

'Yeah,' was the only answer she received. *What a bunch. I'm stuck up here with nothing to do, all sad-sack faces,* she thought. *Might as well try to talk to the old man and see what makes him tick.*

She watched Heather walk to her tent and crawl in, and then moved toward Shuskin.

As she got closer, she stopped and grimaced. He was grungy up close, and looked completely crazy. He looked back at her with wild eyes and started to shrink back closer to Nusmen and then instead, stood up and walked toward her lifting up his hand. Sheilla was in a panic. He was going to touch her! She closed her eyes hoping it was only her imagination.

'Red,' said Shuskin. Sheilla felt faint and squinted out of one eye. What she saw made her cringe. The old creature was holding her auburn hair in his dirt-encrusted hand. 'What am I doing here?' she said out loud. Then stained teeth grinned at her. This was too much. *Is there anyone sane around here?* Sheilla wondered.

'Shoo, shoo,' she heard the short woman say as the old transient moved away reluctantly. 'Vamos. Out kitchen.' Sheilla looked around, confused, thinking *Kitchen? What kitchen?* She followed the short woman. Now she remembered, thinking back to the Mexico raid. Lola shouted at the boy.

'Pedro, aqui, rapido, ahora.'

He walked at anything but a rapid pace toward the kitchen and eventually said, 'Sí, tía Lo,' as she scowled at him.

'I no your aunt. Why say that?'

'You my other mother but can have only one. So I want you be my aunt.'

She didn't answer for several seconds as she stared down at the dirt. Then she looked up with resignation, 'Está OK. Comprendo, niño,' she said softly, knowing that what he said was true: she would never be his mother.

Heather's tent flap opened and Pedro peeked in. Her eyes red and puffy, she held out her arms to her adopted son. Heather did not understand why a tear ran down Pedro's cheek. Then he collapsed into her arms and they both bawled for several seconds. Their spasms died after a while and they lay relaxed, comforting each other.

Something had changed between them. Pedro opened up to her,

telling her memories he had but kept obscured about his dead family. Heather didn't understand what had just happened. But she could sense a new bond had formed.

'Here, coffee, señorita,' said Pedro. 'Drink,' as he stood staring.

'Thank you,' she said not knowing if he wanted something.

'Touch, please,' Oh, he was looking at her long dark auburn hair too and had probably seen the vagabond touch it. She bent forward letting her hair hang over her head.

'Yes please,' as he delicately reached up.

'Muy bonita, we go swim?'

'I don't have a suit.'

'Nobody has a suit here,' said Heather, surprising Sheilla by saying more than four words. *She's coming out of it,* she thought as she looked at Heather, who suddenly seemed content. Sheilla shook her head, wondering what was going on with this lot. *From happy to forlorn to content.*

She just stood there, then looked at Nusmen and Old Man Shuskin. From behind her, she heard Heather say, 'We'll go in a few minutes. Walking up there and the cold water will help everyone to feel better. Pedro, you go help Sheilla get the things the general left and take them to Brush and Glenda's tent. She can stay there tonight. Then we'll leave.'

'Okie dokie,' he yelped, jumping up and down.

Heather couldn't help but smile, even if only a little. Pedro would be her support.

'Thanks, Pedro,' answered Sheilla, thinking that Heather was talking at last and probably would be the best company for her. No way were they going to talk her out of her panties in a public lake though. She would just watch them swim. All of a sudden, Heather started to laugh, then slumped to the ground putting her face in her hands. Sheilla dropped to the ground too, and put her arm around her. 'Poor thing, don't cry.'

'He'll die. I know he will. I can't live without him and now we have Pedro to take care of,' sobbed Heather.

'Mama, don't cry anymore,' said Pedro as he kneeled beside her, squeezing her arm.

Chapter 39

'I don't like buzzing off like this, General,' said Jim as the helicopter passed the small mountain lake.

'I know it seems cruel but the truth is, you're needed, and maybe the sudden shock is the best way for her to accept what you do and will continue to do.'

'I'm not too sure about that approach,' said Glenda. 'A few days letting her get accustomed to it with Jim next to her might have been better than a few minutes.'

The general looked at Brush who shrugged and then added, 'She's probably right.'

'Ah shit,' said the general. 'I'm a general not a babysitter. This is the army for Christ sake, or close to it.'

Brush raised an eyebrow and looked at Glenda with a twisted smile. Then Will abruptly raised the chopper's nose almost straight up and, rolling to the left in a steep bank, he turned it back toward the meadow.

'Wise choice,' said Glenda.

'I hope it is…Glenda, with your flight leaving at twenty-two hundred tonight, this will give you less time to prepare.'

Brush arched both eyebrows. In his past, he had never worried about leaving a woman. There was always another out there. But to have his woman leave him for a mission was a new sensation. Reaching over, he squeezed Glenda's hand. He wasn't sure if he liked this new feeling. Glenda sensed it.

Glenda lifted his headset off one ear, pulled the mic away and said, 'It's going to be like this, we'll be OK.'

The general throttled the chopper as fast as it could go and headed back to the meadow. The sound that had made Heather nauseous just a short time ago now lifted her spirits. Sheilla and Pedro poked their heads out of Brush and Glenda's tent as the whop, whop, whop of the blades grew louder. The chopper came in fast, lifted its nose slightly, momentarily slowed a few feet over the meadow and lifted into the sky, turning back toward the west.

Pedro ran out of the tent. Heather raced across the meadow as fast as she could run, both converging on the lone figure standing in the meadow as blowing debris settled around Jim.

'I don't care why you are back or for how long. Just that you're here,' said Heather with tears streaming down her cheeks. Blood was flowing back into her brain. She was whole again. She was alive. And she squeezed and held him with all her strength.

'Dad, Dad. You back.' Pedro wrapped both arms around Jim's leg. Jim reached down with his left arm and scooped him up, his right around Heather's waist as they moved lightly across the meadow toward the camp.

'Boys and girls,' said the general to Brush and Glenda as the Huey lifted into the sky. 'We have just enough fuel to make it back. Without the auxiliary tank I added a few years ago, I don't think we would make it.'

'Speaking for the "girls" back here,' said Glenda. 'I hope we do make it back. And I'll forgive you for calling me that after that act of compassion.'

'Calling you "girl" means he likes you, honey,' said Brush.

The general rolled his eyes. Women. *What was I thinking when I brought them into my nice little world?*

Chapter 40

She didn't expect anyone to return soon to the deserted rooms. Possibly it might even be several days. Najma would wait as long as it took. She wanted to get her hands on them but sitting here knowing it would happen gave her a feeling of pleasure.

She was confident they would return eventually and she would be waiting. She didn't know what its purpose was. But the room had a special function and they would be back. Najma ignored her throbbing head and bruised body. Her anger subdued, allowing her to focus on her task.

They would not be quiet and she would hear them walking up the steps and entering the hall, however, she would have to watch the kitchen entrance in case someone came that way. She looked carefully around the room and saw nothing that would let her believe this was anything other than a meeting room. Why meet here and not at the general's or the mayor's office?

She decided it didn't make any difference. She quietly gathered up her refuse and silently walked into the kitchen, stuffing her wrappers and empty bottles into trash bag. She reassured herself that she had relocked the exit door from the kitchen after she had explored the empty premises earlier.

She closed the kitchen door. It squeaked on little used hinges. She opened another burrito that she had been saving for later. It oozed grease. She poured a small amount of the oil onto each hinge and worked the door back and forth. The friction disappeared from the old metal hinges.

Nusmen sat on the ground, pouting. His new charge sat fiddling with some sticks about three feet away, which was as close as Nusmen would let him get.

'Feel safer now,' said Lola. 'They no men,' pointing at Nusmen and Shuskin.

'Nusmen knows his way around the woods, Lo,' said Heather. 'Let's go to the upper lake.'

Jim turned her to him. 'The general, in his infinite wisdom, and with a little push by Glenda, decided that it was not fair to surprise you like he did. He means well but his social skills are not always his best attribute.'

'Will Sheilla want to go to the lake? I know Pedro does. We'll all go and then they can watch out for Pedro while we sneak off for a while. OK?'

Heather pulled Jim to her, looked up into his blue eyes and gave him a kiss. 'I'll try to be OK.'

The light shifted to gray and then to charcoal. The night drifted along slowly for Najma as she sat in one of the lounge chairs, eyes open and empty as the night. The darkness lifted and a small prism of light projected on the floor through the windowpane, reminding her of the ebbing light just two days ago in the desert. She could not remember more but, just as Bertrand was doing across the continent, she constructed a story. Reconfirmed it over and over. She would leave the large guard and all the others alive long enough to tell her what had happened, who was responsible and who had violated her.

'I no stay here by myself,' said Lola.

'I'm afraid you have to stay like last time. Remember someone has to watch the llamas.'

Lola shook her head.

'You will be OK. I need you here. I could ask the old man to stay with you?' Lola puckered her lips and shook her head sideways.

Pedro came running back from Sheilla's tent. 'She has no swimming suit.'

'Go back and tell her, her underwear will be fine and bring a towel.'

Pedro ran back arms waving excitedly. Heather looked at Jim and smiled. 'But what are you going to wear, big guy?'

The group of seven filed across the meadow, dark silhouettes along the small ridge toward the lake that was like a chalice full of clear liquid held up to the gods. Heather and Jim followed Pedro who skipped and jumped holding Sheilla's hand. Nusmen, at the back, grumbled his way along, shadowed by the old man.

'Guess Nusmen wants to go back to the center and his experiments. Is he always this taciturn out here?' asked Jim then continued. 'It worries me a little that the general is putting so much faith in him. His science might be good but is he trustworthy? Will he stay rational?'

'He's smart. Knows his stuff...truthfully, his social skills are none too good, just like some other nerds I know. Mentally they are always close to falling off the precipice. From what I know of him, he is probably crazy about working there.'

The collection of tall people, small people, young, old, happy, and disconsolate, followed the trail under the hazy late August sky.

'Beautiful up here,' shouted Sheilla from twenty feet in front of Jim and Heather.

'Yep, it is,' Heather shouted back. 'Jim, I grabbed some soap and shampoo. What do you think are the chances of getting Nusmen's friend a scrubbing in the lake?'

'As a microbiologist,' said Jim, 'I have only one request—after we get out, not before we get in. Who is going to scrub him?'

'You think Nusmen might?' asked Heather.

'I don't think anyone is going to unless we tie Shuskin up,' said Jim. 'I have a feeling he is afraid of water and soap. And I doubt Nusmen is happy enough about the situation to help.'

'Hum, I'll try talking to him anyway,' said Heather.

Pedro ran for the lake as it came into view. 'Swimming,' he shouted.

'No diving. It's shallow,' yelled Heather.

'Wow,' said Sheilla as she stared at the shimmering crystal-clear lake. 'It's small, like a special gem set way up here. We saw lots of lakes on the flight over on the other side of the mountains and then this one flying in. It's nice to see one up close. Is it cold?'

'It doesn't have much water volume so it depends on the time of day and the outside temperature. It should be warm enough now,' added Jim.

'Well, here goes,' said Heather.

'Good luck,' said Jim giving her an encouraging smile.

'Nusmen, we have to get Old Man Shuskin cleaned up. He looks awful.' Nusmen just stared at her like she was crazy. 'I take it you aren't going to do anything? He likes you, talk to him.'

'I'm not going to touch him,' said Nusmen, sounding churlish.

'Come on, Nusmen, buck up,' said Heather. 'What's your problem anyway? Instead of jail you have been given your dream job. You're wanted and you have a chance to do some good. So why not remove that sad face and get in the water with Shuskin and help him out.'

'But I can't, I can't touch him.'

Heather peered around Nusmen. 'Shuskin, I always liked it that you found your home in the mountains and not the city but even up here people stay clean and you definitely need some cleaning up. Have you always been this dirty? Will you get in the lake and scrub up for me?'

Shuskin looked down, moving from foot to foot looking agitated, and didn't answer.

'Nusmen, walk with me and then strip off and get in the lake. Let's see what he does.'

'I think he likes you, Heather. He acts differently around you than the others.'

'She nice,' said Shuskin looking at Nusmen. 'Nice to animals. I brung her llama.'

'What did you just say? What llama? What? Tell me,' demanded Heather.

Shuskin scrunched up behind Nusmen. Her excited voice scared him a little.

'Old man. Look at me. If you brought Pipey back, I'll love you forever. I'm not angry, just shocked, very surprised and very happy. You really did that?'

'You's a nice lady in the mountains. You's nice to critters. Llama lost. I help.'

Heather beamed then almost choked and a different sort of tear rolled down her cheek. 'Mister, you are wonderful. I love that llama. Thank you so much for returning him to us. I'll never ever forget it.' She stopped just short of giving him a hug.

Shuskin stared at her, still not knowing if she was happy or angry. Finally, her beaming smile convinced him. He grinned, a black smile. It was difficult to tell the dark gaps where his teeth were missing from the dark stains on those that remained. *How did he manage to get them so black?* she wondered.

'I'll go in the water with you and so will Nusmen. Then you can tell me how you found Pipestone.' Heather glared at Nusmen, telling him he had no choice. 'Let's go, both of you.' She marched off toward the lake, followed by a reluctant Nusmen, trailed by an even more reluctant Shuskin.

'You coming in, Jim? Don't think Shuskin will mind if you go with no suit.'

'Sorry to disappoint. I have my trunks on under my jeans.'

'Oh.'

'Maybe you have,' said Sheilla. 'But I have nothing to wear.'

'Underclothes will do out here. Most of the time we go sans clothes but not today.'

No way I'm going to jump in the lake half naked with Nusmen and Shuskin, or any of them for that matter, Sheilla said to herself.

Heather sat on a stone and unlaced her shoes. 'Come on you two, get with it,' she called. She quickly removed boots, socks and then pants and jumped in the lake still wearing her black T-shirt and pink underpants. 'Pedro,' she shouted. 'Jumping is OK but don't you dare dive.'

Jim looked at Heather and then Nusmen, glad she had left her top on: she always had the same effect on him, it never changed. He could feel himself stirring as the wet shirt clung to her skin. He knew it was crazy to leave her, but he felt empty without a mission.

Chapter 41

The morning stretched on. Najma sat without expectations. Time meant little. Infinite patience with the stillness eventually erupting, as she knew it would, into intense action. It was like all battles: boredom transfusing to adrenaline. Her mind wandered to her youth and the men her father had allowed to ravage her young body, and how she had eventually killed them all with her knife. A smile flitted over her lips; she would do a much better job with these assholes as an adult than she had done as a teenager.

The steps creaked; voices and footfalls moved closer. She moved light-footed, quickly stepping into the kitchen and closing the oiled-hinged door, leaving only a small viewing crack. The large guard walked into the room, briefly scanning it, followed by another. 'Está bien,' he said to the, as yet, unseen men behind him. Najma allowed a small smile as her two targets walked in together. Then two more men she had not seen before also entered the room followed by a third carrying a briefcase. The three extra men complicated things.

The large guard moved against the wall and the other moved to the window. She had anticipated that the guards would remain outside. As the hall door closed, she moved into the room carrying a silenced MP5, coincidentally Jim's favorite weapon. Time and the room's inhabitants froze into stillness, except for the large guard who reached for his shoulder holster. She shot him low-down in the stomach just above his groin, not to kill him but to cause as much pain as she could while she dealt with the others.

As she looked at the immaculately dressed general, she said in a whisper-like purr, 'Tell the others outside to get in here now.'

He hesitated and she raised the gun, pointing at his head. Her eyes, not focused on him or anyone, taking in all the others in the room, waiting to sense any movement. She stepped to the left toward the wall where the large man lay moaning, withdrawing her small pistol with its oversize silencer. The door flung open and a smaller thin man entered with a pistol raised. Directly behind him another man followed on his heels.

From eight feet away she shot the first guard in the shoulder and in the next fraction of a second the other man in the only place visible to her, his head. She now had control of the room but didn't move or speak. Her original quarry sat in silence at the table. The only guard that had a large stature lay on the floor. She glared at him.

She said without looking at the guard. 'Silence or I will shoot you again.' He moaned; she raised her small silenced pistol and from only five feet away, and shot him in the upper arm. Blood trickled from his untucked white shirt. Carefully she bent over and removed his large stainless steel revolver. She tossed it in her hand admiring the solid feel of the Smith & Wesson .357 Magnum.

The other guard she had shot in the shoulder lay silent, apparently passed out, surprising as the small caliber twenty-two bullet did not have a shock effect. Najma smiled at the men at the table and moved to the seemingly unconscious guard. Before she bent over to search for his weapons, she sensed him tensing. 'Open your eyes,' she said with a level voice. 'Do you recognize me?'

In the swirling monochrome fog of her memories, she remembered a large man and a smaller one. He opened his eyes and looked at her.

'I remember your tight little ass,' he smirked.

Did he think he still had power over her or was it that he'd already assessed that he would not live through the next few minutes? Or was it just male bravado or stupidity? Perhaps he thought he could anger her and die quickly. Whatever the reason, he would soon regret his choices, both of two nights ago and now.

Najma felt as though she had been here before. This man she would punish beyond his imagination just as she had done to others before. The man grinned at her. She fired one bullet into his other shoulder followed quickly by a round into each kneecap.

While holding the MP5 in her right hand she ejected the clip from her pistol and replaced it. She looked at the only guard that was not wounded and said, pointing at the skinny guard, 'Take off his pants.' He just stood looking at her.

'Quítate los pantalones,' said General Ramos.

Martin Pearson sat nervously in a dusty Tubutama café, wearing what he thought would pass for old clothes and sprouting a four-day-old salt and pepper stubble. He wore an old bleached burgundy Redskins baseball cap and dark sunglasses. He sat stretched out with his Nike tennis shoes crossed over the bottom of his nearly new Wrangler jeans. He was not happy about the gray in his beard and less comfortable pretending to while away the day at this cafe. It was not his sort of place, although he thought he was playing the role well.

He might as well as have been wearing a Brooks Brothers suit, as he looked nothing like a local, a bum, or even a tourist, which caused all the more gossip among the residents. The police had started to wonder who he was. Martin's tradecraft lacked, as did his command of the situation.

'You need to leave your location now,' came over his earpiece.

'Why?'

'You are being observed,' answered Eduardo.

'Shit,' mumbled Pearson into his mic.

'What is this guy doing down here? This is a fucked operation. Too dangerous in this town to make a mistake. We never should have let him go out there,' Eduardo, the assigned CIA operative who was a specialist in northern Mexico, said to his partner, Thomas.

'No argument from me on that,' said Thomas.

Eduardo toggled his talk button. 'Stand up, look at your watch and walk up the street to your right. And don't fucking answer me turning your head toward your mic.'

'Stupid fucker,' said Thomas.

Martin's throat was dry. He had thought he could play the role. It had all sounded good in the room when he pushed to be part of the operation. Now he would be a laughingstock. He got up and did as Eduardo told him to.

'Shit,' said Eduardo, as he watched the office jockey boss he had been given. 'There's a whole shitload of people on him. We got to get him out of here. He might be a stupid son of a bitch but it'll be our ass if we lose him. Go to your room,' he ordered Martin, getting more upset by the second. 'On the way in, tell the clerk you are going to check out, say there's nothing to do here. Quote me, "one boring town." Then say you are going to head over to Nogales. Then do it. Get in the red Nissan and drive there.'

'I can't leave,' Martin managed to get out before Eduardo cut him off and said, 'Don't say anything else. Just walk and don't look around unless it is at a woman or dog. You'll look suspicious if you look behind you. Don't talk!'

He turned to his partner. 'This guy ever been in the field? Supposed to be smart, right? And worse he's in charge!'

'I heard he was a smartass,' said Thomas. 'What do you want to do?'

'We can't go and get one of the top office jockeys killed, like I said. Why didn't they send Turnbull or Jackson? They've got hundreds of better field operatives. Why send this guy?'

'Call operations and have them arrange a room for him in Nogales. Tell them that we can't spare anyone and to get somebody to watch him, emphasize, unless they want to be responsible for losing him. We'll figure out a way to get him back in the loop where he can pretend he is in charge. Let's hope he makes it to Nogales.'

Lazaro did not like to bother Guillermo with trivial details: Captain Rodriguez just reported the odd behavior of the man at the café. It was probably nothing. The police captain was having the man followed; still Guillermo had told him to report anything unusual. Lazaro rose through the ranks of the cartel based on smart decisions. He was ruthless and smart, not brazen and showy. He had probably killed more people than many of his men but he was also thoughtful. He never rushed into anything with anger and although he was now one of two lieutenants in the cartel, he walked and acted carefully around Guillermo.

He pulled out his cell phone and called El Padrino.

'There is a gringo acting strangely in town, and I was told he was talking into a radio transmitter. I am having him followed and the police captain has gathered a drinking glass the man touched. It will give it to the Russian to check the computers for matching fingerprints.'

'Tell Vladislav to call me when he has an answer.' Guillermo clicked off his cell, wondering what this meant. He sat thinking for a long time. Eventually he pressed the number two on his cell phone, speed dialing his other top lieutenant. 'Vega, make sure Najma's double is ready.'

Just as he was setting his phone on the table, it rang.

'Lazaro said to call you. The fingerprints are locked in a special government program. I can't get them. That means he is probably not DEA, possibly CIA, maybe NSA, possibly BWC. You want me to keep looking?' asked Vladislav.

'No, not now. Your best guess?'

'CIA has been asking questions. My guess is them.'

Guillermo thought for a moment and called Lazaro. 'I want you to move more men into town. Make inquiries and make sure the man is carefully followed and alone.'

Lazaro knew that Guillermo was always cautious but he had a feeling this might be more than caution. 'Tio, get me men to follow the gringo, rapido.'

Lazaro's phone rang; it was Captain Rodriguez. 'The man has checked out of the hotel. He is driving east toward Nogales. I have a car tailing him. What do you want me to do?'

'No radios use only cells. Don't be seen. Give me the follower's phone number. I will take over from here. And ask questions in town, but carefully.'

Sergeant Ricardo was humming to himself as he drove casually along, following the slow-driving Gringo. He was trying to ignore the snoring of his partner when his cell phone rang. 'Sí. Ricardo,' he answered sounding bored and then sat straight up in his seat with his arms rigid against the steering wheel. A half second later, he hit Pas's arm to stop his snoring.

'Sergeant. Listen carefully. Do not let the man you are following out of sight. Comprende?' Without waiting for an answer, Lazaro said, 'Tio will be in touch with you.' He then called Tio and said, 'Get on the road now and catch up to the man the police are following. I want you to get two more cars. Then get rid of the police. I want to know everything this gringo does.'

Chapter 42

'What do you think?' asked Brush.

'The one thing I learned about the CIA was to never trust them,' said Glenda. 'I think they decided to use her, not that they need another assassin. An escape seems unlikely.'

'Except for one thing, gorgeous: why ask questions about her if they let her go?'

'A ruse?'

'Maybe, doubtful.' Brush shook his head. 'It doesn't make sense, unless Najma is not there. But how the hell could she get out of Gitmo? She was practically dead, and I am sure the CIA had her locked up tight.'

'Well, search me.' Then she stopped and caught the look in Brush's eye.

'Anytime, beautiful.' He smiled.

Brush pulled her to him. She laid her soft, light ginger-red hair on his shoulder and nuzzled his neck. His thoughts were a jumble. Planning and executing missions with Jim had been his life. In between, he'd said goodbye to a parade of women and was happy to leave but he didn't want to say goodbye to Glenda. Not even for a few days. Especially not now as he held her.

Another part of him didn't want her going where he couldn't protect her. Even if he knew that he felt that way, he shouldn't say it to her. She was capable of taking care of herself and maybe even safer without him distracting her. Then he thought, *I can say what I think because she understands and probably wants to take care of me too.*

Then Brush made a decision. No matter what, he would never deceive her. 'Jim and I are going to be not far away. The general wants us as backup.'

For a moment anger welled up in her. Then she realized what Brush was doing. Putting their relationship ahead of the years with the Jim and the general. He trusted her, to say that. The anger dissipated as fast as it had appeared.

She squeezed him, wondering how their lives would play out. Would they grow old together? 'What's the plan?' she asked.

'I don't know yet.'

'Whatever you are doing, you be careful.'

'I should be saying that to you. Kramer might be smart with paper and pencil but he could just as easily get you both killed. You'll have your hands full watching out for yourself and him, even if this probably is not that dangerous.' His hand strayed to her bottom. 'Let's go home,' he said.

'Look who's got his hands full...' She laughed then said softly, 'Home. A nice ring to it. I wonder how much time we will be able to spend there. More the better but...'

'All the more reason to get there now. Our little base house sounds like just the place to be. How much time do we have?'

'I will need to be back here in two hours.'

Najma looked down at the Mexican general's guard who now lay naked from the waist down with red dripping from both knees and his shoulder. She leered at him. Then she turned to the general. 'Ask your guard what he knows about raping me the night before last.'

The general turned to the man and did as she requested. The guard's eyes wavered left and then he looked down. Then he pointed to the skinny guard and the large one.

The general erupted into a string of profanities. His face turned red. 'Señorita. Give me your gun and I will shoot them myself.' Najma laughed and casually turned to the man who had just confirmed the identities of her two assailants. She turned and shot him in the heart.

'Why did you shoot him? I do not think he had anything to do with rape—ah, hurting you.'

'I agree. A quick death is my present to him. You will help me more, General, yes? Who are these other men with you?'

The general was feeling better. This woman was here to avenge her mistreatment, not to harm him. He would ingratiate himself with her. In a more relaxed voice he said, 'Señor Gomez, Mr. Hook with the briefcase, and Señor Perez wearing the red and blue shirt.'

In a blur, she shot all three men before anyone could react. The general sat stunned and sweat beaded on his forehead. He managed to ask, 'What do you want from us?'

'I came here to kill you, General, but first things first. I want you to see what happens to the enemies of Guillermo Vasquez.'

A visible shudder went through the general's body. At the mention of the cartel leader's name, the fat mayor slumped in his chair and started to heave and bawl like a child. He was barely able to blurt out, 'I knew I should not trust you, General. You have killed us both.' With a sudden surge of fear-driven energy, he lifted the table up and propelled his stubby legs toward Najma and the door. A dark dot and then a widening smudge of red appeared above his pink suitcoat pocket. He fell into the wall and landed on top of the dead guard in the doorway.

'Stand up, General.'

'I will pay you a great sum of money,' he pleaded. 'Here take this case, and I will get you much more.' He reached down for the case that had fallen to the floor. Najma let him bring it to his lap and open it.

'Show me the money.' He did so, holding up a neatly bound stack of US hundred-dollar bills. Before he could react, she released a short burst from the MP5 into his chest. She had no more interest in him. She came here to kill him and the mayor for Guillermo. Moans came from the mayor. The big guard was biting on his tongue so hard that he nearly severed it. He wanted to keep quiet, holding to the delusion that this woman would not hurt him more if he remained silent.

Najma's lips turned up slightly as she regarded the rotund mayor in his pink suit and the two men that she was now certain had violated her. She nudged the large man. 'I want to know what happened. Every detail.'

The mayor screamed through foaming red blood, 'Get me a doctor. I need a doctor.'

'Shut up, fat man, and perhaps you will live.' For some reason she wanted to prolong his death and toy with this absurd man a little.

Instead, the mayor let out a terrifying scream. Najma stood over him and jammed her shoe on his throat and then pushed, observing his beady eyes. The mayor's fat body convulsed gasping for air.

Martin drove toward Nogales, annoyed at his dismissal by underlings. He didn't see anyone following him. He kept thinking Eduardo was all wrong. His disguise had been OK. He pulled over and dialed Eduardo. 'I'm on my way back.'

'Martin, you do that I will shoot you. I promise. Don't even think about it. Get your ass to Nogales and don't call me again. The special operations team will contact you when you arrive. They are supposed to be heading here but now we may have to do without them while they take care of you.'

'Screw you, Eduardo. This is my operation.'

'Fine, call it what you want, just stay away from us or you'll get fragged.'

'You would not get away with it.'

'Try us,' Eduardo disconnected.

Tio had no choice but to drive past the gringo until he was out of sight. He then pulled behind a small building and waited. 'Jose, stop and wait for me to tell you to start up again.' He called Lazaro. 'The gringo has stopped.'

It suddenly came to Martin. Dust and gravel flew as he jerked the steering wheel hard to the left. He raced the car back to Tubutama. This was his operation. Hell yes, this was his opportunity. They would never shoot him. He had to assert himself. *Eduardo is bluffing. They're wrong about the danger. I am going to do this right,* he thought.

Martin's car blew past Jose's. 'Hijo de perra. Pinche culero,' swore Jose. He gunned his police car and called Tio. 'The son of a bitch turned around and he's going real fast. Son of a bitch.'

'Stay back but don't lose him,' ordered Tio.

Jose rubbed his head and mumbled, 'Fuckin asshole.' He could just see the gringo's car ahead. He looked at his speedometer. It read one hundred and forty kilometers per hour. Where was the gringo going? Where was Tio? *My car is too old for this crap.*

Tio called Lazaro. 'The gringo is headed back to Tubutama and in a big hurry.'

'Don't lose him.' Lazaro then dialed Guillermo.

Guillermo paused for a second. 'Have the police pull him over for speeding, arrest him and bring him here.'

Chapter 43

Brush was not sleeping his usual sound slumber. He was thinking about Glenda and Kramer. The captain was smart with facts and numbers, as well as languages; still Brush wondered if he could shoot a palm tree from ten feet. Must have qualified in marksmanship during his training but shooting paper targets didn't mean anything. Brush shook himself. He was used to being the one in harm's way while his ladies fretted for him back home. Leave it to Glenda to turn the tables on him like this. She was tough, she was capable, and he was going in as backup: it would all be OK.

He got up, shaved, dressed, and walked to the BWC, entering on the office side. The guard nodded as he swiped his pass card, then walked to the back of the building and took an elevator down.

'We don't usually see you looking serious this early, Brush.'

'Morning, General. Couldn't sleep so thought I would come in and work on some things.'

'Good idea. Just in case you happen to wander into the control room for Glenda and Kramer's operation, try not to cause any trouble. Their plane is about to touch down at Guantánamo.'

'Never crossed my mind,' said Brush, knowing full well that the general knew why he was here so early.

'You have to boot-up later today. I want everything ready as soon as I get Jim back here this afternoon. I want you, Jim, and the Special Forces on-site tonight.'

'You got it. Sheilla is still convinced Najma is on the loose? Jim will be none too happy if she is. He thinks she will come for him.'

'Well, it's about time we found out something concrete.' The general looked at Brush knowing why he was really in this early. 'Move your sorry ass into the ops room, I want you to make sure Glenda and Kramer hook up with Grant OK.'

'And I thought you were a hard ass,' mumbled Brush under his breath while he chuckled.

General Crystal was pretending to himself that he could not understand why he was in his chopper and flying back over the mountains again. He thought of himself as an ultra-realist, or always had done. This personal obfuscation was unusual. *Damn it to hell. Is this what women do to you? What a mess. I like the old ways with Jim and Brush. Now I've got all these women to deal with,* his inner voice said as it talked to another inner self. Then an image of Sheilla formed in his mind. A strange feeling coursed through him. He felt a little numb as he stared straight ahead in a daze.

Suddenly he looked down. For a split-second, he felt disorientated. The peaks below were moving away from him. *I don't believe it. I've never done this before. I've lost my discipline!* he said to himself. He eased forward on the cyclic, dipped the nose slightly, and started moving forward again. In only a few seconds, while he imagining Sheilla, he had allowed himself to move back on the cyclic, stopping his forward motion until he had not only ceased flying forward but started to travel backward.

I better get my act together and get rid of these thoughts. Balderdash and all to hell. I still have lots to do with my career and no time for this sort of funny business, he told himself with certainty. 'Shoot,' he bellowed into his mic.

Lake Chelan, long and slender from the air, glistened in its fifty-mile stretch to his right as he flew north to Oval Lakes. He rubbed his chin and took a deep breath as he rolled his eyes, eased back on the cyclic and started to descend to the meadow.

The beating of the large blades compressed the air, sending the message of his imminent arrival. As the helicopter settled onto the far side of the meadow from the campsite, the emotions of the campers could not have been more diverse. Pedro jumped with excitement. Nusmen vacillated between a little hope that he would be returned and the morose knowledge that he probably would not go back to his new home for another twelve days.

The old man stayed a few feet behind his new friend, afraid of what the helicopter would mean for him. His body was scrubbed. However, it would take more than one cold-water bath to remove grime embedded deep in his skin. Not to mention his teeth. Heather had given him a toothbrush but it would take a dentist to remove the stains on his few remaining teeth.

Heather looked resigned. She didn't want to lose Jim to his other life. But after their night together she had realized she would lose him if she continued being selfish. How could she make him understand; they were parents now, he had a bigger obligation. She knew she had to try and set aside the agitation she felt. Still the conflict was not resolved: Which man was truly Jim, the lover of some humans, especially her and his buddies, or the killer of others?

Jim, for his part, was torn between wanting to stay with her and wanting to get back to field operations. When he was in the field, he wanted to be home with Heather. When home with her, he wanted to be in the field.

There were no demands on his emotions in the field, just a mission to accomplish. Here in the mountains with Heather, he had felt pressured, almost trapped. More than anything he wanted to shed the sad feelings, see Heather smile, hold her close and feel their love permeating their bodies and, above all, have her get rid of her expectations that had so recently turned to demands. Just be with her.

Solving problems came naturally to him; logic and reason were his tools. But they betrayed him when it came to emotions. The only solution was escape: escape to what he knew.

Sheilla woke surprisingly content and then immediately her mind turned to her job, and she became anxious she was not there to help with planning and the still unresolved issues with Najma. Yet she had slept well, much to her surprise, better then she thought she would in the wilderness. The air felt fresh, no bugs had nibbled her body. She had found the evening pleasant, drinking wine and talking, mostly to Pedro and Lola. Pedro had been animated, just as the others had been subdued. Jim and Heather stayed by themselves talking. Minus the glum Nusmen and Heather's somberness, Sheilla found her first wilderness experience enjoyable; the swimming turned out to be a blast after all. Nevertheless, she looked forward to the helicopter ride back and sleeping safe in a real bed tonight.

Standing alone in the meadow, long auburn hair blowing against the greens and browns, she watched the approach of the helicopter. Will Crystal could see her smile as he got closer. He raised his right hand and waved, then deftly settled the helicopter onto the meadow and slowed the rotor blades.

Sheilla walked slowly, almost hesitantly out toward the helicopter. Then she heard shouting off to her left as Pedro came running, followed by Heather carrying a bag.

'You catch some fish, Pedro?'

'Niño fish, not big one. I have ride now?'

'Pedro. Say it properly. May I have a ride now, please?'

'OK, Mama.' He smiled, not about his grammar but about the ride and still didn't say it as she had requested.

Heather patted his shoulder as the general stepped out and started to walk toward them. He looked at Sheilla and said,

'Beautiful afternoon isn't it?' and then looked down at Pedro. 'Bet you want to go for a ride?'

'Sí, yes,' said Pedro eagerly and then looking up at Heather, added 'please.'

'Short one in a while, OK?' said the general. Then added, looking directly at Heather, 'It has to be very short so I don't run out of fuel on the way home with Sheilla and your dad.'

'Promise?' asked Pedro.

'Generals never promise but you have my word.'

Jim walked over carrying fishing poles and a daypack. 'Good flight?'

The general knew he was asking about more than the flight.

'Yes. Did you have a nice night?'

'We did, General,' said Heather.

'Call me Will, especially out here.'

Will excused himself as his oversized satellite telephone chirped.

Heather looked at him, wondering if he was ever was away from work. He was not much taller than her five feet six inches. A few gray hairs at the temples. Stout but not as stocky or muscular as Brush. He had a pleasant face. None of this matched his booming voice. Why wasn't it as loud as usual now?

He was a tough seasoned military man, but bringing Jim back to her, if only for a night, meant to her that underneath he was human. 'Right-oh, Will,' she said and with a sincere look added, 'Thanks. Let's get you some coffee. We had lunch by the Oval Lake while this guy caught our dinner. You hungry? Sheilla, you have lunch while we were fishing?'

'I was just thinking that I am hungry,' answered Sheilla. She turned to the general. 'I am surprised I didn't get any calls on my sat phone last night?'

'I had your calls come to me last night and this morning but you are up now so I expect your vacation in the woods has ended.'

Sheilla was perturbed to be cut out of the loop. She was one of, if not the key planner. 'Why, General?'

'Will, out here please, Sheilla. A little break never hurt anyone and as soon as the mission starts you can't have one.'

'Here's an idea,' said Heather. 'How about Lo makes you a picnic lunch and you and Will can go up to the lake? Will, you said you might want to yesterday, didn't you? Maybe Pedro wants to go too?'

'I'll go up but I'm not swimming again,' said Sheilla. 'I'll watch and have some lunch. How long before we have to leave?'

'Two hours at most,' said Will.

'Pedro, you help Lo get the sandwiches and then go swimming; I want to talk to Jim for a while.'

'Yes, Mama,' answered Pedro trying to be good so as not to ruin his chances of a helicopter ride.

Lola put food into a small red daypack. The general slung it over one shoulder as Sheilla, leading the way, holding hands with Pedro, walked past the helicopter and up the small incline that would lead them to the lake. Jim and Heather walked into the meadow and checked the llamas who, other than Pipey, were safely staked out on their long multicolored leads. Pipestone stood and gave a little sideways kick as they approached then put his head down and resumed eating.

'I'm going to move Meteor to a better spot and then let's sit over by that big rock again,' said Heather as she squeezed Jim's hand before letting go and walked toward her old, reliable dark brown llama. 'Meteor's getting old,' she said, looking back at Jim.

Najma admired the perfectly dressed general with his new decorative red blotches on his thin chest. Red and tan, a nice combination. She had a job to do and now it was nearly finished.

Almost time for pleasure. She said to the big guy, 'Was that fat blob of a mayor involved in your fun and games the other night?'

He rolled his head back and forth. Najma turned to the rotund mayor and stood over him as he tried to breathe. She stared into his eyes, and slowly pointed the MP5 at his face. Terror filled his eyes. She waited and watched as yellow fluid leaked onto the floor through his pretty-pink suit pants.

He closed his eyes. She kicked him. He opened them. She raised the barrel again, pointing at his open mouth, smiled and squeezed the trigger, ripping through his tongue and spine. His eyes went dull. This was not what she had envisioned for the mayor and the general, but her duty to Guillermo was completed. Now she could deal with her two rapists.

Chapter 44

Heather sat looking at the meadow below her feet and then at Jim and back again. He sat patiently, saying nothing, waiting for Heather to say what was on her mind. He knew what it would be, or he thought he did.

'We can't go on like we are.'

It was not the statement he'd expected. He waited again. She had been fine last night and earlier. Not bubbly as usual, but at least accepting that he was going to continue his assignments.

'We love each other. You know how much I love you, Jim, but I don't trust you the way I should. How can I? I don't really know you. I thought I did but I don't. I wonder sometimes who it is that I love. I love your body. I love your mind too, but only the part I know. I don't know if I love the rest or not. You keep it locked up and won't share it with me.'

Jim knew she was headed to a different place, a new place. A place that was deeper and that could have a big impact on them both. Her tone stopped him from saying anything.

She continued, 'I know more about you now than I did before Mexico, but it isn't enough. I fill in the blank places with imaginary thoughts, trying to conjure up a full picture. Deep down I want to know. I want to understand you. I resent that you won't tell me what is really in your heart and mind.'

Jim wanted to say something. He realized that the nine months on the ranch living a different life, a normal life, caused a change in Heather. Not to mention the addition of a child and a nanny.

'I...' he started to say. She waited but he didn't continue.

'Jim. We have, I have, everything I want. I have you and I love you, you know that. We have Pedro, you are special friends here with Duane, more than just having him as our ranch hand, we have Lola and our place in the world. But it won't work for me, even as we get so near to being where I've always dreamed about.'

'I don't know why I don't...'

'Why you won't open up, you mean? You can if you want to. I need to know all of you. You have to give me what is inside you. If you can't, I don't want you coming back to me. We have a child now to think of. What could be more important than what we have? Yet you gamble on throwing it away every time you leave. I can feel it inside me; you want to go. But you won't say so or tell me why.'

'I'm not sure I can express it right, or if you would like what you see.'

'What! You think that after Mexico, seeing death and watching you causing death and...and having to be only feet away as those two wonderful women were raped and beaten so horribly...you still think that I can't understand?' Tears welled up and she started to cry. 'Besides, understand what? I don't know what you do. Do you always kill people; is that what you do? Is it only bad people? Or anyone who gets in the way of the mission? I just barely know where you go. You won't share yourself with me. You won't tell me what you feel about what you do. Even last night, when I asked you, when I told you I really needed to know, you just closed up. Nothing will ever change that, but I can't be with you unless you trust me with yourself. Mexico changed me. It made me see what is important and how far I'm willing to go for what I believe in. It also made me understand what is missing, why, no matter how deep we pretend our relationship goes, it's still only superficial. I want to know you wholly, or I want to be free. You have to decide and you have to decide now.'

'I need to gather my thoughts. Let's go to the lake and we can talk later.'

'No. No, Jim. I'm done waiting patiently for you to return, for you to be ready. You talk to me now.'

'I...'

'You talk to me now. Right here. Everything. It's the time and the place. I never thought I would ever say this to you but if you don't—don't come back, not until you can open up. I'll take Pedro and move into the valley; I'll finalize the adoption as a single parent. You can go on as many missions as you like then. We can't pretend to have something special when it isn't. When it's full of half-truths and lies. We need to be complete. To blend our minds and really be together.'

'You didn't like what you saw of me in Mexico. What if that is a large part of who I am? You won't, can't understand. You don't have the experience; you have been too shelt—'

'Look at me. I'm not made of glass. I didn't like what I saw but I was—and am—glad that what you did saved my life, saved our friends' lives. Could I have done it? No, never. But maybe I can understand why you do. And you are going to have to take that chance. I might be naive about a lot of things but I know you in more ways than you might believe. You have to trust me...have to be with me completely. I want you. We need you.'

Jim felt a fear that he had never felt in the field. He could feel jitters vibrating inside him. *This is not the Heather I know. What is she doing?*

'You do know me. You know I think before I can let things out.'

Jim reached over and put his hands on the sides of her head. He looked into her eyes with eyes he fought to keep from misting over. Then he stood abruptly and walked away.

Chapter 45

Sheilla's satellite phone rang as she packed up her tent before heading to the lake.

'Sheilla, it's Mark.'

'Katarina just looked at a report from Mexico. A border town not far from Tubutama. Nine men shot. Two, however, tortured. I won't relay the whole gruesome scene to you but those two died very slowly and, ah,' he hesitated, 'by choking on cut off penises, um, not their own but each other's. And, ah, there were chair legs sticking out of their rectums. There's more if you want to hear it? Katarina said this definitely fits Najma's profile.'

'You are right to call me. I don't need to hear any more. I'll see it when I get back.'

'Talk to me,' said Will.

Sheilla ran her hand over her forehead and through her hair. Squeezed her upper lip with her right hand, holding it for a few seconds while she thought. 'Let's take a walk.'

Out on the meadow she said, 'This is Najma. It's her method more or less. Nine guys executed and sexually molested. Sounds like her but this seems a little over the top even for Najma. Something else is going on. Something doesn't add up still, someone like her—no, it's got to be her but...'

'We stop pussyfooting around. I want some real answers, facts.' The general put the satellite phone to his ear and gave a rash of orders. 'I'm not going to let Glenda and Kramer know that Jim, Brush, and Nielly's team are going to be on a ship just offshore. Jim doesn't know yet either. I want to know what is going on first with the CIA and what happened to Najma. If she is gone, they can deploy to Mexico if it seems right.'

'What about sending someone to Mexico first?' asked Sheilla.

'Probably would not be able to find out much in a cartel-run town. Even drones aren't going to tell us much. If she is on the loose, we have to worry about what she might do.

'We verify she is not at Gitmo pronto. Sheilla, that's your number one task back at the office. In the meantime, we look at what we should or can do if she is back in Tubutama and figure out what is going on with the CIA and its director. I feel sort of naked without more info.'

'You have anyone to call there?'

'I might,' said the general. 'There are a lot of good people there and I have a good relations with them. Let's not tip our hand yet.'

The quiet haze-filled translucent sky promised stifling heat. Thin, short-haired Captain Russ Kramer walked across the warming tarmac, his head seven inches taller than Glenda Rose Stuart's. Her fine ginger hair, pulled into a ponytail, protruded through the back opening of her navy-blue baseball cap. Walking briskly with them was a senior petty officer who had met them when they disembarked.

Glenda wore hiking boots and work clothes, befitting her role as a security inspector sent by the US Navy, but try as she might, she could not disguise her buxom shape. They made a colorful trio; the light-brown-skinned Kramer, who was also dressed in work clothes, contrasting with Glenda's translucent pale skin and Senior Petty Officer Gould's shaved head and shining black skin.

Gould wondered what this inspection was for but he had learned a long time ago not to attempt to understand the working of the navy. His first job was to make sure these two had what they needed for whatever it was they were inspecting. His real role was to protect the CIA's interest at X-Ray. Inspections like this were not normal so he was curious.

The three stopped when a seaman walked up to Gould, addressed him as Senior Chief Gould, and presented him with a piece of paper. Gould studied the sheet for no longer than two seconds, then nodded his head at the young seaman who turned and walked rapidly away.

'Per the request, you will have two experienced petty officers and a seaman that will help you. They are waiting at the gray building in front of us. If you need anything, have one of them find me,' said Gould.

'They have security clearances, access, and know the base well, I assume?' asked Glenda.

Chief Gould ignored the question and said, 'They have detailed maps in the office and will brief you on the base. Camp X-Ray is off-limits, other than that, you can all roam wherever your inspection takes you.' Kramer looked at Glenda questioningly as they walked to the building.

Glenda looked at the three men and asked, 'Who is senior?'

'I am,' answered Dougal.

'Do you have the engineering maps of the base?

'As much as we could find on short notice, ma'am.'

'Ms. Stuart will do for now. Let's get started.'

Chapter 46

Guillermo had formulated his plan to kill the American agents and, if all went well, the serpent's head at the bio terrorism center, Major General William Crystal. Immediately after Najma provided him with the information about who had destroyed his headquarters, he'd moved eight cartel members into the United States. They were now living in orchard houses less than forty miles from Wolf Canyon Ranch, near the town of Okanagan. They were experienced and carefully chosen. He wanted no mistakes.

Yet, as he sat there pondering, he wondered if a small incisive approach with Najma might be better than involving too many of his people. Maybe he should involve none at all. Let Najma do what she did best on her own. As he looked at the issues from all angles, Guillermo wondered if just killing the general would not have as much impact on his reputation, or if it would raise the ire of the US government. No, he thought, Colonel Johnson was the main target.

Most citizens of the United States had heard of cartels, but few suspected how pervasive cartels had become in the US. Cartel gangs supplied most of the drugs to US cities. The Siastra cartel was one of the largest. Guillermo could call upon hundreds of gang members in almost any part of the United States. There was always a question of DEA penetration into his organization, so, if he went ahead with the big operation, he wanted his men from Mexico in the US this time. He would use some locals but they would not know much about the plan until the last minute. Information was critical and he had no difficulty penetrating Fort Lewis. Drugs were as much a part of the military as guns and prostitutes. There was a user that worked for the general at the BWC and Vladislov had pulled a history.

The large plan that involved taking out the agents and the general, involved a key person who was not Mexican, nor a member of the cartel: he was simply the best assassin known to Guillermo—that is if there was anyone better than Najma. Alva Gager was trained originally by the Mossad; he now freelanced for governments and anyone with enough money to pay. He came at great cost. Guillermo had to pay two million up front and another two million to Gager when the job was complete.

Vladislav had three computer techs checking every detail available about Colonel Johnson, Major McGuire, and General Crystal. He had assembled detailed maps of the ranch terrain, where the phone lines had been installed, the electricity and the details of each building, obtained from the county records. All public and easily accessible.

In a few days, the bow-hunting season would start in Washington State and Guillermo's men could move freely near the ranch, posing as hunters. Then it would be time to bring Najma into the plan. She would assume control with the Israeli assassin as her second.

'Lazaro, bring in the woman,' commanded Guillermo.

Guillermo waited impatiently, which was not his nature. He paced the floor, walking erect in his London-tailored blue suit with a light blue shirt, open at the collar.

'Enter.' He turned as Lazaro walked into the room with Najma. But it wasn't Najma. Guillermo couldn't help but smile as he walked toward her. She looked nearly identical with one exception. Her eyes were not those of Najma—Najma emanated evil, while this woman's eyes were soft and caring.

'Please sit.' He nodded to Lazaro to leave.

'Has Lazaro explained your task?'

'Yes,' responded Ayla. Vladislav had searched hundreds of thousands of driver's license photos in the US, using a facial recognition program he had written especially for this task of impersonating Najma.

'You are comfortable in your room?'

'Yes, Mr. Vasquez, very comfortable.'

'Very good, Lazaro is outside the door and will escort you back and I'll see you in the morning.'

'Good night, sir. I can't tell you how much I appreciate this opportunity.'

Guillermo remained on his sofa and waved as if to say it was nothing, while she turned and left the expensively decorated room.

Ayla, whose family was poor, had been told only that it was legal and Guillermo needed an actress for one week in order to catch a thief. She would live in a large house, be well guarded and come to no harm. Cartel men, dressed in well-cut suits, had approached her at her home in El Paso. A man presented his card embossed with his Dallas-based law firm's name. He'd explained that his employer was very rich and needed an actress for a business reason at his estate.

Shown a picture of Najma, the family were stunned by the similarity, all except for the eyes. Their coldness transcended the picture. They handed the picture back and their thoughts turned only to money. The employer would pay her the sum of one hundred thousand dollars if she agreed to leave now and another like sum in a week when she would return home.

That amount of money was enormous to her and her brother, mother and father, and the thought that they would be rich in another week glazed their minds. The man repeatedly said she would be safe. There was never a thought of saying no. The cartel man passed a small shiny-brown leather designer briefcase to the father who stared with wide eyes at the money. They said if she accepted the offer that time was important and they would have to leave immediately.

Blinded by the money and the well-dressed lawyer, the family could think of nothing other than they had finally won a lottery.

'I need to pack first,' responded Ayla.

'There is no need. We will be at the airport in less than thirty minutes. The plane is fully supplied with anything you might want and no doubt much more. You will be able to keep any of the clothes and other items when we return here. Your new employer is very generous.'

Ayla looked back at her mother, father, and brother as she walked down their front steps along the sidewalk. Near the intersection, a black BMW pulled up beside them and after they got inside, it drove rapidly down the street. The cartel didn't want a nosy neighbor to see a fancy car parked in front of Ayla's house.

When she looked back at her home, she couldn't see it well. The overly bright streetlight that usually made their front yard seem like daytime must have gone out.

The family waved goodbye to Ayla and went back inside their home all smiles. Two men had remained with some papers for them to sign.

'Can you believe it,' said the father as he lovingly punched his son's shoulder.

'Why don't you three sit on the sofa and I'll explain these documents and you can sign them.' The sofa faced the TV and the front door, dividing the small room from the kitchen.

Guillermo's man smiled at the family, giving no indication as the other man quietly walked up behind the sofa. He hit the father with a leather wrapped pipe. The man in front quickly grabbed the teenage boy while the other man placed a plastic bag over the women's head, holding her while she struggled, the bag blowing up and sucking in as she tried to breathe. Then her body went limp. The man moved behind the boy and took out a syringe, pulled up his sleeve and gave him a large dose of heroin.

The boy slowly slumped on the sofa. They then picked up the man and rammed his head against the doorjamb, pulled the plastic bag off the woman and carried the boy to the kitchen where they dropped him on the floor in front of the gas stove. The dose was not enough to kill him. It was not their intent. They just wanted him unconscious.

One of the men turned on the gas stove and placed a book of matches by the limp boy. The other went into the living room and lit two candles on an end table next to the sofa. They turned and walked out the back door. The alley was completely deserted as they walked out and around the first street corner. A car quickly pulled up and they sped away. They drove two blocks to the front street and waited at the corner.

Several minutes later the house exploded in a fireball, ballooned out and then collapsed on itself. The driver, dressed in work clothes, turned to the two men in suits and said, 'Why all the fucking trouble? Could have just shot them. No big deal in this neighbor-hood. People die all the time.'

'Let's get out of here. We just follow orders. We were told it had to look like an accident.'

As they drove down the street, three houses were on fire. No one looked in the departing car's direction.

Guillermo picked up a printout of a story from the *El Paso Times*. The gas explosion had killed three people and a fourth was missing. Before the fire company could get there, two other houses had burned nearly to the ground. After autopsies of the badly burned residents, and an arson and police investigation, it had been determined that the family's teenage son had been high on drugs. He had started the gas stove, then passed out on the floor. Candles in the living room ignited the gas, destroying the house. The explosion threw the father against a doorjamb, probably killing him before fire consumed his body.

The causes seemed obvious to the police. They never questioned why there was no searing of the woman's lungs, perhaps she had died immediately from the explosion. Nor why the son had passed out on the kitchen floor. The morgue was always busy with deaths from the poor part of El Paso. They closed the case, stamped it as accidental deaths and went on to other investigations.

Martin was terrified and his head ached. He knew he had been abducted but could see nothing out of the smelly hood that covered his throbbing head. He was coming to and had no idea how long he had been in the car as it slowed and drove over some paving stones, making his head hurt all the more. Moments later, it stopped not more than thirty feet from where Lazaro had just walked Ayla back to her room.

They escorted him several dozen yards, threw him down on a hard floor, pulled off his pants and underwear, tied his hands and feet, and then he was strapped to a chair. Someone jerked the hood off and slammed a door shut, leaving him in the dark.

Chapter 47

A light breeze scented the warm rising noonday air with pine on the ridgetop. The last of the night's dampness ascended from the valley below the small lake.

Pedro had wasted no time getting in the lake and was splashing, climbing in and out and jumping in again.

The general was thinking that kids had more energy than he could deal with and maybe a family wasn't such a good way to spend his retirement.

'General, we need to get back. I feel like an idiot sitting out here. It is making me nervous. We have the mission starting in Cuba and the whole thing with Najma leaves me feeling jittery.'

The general moved close to Sheilla, his face turning serious, and said, 'I learned something a long time ago in combat. In between action there is always some downtime. If only for a few minutes, you embrace it. Take every second of it. We have sat phones to communicate. Glenda and Kramer are just getting their bearings at Gitmo. Everything is planned. This is our few minutes of downtime. Carpe diem, Sheilla.'

As if on cue his sat phone rang.

He put it down and said, 'Not really away at all, are we? Neilly's arrived just offshore from Gitmo.'

Sheilla puffed out her cheeks, then exhaled the air. 'This is hard, General. We go back soon, right?'

The general didn't answer and just stood looking at her. Then a look of resignation came over her face. 'OK. Do you want to go swimming?'

The general looked around as if he expected to see other people. Then he looked at Sheilla.

She relaxed a little. A few minutes wouldn't matter. 'Hey, no worries. I found out yesterday that I had to get over the idea that my underclothes are any different from a bathing suit. Just terminology as Jim said.' The general raised an eyebrow thinking that there was a transformation in her today. And then he thought, *What I know about women's underwear you could pack in a sardine can.*

They both alternated between acting as if they were ignoring each other and happily talking as they stripped down to their underwear. Sheilla had on a black bra mostly obscured by her long auburn hair and lacey black panties. Her skin was pale against the smooth black rock surrounding the lake, while her hair shimmered in the bright light as it swayed with her movements.

The general was sturdy and compact, covered with light brown hair and wearing army olive-drab army issue boxer shorts. As far back as he could remember he had swum in rivers and lakes with his men, starting with B-52 craters filled with murky water in Vietnam. He could never remember being alone with a woman at a remote lake like this before. As self-conscious as he was, underneath he wanted to be here.

'Last one in is a rotten egg,' yelled Sheilla as she moved quickly to the rock edge and jumped in.

'Not fair,' boomed the general as he started to dive in.

'No, Will, don't dive.' But he was already in the air. A gush of water covered Sheilla as the general tucked into a cannon ball.

She held her mouth and then his head popped out of the water.

'No worries, girl, I could see you were only waist deep.'

Sheilla reached out and splashed water at him shaking the dark strands of wet hair and pursing her lips. 'You had me scared for a second. I flashed on that guy in the movie in Australia that dove in and killed himself. He was Japanese, um...'

'No idea,' said Will.

'I got it, *Japanese Story,*' said Sheilla jubilantly. 'That's it, all right. The title doesn't fit the outback in Australia.'

The general pushed off the bottom: floating on his back he looked at the sky thinking this was OK, being here. A private pool in the mountains.

Pedro frolicked in the background of his thoughts but barely penetrated his conscious mind.

The general was having a good time, mostly relaxed but tinged with a little apprehension, having nearly zero experience with the opposite sex other than at a professional level. Sheilla, for her part, was oblivious to the general's thoughts. Even if she had an interest other than friendship, she wouldn't know how to cross that boundary any more than he did. In spite of his inexplicable underlying tension, the general was happy they were together and having fun.

Sheilla laid a towel on a smooth flat black rock near the shore. They both lay down feeling the heat of the early afternoon sun removing the chill of the water. There was no getting Pedro out of the lake.

'Thank you, General, for bringing me. It really has been special and you were right, it is safe out here. Nobody, except the office, even knows where we are and I haven't seen another soul. Safer than the city.'

'Sheilla, out here away from the center, please start calling me Will.'

'OK then, Will.'

'Maybe sometime we could do something I have always thought about and never gotten around to: landing in a mountain meadow and having a picnic.'

Sheilla smiled. 'That sounds wonderful,' she said, wondering why the general was talking with such a soft low voice again. Maybe because it was so quiet out there, she reasoned. 'What happened to your voice, Will?'

'Not commanding anyone and I was enjoying the quiet and didn't want to throw my big voice in with the softer sounds of nature.' He wondered if that was the real explanation. He looked up toward the sun, shading his eyes with a hand. 'Time to start back.' He turned and gave her a small, serious-looking smile and then stood up. He was unsure what he should do. For a second he wanted to move over and kiss her but whether it was remembering she worked for him and he couldn't be involved with an employee or the fact that he had not kissed a woman for years, something stopped him. *Nonsense, mountain air,* he said to himself. He started to put his clothes back on.

'Thanks, Will. This has been a beautiful and wonderful experience.'

'It has for me too. When we get back to camp with Heather and Jim, I have a feeling that is going to change.'

'Yeah, neither of them have been jumping up and down happy.'

They grabbed their things, managed to get Pedro dry and set off down the ridge toward the meadow.

'Nothing for it but to do it,' said General Crystal.

'Funny sort of a saying.'

'Just something I remember from my early officer training.'

Lola fidgeted with the kitchen things. Nusmen had his back to a tree with legs stretched out. To a casual observer he would seem to be reading a novel. And it did bring him pleasure being absorbed in a book, even though the title was *Macro Molecules*. Shuskin was about six feet away with his rucksack open, arranging his new belongings. He lined them up in the dirt, toothbrush, toothpaste, hairbrush, penknife, an unused red handkerchief; three candy bars, four granola bars. He had never owned so many new things. He just liked looking at them as a child would her dolls or the same way that Pedro admired his knife.

They were all fixated on what they were doing and didn't see the general, Sheilla, and Pedro walking past the helicopter in their direction. About twenty feet out the general boomed, 'Nice day isn't it.' Lola took a deep breath, crossed herself and said, 'Mon Dios.' Shuskin started to cover his things. Then as they neared the kitchen area, the general laughed when he saw Nusmen reading a chemistry book. He looked at Sheilla. 'Amazing. He never stops, even out here. Let's get Jim and load up. Enough R&R for one day. Sheilla, see if you can find them and get Jim ready.'

Jim walked to where he had left Heather. He looked back at the camp and didn't see her. He had no desire to talk to anyone. He took what he thought was the next best course. She probably did not want to talk to anyone any more than he did and had gone into the woods, or headed to the ridgetop. He circled slowly around where they'd had their argument.

He found an upturned decaying piece of wood. He went past it and immediately spotted some other signs of someone having gone through the dense trees. Following his sixth sense as much as looking for signs, he walked, pushing his way through straggly small conifers struggling to get out of the undercover and into the open. Not far along, he found some bark and moss scraped off an old deadfall where her shoe had slipped. He picked up his pace as best as he could. She was staying at the same elevation, not climbing.

As he walked out of the dense trees into a small meadow, he saw her sprawled facedown in the short mountain grass. He watched her for a minute, she wasn't moving. He walked straight to her. A few feet away she abruptly turned her head in the direction of the approaching steps. She didn't move. He continued straight to her and seconds before he arrived she turned on her side, held her arms out and they collapsed together in a tight hug.

For a minute, neither said anything. Then she started to cry again. 'I'm sorry; I don't want to lose you. I don't understand what I'm feeling,' she whispered and started to really cry, gasping for breath between the sobs. 'I-I can't be without you. I'm afraid. Please, Jim. Please, please, please.'

He put a hand on each side of her head and turned her face to him. He looked into her red-rimmed eyes, held her tight and put his forehead on hers. He held it there with both looking into bleary eyes.

She could feel his eyes start to curl at the edges. She started to rotate her head slowly back and forth. He did the same in the opposite direction. Then in spite of herself, she started to smile, and almost as fast let out a gasp and tears started again. Suddenly a hiccup and another. 'Oh,' a fast inhalation of breath. 'Oh no.'

'I'll come back to you; both of you.'

She looked at him in between hiccups and tried to kiss him but it didn't work as her lips jumped to his nose. 'Try to pretend you are drinking out of a glass backward,' said Jim.

'Just hold me for a while.'

Little by little, the hiccups slowed as she clung to him as hard as she could.

A knock on the office door. Seaman Smith opened it. 'Ms. Stuart?'

Glenda opened the envelope she had just been handed and read, *Called off base for emergency ship repairs in the harbor. Meet at your quarters 21:30 tomorrow night. Grant.*

Glenda's face tightened. Was the general's old friend putting her off or was he really called away? Well, it would be an opportunity to make the cover look good doing some inspecting and maybe they would learn something. She turned to Dougal. 'Show us our quarters, then take a break. We meet here at fourteen hundred.'

Heather and Jim walked back into camp.

The general watched them move past the grazing llamas and toward the kitchen where they were all having coffee surrounded by the primary colored panniers, including a reluctant Shuskin who had almost forgotten what coffee tasted like. General Will Crystal imperceptibly nodded to himself. *One problem solved,* he thought.

Pedro sat whittling a stick with the knife Heather had given him with instructions to be careful. It was a peaceful idyllic camping scene.

No one said anything except Lola, who was muttering about not having a proper stove. Heather tucked her lower lip up and held it tight. It was something she did when serious. Still holding Jim's hand she sat on the ground and pulled him down beside her. 'I could live here my whole life,' she said.

'You no serious, we no live here. This no home.'

'I didn't mean that we would live here, Lo, just that it is very nice here.'

The general lifted his coffee cup. 'Here's to special places and special people. Now let's move out.'

'And new experiences,' said Sheilla.

Heather looked at the slightly cleaner old man. 'Shuskin, you going to toast with us?'

He looked down sheepishly, made a tight-lipped forced smile. Not showing his stained teeth, which added to his cleaner look. Then he lifted the Lexan coffee mug. As Heather watched him, her look showed that she was pleased.

Nusmen just rolled his eyes, still feeling agitated.

Heather turned and looked at the group, Shuskin, Nusmen, Lola and then took Jim aside. 'You taking anything with you?' Jim shook his head. 'In that case let's walk out by that boulder.'

Old Man Shuskin watched them cross the meadow. He had been watching people in the mountains much of his life. The two stood far off with Heather rubbing Jim's arms, giving him a hug and a kiss. Then they did something strange. They put their foreheads together for several seconds.

'I'm glad we could do this,' said General Crystal in a normal voice, glancing at Sheilla. Then in his booming voice, he continued, 'Time to rock and roll. Load up Pedro. You ready for a short ride in my chopper?

'Yes sir.'

'Get a move on it then.'

Minutes later a wide-eyed excited Pedro jumped out of the general's helicopter, stood straight and saluted. 'Thank you sir!'

The general walked toward the camp and said in his commanding voice. 'Everyone ready? Nusmen carry their gear over.' Then he walked up to Nusmen and looked in straight in the eye. ' After we leave you've got a job here. Help them pack out and do it right or I'll extend your vacation.'

Chapter 48

Alva Gager walked slowly around Guillermo's living room, studying the paintings. Alva had been born in Italy near Rome. His father was Israeli, giving Alva dual Israeli-Italian citizenship. Six feet tall, he had a Mediterranean complexion with a dark three-day stubble that matched his black, slicked-back hair.

'Remarkable use of purple,' he commented as he admired a five-foot-tall Francis Bacon painting. Nearly one third of the canvas contained a mesmerizing lavender-purple rectangle. Above it was the more typical Bacon trademark distorted figure. 'I admire him but have never been a great fan. This, however, is truly wonderful. And this too,' he added as he stood admiring a painting with a large gray field overlaid with tiny maroon ellipses. 'The best era for Poons, I think, yes.' Each wall held paintings from various eras, Miro, Duchamp, Picasso, Magritte, Stella.

'I am very pleased. Many people enter this room but few appreciate what's on the walls as much as you have.' With a rare and twisted smile Guillermo continued, 'If I could hazard a guess, I would say most who have been here dislike them. Please sit, Alva.' The manservant appeared and they each ordered a brandy.

'You are comfortable?' asked Guillermo.

'Very, your hacienda is as remarkable as these paintings. The outward appearance is, shall I say, an interesting façade. It disguises a formidable set of defenses, I think.'

'It is adequate, yes.' Guillermo held up his glass. 'To an agreeable ending. I might say an interesting challenge for you.'

'She will not be a compliant target,' said Alva. And then, 'It is always easier to kill someone than it is to keep from being killed.'

'Yes, the hunter has the advantage.'

'I have watched the footage you sent and I must compliment you on her look-alike.'

'Since we first discussed this, something has happened that provides an opportunity.' Guillermo sipped his brandy and then continued. 'We captured a man today in the village, an employee of the CIA.'

Alva remained quiet looking at Guillermo, not liking the sound of the CIA's involvement.

'For some time I have been disturbed by the fact that there was no news of Najma's escape. As you know, my plan assumed that it would be brought to the attention of those we are interested in, the general and the colonel. That has not happened.'

'And you have discovered the reason why not, I presume?'

'The CIA has kept her escape a secret for political reasons. I do not know how but they have traced Najma to me here at the hacienda. In other circumstances this would be a problem, however, now I see it as an opportunity.'

'They have sent a team to recapture her. She goes back to Guantánamo and no one is the wiser about her escape. My idea is simple, we allow the CIA agent to observe our fake Najma's death, then allow him to escape so he will take the news back with him that she is dead. I imagine they can then find a way to say she died without fear of political repercussions.'

'The Americans will not be expecting Najma.'

'It is necessary as the Biological Warfare Center and the CIA are all looking for information on each other's computers, just as we are on theirs, so my computer tech has informed me. It is better that we stop their interest now. It would not be beyond the general's warfare center to send people here to get her perhaps as the CIA has done.'

Guillermo once again sipped his brandy and looked at the assassin who enjoyed his paintings.

'This is very good,' said Alva, sipping his brandy.

'Tonight we will allow the CIA man to see Najma. He will be bound and she will go to him with orders to torture him but do no serious damage. Later a guard will make it possible for him to undo his restraints and escape the only way open to him, down a hall that leads to a tunnel and the desert. Najma's double will be near the end preventing him from leaving. My men will start shooting at the man but will hit Najma's double and kill her. The CIA agent will see her die in front of him and then we will allow him to escape.'

'There are many possible complications, no? He might not try to escape for instance.'

'That is possible but not probable when you think about it. Perhaps the man will take her weapon and put a bullet in her head before he escapes; that would be a fortunate development for us. We observe him and in the morning send a vehicle with some peasants who will be convinced to give him a lift into town. He tells his story and, voila, everyone thinks Najma is dead and neither the CIA nor the general will bother us further. Neither Najma, nor you, Alva, will be expected. You should be able to terminate the agents and the general easily.'

'It's too hot to be out.'

'Knock it off, Kramer, you really are a desk jockey. Can't work without air- con.'

To make their cover look good, Glenda Rose and Russ Kramer visited the guard stations, busily taking notes, and were now walking the perimeter fence with their helpers.

'Those buildings ahead are X-Ray. We can't go in there but we can walk between the building wall and the fence,' said Dougal.

'What's the big deal about this X-Ray?' asked Glenda.

Kramer wiped his forehead with a handkerchief that was already soaked with sweat. 'There's shade by that building, let's sit down for a while. I need a drink.'

Glenda didn't know if Kramer was actually trying to be smart and get them close to X-Ray or was really as exhausted as he was acting. They wouldn't learn anything just sitting there, so why bother? He must really just want to sit down, she concluded.

They walked over and lined their backs up against the shaded wall.

'Oh man, sitting and water never felt so good.' Kramer sighed contentedly.

They sat for a minute and then Seaman Smith said excitably, 'Holy shit, look at that!' He pointed to the fence almost directly in front of them. 'An elephant could walk through that.'

They jumped up except for Kramer and trotted to the tall gash where the fence had been cut.

'Dougal, get the CID out here. Maybe they can figure out why it has been cut. Maybe someone is going in and out. Kramer! Get over here now,' yelled Glenda. Kramer struggled to his feet and walked to Glenda.

She said quietly as they walked a few feet away from the others, 'Go back to your shade and call the operations room and tell them about the fence. Tell them I had no choice but to ask for the MP investigators, otherwise it would look funny for us as inspectors. Tell them too that the hole is right next to Camp X-Ray.'

Najma's hair was growing longer, regaining its raven-black luster. It was now long enough to obscure the raised, red starfish mark behind her right ear.

She looks slightly more at ease, thought Guillermo, *a little more open.*

'Will you lunch with me today, Najma?' he asked.

'All right.'

'What would you like?'

'Whatever you are having.'

'I am pleased with both your actions in Nogales and with our enemies in Mexicali. Are you ready to venture north?'

'Of course.'

She never said much, and her terse way of talking would have earned anyone else a shallow grave. Guillermo though was not concerned, knowing she would soon die. She had served him well but she would be too much of a liability after killing American officers in the US. They would never stop searching for her and likely him. The better plan was to have her die and end it.

'Perhaps another week and the plans for our termination of the Americans will be in place. I will discuss them with you then. In the meantime, I want you to stay inside the hacienda. The CIA will be looking for you by now. You are comfortable here, aren't you?'

'Yes.'

'Good, I have a little activity for you here. It may bring you some small enjoyment.'

Guillermo held up his glass of Chateauneuf-du-Pape. 'To the end of our mutual enemies.'

Jim watched Heather and Pedro grow small in the meadow from the back seat. His thoughts, never far from reality, knew that he was happy with Heather and that he was also happy to be leaving. He wondered how to explain that to her, how to explain it to himself. *It is just the way I am.* His world was out there somewhere and he knew he couldn't do without it. If he had to choose? He dropped the thought. He didn't want to think about it. Go with the flow and things would work out, or change, as the case may be and the choice would be made for him.

The general said into his mic, 'Turning out right.'

The Huey lifted under the general's steady hand with Sheilla in the co-pilot's seat. They waved out the front and then the general turned to his right and hovered for a few seconds. Jim had immediately moved to the side. Heather stood holding Pedro's hand forty feet away. Behind them, near the kitchen, Nusmen, Lola, and Shuskin. Off to their right, the closest llama, Cinnabar, tugged at the end of his lead line as the heavy helicopter beat the afternoon air on what had been a peaceful meadow in the mountains.

Heather's hair blew wildly but she managed to ignore it and sent Jim a kiss with her hand, and then made a fist with a thumb up. The chopper lifted higher and lightly banked to its left, heading toward the top of the ridge, the small lake below and the soaring Cascades ahead. Jim continued to look back as Heather and Pedro grew smaller, then disappeared behind the trees. Remorse set in. Now that he was leaving he wanted to return to her. *A safe thought with the general flying in the opposite direction.* Jim knew his thoughts and wants were a contradiction. *Nusmen better take care of them. Probably more like Heather taking care of him though,* he thought.

The general adjusted gauges and announced to Sheilla, 'We're heading one-niner-five through that low part of the mountains straight ahead and then directly to the BWC. Take that stick, the one between your legs, and hold it steady. You have it?'

'Huh, yeah.'

'It's all yours.'

The general turned around and winked at Jim. They both knew that for a few seconds nothing would happen and it was not difficult to fly a moving helicopter. The general had locked the power and the rudders could take care of themselves for a short while. He then looked at Sheilla who was holding the cyclic for dear life completely rigid.

'Hold your hand steady but otherwise you can relax. You have

to feel the subtle movements. Keep holding it, I have the controls.'
He then pushed slightly to the left and then the right. 'See how a
slight movement causes it to change direction. You have the
controls.' And he let go. 'Go ahead and try it.'

She still looked nearly petrified but did as he told her. Then she
got a huge smile on her face and turned to Will and said, 'Who
would have ever thought? I'm flying a helicopter.'

'You are indeed and a mighty fine job too. You want a little
music? Nobody out here to talk to on the radio and the music player
will cut off if someone calls.'

Sheilla was interested to see what his choice of music would be.
Wagner like in *Apocalypse Now*? The general hit a switch that cut
Jim out of their communication. 'This has been a nice day, or did I
already say that before?'

'You did and it has been.'

'I cut Jim's mic off, he can't hear us. He's OK. He just likes to
ponder on his own. At first he won't like music cutting into his
thoughts but then I think he'll be all right with it. Might relax him.'

Will turned a knob and the volume came up, Sheilla was
amazed. 'Who is it?'

'Jefferson Airplane. I thought it would be appropriate. The one
playing is "3/5 of a Mile in 10 Seconds." One of my favorites.'

'Cool, sixties oldies.' She looked over at the general and could
see his eyes dancing to the music. Then she started a slight dance,
moving her hips to the rhythm, relaxing but still gripping the cyclic.
Will took back the controls as another song started out more softly
and built up. The general followed the sound, banked the helicopter
down and to the left, picking up speed as it dropped lower and then
back to the right in a steep ascending arc that felt to Sheilla as
though they were floating straight up.

' "Embryonic Journey," ' said the general.

'Is that what the maneuver is called?

'It's the song's name. It's fun flying with the music sometimes.'

Will glanced back at Jim who squinted his eyes at his boss and old friend, then gave a slight, lopsided smile. The general knew the music had gotten to him. ' "White Rabbit" is next.'

Sheilla sat listening, thinking that people were strange, or was it they were interesting? She never expected the general to play music and certainly not this kind of music. Apparently, the general knew that Jim liked it too. She had only thought of them as serious and perhaps that was the way they thought about her too. Now she was seeing another side to them.

The mountains approached with snowy peaks rising on both sides. They skimmed over ridges as they streamed along an invisible road between higher peaks.

'It's wild and beautiful. I could stay up here all day,' said Sheilla, meaning every word.

Chapter 49

Martin had never felt worse in his life. Last night he had tried to sleep but his head still ached. His hands were bound behind and tied to a chair. A chair that did not even wiggle when he shook his body. It was attached to the floor but he could not see how. His bare bottom felt dead, sitting motionless on the hard wood, and the circulation to his legs was cut off, leaving them numb. There was blood crusted on his right eye and he could do nothing to remove it. His lips were parched. They had fed him nothing, nor given him water.

He considered that might be for the best since they had not allowed him to go to the bathroom either. He had finally given in and peed, and grateful that that was all he had to do, at least so far. His urine had quickly run off the chair. Maybe that is was why they had taken his pants. The smallest sliver of light penetrated into his room from outside, which told him it was still light but its color was dimming by the minute. *Evening.*

Suddenly the door opened. At first blinded by the light, his eyes quickly adjusted as it was only a faint light from the setting sun. Then a single central bright overhead light came on. A very tough-looking Mexican pulled out a long knife and jabbed it into a wood shelf, then casually reached behind the knife and took hold of a wooden baseball bat. The man had massive hands attached to his oversized body topped with a bald head. The bat looked like a toy in his grasp. He started to walk toward Martin, slapping the bat on his other hand. Martin began to tremble, realizing just how much trouble he was in. He fervently wished he'd gone to Nogales.

Another shadow appeared in the door. Martin could not see behind the man and was certain that he was about to be beaten to death. Then a woman's voice said, 'Step aside.' The man slowly obeyed. Najma walked over to the giant and took the bat. She immediately jammed it into the big man's stomach, doubling him over, then said, 'Out. You have to wait your turn.' She walked back and closed the door behind him as he shuffled out.

Martin relaxed. She had saved him. Then shock penetrated his foggy brain: *Najma.*

'What's your name?' she demanded.

He stuttered for a second and then said, 'Martin.'

'Very good, Martin. What is your occupation?'

'Ah…a teacher on vacation.'

She walked over to him and said, 'Not so good, Martin.' She tapped him on the side of the head with the bat in nearly the exact place that the policeman had hit him. It was not hard but it made his head feel like it was going to split.

'Would you care to repeat that answer?'

'I work for the government,' he blurted out.

She took off her shawl and carefully hung it from a nail. Martin was dizzy but he could still see that Najma was wearing a thin blouse showing well-shaped breasts and skin-tight black leather pants. His confused mind wobbled between the pain, fright, and her. Exactly what she wanted.

She walked to him and straddled his legs, sitting on them, looking directly into his eyes: she reached up and wiped the crusted blood then the fresh blood now running down from his ear. Her touch caused him to grimace. Her coal-black eyes never left his. In spite of himself, he began to shiver. Then the realization crept into his mind, *She's going to kill me after she tortures me.* 'Najma,' he whispered.

'Government man, just how is it that you know who I am?'

'I, ah, heard the guard say it.'

She reached down with her right hand to his testicles and played lightly with them, massaging them in her fingers. Then she rubbed his penis softly. Martin's mouth dropped a little. 'I do not get you excited?' She moved closer, continuing her massage. She rolled her tongue over her lips and rubbed her breast with her left hand until her nipple pushed hard and firm against the thin black fabric. In spite of himself, Martin could feel himself responding.

'You had me worried for a minute, Martin.' She made a deep low groaning noise that sounded more animal than human.

Martin's breathing became more rapid as she continued with expert fingers. His pain was leaving him as she stroked his now rigid penis. He closed his eyes wondering why she was doing this. She moved her hand and cupped his testicles. He opened his eyes and looked at her with softer eyes.

The searing pain shot through every part of his body as she clamped both testicles in her hand. He instantly became nauseous; his torso felt sick and weak, sweat beaded on his forehead. He could feel her looking at him but saw only flashing lights. Then he heard a voice as she relaxed her grip.

'Martin, when I ask you something, try to be specific. Who do you work for?'

Martin hesitated and she instantly squeezed again.

'The CIA,' he blurted; he couldn't help it.

'That is better, much better,' she purred.

Najma would have enjoyed herself if she knew she could carry on and eventually watch this man die. But she had been told under no circumstances to hurt him so much that he could not escape. Which meant no broken legs.

Suddenly, in her hand she held a small double bladed knife. She touched its point on his forehead and slowly pulled it down the bridge of his nose, across his lips, and continued down the front of his shirt, easily cutting off a button with the razor-sharp blade. She grasped his now limp penis, holding it just below the head and then positioned the knife so as to be able to slice off its end. Martin felt his head spinning. *She is going to cut off my penis,* he screamed to himself.

'Another question for you. Exactly what do you do for the CIA?'

'I'll tell you everything; just don't cut me, please.'

With lightning speed, she sliced a small piece from the tip. Martin began screaming. He had never screamed so loud before. Outside the cartel men looked at each other with knowing looks. They were glad the bitch was on their side.

'Shut up, Martin, you make so much noise. If you don't stop I will cut something else.' She placed the blade by his ear. He thrashed his head sideways in a panic, yelped, and she instantly clamped his testicles again. He felt paralyzed. Through the pain he didn't realize that he still had his balls. She put the knife under his earlobe and looked at his distorted face. 'I believe you will tell me what I ask.'

Through a raspy voice she heard, 'I will. I'm just an office worker on a vacation.' She smiled, at the same time grabbing his head in her left hand and slicing up, smoothly severing his ear. This time Martin surpassed his other screams. Outside the cartel men began to look uncomfortable and muttered, 'The devil is in her. *El diablo es temido por todo el mundo.* The devil is feared by everybody.' They crossed themselves saying, 'She is not human.' The larger man knew he was going to have to go into that room soon. It would be playacting, but still he didn't want to go. He was to throw her out of the room, breaking Martin's chair loose and then dropping a knife near his feet. He wondered if that meant she would come for him later even though it was acting, and a quiver passed through his massive frame.

Najma stood, casually bent over his ear, which was lying on the floor, and speared it with her knife tip. Then she held it in front of him. 'Are you hungry, Martin?'

'I'm Martin Pearson, head of analytical operations,' Martin spit out rapid-fire. 'I'm thirty-nine years old. Worked for the CIA since college.' He would go on forever if she didn't hurt him anymore. 'Started working in Guiana because French fluent. Ask me anything. What do you want?' Martin said, sobbing.

'Well, Martin, truthfully, I don't really care about any of what you just said. What I want is to hear you scream.' Martin almost fainted. His mind went blank. This woman was going to kill him bit by bit. Then in desperation he pleaded, 'Please stop, you must want something. I'll do anything. I'm not poor, I can get you things. Passports.'

What Martin didn't realize was that he was trying to reason with someone whose language he did not understand. She had just told him what she wanted. 'Martin, I want to kill you but very slowly.' She walked behind him while he squirmed uselessly. She would have to do this right. Najma grasped his bound hand and pushed her blade under his thumbnail. Martin could not help himself, he wailed liked a lone crazed animal until his eardrums hurt, his missing ear matching throbs beat for beat with his wounded thumb and penis. 'Very good, Martin. That was good. Perhaps I won't cut it off now,' as she captured his eyes with hers. Then slicing through flesh and bone, she did. He screamed but his voice was getting hoarse and he was almost beyond pain. Najma needed him distracted.

What he didn't feel was her cutting through most of the cord that tied his hands. If he tried, he could break free. It was time. The door burst open and the large man walked in. He pointed at Najma and said, 'Out, now.'

'Make me.'

'Orders. You can have him after we're finished.'

'I don't care about your orders.'

She held the small blade pointed at him, between her index and middle finger. He extracted the knife from the wood shelf and casually walked toward her. She jumped behind Martin and the big man swiped a hand at her, hitting Martin on the shoulder. It felt like he had been hit with a massive club. The man then pushed sideways, tipping over Martin's chair and ripping out the bolts securing it.

Najma jabbed at him, catching him in the hand. He bellowed and dropped his knife at Martin's feet, then Najma walked out the door with the big man close behind. The door slammed, closing behind them.

Martin lay bleeding, wishing he was dead. His penis was on fire, but his ear, or where it had been, sent a throb into the center of his brain. He didn't know what was missing from his hand but it beat its own pain-rhythm. Then he remembered that she had cut off part of his penis and he lost himself in tears. This couldn't be happening. She or the giant would be back and it would only get worse.

Najma sneered at the big man who was holding his hand. Lazaro walked into the hall and motioned for the men to follow him. 'Najma, you are finished for the night,' he said and then added, 'Gracias. Beno, get that hand taken care of. The rest of you know what to do. I want one of you sitting there where you will pretend to be asleep. Another standing there, facing away from the door. That only leaves one way for him to go. After he leaves the room, give him a few minutes and start talking loudly. He can only run down the tunnel. It may take some time. Do not look around, he has to think he is getting away without you seeing him.'

The men gave no thought to disobeying. Lazaro was the top enforcer and would have them killed or worse, turned them over to the loco woman if he was unhappy. They knew this was serious, straight from Guillermo. They silently obeyed. Lazaro walked into the room. He looked at Martin and said, 'Leave the worthless Americano where he is until Beno gets his hand taken care of. He will be very angry, the Americano's fault. He likes to break bones with his bat.' Then he shook his head, as though sorry for Martin. Then he walked out without latching the door.

Heather felt tired, still upset to see Jim fly away. She needed to calm down. Her best way was to sit with her notebook and try to write a poem. 'Lola, I am going out by the llamas for a few minutes. Pedro will help you if you need anything. Talk to him in Spanish. He starts school in a month and they will only speak English. He needs to keep up with his Spanish.'

She pulled her notebook out of her rucksack and walked over toward Meteor. She sat against a large rock and watched him for a few minutes, wondering how long he would live. Packing wouldn't be the same without him. Then Shasta and his limp made her even more sad. The thought of losing them made her remember almost losing Pipestone to the cougar. She looked back at Shuskin huddled over his stuff and wondered what she would do with him.

She opened her well-worn black notebook and thumbed the pages until she got to her last entry. She had written a poem title but then couldn't think what to say. She looked down at it: *Love is a long way to drive.* Sort of a seventies rock sound. She had no inspiration and then decided that writing a poem was beyond her today. She would just write something and maybe it would help her relax.

She put the blue ballpoint pen on the page and held it there thinking about Jim and how he was away again, not there to wake up with her in the morning, and she started to write.

If I could live just one way each day, it would be to wake my conscious mind with the feel of your breath mingling with mine. To feel the soft touch of your lips on my neck, the caress of your fingers in my hair and the vibrations as your skin touches mine as the first light crests the mountain ridge. To look into your open wondering blue eyes, projecting a clear late summer day and know that all I want this season, this year, forever, is to feel this way every day. Please come back, Jim, hold me, and one day soon, say you will stay with me.

This could be a poem, she thought, but Heather couldn't really concentrate. *I'll make it into one some other time,* she thought, sitting motionless, head hanging with eyes fixed on the paper. With the turmoil of the day, her emotions welled up. Salt and water dripped, mixing with blue ink diffusing on the paper in colorful spots as her words turned to puddles of longing.

Chapter 50

The huge hangar doors were sliding open as the Huey approached, hovering five feet above the tarmac. The general gently settled down twenty feet outside the door. On occasion, he had flown directly into or out of the hangar, but the ground crews were never happy when he did. They kept the football-sized hangar floor spotless and flying in brought debris from the outside.

The general looked at Jim. 'You're on a mission tonight, back up in Cuba. Mason is getting gear together. Mark and Katarina will brief you.'

Within seconds, the ground crew arrived and towed Six Centaur inside. Before they stopped, Jim was out and heading toward the elevator. He knew he needed to return to Heather as fast as he could, therefore his efficiency mode kicked in; not a second was to be wasted. The general and Sheilla moved much more slowly with Will talking her through the shutdown procedure.

Will and Sheilla undid their harnesses. The general reached for the door handle, hesitated and then said, 'Are you ready? Don't worry about your gear. Mason will send someone up to get it.'

Sheilla opened her door to leave, oblivious to the general's personal thoughts. The general didn't know what to think about what was going through his head these days. Sheilla was his subordinate, he could enjoy her company but that was all. Maybe he was just being a crazy, lonely old man. The thought made him angry at his feelings. Within minutes, they were in the elevator down, heading back to their normal world.

Jim went straight to his office, picked up the phone, and called Sergeant Mason. 'We ready to go?'

'General Crystal briefed me on the mission…Everything I think you will want is loaded and packed, there is a cargo manifest in your email. I can have it on the plane in fifteen minutes when you give me the order; let me know if you'd like anything else.'

'I'll check it out and be there in a minute.' Sergeant Mason ran a tight shop. The weapons were always in perfect working order and supplies neatly arranged. The field operatives used a large variety of equipment. In his supply area, he had everything from civilian clothes to hazardous materials suits and a large variety of equipment, from small robots and lock picks to sledge hammers. The arsenal was loaded with enough weapons for a platoon. He knew what Jim and Brush preferred; however, many times a mission required different tools, clothes, or weapons. He packed this mission for the Caribbean as a stealth mission with quick insertion.

He opened a heavy door and walked down a long hall to a bunker accessed through a tunnel away from the warfare center's laboratory and the headquarters' offices. Another tunnel connected the ammunition bunker to the hangar.

He packed a small case with several grenades and flares and walked back to the supply area.

Jim picked up the internal pager. He punched in the four-digit code for Brush. Brush called back seconds later and Jim asked, 'Whatcha up to?'

'Heading to supply. Want to meet me there?'

'Sure, one of my favorite places. I like it there, all my favorite toys on shelves.'

'Then we are having a briefing in thirty minutes.'

In the supply room, Jim and Brush added a few items to what Mason had packed.

Mason looked at Jim. 'Don't you forget, Colonel, before I retire at my forty years, I want to have one last taste of the field.'

'Miss it, eh?' said Brush.

'You bet. I like all the fancy shit in this room, but I don't want to have my last memories being a supply donkey.'

'I have to admit I understand. We'll find something where you can have some fun.'

'Still nothing, Pearson's ride was found down a dirt road not far from where he said he flipped a bitch,' said Dino.

'Jeez, Dino. Where do you guys come up with the talk?' replied Bertrand, who prided himself on his correct use of language.

'Sorry, boss, I forget you office boys don't get out on the street much. It means U-turn, like bust a U-ey.'

'Dino, you're insufferable sometimes. Just go find our boy. Martin knows too much for us to have him spilling information. It was my mistake to send him, but what possessed you to let him out of a secure place?'

'You're not the first person who I have had that conversation with in the last day. We were told he was in charge and to cooperate.'

'Well, OK. Just find him and get back fast.'

'Look, I've pulled in as many of our people as I can. They won't be much help. We can't go asking everyone questions. The cops and most everyone else are in the cartel's pocket. If you ask me, there isn't much doubt they have him. He could be in Bogota by now. But I can't storm into Siastra's headquarters, even if we knew he was there; we'd need an army.'

'You're not going to get one. Mexico's intelligence service got upset that we were running an operation in their backyard and we didn't inform them. They won't help. Money is your best tool. Somebody will cooperate for the right price.'

'Yeah, and what are they going to tell us. The cartel is cutting his balls off and he's squealing like a pig. Fuck, I'll call if we find anything.'

'Jesus Christ, I hurt,' said Martin. Then he looked at the door, afraid that someone would hear him and she would come back. The thought scared him so much he tried to kick his legs and pull his tied arms from the chair, violently shaking in frustration. Nothing happened. Najma's cut had left too much cord for Martin to break. Then he saw the knife lying there right in front of him. He tried to wiggle over but he couldn't. Something was still holding the chair. He didn't have the strength to free it.

'Oh God, please help me. Kick hard and maybe the chair will come loose and I can get the knife,' he mumbled to himself. Then he realized that even if he could work his way around, he couldn't hold the knife and cut himself loose.

He started to work his arms back and forth and then let out a shriek. He had rubbed what was left of his thumb on the floor. Martin jerked to try to lift it up. Then he felt it. The bonds were not as tight as they had been.

He stared at the door. Had he made too much noise? He held his breath and grimaced at the pain. He slowly counted down from ten. The door didn't move. He heard no one. He closed his eyes and said, 'Thank you, God.' He pulled and twisted his wrists and arms and little by little, the cord unraveled. He hugged his aching arms to his sides.

Martin lay for a second, just relieved, and then brought his left hand slowly up and looked at it. The mangled and bloody stump where his thumb had been made him nauseous. He hesitated then gritted his teeth and sat up. He didn't dare touch where his ear had been. The pain in his head told him it must be bad and he had seen his ear sticking on her knife. Then his mouth set in a thin line as with his other hand, he reached down and gingerly took hold of his penis. He closed his eyes and then the flash, 'I'm holding it, it's not gone,' he whispered and finally forced himself to look down at it.

It hurt like hell. He thought she had severed half his penis. To his immense relief, he discovered that it was mostly still there. She had sliced only a small bit of the tip, but the rest was still intact. Then relief drained away with the thought that she had cut off the best part. He wouldn't be able to feel anything. Anger surged bringing adrenaline with it. 'I'll kill the witch. I'll find her and I'll kill her,' he vowed. Just as fast, he realized that she could be back anytime. He reached down, took the knife, and cut his legs free. With his good hand, Martin rubbed them and looked around the room. His Wranglers were on the floor in the corner next to his bleached out Redskins hat. *I love that hat,* he thought randomly.

He carefully got up and went to the corner. He picked up the jeans with his right hand and almost fell over trying to get a foot into the pant leg. He sat on the floor and stifled a yell as the tip of his raw penis touched his jeans. Martin took a deep, ragged breath. He tugged and wiggled his way into the jeans but when he pulled them up the pain was too much when he rubbed on the coarse fabric. There was a coffee cup sitting on the shelf. He hobbled over, carefully tucked his penis inside and then struggled to hold it with his bad hand and pull the jeans over. It still hurt but not as much. He managed to zip the Wranglers, fasten the top button and then put on his hat and shoes.

'The American is up playing with his dick or what's left of it. He'll try to come out soon,' Vladislav said as he watched his monitors. There were cameras installed everywhere in the hacienda except for Guillermo's house. For this operation, he had added a few to monitor every angle in the American's room. He had seen a few bad things in his life but watching Najma was almost beyond his imagination. The woman must not have any feelings. He was wrong in that assessment. She did have feelings, but compassion wasn't among them.

Now Martin was afraid again. What if he opened the door and someone was right there? The big guy, or worse the woman? He put his good ear up to the door and listened. Nothing. Then he carefully pushed down on the handle. Fortunately, it didn't make any noise. He thought for a minute, afraid to do more. Then he pushed down all the way and cracked the door open. He had to get away. Anything would be better than facing her again. He gripped the knife hard. If he was going to die it might as well be now.

He didn't see anyone and slowly opened the door farther, easing it to about two feet, then three, and put his head out. He quickly drew it back; there was a man in a chair a little farther down. Gaining courage, he looked again. The man was softly snoring. Martin looked down the hall and saw another man leaning against the wall but with his back turned to him.

Slowly he moved into the corridor, starting to shake as he did so. He moved a few feet and there was another hall to his right. He inched toward it. He wanted to run but knew it would be a mistake. He made it around the corner and was now out of sight of both men.

Vladislav said, 'He's in the hall.'

Martin took a quick look behind him and saw no one. Then he became frantic. He had left his door open. They would see it any second. He started to move as fast as he could now, with his good hand holding the coffee mug bulging in his crotch and his hand with the missing thumb up in the air. It felt better that way. His ear throbbed with every step.

The hall ended in a door several feet away but there was another hall off it. To his amazement, there was a lit, green exit sign, which Vladislav had thoughtfully placed for him. There was still no one and he set off again, head turned to his left. It felt better when the moving air did not hit the exposed flesh and skull, which not so

many hours ago, had been covered with his ear. Thumb stump held
high and good hand steadying the coffee mug with the knife
alongside it pointing straight ahead, he moved as fast as he could
down the hall. It looked endless. Nothing but closed doors. He heard
and saw no one.

He didn't know that just moments ago he had passed Vladisav's
computer facility. His spirits lifted as he moved farther on. Abruptly
he heard shouting and yelling behind him. *The fucking door, stupid,*
he said to himself and ran as fast as he could. Ignoring the pain of
his penis flapping up and down in the ceramic coffee mug, trying to
keep his eyes forward with his head turned against the wind,
grimacing.

Vladislav and three others watching the screens couldn't help
themselves. Vladislav started to laugh, something he rarely did. He
could hardly contain himself as he pointed at the screen. 'Statue of
Liberty,' one of them shouted. 'She doesn't hold her balls,' retorted
Lazaro with a sneer. 'We're recording this, right?'

'We're going to send this to a reality TV show,' said Vladislav,
catching his breath. 'Now watch this.' He flipped a switch and
spoke into his mic. 'Ready with the girl?'

'Sí. Ahora?'

'Trenta segudos.'

'Señorita. Now you earn your money. All you do is stand in the
middle of the hall holding the gun. The man will stop when he sees
you.'

'Nothing was said about guns,' said Ayla now afraid.

'No worries, nothing will happen to you. A few more things the
next couple of days and you will return home a rich lady. Step out
now.'

Martin could hear the shouting getting closer. He was not going
fast enough. Then as he looked at the end of the hall, bile hit his
throat. Najma was standing there, not more than twenty feet in front

of him, holding a gun. He almost turned and ran back. His heart sank. 'I'm finished,' he whispered.

The clamor behind grew closer and there was nothing he could do. From behind he heard, 'Kill him, don't let him get away.' Then shots rang out, deafening in the tunnel as they ricocheted on the wall. He could feel them passing so close the air moved. *If I don't move, I'm dead,* he thought. Martin decided to charge the woman. What choice did he have? As he moved toward her, her chest turned red with blood. She was hit. He started to move faster. The shots continued. He was almost to her. The bullets miraculously continued to miss him but two more hit 'Najma.' Her head nearly exploded just as he neared her, peppering the wall with blood, brains, and bone. He started to cackle. Then he yelled, 'Good riddance, bitch. Yeah!' as a heavy metal gate began to slide shut just beyond her, cutting off the exit. He moved fast toward it. He knew he should have taken her gun but he had to get out. He made it through the gate, jumped to the side and, stumbling, fell painfully to the ground, just before it closed.

Then a realization hit him. He had just watched a human, even if only a half human, gunned down, her head erupting and he had laughed. Martin tipped his head to the side and threw up. But there was nothing there, his stomach was empty. His shame overcame his elation as he got up and moved away as fast as he could, wondering what kind of person he had become.

There were stars out. A crisp brilliant moon. Cup in hand, mutilated hand held high, he half hobbled, half limped across the desert trying not to run into anything. The men on the wall laughed as they watched the crazy gringo but not with much enthusiasm. They were still thinking about the she-devil who had sliced his penis. They were hard men but some things were sacred. Other men stationed in the hills watched Martin with night-vision goggles. His new nickname was SOL, they pronounced it 'Saul,' short for Statue of

Liberty. They knew something the running man did not: he was free.

His hand held high, as if he was holding a torch and the bloody stump feeling like the torch's flame, a missing thumb that would later become a symbol of his emancipation. As he half ran, half stumbled to his liberty, his thoughts and habits escaped the confinement of his past. His experiences were changing him. It would take Martin days to acknowledge the full change, and longer still to understand it.

'Let loose a few,' came Lazaro's voice over the radio. 'Make sure you don't hit the gringo. Shoot wide. This gringo is so stupid he won't know the difference.' The expert shooters on the wall sent half dozen rounds a few feet wide of Martin before he disappeared over a small rise.

Chapter 51

'General,' said Sheilla, 'Glenda reported they found a large cut in the fence of Guantánamo just outside Camp X-Ray.'

'Let's walk to the conference room. Anything else?'

'She said she would call in if there was. She has CID taking a look. Since she can't meet Grant until tomorrow night she said they are inspecting. Added that Captain Kramer is a wimp.' They both shook their heads.

'I wanted to know what he is made of. He's probably useless out of the office.'

'Why send him out?'

'It's not that dangerous of an assignment and Glenda is capable. You never really know how someone will act until you give them a chance. I wanted to give him that chance. He's a good intelligence officer and that's where we'll probably keep him. Besides no military types will recognize him there, or Glenda for that matter. Jim and Brush might have been recognized by someone.'

'Oh,' was all Sheilla could say. The general had been several steps in front of her. She bit her lip.

They were the last to enter the conference room. Sheilla added a pile of papers to the maps and papers already on the conference table.

Jim sat at the head of the table with Brush on his right and the general on his left, sitting next to Sheilla.

'What I want,' said Jim, 'is a quick synopsis from each of you.'

He looked at Mark, Fred, and Katarina. 'There is a lot of material sitting here. Bring me up to speed, what do we know about X-Ray and their security? The mission is simple—Glenda finds out whether Najma is or isn't at G. We hook up with Neilly and stay flexible. If Najma isn't there, we track her and get her back.'

He turned to the analysts. 'Quick summary from each of you.'

When they were finished Jim looked to his left. 'Anything to add, General, Sheilla?'

Neither added anything.

'We'll review this on the flight. Secure satellite communications to the sit room here and the SOF team is all set. Frank, everything loaded?' Jim looked at Sergeant Mason, who glanced up, surprised to hear someone using his first name at an official meeting.

'Yes, sir,' he quickly added, pleased.

'Sergeant, get these folders to the plane.' Frank nodded as Jim stood up, looked at the general, and briskly walked out with Brush. Jim was ready. He felt good, like himself.

Martin seemed to have pain coming from all parts of his body. As happy as he was that he had gotten away, fear returned. He wanted to be far away and out of Mexico. They wouldn't capture Najma but at least she couldn't cause anyone else pain again. The director and Flayback would work some PR magic and the whole episode would fade into history. *But not for me,* he thought.

He was starving. He stumbled on a small puddle of water in an old stream bed, and quenched his thirst. Still exhausted and riddled with fiery pains, Martin sat down on the granular desert soil and leaned against a lichen-covered rock. Despite his headache and a thumb and ear that hurt like crazy, even though they weren't there anymore, he worried about 'the artful throbber,' his name for the body part that Najma had almost cut off. Almost, but to his immense relief, unlike his ear and thumb, it was still there, most of it anyway.

Despite the stinging and pain, he was overcome with exhaustion and fell into a deep sleep. His last thought before his consciousness vanished was, *I wonder if snakes like the smell of blood?*

Martin woke up under a hot sun. He opened his eyes groggily and for a second wondered where he was. His head radiated a raw pain. There was buzzing all around him. 'Shit, damn,' he muttered as he hit at flies buzzing round his face and his oozing-crusted thumb-stump.

He pulled the knife out and decided to cut a bandage for his thumb from his shirttail. He wanted to get the ugly stump out of his sight as much as get it away from the flies. He looked down toward 'artful' and noticed bloodstains on his pants. A flash image of the sadistic witch's head exploding crossed through his thoughts. *The blood must be from Najma,* he figured.

Then groaning and throwing out a few expletives, wondering how much damage was done, Martin unzipped his pants. He started to lift the white coffee cup and yelped. Artful was stuck to the side. He decided best to leave it alone for the time being. He didn't have to take a leak; being dehydrated had its advantages. Then he remembered hearing that urine was good for healing wounds. A solution struck him and he giggled. When he had to pee, he would do it in the cup. The urine would unstick it and maybe do some good. Life was full of surprises.

His preoccupation with his wounds suddenly left him. He quickly scanned the desert. Someone might be looking for him. He had walked a long way last night; maybe he had gotten farther than they would be looking. Martin began thinking about what to do next. He had better get out of here and find a hospital. Not a good idea, they would be looking for him there. He had to get to Eduardo. But how, without being spotted? Eduardo was right, they had been watching him and they still would be. He had been a fool and paid a price for his ignorance.

Looking around he tried to figure out where he had come from. *Shit. I could walk right back into the cartel's arms.* He should have thought of that last night. *I really am a piss poor field operative,* he told himself. He was starting to swear and talk aloud to himself just like an old prospector. Then he began to think more rationally. North was the US. He had no choice, it was better than heading toward Mexico City. The sun rises in the east. He turned ninety degrees and looked for the best way to walk, just as Najma had done from her unknown desert location.

Two hours later, Martin was roasting in the desert sun. He was starting to think about eating cacti or lizards for food and water. Then fear gripped him as he heard something out of place. He stopped and listened. Now he could hear a car approaching. They were onto him. He dropped to the ground, watching his thumb and hit the mug with a clang on a rock. Thankfully, it didn't break. He might be parched but suddenly he had to pee. He unzipped again and peed but a searing pain hit him as the urine not only stung like crazy but forced his penis to pull from the side of the cup rather than dissolving slowly away as he had thought it would. Then he started to laugh at the insanity of the situation. 'I think I'm going off the deep end. Maybe heatstroke.' *Shut up, Martin.* 'They're getting close,' he whispered.

The vehicle stopped not far from where he lay. His first thought was to run but then reason took over. Maybe they didn't know he was here. *Not much chance of that,* he thought. He listened but they didn't seem to be coming his way. It sounded like several people jabbering away. He peered around a prickly pear cactus. He pulled himself sideways to a sagebrush and lifted himself up. There was an old blue pickup with four men sitting on the ground. They looked like peasants or Indians. He relaxed and watched, not knowing what to do. Not cartel. Maybe they worked for the cartel? Finally, his need to get away overcame his fear. He slowly got up and walked toward the men.

One stood as he approached. 'Aloha, señor. Buenos dias.' Martin's French was not much help so he asked. 'English? You speak English?'

'No, señor, no Inglés, pero José habla poco.'

A small man stood and swatted dust from his pants, saying, 'Lost, mister?'

'Yes. Small accident. Can you take me to the hotel in Tubutama?'

They talked amongst themselves as if discussing it. Just as they had been instructed. 'Can you pay?' Then more talking. The man turned toward Martin and held up five fingers. 'Five dollars.'

Martin almost yelled with relief. 'Take me right to the front of the hotel and I'll give you fifty dollars!' Then he added, 'But I have to hide from my wife. Do you have a poncho and a hat?' Martin figured that wearing the same clothes and his red baseball hat would be a sure giveaway.

Excited talking and the men all jumped up and pointed at the back of the truck. With what the cartel was paying them plus fifty American dollars, it would be a very good day.

They helped him climb in and put an old dusty blanket by him. One man gave him a frayed blue baseball cap with the remnants of a green tractor on the front. 'Perfect,' said Martin. 'Gracias.' He carefully tilted it so it didn't come close to the raw flesh where his ear had been. It never occurred to him that they said nothing about his wounds.

The truck went slowly, bumping and rolling over the uneven ground and reached a rutted dirt road and then a paved road. Martin was getting excited. He was going to make it. Just as they started down the road, a police car drove up behind them. He pulled the blanket up and looked down. 'No, no, no,' he eked out. José patted his knee and grinned. 'No hay problema, señor.' The police car followed for a minute and then pulled to the side and stopped. Martin's breathing slowed.

'I'm going to die of a heart attack before I get out of here,' he said and then laughed. José looked at him and whispered to the other man in back, 'Loco, no?'

The truck creaked and sputtered its way along, but the men just grinned and didn't look worried. They reached town and stopped in front of the hotel. Martin hoped Eduardo and the others were still there. The men helped him out of the truck and stood waiting expectantly for their money. Almost immediately, a man dressed like a local walked up to him and said, 'Martin, we're from your company.' Then another joined them.

Martin became skeptical and scared. What if they were cartel? 'You know Eduardo?'

They looked at each other with their mouths open and then looked back at Martin. 'Move your ass inside. It's dangerous out here.' The man got out his phone and said, 'We got him. Yeah, he's right here in the lobby.'

Martin gulped. Acid rushed up from his stomach, Martin's throat felt like it was on fire, then it was if his breathing was cut off with a tightness in his chest. He moved inside with pain and relief.

Seconds later Eduardo, followed by Thomas, Dino, and two more men rushed down the steps. 'Son of a bitch,' said Eduardo.

Martin's face was red and he couldn't talk. They all stared at him.

Eduardo said to the first man that had approached Martin, 'Go see what the men outside want.'

Maybe some kind of panic attack, Martin said to himself. Then he managed to say, 'You have any money to pay these guys for bringing me out of the desert? I promised fifty bucks.'

'US dollars? They would have been jumping up and down for a couple of bucks.'

Martin looked at the men. 'Long ride. I say fifty American each.' He felt defensive about his rescuers and wanted to assert his authority after his humiliation at the hands of the cartel. Not to mention a little bluster to cover his own embarrassment and stupidity.

'Give 'em the money, Thomas,' said Eduardo. He didn't care

about the money. They had plenty of cash for bribes but could never find anyone to take it. The town belonged to the cartel and taking money from the Notrè Americanos for information would be tantamount to a death sentence.

'Jesus, Martin, I think you need a doctor; you look like shit.'

Martin felt calm and strangely happy; he found he didn't care about the pain. He was getting used to it. In fact, he found himself embracing it while enjoying the men's response. Before they had looked and talked to him disrespectfully and he had deserved their condescending behavior. This newfound acceptance he was feeling from these experienced field operatives seemed important. He felt comfortable being this Martin, a bloody mess but a wily survivor. It was who he had become. He hadn't captured Najma, but she wasn't a problem anymore; she was dead and gone. Game over. He tried not to grimace, unwrapping his hand and holding it up.

They stood agape, looking at the blood-encrusted stump where his thumb had been. 'Yep, I think some medical attention would be very nice,' he said coolly. 'And a new ear if you've got one.' Then they all looked at his jeans and then each other, obviously wondering what else was missing. Martin let them stand mouths open for a minute—'Oh, the jeans. It's a ceramic coffee cup. Nice white one.'

Chapter 52

'Shut-eye time,' said Brush as the Citation X taxied for takeoff toward the southeast end of ten-thousand-foot runway number zero one zero. 'What's the flight plan?'

'Straight through, no stops.' Brush rubbed his chin.

'Piece of cake,' said Jim, with Brush knowing what he was thinking. Sixty knots, westerly tailwinds sandwiched between a huge departing low and a high moving in on the route.

'You sure you don't want some help with that pile of papers?'

'Nope, you go ahead. I want to go over everything.' This was a normal division of duties. Brush let Jim do the planning.

'Well then, wake me up at the other end, partner. Or wake me up if there is anything about Glenda.'

'Uh huh, pleasant dreams, pal.'

The distance capability of their plane was extraordinary but having a tailwind made this nonstop trip doable. Not so if they were bucking a headwind.

Sergeant Mason and his men had reconfigured the twelve-person plane for two sleeping berths and a table and comfortable lounge chairs. Jim settled into one of the chairs and picked up the first file.

Guillermo's manservant escorted Najma into the dining room. Not to eat but to discuss the attack to the north and, unbeknownst to her, to meet Alva Gager. She was not prepared for this. At six feet, she was a few inches shorter than Guillermo. However, they contrasted sharply. Guillermo was thinner, lighter skinned with a prominent beaked nose and clean-shaven. This man had a heavy black stubble, dark olive skin, and long black hair slicked back. She could sense taut hard muscles under his tan chino pants and light blue linen oxford shirt.

Guillermo politely introduced them. They nodded to each other. A brief encounter with this man and Najma instantly knew he was not only an adversary but a capable adversary. Guillermo broke into both their thoughts, 'Alva is a

long-term associate and knows the northwestern United States well. He will be a great help to you.'

They stood face-to-face. Neither averted their eyes. Najma sensed his confidence. *What was his purpose?* she wondered. This man's eyes and steady gaze told her he was dangerous. He was extremely fit for, probably, forty years old. They shook hands, although he didn't grasp hers heavily.

Not using that strength suggested to her that he had a capable mind. She looked at his hand before releasing it. It was not a farmer's hand although there were many scars, including a three-inch line that went straight from his index finger to his wrist. His face was unblemished. If he was a fighter, he had avoided being hit. His hands suggested he had done the hitting. He stood relaxed, feet slightly apart and well balanced.

Alva was going through much the same analysis with an advantage. He had seen videos and had her described to him in detail. He wondered if the 'she-devil' was as dangerous as her legend. She had survived many battles. She had been the sole survivor in the terrorist attack in Seattle. She evaded the Americans in their country. Just as Najma had surmised about him, he concluded that she was a dangerous adversary.

People in his line of work understood one important thing, however. It was always far easier to kill someone than to avoid being killed. Surprise, and thus the advantage, always belongs to the assassin. She was tough, a skilled killer, but would be no match for him when he chose to fulfill the final task in his contract with Guillermo.

Then he casually studied her body and wondered if he might seduce her first. She looked worth the effort. She reminded him of a panther, tense and sleek. And he was attracted to strong, capable women. An interesting challenge. Alva had a long list of conquests. They were easy for him. He fit the tall, dark, and handsome media profile of many women's fantasies. He liked to think that they had not been disappointed.

Heather settled into resignation again: Jim was gone and would keep going away as long as he was able. Her feelings and concerns had no bearing on the matter; she understood that now. She had not fully made up her mind if she would accept that or not. She had wavered back and forth for the last two days. She loved him but could she say more than anything? There was Pedro now and she wanted a 'normal' life with her family. She wanted her partner with her every day. Sure, he could go off to work in the morning but she wanted him in her bed at night and home on weekends; her vision of normal.

Pedro had changed her. Before, she had no aversion to leaving home and spending weeks on field trips. In fact, she had loved it. Now she belonged at home. They could travel and camp in the wilderness as much as they liked during summers and school vacations. But her duty and her life were at the ranch. She had lived there for so long, she thought of it as much hers as Jim's, but that wasn't true. It was his. She was nothing more than an interloper, a transient, no different from Shuskin. If she left Jim; she would also leave the ranch.

She walked to the old man. 'What do you do in the winter? Where do you live?'

Old Man Shuskin just stared at her with a blank expression. *Well, progress,* she thought. He didn't cower behind Nusmen. She turned to her ex-colleague.

'Nus, what are you going to do with Shuskin? Does he have a first name? Come on, Nus. You plan to go back to the lab just as fast as you can. He can't go with you. So what's your plan?'

Neither Nusmen nor Shuskin said a word. Heather gave up.

'All right, I might as well be talking to a pair of trees. Lola, get that the spaghetti boiling and heat up the sauce we talked about, OK?'

'Sí, señora, no problema.'

'Why did you say señora? You never have before. What gives?'

Lola with her round face gave her a resigned smile. 'You mother now, you señora.'

'Oh...then gracias, señora. We both are his mothers. You will be as much a mother to Pedro as I will be.'

Lola acknowledged Heather with a grateful look. Pleased that Heather said what she had, Lola still understood that she would never have a son of her own again. She would always be grateful to Heather and Jim for allowing her into their home. It was a dream-world compared to her life in Mexico. Lola would do everything in her power to please them and take care of them and Pedro too.

'Pedro, let's check the llamas before dinner.' Then she looked at Nusmen and Shuskin and added, 'Better talking to llamas than these two.'

'Heather, knock it off. What's turned you so sarcastic?' asked Nusmen. She just nodded a little and fluttered her hand. She knew he was partly right and while she didn't feel like saying she was sorry, she hoped he knew that she accepted his verdict of her behavior.

She turned and took Pedro's small brown hand. *I will do better,* she said to herself. *I have a reason to,* and she smiled down at him as they walked into the meadow. She stopped and turned back to Nusmen. 'What time would you like to leave in the morning? It won't take that long to get down. I'd like a swim first.'

'Whatever.'

She ignored his surly attitude. Maybe they both were being curmudgeons.

'Let's say noon then. We could all go swimming again,' she said as pleasantly as she could.

Nusmen mumbled, 'One minute she's ragging on me and the next bonding.'

'Me swim, Mama?'

Heather almost corrected his usage and then remembered he had only another few weeks before school. She wouldn't correct him anymore. He would get more than enough correction soon. She would try to let him just be and enjoy his new world. 'After dinner, Pedro, let's play some catch. What do you think? Want to? Or, I brought a Frisbee too?'

'Frisbee, please.'

'Let's see if we can't get Nusmen to join in. I doubt Shuskin will or can.'

Pedro scrunched up his nose. Heather nudged him playfully. 'Hey, buster, he's an old man. Everyone is special in their own way. He could probably tell you some really interesting stories. Well, I used to think that about him out in the mountains, anyway. Underneath, maybe he's a sorcerer. You think? Or a shaman.'

Pedro's eyes grew wide. He recalled stories about a shaman in Mexico and during a celebration he saw him with tall feathers on his head, drinking a potion from a giant shell, his body painted turquoise. The boy shivered.

The following afternoon, the white Ford with its red wood sides drove slowly up the ranch road to the main barn. Heather backed against the loading dock. Coming back without Jim was not how she'd planned to end this trip. Heather shook herself out of it. She had always been fine without Jim.

'Pedro, would you go back and open the gate into the holding pen for me?'

'Sí, I do it, Mama.'

Nusmen drove in with Shuskin, parked and jumped up on the loading dock. 'I'll give you a hand. What are you going to do with the old man?'

Heather stopped, put her hands on her hips and said, 'Nus, you kidding me? What do you mean: what am I going to do with him? He's yours and you just assume I'm going to take him?'

'I can't take him. You know that.'

'Yeah, I assumed that would be the case but you could at least ask, you turkey. Sometime you should try not being such a jerk.'

'I'm sorry. I didn't know he was just going to attach himself to me like he has and I've been upset.'

'You're welcome, Nus. An apology represents progress. I already assumed that it would be up to me but I didn't want anyone else assuming it, especially you. I was thinking about letting him stay in the cabin. Not sure if he will stay there without you or if he'll stay at all. Any ideas? I don't know if he would even sleep inside.'

Nusmen stood speechless. He had friends now in the lab, something he had never really had before, and one out here in the world, maybe even two if you counted the old man.

Heather sensed where his mind was. 'Let's get the llamas' halters off and unloaded, then we'll just ask him. Maybe he'll stay. It's up to him. I'm not going to force him. Pedro, could you drop some hay into the feeders?'

'I do it fast and then we eat?'

The llamas tussled and pulled, wanting to get out of the truck. One by one, they took the halters off and let them out the truck's back gate. Shasta ran up to the fence with his ears folded back and head jutting out. Pipestone walked toward him but ten feet from him he jumped forward and then bolted to the far side of the pen.

'He's teasing him. I wish I knew what they thought. It's like he is saying, look at us back from an adventure, and you were stuck here and no way are you going to spit on me from that side of the fence.' Heather grinned at her own whimsy. 'Shasta's leg looks better. He didn't seem to be limping.' Then she walked directly to him. He put his head up as high as he could stretch it and folded his ears back in his most menacing way. She walked straight to him but with her eyes slightly lowered. Instead of spitting, as anyone who understood llama-body language would expect, he lowered his head and stretched it to her, nostrils flaring, and puffed a small amount of breath toward her face. Heather returned a soft breath. It was a sign of love and caring. Then he jerked his head back and walked off as if to say, *A tough llama can only handle so much smooching.*

'Jeez, Heather, I thought he was going to plaster you but good.'

Heather turned to Nusmen and Shuskin with a contented look. 'Let's go in the barn for a minute.'

When they got inside, Heather walked into the barn office. Next to it was the veterinary room, with a shower and a toilet attached to the side. She turned to Shuskin. 'What is your first name, Shuskin? Come on, you can tell us.'

Shuskin just shook his head and then looked down at his feet.

'Until you tell me your name, or what you would really like to be called, I'll have to call you Shuskin.' He peered up at her without raising his head much. 'OK then, do you think you would like to stay here in the barn? It is comfortable, woodstove and water. You and Nusmen can stay here tonight.' Heather glowered at Nusmen letting him know he had no choice. 'Or let's stop at the old homesteader's cabin on the way up for dinner. You two can spend the night there, if you'd prefer.' *Shit, why did I offer the barn, too dangerous. He might burn it down. I'll make them stay at the cabin*, she said to herself.

She looked down at Pedro who was looking up. He whispered, 'Please, I'm hungry.' She put her arm around him, 'Let's go get some food! On the way, just one little stop at the cabin. Nus, you and Shuskin ride on the four-wheeler.'

Heather laughed as the old man slowly climbed on the red Honda and put both arms around Nusmen. 'Nusmen, you should see your face!'

Chapter 53

Brush walked into the communication center on the navy's smallest aircraft carrier. Only one hundred and thirty-one feet long, it was used originally for helicopter training. After landing in Guantánamo, they had transferred with their gear to the small ship in the SF team's helicopter.

Jim hadn't seen Chief Warrant Officer Marilyn Cutter since they were both injured in Mexico. They gave each other a long hug; a bond between survivors.

Will Crystal had practiced flying with Marilyn before their mission over the Mexico border and said she was one of the best pilots he had ever flown with. Not a light compliment coming from a man who was critical of anyone who didn't meet his standards. Marilyn was accomplished, brave, and talented; she had also nearly died of her injuries last time out.

Most of the ship was a flat-back deck with the SF team's specially equipped Black Hawk sitting alone in the middle. Sticking high up only a few feet from the bow was a pilothouse. Completely covered with antennas and dish shaped satellite receivers, the exterior looked unruly, contrasting with the stark flat stern. Inside, one deck below, Mac sat looking at an array of communication devices.

'Mac, can you try and connect me up for a sat call?'

'Yeah sure, number?'

Mac looked at Brush when he recognized the number. Glenda,

who they were secretly here to back up. 'You want, you can go over there and plug this in, more privacy.'

Brush looked a little guilty. 'Yeah, OK. Thanks, Mac.'

Mac flipped a switch. He was monitoring all her communications back to the control center at the BWC.

Mac pushed a quick connect button to her secure satellite phone. As a courtesy to Brush, he locked out himself and Sheilla's op center. Seconds later they were connected.

'Hi, babes. I miss you like crazy.' Brush looked around but no one seemed to hear or be listening.

'That's an understatement for me, big guy. Not at all like being in hot places with you.'

'Kramer is keeping you company?'

'Knock it off. Kramer isn't keeping me any way and you know it.'

'Yeah, I know but how could anyone not want to at least flirt with you a little?'

'Kramer is too overwhelmed by the heat to think of much else. Besides, most men are afraid of assertive women.'

'Fear never crossed my mind. What you up to?'

'Not much yet, just working our cover, inspecting, and surprise, found a big hole in the security fence only a few feet from X-Ray. You?'

'Talking to you, enough to keep any sane man happy.' Brush knew the message she was sending was: *We are on a secure phone but one never knows who can monitor.* It was hard not telling her they had arrived and were just offshore. The thought of sneaking into Gitmo and her quarters passed through his mind. It reminded him of his teenage summer camps, sneaking over to the girls' bunkhouse.

'You know, you better take care of yourself. I want to see you looking me in the eye as soon as you can.'

'Right back at you.'

'Nus, drop yours and Shuskin's gear here; see if you can tell if he might stay inside, and then come up on the four-wheeler. See you for dinner in about thirty or thirty-five minutes.'

Nusmen looked at Shuskin. He was feeling a lot kindlier to him now that he knew Heather was going to take him off his hands. They dropped their packs and Nusmen opened the cabin door. It was made of aged boards spanning twelve by fourteen feet. A porch sloped sideways and needed some better support. Still, it was in good shape for being nearly a hundred years old and sitting on a foundation of small rocks sinking into the damp, soft soil next to the aspen grove. The water floated on a bed of clay and provided nourishment for the trees that snaked their way down the canyon alongside an intermittent stream.

Nusmen opened the door and motioned for Shuskin to go in. He didn't move. Nusmen was getting used to this so he walked in and went around the corner, then turned back. Shuskin was poking his head in, trying to see where Nusmen had gone.

'Well, come in and close the screen door,' he said. Shuskin shuffled in and then walked over to a shelf that had some rocks and crystals, quartz and other stones that Jim and Heather had picked up hiking near the ranch.

He touched one and then the other until he had touched them all. Then he walked over and prodded the mattress up and down a couple of times with a single dark finger. It was old and had a hole or two where mice had managed to make their winter home. The bed was dark metal with crisscrossed wire supporting the old mattress. Nusmen watched him and then ventured, 'Nice cabin, huh? You want to sleep here tonight?'

Shuskin turned to the sink set slightly askew in an old wide board. There was no running water but it drained outside to a makeshift septic tank in an old barrel. Above the sink was a rough-hewn wood shelf with dishes and some cooking equipment and a small amount of food. He reached up and touched a can of peaches. Next to the sink was an ancient woodstove and just beyond it in the corner stood a small pile of stacked wood. In the center of the room was an old painted wood table with an oil light hanging above it.

Then, surprising Nusmen, Shuskin walked over the worn green shag carpet that the table sat on, moving to the wall above the stacked wood. He put up a crooked finger and touched yellowed newspaper attached to the wall. The headlines on the one he pointed to read, 'Pearl Harbor Attacked.'

Glenda sat drinking coffee in her quarters. She was feeling the effects of hearing from Brush. It made her feel whole to hear his voice and know he was out there and feeling the same way she did.

While her career with the FBI had been disappointing, it was simple and uncomplicated. General Crystal, recognizing her abilities, gave her tasks worthy of her talents, or would in the future she was sure. She nodded to herself. *I have everything now,* she thought. A knock on the door interrupted her thoughts.

The door opened slowly and Kramer walked in, pushing it closed. He looked at his watch. 'It's nearly twenty-one hundred. What do you want to discuss?'

Another knock on the door. Kramer opened it.

The man, a medium height Asian, ignored Kramer, looked at Glenda, walked over, and took her hand. 'How is your inspecting going?' he asked.

The general had told her little about Master Chief Grant, other than he was a trustworthy Asian, who would greet her with the question he just had. Her challenge response was simply, 'The same as always.' It wasn't exciting code but to any observer it would sound normal. Grant put his fingers to his lips and turned to both of them. He took out a small black device, pushed a button and said, 'It is a pleasure to meet you.' He walked around the room checking for listening devices. 'That coffee looks good. Mind if I pour a cup?'

'Kramer, pour the senior chief some coffee and yourself too.'

Grant moved all over the room, his wide face looking closely at several items. Kramer handed him a mug of coffee. Glenda said, 'Have a seat.'

'Before we settle in and talk, it's a spectacular night out, if you like stars and I do. There's no moon tonight and the constellations are as bright as they get.'

Glenda took the cue and to her surprise, Kramer seemed to grasp the situation as well. Glenda didn't think he was stupid, just inexperienced, so of course she did not expect him to be as fast on the uptake as he seemed to be. 'Great, maybe you can show me how to recognize Orion. I never have been sure I have the right group of stars,' she replied.

They walked out the door to a clear area away from the lights. Grant pointed up in the sky and said softly to Glenda, 'I've been watching your quarters for the last hour. I'm not the only one. Your room has enough listening devices to catch every whisper.'

'Shit,' she whispered, feeling stupid for not thinking about listening devices. She also realized what she had not done wrong. No secret conversations with Kramer and she had been worried about eavesdropping when she was on the phone with Brush, so she had been careful. However, she had not considered that her room was bugged. A lesson learned without causing damage was not a bad way to learn. 'What do you have in mind?'

Grant smiled. 'Don't worry about it.'

'Let's go back to your quarters and follow my lead.'

They walked back inside and Glenda said, 'Another coffee?'

'I've had enough. Do you have anything stronger? I could use a drink after being out on ship all day.' He shook his head slightly.

'Afraid nothing at all but I wouldn't mind one either. What about you, Kramer, you want to go find a drink with us or you want to turn in?'

'As long as it has ice, count me in.'

'Tell you what, let's go back to my place. I'm pretty well stocked up.'

They strolled looking at the stars until they came to a small house. Once inside, Grant did a quick scan around the house with his device, all the while talking. When he was finished he said, 'I check it all the time but just wanted to make double sure nobody is listening if we're going to go to X-Ray tonight.'

'Jesus, we going to do that?' asked Kramer.

'I designed the security. No problem. What is a problem are the spooks. I don't have any idea why they are interested in you. There was only one man watching your place and maybe with the bugs they are just being cautious. You never know with them. Even though I was one of them a long time ago, I'm never sure what they are up to.'

'That where you met Will Crystal?'

'Yep, Captain Spook we used to call him.'

Grant turned on some music, poured them all a drink, and with a bottle in one hand walked to the window, standing just long enough for someone to see him, and closed the drapes. Then he set his glass down and said, 'Fill me in on how the general is. We were in some spots together in Nam.'

'I haven't known him that long but we have already had some exciting times.'

'That sounds just about right for him. We'll chat for a while, I'll get a call telling us where our spook followers are situated and we'll head to X-Ray in a way that they won't know, if you are sure that is what you want to do.'

Glenda said in a whisper, 'They have a prisoner that we are interested in.'

Outside, in the shadows, Dougal picked up his radio, checked that the volume was low, and called Gould. 'Nothing. Just looking at the stars and now drinking booze.'

'Let me know when they leave, if they do. Grant likes women and that one's worth his attention. Probably trying to get her drunk.' So far, they hadn't overheard anything suspicious and Gould wasn't concerned.

Chapter 54

Grant, Glenda Rose, and Kramer sat in the senior petty officer's small, sparsely furnished but comfortable living room. Glenda and Grant drank Cokes. A small table sitting between them and two green reclining chairs. Kramer sat on a brown leather sofa. Grant looked at his watch. 'Twenty-two-hundred. My guy will be coming on duty now. We give him fifteen minutes and then we'll work our way over there.'

'What about whoever is watching us?' asked Kramer.

'I'll make sure we know where they are and we will leave the house on the opposite side.'

'How?'

Simple. I have someone watching and they will continue to cover our backsides when we head to the camp.'

He picked up a small phone, dialed and said, 'Speak to me.'

'Just the one guy to your front side. I got a quick look; he was one of the petty officers with them earlier.'

'We're out in about five minutes. He moves, let me know.' Then Grant called another number. 'OK? Get it open as soon as you see us at the gate.'

'The plan is this,' said Guillermo as he pointed at a government quadrangle map covering a square mile that included Wolf Canyon Ranch. 'The men will come down this ridge, Coyote Ridge, to the east of the house and barns. More men will come from the north. They will park at the ski area here called Loup Loup about a mile behind the ranch. Then walk east alongside Wolf Mountain.'

'How many men?' asked Alva.

'Twenty-five total, not counting you two.' Guillermo had two more men that were expert snipers but he had no intention of telling either Najma or Alva about them. They would be his insurance in case Alva failed to kill Najma.

Najma sat looking at Guillermo and not saying anything. Guillermo knew why and said, 'These are my thoughts and plans, Najma. It is your mission. You have never failed me. Your thoughts?'

'I don't want anyone else there,' she said, looking at Alva. 'I can handle this by myself. I will handle it alone.'

'The men are experienced and can aid you. It is, of course, up to you. Eliminating the general at his army base will require help.'

'The general will come to help the colonel,' said Najma.

'He might bring the army if he does.'

Najma scowled. 'Get me to his ranch and I will tell you what I think should be done.'

'She's dead alright,' said Martin. 'I saw her shot multiple times and her head exploded right in front of me. And the blood on my coat matched hers, DNA will prove it's her.'

He sat with Sorenson, Flayback, and Bertrand in the director's office. His head was wrapped with a white bandage and his left hand was in a cast to protect the stump where his thumb had been. The doctors had quickly assembled a team of surgeons and started the reconstruction of his ear. They assured Martin that they could do a replantation of his thumb using a toe and that it would be presentable. After some thought, Martin decided that the missing thumb was a visible sign of his indoctrination to field craft, or at least surviving torture. He decided that he could get along without it just fine.

While he kept quiet about the slice missing from his bandaged lower member, somehow the information leaked and spread among the analysts, adding to the lore of his torture by the psycho woman. He never talked about it with anyone. Three times women approached him in the office hinting at going to bed with him. This had never happened before his cartel adventure. What he didn't know for weeks was that a secret office pool had been formed betting on how much of his penis Najma had eliminated.

No one seemed to know that the damage was minor. The doctor told him that it would heal with no significant loss of feeling and perhaps new nerves would form adding to his sensitivity and pleasure. Martin wasn't sure if doctor was just saying that, nevertheless overall, he was pleased. He felt respected and consequently felt better about himself than he had for a long time.

'As I said in the report, I didn't give them my real name,' he added.

Of course, the three people sitting across from him had read his report and listened to his debriefing. Helen thought about the missing parts. Mostly she thought about Martin's penis, curious.

Sorenson sat wondering how he could use this to secure his position with the president. He could say that Najma had escaped but that they had quickly hunted her down and terminated her. *No,* he thought. They had allowed her to escape to lead them to her terrorist boss.

Bertrand Gupta was puzzled; he had put the story together with Martin's help, a man he now viewed in a new way. Wisecracks were no longer Martin's primary method of communicating; he was focused and calm. He had not called him Bertie since he returned. He had not lost his sense of humor but he didn't use superficial wise-cracks; rather, a deep subtle humor became part of his personality.

There was a new maturity and strength to Martin Pearson. He was widely talked about in the CIA as a hero. He was an analyst who had tasted the field, survived torture and amputation by a psychopath, and been party to killing her while escaping a notoriously secure cartel headquarters and crossing a desolate desert without detection.

For his part, Martin stayed close to the truth. He tried to tell it like he remembered. Perhaps his memory did not remember it all exactly as it had happened but he had not fabricated, not even embellished what had happened at Tubutama. Nevertheless, as the story replayed in the agency, it expanded little by little. Like many heroes, if the whole story was known—if he knew himself—that he had been set up and allowed to escape, his newfound self-esteem would be lost forever.

The facts were indisputable. He had been kidnapped by the cartel, tortured and escaped. He had suffered the loss of an ear and a thumb and some unspecified damage to his penis. No one else of the thousands that worked at the agency's analytical branch could say the same.

Sorenson took full credit for Najma's death, on behalf of the agency, and reported that the CIA had used her to lead them to the planner of the terrorist attack on Seattle. The president and the White House staff were not entirely pleased. The story had several holes such as, the operation to have Najma lead the CIA to the planners of the US attack—what did it accomplish? If indeed she had led them to the planners of the attack what if anything would anyone do about it?

The story leaked to the press said simply that with determination and strong leadership, a woman terrorist involved in the attack on Seattle had been tracked down by the CIA and was now deceased.

The press bought in, building up the agency. Press relations were the one area where Flayback excelled. America should be proud of its clandestine agency and its capable director.

Glenda, Kramer, and Grant, doing a little drunken hooting, walked out of the front door and looked up at the stars. On unsteady feet, they walked back into the house, slamming the door behind them.

'Nice job, you two,' said Grant. He went straight to the back door and they all walked out. Grant was unaware that there was a listening device on a small storage building not far from his back door. They walked past a couple of buildings and he pulled out his phone.

'Are we clear?' He listened for a second. 'Good,' he said shortly and put the phone away. 'We'll walk around a little and then head to X-Ray,' he told them. 'It's risky. I'd hate to see my pension go up in flames. But Will would do it for me.'

Quietly, making sure they weren't followed, the three approached Camp X-Ray. They stopped opposite the gates in the shadow of a building. Grant told them to stay put. He walked across to the entrance gate. It opened immediately and he disappeared inside. A minute later, he hurried back out the gate, walking quickly and said in a low voice. 'Something's not right, let's get out of here.'

Suddenly they heard another voice from the shadows. 'You just arrived. What's the hurry? You'll all feel more comfortable inside,' said Gould as he walked closer holding a pistol. Grant started to move and Gould added, 'Not a good idea,' as three others emerged from the shadows with weapons. Kramer, Grant, and Glenda were ushered to the entrance gate at gunpoint. It reopened and clanged shut as they disappeared into Camp X-Ray.

Sheilla sat telling the general what the press release was going to say. 'It's a spin for sure. The real story is Najma escapes, the CIA is embarrassed and keeps it concealed, they send out inquiries and they suddenly stop. They must have tracked her, and then terminated her.'

'Sorenson,' said Will, shaking his head. 'The old company did everything it could to keep from talking to the press. Maybe politics is the new face of the CIA. One thing for sure, if the White House is releasing the story, it means that CIA has assured them Najma is done dancing.'

Chapter 55

Heather liked her coffee in the morning just at sunrise. She woke up as the first rays filtered through the trees and into her thoughts. Within a fraction of a second, she realized she was at the ranch and the space beside her was empty. She had become accustomed to Jim being there.

She heard soft steps and Pedro tentatively poked his head around the low bookcase headboard that separated the welded metal steps from the back of the bed. Heather patted the bed and Pedro, as if he had been restrained by an invisible elastic band, now severed, catapulted onto the bed and wrapped his arms around her.

After a few minutes, she asked if he was hungry. 'Let's go get some food then. I want to check on the llamas and let them up on the hill to graze. We'll take some food for Shuskin and Nusmen on the way to the barn.'

Lola heard them coming down the stairs and padded out of her room wearing large pink fluffy slippers. 'I cook, what you want I make?'

Pedro said, 'Ah, dollar pancakes and Frosted Flakes.'

Heather went to the stove and started some hot water for coffee while Lola started on Pedro's breakfast.

Nusmen had his head inside his sleeping bag and didn't hear them drive up.

Pedro ran ahead through the wood-pole gate and patted the sleeping bag on the porch. A wild shock of frizzy hair poked out followed by two sleepy eyes.

'I thought Shuskin would be in the bag. Where is he? Not off in the woods?' Heather asked.

Nusmen pursed his lips and nodded his head toward the door.

'He's in the bed.'

'No contact with Glenda, Kramer, or Grant. It's been two hours,' said Will.

'Maybe they're in Camp X-Ray?' asked Jim.

'Maybe. We'll give it a little more time. You go storming in there and it will cause havoc with…'

'Brush will be fine, Will,' said Jim to put the topic to rest, hopefully once and for all.

'One more thing, the reason I called you, the CIA and the White House say Najma is dead.'

'How?'

'The press report states they tracked the last remaining terrorist to a cartel headquarters in Mexico near the US border.'

'Tubutama, huh? What's the inside story?'

'As the released story goes, she was allowed to escape so she would lead them to the planner of the Seattle attack. She led them to a Mexican cartel hacienda, then she was killed there. The one and the same apparently rebuilt. They have a high-level eyewitness and blood splatter on their agent's clothes. Apparently, this higher-up was captured and then tortured by Najma. Get this, they say it was Martin Pearson. He escaped and then was only feet away when she was accidentally shot by the cartel firing at him. They'll have a DNA match soon.'

'Doesn't feel right. The only person killed is Najma. They have her blood so a DNA match proves nothing…no way they would put someone like him in the field. He's a desk jockey.'

Jim felt adrenaline enter his bloodstream. He could not relax until he knew the real story. Even with the general's higher-up contacts and the operatives Jim had become friends with, they were not likely to get the truth through official channels. He thought back on the hacienda and the limited possibilities of someone escaping. He understood the way she thought: she would come for him. And when she did, it would be in his backyard, his home, the ranch.

'Fred, check with the Wolf Pack.'

'I did and the colonel said busy and hung up on me. Then Misa called back and said the kid genius has no manners. She said they know someone else is in all the computers and they can't figure it out. She said the two babes were pissed that someone was getting the better of them. Then she hung up.'

'Well call them again. I don't want to drop Najma just yet. The general said Jim didn't buy the CIA story and neither does he, but the priority is Glenda right now. Ask whether they will stay live com with us.'

'How am I going to do that? They won't even talk to me.'

'All right. I'll call them, you take a break and get Bridget in here. Katarina needs a break.' Sheilla smiled, she had a feeling the rest of the night would be anything but boring.

Heather sat with the phone in her hand, wondering where Jim was and what he was doing. Thinking the same thoughts over and over. Would their relationship, that had once seemed so solid, really recover from the surfacing of such differences? Her mind went in circles finding no new thoughts.

Could she carry on living with him, when he was so often away and in danger? Could she continue sharing every part of herself with him while he kept so much locked away?

Heather lifted the phone and dialed her friend and attorney in Twisp. 'Hi, Jean. How's the legal business?'

'You know Twisp, there aren't a lot of high rollers or even people that pay their bills on time. What's happening with you?'

'Just came down from the mountains. You remember the phantom of the wilderness, the old man people used to talk about but rarely saw?'

'I think I remember people mentioning him but I don't like going out very far anymore. What about him?'

'It's a long story but he's here on the ranch and I have a feeling he is going to be here for a while.'

'You think that's wise? Is it safe to have him there?'

'He's old and it's kind of funny. He saved Pipey and I owe him for that. It's getting closer to winter and I don't want him freezing to death. I'll tell you the whole story sometime over coffee. What I wanted to ask you is if you think your husband would do some pro bono dental work?'

'It wouldn't be the first time. You want me to ask him for you?'

'I'd appreciate it. You might want to tell him his teeth are pretty bad.'

'Oh boy, OK, I'll ask. He'll probably do it out of curiosity.'

Chapter 56

Lights blinked and monitors flickered in the subdued lighting in the underground room that the Huachuca Wolf Pack called home.

'Misa, you want to tell me how you got past the CIA zebra-level computer security without leaving any trail? I mean, I break in all the time but do it through proxies. We play cat and mouse for a while and then they kick us out. Looks like you can live in their system and they don't have a clue. You've come a long way since Atari, Grandma.'

Misa rolled her eyes. 'Yes, I'll enlighten you, my young pup. Not today though. I need to do a few more things; I'll fill you in tomorrow. Right now if you can wheel over my mobility scooter, that'd be a huge help,' said Misa, teasing the young illegal hacker turned white hat, or more like gray hat, *or maybe even closer to charcoal,* she thought. 'Then I need to get into the cartel's computer. Just a feeling that your mystery chase will end there.'

'What is Sheilla still concerned about? The lunatic woman is dead, right? And what do you mean our chase will end there?'

'Well, that's what Sheilla wants to confirm. She wants us to monitor until there is more proof that Najma is dead. The CIA says so but that doesn't make it so. If the cartel is up and running, I'll bet so is their computer center.'

'We'll leave Jason monitoring things around Jim and Brush until they get out of the country. Maybe between the three of us we can hack their computer. Should be easier this time.'

'So you say. I've been trying; I keep running into firewalls I can't break through.'

'Ha, can't be that hard, you just busted the CIA's system,' said Jason, sensing an opportunity to get even if he could hack into their computers.

'Word is that a character named Vladislav was recruited or kidnapped or whatever from Russia by that Guillermo character.'

'Never heard of a Vladislav,' said Jason.

'Figures, he's not mentioned in comic books,' Vidya shot back and then said, 'I've been looking into his past, thinking maybe that would help us break his security. You remember the hacker that went by the handle Griswald?'

'Fuckin' a man, he's famous but dead.'

Vidya smiled and said, ''Fraid not, my young padowan. I think Vladislav is Griswald.'

'Wow, cool! Makes this interesting.' Jake cracked his knuckles and sat down in front of his three monitors, put on his headset that blared heavy metal and started typing at a furious pace as he bobbed and swayed.

Vidya looked at Misa and asked affectionately, 'Mike, you want a snack before we go at it again? We're going to be here for the rest of the night.'

Misa looked at the kid hacker bobbing to his music while he typed and said, 'Not right now, Vid. That youngster might actually get ahead of us. I can't stand either of them when they're smug. Let's teach them another lesson in humility, shall we?'

Director Sorenson looked at Bertrand and Martin and said, 'Tomorrow will be a great day. President eats crow while I stay the director.' In the past, Martin would have made a wise crack. Now he just looked with disdain at the director. Then he exchanged a look with Bertrand that said, *Great for who? Certainly not the CIA.*

'Bertrand, I'll do the morning briefing with the president and then I want you and Martin in the White House by zero eight hundred for a meeting with the secretary of state and the director of the FBI.'

Sorenson got up and left. 'Put it out of your mind, Martin,' said Bertrand. 'He'll find a way to lose his job without any help from us.'

Alva Gager and Najma deplaned the STOL modified Cessna 206 and climbed into a Land Rover, which promptly raced down the dirt road that had also been their runway. Thirty minutes later, they boarded a sleek Beech King Air at Bisbee Municipal Airport. The Land Rover sped away as the pilot turned onto the runway and taxied to the end, turned around and pushed the throttles forward. The fast twin-engine plane nearly jumped off the runway, climbing fast it turned north toward Washington State.

Alva had given up trying to talk to Najma. He picked up the satellite phone, dialed the hacienda and handed it to Najma. 'Your operation,' he said. 'We are leaving Bisbee,' Najma informed Guillermo, who picked up the phone immediately.

Guillermo was pleased that the plan was going smoothly. His men had secured the pickers' cabins at an apple orchard in the town of Okanagan several miles from Wolf Canyon Ranch. Najma and Alva would fly to the larger town of Wenatchee where their plane would not be out of place when it landed. It would arrive near sunup and then his two assassins would be driven to a private house mixed in with the pickers' cabins. His plan assumed they would have no contact with the others until the day of the attack.

Esteban, Gonzalo, and Lazaro, along with four other cartel members, had already spent a day walking across state game land to Coyote Ridge and observing Wolf Canyon Ranch below. They were pretending to be hikers and bird lovers that were watching the dozens of eagles that soared on updrafts near the ranch and Wolf Mountain.

Gonzalo and the thinner, younger Esteban were enforcers for the cartel in north central Washington. They both had green cards and spoke fluent English. They stood on Coyote Ridge overlooking the ranch.

Lazaro pointed across the canyon to the ridge opposite, which rose directly behind the ranch house. 'There are no windows on the back. We can walk down from that side to the house without being seen. All the windows are facing down the valley with just a few looking this way. The woods directly below us could hide an army.'

'That is a big dog with a big bark,' said Esteban.

'Big dogs make an easy target. Najma has a nearly silent weapon and can shoot it without anyone hearing. My men say the dog always stays on this side of the house,' said Lazaro and then continued. 'Esteban, you will have six of my men and come down from behind the house. I want you to take at least two men and put them down the canyon to keep anyone from driving up. Gonzalo will take the rest and come from the woods at the top of the canyon. You see anything wrong with this plan? It is the one that Guillermo gave me. I think it is good and don't see how anyone can escape.'

'We are certain they have no other way to call for help?' said Gonzalo. 'I do not worry about whether we can kill everyone but it is a long way to get back to the cars if they get others to come. What do we do if the army or sheriff brings a helicopter?'

'Yes, it is the one thing we can do nothing about, the long distances back to the cars. The phone line is buried but easy to cut at the junction boxes along the road. The two men guarding the road will do it.'

'Radio or cell phone?' asked Esteban.

'Possiblemente, pero…'

Lazaro cut off Gonzalo, 'Speak only English.'

'Está bien,' smirked Gonzalo. 'OK, OK, but they will never know what hit them. Even if they did, there is no one close to here except the couple of deputies in Twisp, and the fat, lazy sheriff deputies in Okanagan. No helicopters close. We can get away in the hour it would take them to get here.'

'Quickly kill them and leave. We will still be cautious. The two Americans I showed you the picture of are highly trained. We have many more men and surprise on our side, which should give us the advantage.'

'We hear rumors about this woman. Why bring her?'

'Shut up, Esteban, and don't even think about messing with her. Guillermo says she will be in charge when she arrives. If you have a problem, take it up with him. Personally, I wouldn't cross her or even say anything to her or you might find yourself dead.'

'No woman will kill me,' said Esteban.

'You will follow orders, Guillermo's orders and mine or she won't have to kill you,' said Lazaro as he moved in close to the shorter Esteban and then looked at Gonzalo. 'Understood?'

Chapter 57

Captain Jasper Neilly, Jim, and Brush, along with Marilyn and Gaston Reese, Neilly's second in command, sat around a small table in the mess hall, its size appropriate for the smallest ship in the navy. 'We're pretty incognito on this ship. All it's ever been used for is helicopter-landing practice. That is what is being set up with Gitmo for our cover. They start practicing next week.'

'Glenda's in trouble. I can feel it,' said Brush.

'Too early to tell but maybe,' said Jim. He looked at Neilly. 'We don't have a clue exactly where the hell she and Kramer are.'

'Last communication they were headed to X-Ray.'

'The problem,' said Jim, 'is we don't know for sure they are in X-Ray and storming a CIA facility might cause a little trouble.'

'We bust someone's head and find out,' said Brush. 'Maybe one of the seaman escorts.' Looking at Jim, he then added, 'Yeah, yeah OK, not a good idea, but I don't have any better ones and I feel stupid sitting on my ass doing nothing, eh.'

Jim felt for him, knowing he was frustrated. 'Must be some communication we can tap into. Get Mac to connect up with Sheilla and see if her group or the Wolf Pack can tap into X-Ray's communications.'

'Right, Jim. If they were caught in X-Ray, someone would have notified the CIA's night desk at Langley.'

Najma and Alva stepped off the plane as soon as the large metal hangar door closed and stood together near the edge of the Wenatchee airport. Two men immediately started to unload the plane's cargo into a van. Najma and Alva walked to an older, nondescript, green four-wheel drive Ford Explorer. Najma opened the passenger side door and climbed into the backseat, planning to keep Alva in front of her from now on. She didn't like him nor trust the reason he was here. Guillermo's insistence on his presence had increased her misgivings.

They drove alongside a wide slow-moving river. She watched the driver's face in the rearview mirror and looked behind them in the outside mirror. Alva's head topped with slicked-back hair lolled slowly back and forth as the SUV wound its way north, past undulating rows of apple trees covering the hills as they ascended above the river. Along the way, migrant workers stood on ladders picking red apples.

The picking shacks where they headed were now empty as the orchards surrounding them were Gala apple trees. Gala harvesting had finished in mid-August. The timing was good: busy area with lots of people moving about leaving them unnoticed, but they would have Brixton Fruit Orchards to themselves. As if anyone would dispute what the cartel members wanted to do with either the migrants or their living quarters.

She had had no interest in listening to Alva on the flight as he made conversation, telling her the history of the area and expounding on the problems of the orchardists and how they couldn't survive without illegal migrants. There were not enough people who would do the manual labor in America. So the cartel brought them across the border, took most of their wages, and ran drug operations and protection rackets much like the old Mafia.

Local law enforcement not only had their incomes supplemented but their jobs were made easy by the cartel who kept the migrants from making any sort of trouble.

Najma wondered why this man had any interest in talking about local law enforcement's uneasy truce with the Siastra cartel. The apple pickers meant nothing to her, nor did the cartel. What happened between them was of no concern.

Alva's discussion was part of the way he disarmed people like Najma. Prattling on deflected them from his real character. Alva was a Hebrew variant of Alveh, meaning evil and iniquity, the name he assumed in the Mossad. An apt characterization as Alva, calm and analytical, was as cold underneath as Najma.

The dull green Ford with its dark tinted windows, pulled along-side a small house in a row of similar but smaller houses and shacks. They were dingy, dirty-looking buildings with paint peeling and ripped screens, built years ago with cheap materials. Derelict cars, shoes, and debris sat outside, remnants from the poor migrant workers who had gone on to pick at orchards with later maturing varieties of apples.

The car stopped directly in front of the entrance door leaving just enough room for the car doors to open. The driver asked Alva and Najma to get out on the house side and go straight in. He passed them scruffy baseball caps. 'Don't look around or go out in case DEA or the border patrol is watching us.'

Flayback happily had spent the day orchestrating a public relations campaign for her boss and getting her hair done for the press conference. Sorenson gloated at his victory and the power that he wielded at the world's largest intelligence agency. The president and secretary of state had little choice but to embrace him with careful if minimal comments from the White House PR arm stating that the agency had performed well under the senator's direction.

Sorenson, however, didn't like the new attention that Martin received within the agency. He, as the director, should be getting the staff's—his staff's— respect, for his skills as a politician, not some lightweight like Pearson who'd only managed to get his dick cut off. Instead, most of them ignored Sorenson, staying away from him whenever possible. Only the likes of Flayback scratched his ego. However, everyone now treated Martin Pearson with respect, and to his credit, the man acted in a relaxed and serious manner. He had always been good at his job; it was his unbearable personality that made him hard to put up with. Now, Sorenson hated the respect he was getting.

He decided to bide his time and then manufacture some way to fire the man. The thought made him happy. He daydreamed about having the smart-ass Martin escorted out by security, followed by his personal items in a few boxes and dumped in the parking lot.

Martin grew comfortable with his new status. While he had told the truth about his capture there were some things he had omitted. He didn't like remembering the pain and how he had screamed. If he had known that the cartel had laughed at him and nicknamed him 'Statue of Liberty' he would have felt very embarrassed.

Behind both his old and new personalities, Martin harbored an intelligent mind and, once or twice, the idea that he had escaped so easily, or was able to escape at all, passed through his thoughts.

Chapter 58

Glenda, Kramer, and Grant had been prodded into a hall lined with cells. 'Any of you want to tell me why the hell you are breaking into a secure government facility that is totally off-limits? Of course, you knew that. I have a feeling you are all going to do some big jail time. I could say a good word on your behalf if you cooperated.'

'Are you joking or just overrating your importance,' said Glenda.

Grant didn't respond as he concentrated on his chances of disarming their captors. Much to Glenda's surprise, Kramer said belligerently, 'Fuck you.'

Dougal hit Kramer with a vicious blow to his kidney, knocking him to the ground. Grant sensed the opportunity and grabbed Gould's wrist that was holding the gun pointing toward Kramer.

Glenda started to turn and Dougal wrapped a muscled hairy forearm around her neck while holding a pistol to her head.

Gould leered at Grant. 'Concerned about the little lady, are you? That's good because I am. I want her in good shape when I talk to her later.' He thought back regretting he'd missed his chance with the dark-haired sexpot Najma; he'd almost got her to spread her legs. *Not going to miss this one,* he thought. 'Turn around, slope.' He jerked Grant's hands behind his back and snapped on metal cuffs. 'Get him in cell two. I want her in one. I want him close while she squeals.' He ogled her breasts.

'Whatcha think, peaches and cream?'

He was surprised when Glenda smiled at him. She slowly lifted her hands and touched Gould's black cheek. He didn't stop her. 'Nice color.' Then she kneed him as hard as she could, catching Gould square in his crotch. Pain spread across his face and he stood stooped over and groaning.

Seaman Jones looked at Dougal, surprised to see him looking pleased. 'Get her in the cell and then him,' said Dougal as he pointed, giving Kramer a kick in the side.

Gould leaned against the wall with one hand. 'You're going to pay for that, strawberry shortcake.' Then he walked slowly away.

It was just past midnight at the enclave the Wolf Pack loved. The artificial lights gave no clue to the time of day. It did not bother Jake, Jason, Vidya, or Misa. None cared for sunlight or the outdoors. When they were having fun, none cared about sleep. Their social circle consisted of each other and their banter. Their lives were one they fully embraced, here in their computer room.

Computer keys clicked and information raced by on their screens, illuminating their faces in eerie light. 'I got something,' said Jake. 'Just tagged a call to the CIA night desk about an hour ago. It says three people entering X-Ray illegally were detained with injuries.'

'I'll call it up to Sheila,' said Misa.

'Let them sit 'til morning,' said Gould. 'I'm going to pay that lily-white woman a visit then.'

'You think you'll be up for it?' chuckled Dougal, pleased as he thought he might have made a triple entendre *or was it only a double*, he wondered.

Gould passed a hand over his shiny head, scowled, and walked out.

Sheilla called Will Crystal and filled him in on what Misa had told her. 'Jim might have to sit tight, wait for more information,' said Will. 'Not so sure that Brush will.'

'You want me to tell them anything?'

'Nope. It will be Jim's call; talk to him and only him. Let me know ASAP when you hear what his decision is.'

Chapter 59

Jim and Brush in full camouflage peered through dense foliage ten feet from the fence opening outside of X-Ray. Jim had mixed emotions about being here but there'd been no holding Brush back once he'd heard the word 'injuries.'

They had been here for over an hour and everything was dead quiet. Jim looked at his watch, nearly zero three hundred. He felt good being here, out in the field, with Brush. His thoughts wandered back to Pedro, the months at the ranch, and Heather. He had been happy during those times but the feelings he had now, here on the edge of the Cuba's jungle, were more intense, he felt alive and there was no undercurrent of pressure.

Gaston positioned himself near the fence, twenty meters away from Jim and Brush, with a view of the entrance to X-Ray. Neilly and the team's medical specialist, Jeff, were fifteen meters apart, a hundred meters behind Jim and Brush's position, ready to move up if needed. If Jim and Brush moved forward, they would advance to the fence opening. Tom, also known as Techie Tom, along with a new addition to their Special Forces team, Fleur, a tropical medical specialist, fluent in Spanish and an expert in light weapons, stayed near their landing raft. Mac and the others remained on ship monitoring communications and on alert if needed.

'Two men approaching entrance,' said Gaston softly.

Brush touched Jim's arm and pointed toward the fence opening. Jim turned his head to the left and said softly, 'Moving.'

'Moving up,' said Neilly.

Jim and Brush, crouching, moved silently through the fence opening and against the building.

'Three meters,' said Gaston.

They moved to the corner of the building near the entrance and listened as the two men, talking, walked nonchalantly toward X-Ray's entrance.

A few seconds passed and Gaston said, 'Gate opening...go.'

Jim moved rapidly around the corner with Brush covering their approach. Just before it closed, Jim ducked into the door behind the two men, dressed in civilian clothes, followed closely by Brush.

Jim put his finger to his lips as the two startled men stared. Then he pointed at the taller of the two men and the keypad next to the door. The man hesitated, Jim moved closer with his MP5 pointed at the man's chest. The black man started to speak and Jim shook his finger. The man said, 'Fuck you.' Before Gould could finish the thought, Jim hit him hard with a collapsible steel baton on his left temple. He slumped to the ground.

Jim motioned with the baton for the shorter man to open the door. He hesitated for a second and then with an unsteady hand pushed the keypad. The door swung open. Jim smiled at the man and motioned for him to turn around. He quickly put the smaller man in a headlock and injected him with an unhealthy dose of amnesia-inducing Versed and fentanyl. A large but not fatal dose.

Brush flipped the taller man over, reached in a pocket and quickly secured the man's hands and feet with disposable cuffs. He then injected him, just as Jim had done to the smaller man. Neither Gould or Dougal would stir until the next morning and they would remember nothing. Brush moved up behind Jim within seconds as they walked softly down a short corridor toward an open door that was casting light into the dim hall.

Sitting behind a monitoring station, just where Sergeant Alex Smith had once sat, before the cartel ended his dreams of fortune with a bullet to the head, was a man with his head on his arms, sleeping. On the monitoring screen were several small squares showing the outside, the entrance, and the corridor that Jim and Brush had just passed.

Brush smiled, as if to say, *He's helpful.* Jim nodded and plunged a syringe into the man's neck. His head jerked up, and he looked at the two men with dark streaked faces. He closed his blurry eyes and reopened them as if he was shaking off a dream before slumping back in his chair unconscious. With the three men secured, and now in a deep memory-less sleep, Jim studied the control panel and the monitor. 'Seems no other spooks are at home,' he said looking at the security monitors.

Brush saw the monitor showing Glenda's cell. She looked as though she was sleeping. He couldn't see if she were injured or not. He immediately started out the door.

'Wait. I can see a key pad outside the cell. Dammit,' said Jim.

He did a quick search on the computer. 'Nothing.'

'Old technology,' said Brush and he pointed at a small sheet on the side of a file cabinet labeled 'cell code.' 'Five, four, three, two, one. Jesus,' said Brush. He moved back into the corridor, punched in the door code and walked into the cell.

He knelt down by Glenda's cot and lightly stroked her hair. She turned and with a sudden realization threw her arms up and around him and then looked Brush in the eye for several seconds. 'Nice to see you.'

'Let's get out of here, beautiful, eh.' In his best Canadian accent. The out sounding like 'oot.'

'Maybe we should get Kramer first.'

'Yeah, OK, suppose we have to,' responded Brush. 'You look as beautiful as ever, is the desk jockey injured?'

They moved down to the next room and pushed in the same number on the pad. Brush walked into the dark cell and immediately an arm was around his throat.

'Let go, Grant,' Glenda started to say.

But before she could get it out, Grant ended on the floor.

'Mother,' he said looking up and holding his head.

'Grant, eh. I thought you were Kramer. Sorry, pal,' Brush said, as he reached his hand down and pulled Grant to his feet.

'Gets tiring, getting knocked to the floor,' said Grant.

'In that case I'll forgive you,' said Brush.

'You forgive me?'

'Let's move it,' said Brush, smiling at Glenda.

Brush pushed the code into the third key pad and looked into Kramer's cell more carefully than he had done with Grant's. 'Should have known, sound asleep,' said Brush.

Grant walked over as if to shake Kramer and instead said, 'Playing possum are we, Captain?'

Kramer sat up, holding his rib cage. 'Very happy that it's you. I was expecting that prick that broke my rib. I had a plan to get even.'

'Is that really Kramer!' said Brush.

'He needs a little training but he turned out to be not so bad,' said Glenda.

'A world full of surprises, eh.'

As Glenda, Brush, Kramer, and Grant walked into the control room, Jim stood, going through files. There was nothing about the escape but there was a file about an autopsy for Sergeant Alex Smith who died about two weeks ago of a gunshot wound. He grabbed the file and walked into the corridor.

Kramer stopped as he passed Gould lying on the floor. Smiled and kicked him in the rib cage.

'Guess you did get even,' said Brush.

'Said I had a plan.'

Then to his surprise, Glenda kicked Gould hard in the crotch.

Brush looked at her questioningly.

'He didn't hurt me but he was planning on it.'

'Kick again for me,' said Brush, and she did.

'We clear?'

Gaston said, 'Clear as the night's sky.'

Grant looked at Jim, 'I'm staying. Give the general a howdy,' then added, Thanks. I leave you to your Gitmo escape. I'm going to shower and grab a few things and get my ass out of here.'

'I have a feeling someone will be looking for you in the morning,' said Jim.

'Possibly. I am going to scoot onto a ship first thing. It will take them some hours to figure out what happened. If I'm lucky they won't have any evidence but regardless that dipshit Gould will want me bad.'

'If he remembers anything,' said Brush.

'You think not?'

'Kind of doubt it,' said Jim.

Grant smiled. 'Good idea erasing their security tapes. Might save my ass except someone knew we were coming. I'm going to find out who and how. Pleasure meeting you all.'

Seconds later the group joined Neilly and Jeff as they moved off toward the shoreline. Gaston followed several meters behind.

'Ten minutes,' said Neilly.

Fleur acknowledged. She and Tom waited a few minutes before moving to the raft in the water, arriving just before the returning group. They headed to the small ship. Glenda and

Brush made no overt signs of their mutual affection but they sat close each other, both more content then they had been in the past hours.

Jeff and Fleur wrapped Kramer's ribs and put some antiseptic on his head wound and a small butterfly bandage. Mac called the pilots of the Citation X that had brought Glenda and Kramer to Guantánamo only a day earlier and told them to be ready for takeoff as soon as directed. Marilyn Cutter was busy with the pre-flight of her highly modified Sikorsky UH-60 Black Hawk.

Bertrand sat thinking, not pleased, after having a phone call from X-Ray passed on to him in the middle of the night. They locked up three people. Two were General Crystal's people and the third a navy man and past CIA employee. Bertrand called a quick meeting for six a.m., including Martin Pearson; Eric Sands, head of National Clandestine Service; and his NCS deputy, Eileen Skinner.

'They tell you how someone could penetrate their security?' said Eric, the fit, slightly balding veteran, then added, 'Why weren't we informed before this morning if they were broken into last night? Why the delay?'

'The night desk passed it along but the duty officer didn't think it was worth waking me up over until the new one came on duty at five. She identified them from facial and prints and decided it was worth waking me up.'

'It sounds like this started with the woman's escape and Sorenson's handling of it,' said Eric, who had been more verbal about his dislike of Sorenson than most of the other staff.

'What were they doing breaking in, that's the real question,' added Martin realizing that not everyone knew the history of Najma, which was the only plausible explanation of why the general's men and woman wanted into X-Ray.

Bertrand sat quietly and then said, 'Eric's correct; Sorenson's hiding her escape was a mistake in the first place, but let's stay on the current problem.'

Eileen, whose short light hair, sharp angular features and petite build failed to disguise her quick mind, said, 'Call General Crystal. Tell him two of his people entered X-Ray illegally. Demand an explanation.'

Chapter 60

Katarina, Fred, Sheilla, and the general waited anxiously in the operations room. At zero-four-hundred Cuba time, the communication light lit, followed by, 'Retrieval with no problems, no detection, chickens flew the coop,' reported Mac.

Sheilla dialed Misa. 'Everyone is now safe but we need to know as soon as the CIA finds out and if they know it was us.'

'No sweat. We'll snoop around and let you know.'

'General, what is the CIA going to do when they find out?' asked Sheilla.

'Let's get a full report from Jim so we can assess our exposure. No detection means they got in and out clean and we don't have to say a word.'

'Maybe.'

'Spit it out, Sheilla.'

'Fat chance. They would have cameras and whoever captured them probably sent their prints and photos. They were ID'd before we broke them out.'

The general told his night duty clerk to get Sorenson on the line. A few minutes later the NDC tapped on the general's door and said, 'Sorenson's on the line and grumbling about an early morning call.'

'Sorry, Richard, did I wake you? It's middle of the night out here but I thought you would be up and at 'em on the East Coast.'

'I appreciate your apology. What do you want?'

'What sort of game are you playing with Najma?'

'What do you know about her?' Sorenson was gaining some confidence that this might turn out to be to his advantage.

The general knew he was at a disadvantage and thought that telling it straight would probably be the best course. It usually was but with a politician like Sorenson one never knew. 'We have an interest in the terrorist you were supposed to be keeping at X-Ray. Now we have confirmation Najma was outside of X-Ray and I want to know why.'

'There'll be a formal public announcement from the White House later this morning. I guess they decided to finally put you in the loop,' Sorenson said, smirking, assuming the general had been informed about Najma by the White House ahead of the official press announcement.

'Why weren't we informed immediately?' demanded the general.

'The White House did make a preliminary statement earlier to agencies.'

The general wasn't about to tell Sorenson what they knew with the help of the Wolf Pack. He couldn't resist seeing how Sorenson would play this.

'I'll get a report and let you know, General, right after I see what we can disclose to you.' Sorenson hung up and lay back with his arms behind his head, no longer resenting the call. He didn't like the general and seeing him squirm left him pleased.

'I don't think he knows about X-Ray,' said the general.

'Hard to imagine but I think you are right,' said Sheilla, shaking her head.

Everyone looked at Vidya as he celebrated, flapping his hands, high-fiving himself in the air... 'Oh yeah. Cool. Love this shit.'

'You going to let us in on what's so cool?' asked Misa.

'Sure, Mikey.'

'You know I don't really like you calling me Mike.'

'Sorry, gal, only when I am excited.'

Now she really glared at him for calling her gal. 'Spit it out and quit yelping around like a teenager.'

'I just hacked the satellite phone servers. Easy as pie, never tried it before. Now we need to isolate calls from Gitmo, the CIA, and the cartel for the general. Anybody wanna help?'

'Let's split it up and see if we can find anything useful,' said Misa.

'We need an algorithm to isolate calls of interest.'

'They already have them in their system. I'm skimming through calls originating from the cartel's area,' said Jake. 'Jesus. Look at this. Series of calls first from just over the border and then eastern Washington.'

'National Security Agency records this stuff. See if you can get them, Jason. You're the NSA expert, right?'

Thirty minutes later they had a recording of a woman's voice talking to the cartel headquarters in Tubutama from southern Arizona. No names had been used but Misa went white.

'It's her,' she said. 'I recognize that voice anywhere. It scares me to death that she is so close to us.'

'You sure?' asked Jason.

'I'm sure,' interjected Vidya.

'It's a nightmare voice for me, I'll never forget it,' said Misa.

'Call Sheilla,' said Jason. 'Let's track her. They must think their sat phones are secure.'

'Vladislav's good, right?' added Vidya. 'You think we're secure?'

Mac came out of the Baylander's communication room and

handed Colonel Johnson a message. 'Just came in, Colonel.'

Jim's face became rigid. 'Tell Marilyn to fire up the chopper. Get everyone's gear on board as fast as you can, Mac, and make sure the Citation files a flight plan to Methow Valley State before we get on board. No delay.'

Brush looked at Jim, waiting for an explanation.

Chapter 61

'I'm going alone. I don't want anyone else with me. Get rid of anyone else and get me a car,' she ordered. 'I'll drive myself.'

'Señorita,' said Gonzalo.

Lazaro quickly said, 'That is not our plan or my orders. Your target is not there, he is in Cuba, thousands of miles away. There is no hurry. We can stay here and relax.' He could feel Gonzalo tensing.

Lazaro shook his head at Gonzalo.

Gonzalo ignored Lazaro. 'Fucking punta don't tell me what to do,' he nearly spat at Najma.

Lazaro shook his head once and quickly moved between Gonzalo and Najma.

'She does and so do I. Now shut up, Gonzalo, and that goes for everyone.'

Gonzalo stood muttering under his breath as Lazaro moved away. He was so angry that he didn't even see Najma take out a small knife. The next thing he knew, her knife was at his throat and a small stream of blood dripped onto his shirt. She held the back of his head with her other hand. Najma's eyes were daring him to make a move.

'Najma, we need him,' said Lazaro. She pushed her double-edged knife in a fraction farther. The blood increased, the blade now close to his jugular. She held his eyes and in a fluid move stepped away, keeping eye contact with the Mexican enforcer.

Alva watched, impressed. Her speed, her beauty. The more he saw, the more he admired her. She was capable, ruthless, effective.

Lazaro picked up a walkie-talkie. 'Bring a car to number sixteen.'

The morning sun shone bright as it crested Coyote Ridge. Duane and Ben decided to make an early start. Duane didn't like working in the mid-day heat and the prediction was in the upper eighties. They gathered several steel posts, extra barbed wire and various tools onto the back of a red Kawasaki Mule.

Duane had started working for Jim when he was fifty-five and that was twenty years ago. His legs weren't what they used to be. Getting shot in the leg last year hadn't helped much either. 'I was going to take the Honda. More comfortable for me.'

'Wonder where it got to?'

'Saw it when we rode up. It's behind the cabin,' said Ben.

'Never mind. I'll take my truck up to the base of the hill.'

There was a long stretch of fence to repair high up on the Coyote Ridge in the trees where the ranch and the Forest Service land joined. It was steep. Duane planned to ride the four-wheel Mule up as far as they could. He could have gotten the Honda up higher and didn't relish walking up hill.

'We's got everything but the tamper, Ben. Load it up and drive up to the far Forest Service gate and I'll be along in a minute,' said Duane. He still had trouble not referring to the adult Ben as young Ben, but he knew Ben was still sensitive about anyone thinking of him as a youngster, and he'd more than proved himself an adult.

The road Ben and Duane drove was out of sight of Lazaro's man high up in the trees behind Coyote Ridge. The two snipers had moved into position just as the sky lightened. The second sniper had a clear view of the barns, house, and road lower down but couldn't see the end of the canyon where Ben headed. If he had been doing his job watching, he would have seen them down by the barn and on the road below the house. Instead, a tendril of smoke drifted up while he lay in a little swale, just behind his position, smoking and watching the sky after finishing a snack.

Lazaro chose their positions mainly to cover the area around the house. He expected that the action would be there and Najma would eventually have to move over the exposed ground to get away after killing the colonel when he returned. The snipers would have a clear field of fire.

Ben liked the view from high up at the back of the ranch. The canyon flowed down toward the valley and the mountains looked taller. The air smelled of pine and the vine maples were turning red. Duane's old Toyota pickup crawled slowly up the rough track. He pulled off under a big ponderosa pine and stopped.

'You gonna take up lunch?' asked Ben.

'No, siree. We come down here for lunch and then we's through. I got hay to put up at home. Got plenty of coffee.' He dropped a large green metal thermos into an orange plastic milk case bungeed to the back rack of the Mule. Duane pulled on the metal posts and they felt secure. 'We's ready, I'm a driving, you have to walk.'

'We can both ride.'

'Nope, better just me. Lighter and will crawl up the hill better with just one person.' And he was thinking, *It's steep and not safe.* 'Almost forgot with yous jabbering at me, get the shotgun outta my truck.'

'You're not shooting coyotes.'

'Ain't planning on it, but they's plenty a bear about now.'

'You aren't shooting no mother bears either. They all have cubs.'

'No, sir, Ben, I ain't shooting any critter that leaves us be. But remember when Craig and me run into that big old male bear? He might a killed us if we hadn't gotten up a tree. I'm a too old to climb no trees.'

Chapter 62

'Oh-niner-thirty. Who's on call?' boomed General Crystal to his night clerk.

'Team C, sir. Captain Carter.'

'Fire 'em up. I'm going to be out of here in thirty minutes max. I want them behind me as soon as possible. Is Sheilla on her way back in?'

'She never left, just like you.'

'Then ask her to come to my office in five minutes.'

There was a knock on the door and the general looked up irritated that it hadn't been five minutes. 'Enter. Oh, Sergeant Mason. How'd you know I was just about to call you?'

'I didn't know. I heard you were here and I wanted to ask you something.'

'Unless it's really important, I need you to get my bird loaded ASAP. I want a full set of weapons including a fifty.'

'Yes, sir, then I want to go.'

'What?'

'Colonel Johnson promised me down in supply that if anything happened I could go. I'm good for one last mission before boob-tube time.'

With only a few seconds' hesitation, the general nodded his assent. It would be good to have the battle-tested sergeant with him. He understood what the other man was feeling. 'Don't just stand there, kit up and get us loaded.'

'Yes, sir,' said Mason as he snapped a salute and turned on his heel and was out the door before the general could return it.

'You really think she is headed to the ranch? She could be headed anywhere.'

'Instinct and no time to waste.'

'Jim's ETA?' the general asked Sheilla.

'They have a flight plan direct to Methow Valley State. ETA
thirteen-hundred if they don't have to stop. They're diverting around
storms in north Texas and have headwinds. They are working on
different plans but it seems likely they will have to refuel and if they
do it will cost them an hour.'

'We may be jumping the gun here, nevertheless, better early
than late. Get on the horn and see if you can get Neilly's team here.'

Sheilla smiled a big white-toothed smile and shook her long
auburn hair back. 'Most of them are on the plane with Jim.'

The general slapped the desk. 'Dang it, I love those boys. Good
call, Sheilla.'

The general boomed out for his night clerk and told him to get
Carter on the line and his response team in the air. 'Tell him I'll be
in front of him and to contact me as soon as he's up.' Carter's team
was his best on-site quick-response Special Forces team. *They're
good but not as good as Neilly,* thought the general.

Suddenly the Wolf Pack's monitors showed flashing multicolored dots with what looked like an alien in the middle of their
screens, and then the screens went black. 'Not cool,' shouted Jason.

'What the hell,' said Jake.

'Griswald,' said Vidya. 'That's his signature.'

'Everyone shut down,' yelled Jason.

'Too late, we're already shut down,' said Misa.

'Disconnect your power,' yelled Jason.

'Let's get new computers up.'

'No "dead" Ruskie prick is going to one-up me. Tell Sheilla we're down.'

'This is war.' Jake sounded more excited than angry. 'Let's get up and running and get him,' Jason ordered, like the colonel he was.

Griswald sat smugly at his console. He was thought to be dead but he could not help using his old signature to tell the world, his world, he was reborn. He knew he was the best in the world. No one had ever defeated him. Misa and Vidya had as many years working computers as he had, but they didn't have the hacking time. He had been aware of the Wolf Pack's presence all along and had merely chosen his moment to shut them down.

Sheilla said when Misa called, 'Not good,' just as Fred burst in saying all their computers were out. 'Us too,' said Sheilla.

'Damn right not good.'

This was the first time Fleur had worked with Jim and Brush. 'Why does he look so worried?'

'It's just his way,' answered Brush.

'Meaning?'

'He's always in front of a mission. Works out all the permutations in advance. Worries in advance. He knows she'll come for him. He understands the woman. It's personal between them. The question is when. Why take chances.'

Jim sat on the smooth gray leather seats of the Citation staring ahead. Willing it forward. The pilot knew Jim's urgency. Nothing could control the situation. He could only sit as the plane moved northwest toward their destination, battling the heavy winds.

The dusty green Explorer pulled behind a deserted wood house with peeling, gray-white paint, off Highway 20. Twenty was the main east-west highway, although little traveled between Okanogan and Twisp. It went on through Winthrop and eventually crossed the North Cascades to the Pacific. The old house was deserted and owned by the Department of Wildlife. It was the closest place to Wolf Canyon Ranch that a car could park off the main road without going into the valley below the ranch. The approach from the house was also at a higher elevation, leaving less climbing to gain the top of Coyote Ridge than walking up from Beaver Creek.

Najma slung her rucksack. She carried no food, only weapons, binoculars, and ammunition. Just minutes after she started hiking the undulating ground toward Coyote Ridge, Alva pulled in behind the house. She had ordered him to stay at the pickers' house. He of course had no intention of staying and followed her. His first priority would be to help eliminate Guillermo's enemies and then to take care of the black-haired beauty. A professional, he would observe her and bide his time. He was not happy that Najma had set off in contradiction to the plan.

General Crystal looked at his old friend and said, 'Sergeant, you're riding shotgun. It's just us two. I'm not waiting for Carter's SWAT guys. They'll follow in their chopper. Let's hit it. Into the blasted sun we fly.'

'It's as high as I can get there, Ben. Let's stop for a spell and have some coffee.'

'Sure if you want. It only gets steeper from here. But I think I could drive up another couple hundred feet.'

'Not worth turning the Mule over and messing up our stuff or Jim's Mule.'

The morning sun felt like an electric blanket on Najma's back as she cautiously worked her way slowly west through gullies around small hills, concealing herself from observers with a higher vantage point.

Alva stayed well back. He knew her direction and needn't follow her too close. He looked at the terrain. The ridge far ahead ascended to the right or north toward the ski area and the Loup Loup pass. Sage eventually giving way to pines at the higher elevations to the north. The ground dropped off to the left and ultimately into the lower valley. He guessed she would angle toward the high trees and work her way to a vantage point on the ridge.

Najma slowly scanned the area as she approached the ridge. She felt close to her boy and her nemesis. The undulating terrain gave her exactly what she desired. A large hill protruded from the ridge. She could walk just below it and ascend toward the Ponderosa Pines above. Rocks protruded here and there from the hills but there were no cliffs or rock walls to climb. A 'soft' rugged country. Unpopulated and government owned with eagles, deer, and coyotes. All except for the isolated Wolf Canyon Ranch.

Chapter 63

'We're landing?' asked a sleepy eyed Brush. 'Headwinds are too strong. We're fueling up at Great Falls.'

'Any word?'

'General's nearing the ranch. I'll call Heather shortly and let her know he is going to pick her up.'

Glenda rubbed her eyes and yawned. 'What's our ETA?'

'When we're up again, I figure another hundred minutes.'

'How come you didn't warn her already?'

'Under the circumstances I didn't want to scare her. Not much she could do. Best that they just act normal until the general's a few minutes away. At the last minute I'll have them move above the house to a small flat spot where Will can touch down.'

Neilly sat relaxed in the jet and looked around at his team. They were all each other's best friends. Only Gaston Reese was married. None had time for a home life and they considered the team their family. They rarely added a new member and if they did, they did so carefully. The preferred way to bring a new member in was to ask them to freelance on several missions and then, and only if everyone agreed, invite them in.

Fleur, leaning back on the plane's sofa, legs straight out, between Jeff and Brush's empty seat, was their newest addition, a light weapons expert and qualified nurse practitioner. Five foot six inches, stout legs, slender torso, ropey muscles undulated through her caramel skin and contrasted with her green eyes and dark brown hair.

Joe McDonald, their heavy weapons specialist, lay stretched out on the cabin floor. Tom Bryant, nicknamed Techie Tom, sat in a chair cleaning his unassembled Beretta. Mac Smith's head lulled back as he slept on the sofa.

The others sat or slept, all feeling relaxed and safe in the aluminum capsule as it descended from the cold upper atmosphere.

The steward, a young captain, walked up and handed Jim a box apparatus with a phone attached. 'What's up, Sheilla?'

'Have to call you this way. Our computers are down. Wolf Pack's are down too.'

Jim tensed and sat a little straighter. 'Where's Will?'

'He's close, maybe halfway there. We're trying to get everyone hooked into this radio. I should have the general tied in in a few minutes.'

'Who's the general got with him?'

'Sergeant Mason.'

'That's it?'

'Carter's team just left, they're at least thirty minutes behind the general.'

Jim decided he had to call Heather. He dialed using the satellite phone. No answer. He tried again and still nothing.

'What's up, buddy?'

Jim didn't answer. He wondered if she was upset and didn't want to talk to him. He put the side of the headset that held the mic up to his ear. 'Captain. Can we get by without refueling?'

'Maybe, doubt it. Depends on the wind. We can't chance it past the air base, there's no place to put down on our path in that part of the state past Fairchild.'

'Head to Fairchild and see what it looks like. Don't land here.'

'Will do. We'll burn more fuel at this altitude. I'll let you know our status as we approach Spokane.' The pilot understood that Jim knew things could change and wanted to leave the possibility open. *Fat chance but who knows. I like Crystal and want to get this bird if it will save his bacon. I'll notch things back without giving up much speed and maybe, just maybe...* The pilot fiddled with the power, pulling the levers back while he watched the speed and the fuel-use gauges.

'Give it your best shot,' Jim said, knowing he would do nothing less.

He looked at the others and said, 'Najma's in our backyard. No proof but she's there. Computers are out at the BWC and at the Wolf Pack computer center and guessing maybe no phone at the ranch.'

'Could be she's just not answering,' said Glenda, as much to soften the situation for Jim as anything.

Duane put his cup in an old bleached-out blue rucksack along with his silver thermos. 'Guessin' we might as well get to it. I get the wire and tools and maybe you carry a few of those posts up a ways, then come back and get the tamper. I'll get over into the trees and see what the fence looks like. Darn deer probably made a mess of it.'

Alva watched Najma circle below a hill and follow along its edge up into the high ground just below the trees. She was staying just out of sight below the top edges. He scanned the ridge, looking for anyone else. If Lazaro had left anyone there, they would be focusing down into the canyon on the other side of the ridge, maybe the far side. He probably wouldn't see them.

Najma reached the ridgetop above the house, well below where it ascended into the high pines where Duane and Ben were repairing fences. She stayed in a small group of young pines just behind the ridge crest and carefully peered over the edge. She scanned the area but saw no one. She moved quietly, in a low crouch, stopping and starting, using the natural cover to shield her, searching for the best position. Just over the ridge, by a sage and next to a shallow ravine, she stopped and lay on the ground, pulling out her binoculars. The crystal clear wide-field, high magnification, 10 x 70 binoculars needed to be steady. She bunched some grasses together, making a small natural pillow to rest the big binocs on. Looking at the house first, her face tightened when she saw Heather standing near the house and bending over to pull weeds. 'There is no sign of my son,' she muttered to herself watching the thin blonde. What did Johnson see in this woman? *The wimpy bitch is not worthy of him.*

Najma pulled her thoughts away and quickly scanned the valley and didn't see anyone else. Then a movement near the edge of the binoculars. She slowly turned to her left and stared across the canyon near the top of a dry ridge. Ten minutes later there was another movement. A man lifted a long gun in the air as he shifted positions. The size and scope told her it was a sniper. But whose? *Guillermo's,* she reasoned. Too unprofessional to be US military.

She scanned behind her and saw nothing. Nevertheless, she sensed she had been followed. Was it reason or intuition? In truth it was probably just what Jim did: assess the probabilities and draw the most likely conclusion. Alva saw a glint as the east sun reflected off her oversized binocular lens.

Najma's mind flicked back to Guillermo and Alva at the hacienda. She slowly shifted the binoculars to the house. Heather was gone. She looked at other likely sniper positions. She didn't see any movement or sign of others.

Above Duane and Ben, concealed in the trees, Lazaro's second sniper watched the woman at the house, unaware of Najma, Duane, or Ben. He could see the first sniper, concealed across the canyon, west of the house, lying in a small depression near the far side of Noname Ridge.

It was only a few days ago that Jim traversed the slope just below where Najma now lay, happily walking on a cow trail to meet up with Heather, Pedro, and Rosie.

The sniper on the Noname Ridge was back in his position and out of Najma's sight. That made her wonder if there were others she could not see. As she carefully searched, her thoughts jumped from Guillermo to Alva and back to the sniper. Yes, there would probably be other snipers. Were they to help her in Guillermo's misguided plan to eliminate Jim, or were they there for another reason?

She had sensed something had been wrong all along. Now all her instincts said the snipers were here for the same reason Alva was. All the pieces of the puzzle suddenly made sense. Her double. Guillermo wanted the agents and the general dead, but he wanted her dead too. He wanted to leave no trail back to himself. He wanted it to look like Najma killed them and had died doing so.

'You see the woman?' asked Lazaro over his radio phone.

'No,' responded Noname sniper.

The second sniper above Duane overheard and turned his scope toward Coyote Ridge, but he couldn't see in that direction through the thick trees.

Lazaro called Alva, 'Do you see her?'

'She's just over the ridge crest, probably observing the house. If I move closer, she may spot me.'

Heather decided to go inside and get some coffee. 'Come on.' Pedro was lying on top of Rosie near the back door. 'You want some juice?' He grinned at her. 'Way too early for Coke, young man.'

Pedro puffed out his cheeks. Heather gave him a play stern

look. She drew some water into the kettle and noticed her cell phone blinking. Missed call. There was no one she wanted to talk to so she set it down and put the water on the stove. Opened the cupboard admiring the white French Roast Starbucks package just as the phone rang again.

With resignation, she picked up the phone. There was no caller ID. She held it to her ear as she put the coffee filter over her mug.

'Jim,' she said in surprise after his hurried greeting.

'Just listen. We are on our way to the ranch. The general is only a few minutes from you. I'm closer to eighty minutes away, maybe longer. You are in danger. Get Pedro. Go out the loft door. Stay low and get to the little flat spot just above the house and wait for the general to pick you up. No hesitation. Keep quiet and turn your cell phone to vibrate.'

Najma. Jim didn't say it was her, but she knew. Heather turned so fast she knocked the coffee filter and mug onto the stone floor. Shaking, she moved around the corner to the startled Pedro. 'Walk up the steps,' she ordered. Pedro looked at her and started to talk. She covered his mouth. 'Upstairs now. Right now. Lola,' she yelled.

'Making bed upstairs.'

Pedro hadn't moved and just stood looking at her as if she had gone crazy. Then he started to cry. He sensed her fear. She lifted him, turned toward the metal stairs and ran up as fast as she could, hardly noticing she was carrying him.

'Listen carefully, both of you. Lo, stop working and listen. Your dad just called, Pedro. There is nothing to worry about but he wants us to get out of the house and up by that little lone pine tree. The general is flying over and will take us for a ride if you are very good and do just what I say.'

Lola noticed that Heather had a pistol in her pocket and crossed herself. Pedro's tears stopped as fast as they had started.

He jumped straight in the air and turned a couple of circles yelling, 'Yeah.'

'Quiet now. Listen. Your dad wants us to play a game and pretend we are sneaking out of the house so that no one can see us. He wants you to be very careful because maybe someone will be looking to see if they can catch us. If they see us, you can't go for a ride. Ready?'

Sitting on the flat, waiting for the general's helicopter, Heather started to shake. She huddled below the scraggly lone pine that had been barely clinging to life for the past several years. Its seed should never have settled on the tiny plateau, on the steep hill a hundred feet above the house. Heather had always loved this secret spot, she felt sorry for the struggling tree but now it offered little comfort. She pulled Pedro close to her.

'I wants another cup of coffee before we start pounding those posts in, Ben. Let's sit over yonder. It's a nice view a the ranch from way up here.'

'I'll carry the last of the posts up and come back in a couple of minutes,' said Ben, wanting to get to work and wondering how Duane could drink so much coffee.

Duane squinted as he tried to focus on a llama that stood in the fenced area behind the house. It stood tall in front of the other llamas, with its head held to maximum height. It then started making noises between a bark and a bray. It was a warning call.

Duane stood watching as the llama continued it's braying, wondering what the trouble was. Suddenly rising from a small gully-wash, he saw a black bear. It casually ambled along not a hundred feet from the llamas, angling toward the Noname Ridge. It stopped and started ripping at an old log with its paws, sending the rotten wood flying in all directions. Just as suddenly as the first bear appeared, a smaller one raced out of the gulley, stopped and then another charged it from behind. Both went rolling and wrestling while the mother of the twins searched for ants in the old log.

Duane wasn't as limber as he used to be and his back hurt most of the time so he looked for something to sit against. A lichen-covered rock pushed through the blue-green bunchgrass and sage just outside the tree line. Duane walked over and eased himself down and poured his fourth cup of black coffee into his decades-old green thermos lid and then started tamping tobacco into his pipe. *Life's not so bad sometimes,* he thought.

He sat back, grimaced and adjusted his position and was appreciatively sipping and puffing on his favorite pipe when Ben walked up and said, 'It is a nice view, just like you said.' Then he paused. 'What is that llama barking at?'

Duane pointed into the upper field. 'Lookie there. It's a bear with cubs.'

'They're playing,' said Ben. 'I'd like one for a pet.'

'Best leaving 'em wild, Ben. They don't bother us none unless it's like that big old toothless male that tried to eat Craig and me. Or you get in-between them there cubs and the mama.'

'The llamas are letting them have it.'

'All except Pipestone. He never makes a noise other than a hum,' said Duane.

'I think he's more like people than llamas.'

'The bears'll move on and they'll forget all about them. You'd a think Heather would be out seeing what the ruckus is about. No sign of her.'

'Busy with something or other in the house no doubt.'

Alva studied the ridge where he knew Najma was concealed. He saw nothing. Then a soft unnatural sound caught his attention.

He started to jump to his right. He was too late as bullet passed through his side. As he slumped to the ground, he turned his head. Najma stood only feet away. She studied him for a few seconds as he looked back, considering if he could take her. His rifle lay just out of reach.

Alva stared at the small bulbous gun held easily in her hands. He noted that it was an Armalite .22 shrouded in plastic and a thick silencer. *It must be nearly silent,* he thought. He didn't see Najma's finger as she caressed the trigger. The impact of the bullet on his skull stilled his thoughts as Najma quickly turned and walked toward the car.

Chapter 64

Jim leaned forward in his seat, willing the plane on. He knew the pilot was doing everything possible to use their fuel efficiently without sacrificing speed. He sat tense, not talking. They were still nearly an hour away as long as they didn't have to fuel up at Fairchild air base. That would cost them another forty-five minutes. 'Status, Captain?'

The pilot didn't answer right away and looked at the digital fuel gauge. He trusted the accuracy. The distance to Methow State airport showed on the GPS as 870 kilometers, 410 kilometers to Fairchild. His fuel gauge said they could fly 878 kilometers.

'Can't do it. We'd be burning fumes in the best conditions and if the wind picks up in the mountains...Sorry, Colonel. I'm putting it down at Fairchild.'

'Sheilla has us in permanent open communication now, Jim, so I heard everything,' said General Crystal. 'Sergeant Mason and I are just a few minutes out, passing Oval Lakes Trailhead now.'

'Carter is catching up with you. They're now only twelve minutes behind you, General. I'll tie them into you whenever you want,' added Sheilla.

'Heather's status?' asked the general.

'They'll be just above the house by a small lone pine,' said Jim. 'There's a little flat spot. Perfect place for you to land and they will be easy to spot. Get them to the airport and we'll meet there.'

'You got something in mind, Jim?'

'Yep. We'll leave some of Carter's team at the airport as backup with one of the birds. Get Heather, Pedro, and Lola on the Citation and back to Fort Lewis.

'Should get Nusmen too.'

Jim had to think about that. It would take time to get Nusmen. Time that would put Heather and Pedro in danger. 'Your call, General.'

'We survey the area and if we don't see anyone we set up some ambush points and spotters on the ridges.'

Lazaro was descending the Loup Loup Pass with three men. 'Carlos, that our car on the road; the one Najma took?'

'Sí.'

Lazaro scowled. 'Follow her. Keep way back.' He then called Alva. No response. Then he called his sniper on Noname.

'I've seen nothing.' Then sniper two said he hadn't seen anyone either.

Then he called Gonzalo who had taken his men to the ski area. There was no answer.

Gonzalo, a white bandage on his throat, walked angrily down a path from the Loup Loup with his men far ahead of him. His radio signals were blocked in the tight canyon between Wolf Mountain and the high end of Coyote Ridge.

Lazaro rang Gonzalo again five minutes later.

Bastardo, said Gonzalo to himself. 'OK, OK.'

'Where the fuck are you?'

'Walking in the woods, compadre.'

'You are supposed to only look at the ski area to understand the layout not go walking around.'

'I need to know what it is like between there and the gringos too,' and then the signal broke off again.

Lazaro called and again there was no answer. He hit the padded dash with the radio phone. 'Pinche culero.' He knew right then that he would kill this idiot. He then glared at Esteban who shrugged his shoulders. Esteban rather enjoyed Gonzalo screwing up, as he would not mind seeing Gonzalo cut his own throat.

'Six minutes,' said General Crystal. 'Sheilla, advise as soon as you have full com and computers back up. Jim, let me know your ETA when you're up.'

Sheilla sounded miserable. 'It's just us and the Wolf Pack that are offline, no one else on either of our bases is. We're getting nowhere bringing ours online. I feel worthless.'

'Keep at it, girl—you'll get it done.'

Lazaro's radio chirped. Vladislav telling him that the colonel had left Cuba and was getting close. Then another call.

Sniper one on Noname Ridge said, 'I have three people moving above the house. Two women and a small boy.'

'You see Najma?' asked Lazaro hoping maybe he was wrong about her being in the car he was following.

'No.'

Then Lazaro mumbled, 'What I thought.'

'Say again,' said sniper one.

'Forget it.'

Sniper two above Duane and Ben said, 'I too see the three people. They are moving very carefully. Maybe to look at the bear.'

'What bear?'

'A black bear walking across the field with niños.'

Noname started scanning the fields and Coyote Ridge and then spotted Duane and Ben but no bear.

'I see no bear but there are two men way up on the ridge not far from two's position.'

Lazaro was getting angry. More men. *I need to clean this up.*

'One, get ready to shoot the two men. Two, when I tell you, kill the two women but not the kid.'

'Gonna sit for a spell more and see where that bear a goen. You go and set those posts out where theys needs to be. I'll be along and we'll tamp 'em in.'

He was interrupted by llama brays again. 'They's looking back toward Coyote Ridge and up toward Wolf Mountain now. See anything, Ben? You's eyes better than myen.'

'Nothen, other than some deer running this way from the Loup Loup path. And the bear and cubs are running from something in the other direction.'

'Theys got better senses than we do. Somethens scaren 'em.'

Just then the unmistakable sound of a helicopter echoed up the valley.

'Army Huey coming in low and fast from the west,' said the sniper two above Duane.

'Malo,' said Lazaro, thinking rapidly. *Najma, off like a lone wolf. Then who the hell are the two on the ridge? And why didn't my men see them before?* he wondered. Lazaro had survived many battles by staying focused. He now saw how to turn this into his favor. The general could be in the chopper. Maybe to get the woman and the boy. *First, kill the two unidentified men. The general is one of the main targets and he is flying right to me. This is good,* he thought and nodded twice as if to confirm the decision.

'Mierda,' he mumbled and then accepting the new situation, 'Esta bien.' 'Both of you, shoot down the chopper and then one, kill the two men on the ridge. Two, shoot any survivors, then, three, kill both women.'

Duane and Ben were watching the helicopter as shots echoed both from above them and from way across the canyon. They watched in amazement as smoke erupted from the helicopter and it slowly leaned sideways, started to turn, and drifted toward the ground as if in slow motion.

'Losing RPMs,' said the general. 'Damn it, we're taking small arms fire,' as a hole appeared in the metal just to the left of his head. 'Tail rotor is hit. This what you been missing, Sergeant?' as he fought the controls. 'Where's it coming from?'

'Both sides of us, General. Don't see anyone.'

'We're going down,' said General Crystal. 'God damn it. I love this bird.' He struggled with the foot pedals and the throttle, trying to slow their spinning as they headed into the llama field below them. He tried to counter the spin by pulling in what was left of the power on and off as he jammed the opposite rudder pedal as hard as he could push. 'Can't stop the spin with the throttle. The RPM's are too low.'

Sheilla, Katarina, Mark, and the rest of her staff sat stunned in the BWC operations room just as everyone on board the Citation did. No one said a word. Then they all listened to clangs, bangs, and static hisses as the helicopter blades dug into the dry stony ground not far below the small pine tree where Heather, Lola, and Pedro lay watching, astonished. The tail nearly broke off and a skid crumpled under the impact. The helicopter lay with its left side pressed into the dirt.

Heather knew in her heart Najma was here. Lurking somewhere. 'Stay down,' she said to Pedro as she covered him and hugged Lola to them.

Everyone waited as the radio crackled with static. There was a low groan as the metal fatigued beyond its strength and gave way. Then a faint voice, nearly obscured behind the static, was heard.

'General, General Crystal, please come in,' said Sheilla.

Jim pushed the intercom. 'Get the ground crews ready for fueling. Zero delay, get us minimum fuel and get us airborne immediately.' Then he added, 'The general's helicopter was just shot down.'

After a second of indecision, not wanting her phone to ring, giving away her position, he called Heather. 'Stay put. There is another unit only minutes away. Make sure your phone is off ring. No noise. Can you see anyone at the helicopter?'

'I can only see a dust cloud. And smoke. 'The general...' and then in a whisper, 'is he dead?'

'The women and the boy are too close together for a clean shot,' said sniper two. Then he caught a movement out of the corner of his eye. 'Men, our men, coming into the canyon below me, from the north.'

The helicopter hit the ground on its side. Dust and smoke ballooned around it. Duane had been in combat in Korea and suddenly experience kicked in. 'Get up now, Ben. Get to the woods. I'll be behind. Move fast.' Duane's experience saved their lives. Sniper one, on Noname Ridge, was fixated on the helicopter that they had just shot down. He didn't see the two men moving farther into the trees until Duane, going as fast as he could, was six feet from the first tree. Then Noname fired a hasty shot that narrowly missed as Duane disappeared into the pines. Ben stopped and Duane, breathing hard, nearly fell on top of him as he tripped on a dead branch.

'You shot?'

'Naw, missed me, hit a rock.'

'It's the Pasayten killers. Isn't it?'

'One of 'em maybe. Hush now.'

'Someone is trying to kill us and whoever is in that helicopter,' whispered Ben.

'I hope it's not Jim,' said Duane.

They looked back through the trees from their higher vantage point toward the billowing dust and smoke surrounding the Huey.

Team C listened as the general's chopper went down. Carter shouted, 'Gear check. Five minutes.' Then to the pilot and door gunner. 'You see the shooters—light 'em up.'

He then looked at the GPS on the panel and next at a map in his lap, and pressed the intercom on the cyclic. 'I want you to come up the valley and then up the one canyon over on the west side. Stay below the ridgetop. I'll direct.'

The general's voice boomed over his radio static. 'You got a shooter on the ridge to the north of us and another somewhere on the other side high up Coyote Ridge.'

'Roger, sir,' said Carter.

'He said "us," ' shouted Sheilla. Everyone let out a cheer at the BWC.

'We're getting out. We have a little dust cover and will go out the north uphill side and hunker down.'

A young cartel member, wanting to make a name for himself, heard the shooting and ran out of the steep notch between Coyote Ridge and Wolf Mountain. He bolted down the canyon, leaping over fences, sage brush, and rocks. He reached the house before his boss, Gonzalo even got near to the head of the canyon. He crouched just below the octagonal deck where Heather, Jim,

Duane, and Craig had sat together so often for coffee, lunches, and barbecues over the years. He was excited to prove himself. He watched the helicopter start to spin before it disappeared below the plateau where Heather, Lola, and Pedro huddled together.

He moved under the deck toward the back and listened. He heard nothing. He darted up to the cement wall between the big windows and the long covered entrance at the back. Edging along the wall toward the covered entryway, he peered through the window in a side door. No sound. He opened it and then peered around the corner. Nothing.

Rosie-O-Twisp awoke and raised her head. She was alerted to llamas braying and clanking machinery but those were normal ranch sounds. Suddenly she heard the young cartel man's steps and then his smell. Her hair prickled and her neck ruff stood straight out. She jumped up. The ridged hairs making her look nearly twice her size. She stalked around the front of the house bristling and saw the man just as he turned from the door.

Rosie moved with lightning speed belying her size. A bone-chilling low growl rumbled from her deep chest. The low growl sent a chill through the young man's body and he froze. Shakily, he managed to lift his rifle as Rosie bore down on him.

'Rosie will come for us,' said Pedro.

Heather could barely speak. The evil woman, Najma, was here and whoever was in the helicopter was dead. Jim said the general was coming to pick them up. It must be him. But she couldn't tell Pedro any of that. She took a breath. 'Rosie's sleeping in her spot by the back door. I hope she stays there.'

'Two men by the cabin,' reported Noname sniper, 'and a dozen men coming from up the canyon, Gonzalo?'

'Asshole Gonzalo. Then what the fuck, two more men you didn't see before. Take 'em out then cover Gonzalo's men from the other two on the ridge. You kill the two on the ridge?'

'They disappeared in the trees.'

'*Idiot*. Keep your eyes open. You probably missed several more.'

Nusmen and Shuskin had heard the helicopter, and then the shots, as they were heating water on the propane stove inside the cabin. They rushed out the door with Shuskin hanging onto the back of Nusmen's coat. Nusmen didn't even notice him. Even if he had, the old guy didn't seem so strange to him anymore.

Nusmen took hold of the porch's thin support post and lifted himself up so he could see into the field where the noise came from. He couldn't see anything but a dust plume and black smoke and no helicopter. The sniper on Noname sighted in on Nusmen and squeezed the trigger. 'I wonder where it went?' Nusmen asked out loud, more to himself than Shuskin. Suddenly, he was slammed backward if hit by a sledgehammer.

Heather felt in her pocket. The small PPK .380 that Jim had given her felt heavy. As cold and lethal as it was reassuring. In a sudden flash, she knew she could kill Najma. In the same instant came another flash of understanding for Jim. Her mind focused. She would protect her boy and kill if she needed to.

'That Rosie growling,' yelled Pedro. 'She protect us.' Then a shot rang out and the growling stopped. Before Heather could stop him, Pedro pulled away and ran toward the house.

The instant the Citation stopped moving, a fuel truck pulled next to it. A dangerous move but the pilot had demanded a hot fueling. The air force men stood on ladders, looking nervous as they pumped fuel. The pilot had ordered exactly enough fuel to get to the Methow Valley and then to Fort Lewis safely. The driver gave a thumbs-up and backed away fast as the plane started to move.

The Citation demanded urgent clearance to taxi and emergency departure. He was already racing down the taxiway when he was cleared.

The pilot picked up speed down the taxiway, glanced to his left for landing planes and without slowing at the hold-line, turned onto the runway and pushed the throttles forward. Over the radio, departure control said sarcastically, 'Um, no hesitation cleared for takeoff,' and then mumbled under his breath, 'that lunatic is going to be grounded,' as he watched the jet disappear to the northwest.

Once they reached cruising speed, it would be less than twenty minutes to Winthrop's Methow Valley State airport. The pilot calculated that 18,000 feet would be optimal to get there and get down in the shortest interval. True to his word, he was getting there as fast as humanly possible. What he had done could cost him a dressing down but he would deal with it later.

Jim sat still, except that he kept biting his nails and pinching his lip with his index finger and thumb. Strange thoughts always popped into his mind in times like this. A defense mechanism when he could do nothing.

He always wondered what microbes lurked under the nails he gnawed but was unable to stop the habit. His mind wandered, he could easily culture them but he never was that interested in the lab. Heather told him over and over to stop biting his nails and use a clipper but he never felt like carrying one. And the truth was for some reason he enjoyed it. He disliked it when they became too long.

Then he focused his mind, assessing what was happening

with the general, seeing the canyon, now a battlefield, with Heather and Pedro right in the middle. He knew, however, that there was nothing he could plan. He would react to the situation when there. Why hadn't he seen this eventuality? It was his fault. Their troubled relationship was his fault. He stifled an angry emotion aimed at himself.

Pedro ran down the steep hill toward the house. His speed picked up and he tripped, tumbling onto the upper deck. His arm was bleeding and he didn't care. Images of his family, his old yellow mutt raced through his brain. Rosie had replaced all of them in his mind with good thoughts and happiness. Without her, those brutal images might never die.

The Citation curved in low over the town of Twisp, shaking buildings with its two hundred miles per hour approach to the mile-long number nine runway. The pilot raised the wind spoilers along with pulling up the nose, dropping his speed to one hundred thirty, nose high, the wheels smoked as they touched the runway.

The pilot had floated onto the runway within feet of its start and well before the normal landing hashes. He raised spoilers and jammed the brake pedals toward the cowling. With smoke still blowing from the tires, the sleek plane careened off the center taxiway.

'Green hangar, third on the left.' Jim had his hand on the door and dropped the steps with the plane still moving. He jumped out, followed by Brush and Neilly. Jim opened a padlock and ran to the Enstrom while Neilly and Brush pushed the large doors back.

One man tossed a duffel onto the Enstrom seat. Jim jumped in and started the engine while three men pushed it out of the hangar. Brush expertly undid one outside door and dropped it with its so far unscratched Plexi to the concrete and then ran to the pilot's side and unhooked it just as Jim engaged the main blade and started to spool up.

Then Brush ran to the Suburban and grabbed the key under the mat. As he ran back to the Enstrom he winked and tossed the key to Glenda. She gave him a stern look and mouthed, *Take care of yourself, mister,* then yelled back as she ran to the Suburban. 'I'll be right behind you.'

Neilly jumped into the front of Jim's Suburban, followed by seven of his team. Techie Tom was still inside the Citation charged with taking care of communications. The three men pushing the helicopter would stay and secure the area. Glenda jumped in the driver's side, pushed the key in the ignition and without bothering to close the door jammed the accelerator to the floor.

'Grab us M16's and ammo belts. In a minute the dust will settle. We need to get out now,' as another shot from above them echoed off the canyon walls. Sergeant Mason didn't hesitate. He bolted over the front seat grabbing a large duffel bag that contained the M16's ammo and several more weapons. The general kicked at the door on Mason's side. His side was jammed into the dirt. The door latch broke and he pushed the door open climbing up and out.

Sergeant Mason tossed the duffel over the seat and up onto the door's edge. The general grabbed it and Mason, athletic for his age, swung over the seat and jumped up and out the door. 'No place to go. The dust is settling down and it's mostly flat out there. We're sitting ducks.'

'We hunker down here,' he said to Mason and also into the mic that was stretched to its limit from inside the chopper. They edged back under the chopper as best they could. 'You have binocs in there, Sergeant?'

'Sorry, sir, no. There's some in back.'

'Stay put. We don't need them,' Will said, as the dust started to settle down exposing them to whoever had been shooting.

'You hear me, Gonzalo?' said Lazaro into his radio. Nothing but silence.

'Shit, stupid fucking radio-phone, idiot,' said Lazaro. Then he called Alva. Nothing. He looked at his handset wondering if something was wrong with it. Nothing was going right and all because the loco woman charged off on her own. The downed helicopter would have radioed for help. There were more men on the ranch than he had been told. *Stupidos.* The snipers should have spotted them earlier. He would kill the two snipers for not doing their job along with Gonzalo. In his mind he was lining them up and shooting them.

Lazaro's cell phone rang. He picked it up and tossed the radio-phone onto the dash. He reluctantly answered, knowing it was Guillermo.

Pedro ran around the front of the house. Lying just outside the door was a man in a pool of blood, his throat torn open. Next to him Pedro's best friend lay not moving. Pedro yelled and ran to Rosie. He was only a few feet away with tears streaming down when she raised her head a few inches and her big tail beat the ground twice. Then she let her head settle down and her eyes closed.

It felt as though a hot poker had been thrust into his left arm. He fell back on the porch with Shuskin struggling to move backward as Nusmen crashed onto him. His jacket sleeve turned red.

He felt nothing at first. Then pain set in.

Shuskin looked at the wound and then up the valley toward the ridge. He knew the shot had come from that direction. He needed to get Nusmen inside, out of sight.

Just as Duane remembered Korea, an older memory worked its way into Shuskin's mind.

'No worry,' shouted Shuskin as he jerked on Nusmen's coat.

'Stop, stop it. You're killing me.'

Luckily, Shuskin's old body found the strength to drag his new friend toward the door just as the wood splintered at Nusmen's feet. As he got him inside, a bullet tore through the cabin wall shattering a jar on a shelf just above his head. The small homesteaders cabin offered little protection from the sniper's heavy caliber bullets.

Chapter 65

Najma drove up the airport approach road just as the jet taxied in front of a green metal hangar and its engines slowed. Before it stopped, a door opened and steps were dropped and the colonel ran down and then across the blacktop to the metal-sided hangar.

Before she could pull behind the next hangar for cover, several more heavily armed men raced down the steps following the colonel.

Well behind Najma, Lazaro told Esteban to pull to the side of the road. He counted fourteen running into the hangar. Seconds later, a black Suburban raced out straining under its heavy load of Neilly's men, with Glenda at the wheel. A few seconds after that, three men pushed a small white helicopter onto the tarmac.

'Duck,' yelled Lazaro as the Suburban, engine roaring, sped by his car. He lifted up and saw that Najma was already out of her car and moving toward the helicopter. 'Down to her car. Move it, fast.' If Lazaro killed the colonel and the general was dead in the helicopter, and then he dealt with Najma, he could salvage this. Otherwise Guillermo would be lining him up against a wall.

'Ben, get me that 30-30 off the Mule.'

'I'll get it but can't shoot that far with no 30-30,' said Ben.

'I knows. We's not shootin nothen down below, we's going up above us.'

Duane knew there was nothing they could do for Heather or the downed helicopter, but he could try to take care of whoever was above them with a big enough rifle to shoot all the way down the canyon. His old limbs pushed him up the mountainside, through the big pines with the determination of the twenty-year-old that had fought bitter cold and snow in the mountains of Korea.

Carter's Black Hawk lifted above the ridge, not exposing its full fuselage. Just high enough for Carter and the pilot to observe. The door was open, the fifty caliber manned and ready. Several faces looked out at the ridgetop. Suddenly one hole and then another ripped through the chopper's side.

'Drop behind the ridge,' yelled Carter.

'I saw him, Captain. He's at your one o'clock just over the ridge in a little depression,' said the corporal on the fifty.

'Move back west a hundred meters. Get some speed up, put the tango at our eleven o'clock when you crest this dirt pile. Waste that mother, Corporal.'

The Black Hawk lowered its nose and picked up speed racing toward the ridge, just as Jim and Brush had with Pedro several days ago. They crested the ridge at eighty knots and floated up and over the edge. The fifty thunked rounds with tracers racing red toward the target. The depression where the sniper lay on Noname Ridge erupted in dust and rock chips, bone and flesh as the heavy rounds churned the dirt and the sniper's body.

Another round tore through the windshield, just missing the pilot. Several eyes looked east toward Coyote Ridge. Then the door gunner slumped in his harness, blood oozing from his chest and mouth.

'Take it down,' yelled Carter. 'Get below the hill by the general's bird.'

Ben ran up to Duane, as he climbed, holding the lever action

Winchester. It was well worn. Bright metal showed here and there where the bluing had worn off. The sight had been a peep sight with a tiny center. Duane had long ago removed the centerpiece leaving a large ring. His eyesight wasn't so good: centering the forward blade in the larger ring worked for him and he thought it was maybe even better. His old eyes seemed to naturally center it and he could hit some things better than he could before.

They moved up and up through large pines. Tan and brown bark in odd shapes clung to the large trunks. The bark near the ground was blackened by past fires.

They heard a rifle shot and moved carefully up. 'There he is,' said Ben.

'Where?'

'See that rock outcrop with the bushes in front? Right on the edge of those big trees.'

'Still can't see nobody. You take the rifle and shoot just like we taught you to shoot at deer. Both eyes open, take your time and squeeze.'

Ben took the short-barreled Winchester. 'Is it loaded?'

'Crack the lever and see.'

Ben could see a brass case inside and pulled the lever closed again. Then he pulled the hammer back as he lay on the ground looking up toward the rock outcrop. He aimed and when he thought he could see something move behind the brush just above the rock, he squeezed the trigger.

'You get him?'

'I think maybe.'

'Wait a spell and see ifen he shoots or moves.'

'I think I might have hit him.'

They waited for a minute and heard nothing.

'Let's look then,' said Duane.

They walked slowly toward the outcrop. Nothing moved. They

moved around it. Sitting on the ground was a man wearing green and brown camouflage holding a pistol aimed straight at them. His skin was dark and he grinned. Duane could feel it. He was going to shoot. Duane jumped in front of young Ben just as the man pulled the trigger on the .45-caliber Colt pistol. The bullet tore into Duane's chest tearing through his aorta and out his back. Blood spurted for seconds while the big muscle pumped blood out the hole in his chest. He fell lifeless, not far from the mountaintop he had looked at for so many years, rising high above Wolf Canyon Ranch: Wolf Mountain.

With Pedro a dozen feet ahead already, Heather told Lola to stay put and she ran after him. She held the small black World War II Walther automatic in her right hand as she jumped big steps down the hill and onto the upper deck. Lola had no intention of staying on her own. She went as fast as her stout short legs could run down the hill to the house but far behind the long-legged athletic Heather.

Another of Gonzalo's men made it into the aspens just below the house. He carefully peered through wild roses as a small boy dropped to the ground by a huge animal just beyond a dead man. He started through the bushes toward them just as Heather came around the corner not more than twenty feet away from the man.

Instantly their eyes met. The man lifted a rifle. Having a son to protect had changed her thought process. She immediately went into a two-hand stance like Jim had showed her many times and with both eyes open, pointed the gun at the man. She pulled the trigger over and over, until it was empty, even as the man lay bleeding not more than ten feet from Pedro.

'He dead, Mama. Rosie too,' Then the boy burst into convulsive sobs his head on the dog's chest. Heather ran to him, wrapped her arm around him and tried to pull him to her. He wouldn't move from Rosie. Heather put her hand on the big dog's head to say goodbye and a golden eye opened.

'She's alive, Pedro.'

Techie went back inside the Citation. He had agreed to monitor the radio and be available if Sheilla needed help with her computers or communication. He didn't like missing out on a good fight.

Carter's Black Hawk skidded to a stop next to the general's crumpled helicopter. Two men jumped out on the opposite side, kneeling with rifles up. The general and Frank Mason ran to the chopper. The other two men jumped back inside and it lifted off with its nose so low that the front edge of the blades beat only inches from grass and dirt.

At the head of the canyon and in the shadows of Wolf Mountain, Gonzalo's men ran from the pine forest into the upper fields toward the house. Gonzalo was exhausted trying to keep up. He stopped at the edge of the trees. From his new vantage point, he could better see the odd-shaped house, cut into the hill on one side with the aspens below and a large wall of windows reflecting the sun.

Behind the house a helicopter appeared, nose pointed down at a steep angle and lifted toward the house. He could see it was a gunship. If his men could shoot it down, they had more than enough men to fight. His legs were hurting though. *Sit here and watch the battle,* he decided.

Duane's lunge knocked Ben to the ground. The heavy .45 caliber bullet exiting Duane's back passed inches from Ben as they both fell. Somehow, Ben managed to hold on to the rifle. He looked at his lifeless friend who had been more like a father or grandfather to him after Craig was killed. Was every father to be killed before his eyes? Anger boiled inside him mixing with adrenaline.

He rolled to his left toward the rocks and brought the rifle up just as the man rose above the rock. Ben fired, racked another round, and fired again and again. His first shot struck the man in the neck. The next three rounds missed the man. It didn't matter, the first bullet did its damage, killing Guillermo's last sniper. Ben crawled back to Duane with tears flooding down his cheeks. Salty water leaving his body, just as the adrenaline spent its effect. He collapsed next to Duane hearing and seeing nothing. Duane's still warm body was the only comfort he felt.

Jim pulled in power. The skids wobbled and tapped the asphalt as it started to lift. Brush was pulling grenades out of the duffel and a new issue MP7 that Neilly's SF were using. He nodded appreciatively when a movement caught his eye. Not more than a dozen feet away by the edge of the hangar stood Najma with a small fat rifle pointed at them. The helicopter was lifting into the air when Jim spotted her. She dipped her rifle down a few inches, indicating for him to stay on the ground.

From this distance if he tried to take off she couldn't miss hitting one of them. Instinct took over. He twisted the throttle hard and jammed his left foot on the rudder. Abruptly the tail swung to the left putting it between them and Najma.

She took careful aim at the tail rotor, expecting him to fly away from her to escape, as any normal pilot would do. Suddenly the helicopter was coming straight back at her. Its lethal tail blade spinning like a giant buzz saw directly toward her.

The Black Hawk lifted high to have a view of the battlefield. They saw the three civilians by the house. A man was only twenty yards from them in front of the house on a dirt path. He was between the Black Hawk and Heather, making it impossible to safely fire the fifty caliber or its Gatling guns.

As they flew toward the house, they saw more men approaching from up the canyon, getting close to a small llama shelter behind the house. Two llamas stood with their heads held high, defending their pasture against the intruders, just as they had done with the black bear.

'First,' boomed the general, 'take this new fandangled piece of metal down and scrape that man off that path. Then get six men off this side of the house. Mason, you're out too, check that man and secure the civilians.'

The Black Hawk's pilot flew straight at the man, trying his best to hit him with a skid backed up by nearly ten thousand pounds of metal. They heard noises as the skid scraped the rocks and dirt. The end of its blades chopped small limbs off the aspen trees in front of the house.

He couldn't see through the dust plume to tell if he had hit the man.

The helicopter lifted and the general grinned through the dust, giving a thumbs-up to Heather to reassure her. The helicopter quickly moved a hundred feet and touched down in the grassy flat in front of the house.

The general pointed to six of the SWAT team, 'Out now. Mason, you too. Check that man and secure the civilians.' Sergeant Frank Mason flipped a salute and leapt out of the chopper.

'After the drop below the house, circle back behind the knoll. Come across to the barn. Drop two men behind the barn.' The general didn't need to tell his well-trained men to move to opposite ends of the barn. Everyone understood the deployment logic.

Captain Carter didn't say anything. He knew the general had more combat time and flanking was a smart move. They would have a height advantage and the sun was of no consequence sitting high in the sky. Besides his battle experience, the general was his commanding officer and a few pay grades higher than his company grade status. Keeping his mouth shut was not just the best option, but the only option.

'After the men are out, move back over above the house. We'll have a clear field of fire up the canyon.'

Carter looked up the canyon and added quickly over the intercom, 'Estimate twenty hostiles.'

The helicopter barely stopped, five feet off the ground, thirty yards in front of the house, while six men exited followed by Sergeant Mason. The Black Hawk tipped its nose down, turned, and circled back undercover of the knoll.

Gonzalo watched the Black Hawk nearly colliding with the ground, chopping branches off a small aspen tree with its four blades. Leaves, dirt, and debris spun in the air. The helicopter drifted right, hovering below the house, while six men jumped to the ground and fanned out, staying out of sight below the level of the sagebrush tops, as they moved up the canyon through the aspens, past Heather.

A seventh man didn't crouch as he ran straight up the hill toward the spot where the Black Hawk had just left its mark with the chopper's skid. Then Gonzalo spotted the man lying alongside a gouge in the ground. *Macho pilot,* he thought.

Gonzalo hadn't risen to the level that he had in the cartel for being dumb. He was abrasive and crude and although he was no tactician, nevertheless he was not so stupid that he couldn't see the strategy unfolding. The army men spread out below the knoll and into the aspens by the house. They moved with precision as they advanced toward his men. The Black Hawk turned out to its right, gaining speed and moved back over the general's downed Huey, using the knoll as cover from his men's rifles.

It crested the ridge, above the plateau. *Now they would deposit men using the barn for cover,* he thought. Two men dropped out of the chopper, moved to opposite ends of the barn, flanking his cartel men from the high ground. Perhaps that was overcautious as the chopper could have easily hovered from a safe distance and annihilated his men with any of its weapons.

The Black Hawk flew east gaining speed and then when out of the cartel men's firing range, it swung in an arch turning back toward the house. It hung there menacingly; nose slightly down, with its rockets and Gatling guns pointed toward the overmatched cartel men. The door gunner covered their flank toward the knoll.

Gonzalo's mouth closed tight. He had thought this was going to be easy: his men against women, kids, and ranch hands. Then this helicopter appeared. He didn't recognize it as a gunship at first. Whoever commanded didn't take chances. In fights, things went wrong. This commander understood that well and if the chopper failed to do its job, the men on the ground had superior position. *Battle over,* Gonzalo said to himself. Time to leave.

Heather sat with Pedro and Lola brushing away dust and debris from the Black Hawk's encounter with the plateau; she smiled reassuringly at Pedro who looked at her with large brown saucer eyes. Lola grumbled and swatted at her clothes. 'We are safe now.'

'Mama, you saved me and Rosie from that man. I proud of you.'

The general looked back toward the hillside trail and could see a deep furrow where the thick steel skid had dug into the friable soil and dry plants. A body lay just beyond the gouge. Then it moved.

Just below, Sergeant Mason ran up the hill. *I miss it. I love it,* Sergeant Mason chanted to himself. He charged up the hill feeling like he had shed twenty years, doing what he loved as a twenty-year-old. Storming toward the enemy with his comrades. Even if this one was dead. He let out a blood-curdling yell as he ran straight at the man. First take care of the man and then the colonel's family.

Mason's yell would have raised bumps of terror on most people. The cartel man was young, battle tested, and with limited hearing. He paid no attention to what was to him a muted noise. Instead, he cursed having had the gringo woman in his sights. It would have made his reputation to kill one of the targets. A fraction of a second more and from this short distance his bullet would have hit her in the head. It didn't happen; he had to roll away from the approaching helicopter and his bullet went wide of its mark. With all the noise, typical of a firefight, Heather never knew the bullet had passed by her head.

Now Felipe, the young cartel soldier, watched some crazy person running up the hill into the settling dust, yelling. Felipe stared at the black apparition, feeling slightly stunned from the near encounter with the helicopter and the rock chips and dirt embedded in his face that had hit him like a shotgun blast. He managed to lift his M16 as he lay on the ground and fired two wild shots into the charging man.

Master Sergeant Frank Mason's momentum carried him undaunted for several feet, even as the bullets tumbled and tore through his body. Mason, slowed, stumbled, and fell, his knees hitting the ground as he looked straight ahead at this ragtag Mexican kid only two meters away. To the kid's amazement, white teeth against his chocolate brown face appeared then turned to a wide grin before he fell, face forward, into the dirt. His lower legs pointed straight up as if pulled by an invisible string as his torso pitched forward and then they dropped back, toes down, onto the dry tan soil.

Felipe crossed himself.

Chapter 66

The general had given Heather a reassuring thumbs up through the windscreen that was supposed to mean *don't worry*. Even though her adrenaline was dissipating after she had shot the attacker in the woods; watching the soldier get killed injected a second dose into her bloodstream.

Carter's ground team was too low in the canyon to see the man that just shot Mason. Felipe sat up, got on his knees, and looked toward the house.

Heather grabbed the rifle of the dead man lying next to Rosie and pointed it toward Sergeant Mason's killer. Lola grimaced and put her hands over her ears. Pedro just stared at his mother. The man staggered to his feet and started to point his gun toward them. Heather pulled hard on the trigger of the M16, emptying the remaining twenty-six rounds in the direction of the man. She didn't know the first thing about automatic weapons but luck was with her: she had been holding the gun loosely and pointing low to the left—the gun bucked up to the right as she fired, killing him.

A wide eyed Pedro said, 'You killed another one, Mama.' With wild eyes she looked back at him. Then she threw the gun down and clutched him—barely noticing the dead man, only inches away, his bloody throat tenuously attached to his neck. Tears streamed down her face. Adrenaline, once again coursing through her veins after killing a second man. Pedro strained to pull her arms away and said, 'We have to get Rosie to the hospital.'

The tail rotor blades sheared off as they struck the side of the hangar and sent lethal shards of metal flying. Najma reacted instantly as soon as it registered that the helicopter was coming at her instead of flying away. She had him and he managed to slip out of her grasp again.

Playing against Johnson was like a chess game. She realized his next move would be to bail out on the ground with weapons pointed her way. The three Special Forces men started to move toward the noise and the hangar in a crouch.

Najma ran along the hangar and then jumped into a ditch just behind the access road running behind the hangars.

Brush already had weapons out expecting to go to the ranch. The second Jim rammed the tail of his new Enstrom into the wall, Brush, all in one motion, undid his harness, checked to see if a round was chambered, and jumped from the helicopter. Jim didn't have time to check the MP7 that Brush had pulled out for him but he undid his harness with his left hand as he pulled the cyclic back with his right. He turned the throttle off as he jumped to the hard cement floor landing in a crouched position facing the broken tail of his new Enstrom. Najma was gone. He signaled to Brush to go right and he went to the left edge of the hangar.

From down the tarmac, shots erupted and he turned to see two of the three Special Forces guys go down. Najma was not alone.

Lazaro directed Esteban and Carlos to the right while he and the fourth man ran directly ahead toward the jet. Neilly's three Special Forces had been walking casually toward the jet but turned abruptly as the Enstrom tore into the hangar. They turned and sprinted to aid Jim and Brush, thinking that the helicopter had malfunctioned. Lazaro and Esteban were on their flank and opened fire on them, killing two instantly.

The third SF man dropped prone and placed well-aimed rounds

at the attackers. He killed Lazaro's fourth man. Then a bullet caught him in the leg, then a round hit the concrete blinding him.

Techie stepped into the jet's door and opened fire on Esteban and Carlos. They ran behind the metal hangar but Techie paced the target. It easily passed through the lightweight metal killing Esteban. Lazaro, with a new clip and on full automatic, unloaded on Techie who dove back inside the plane. Blood dripped from his right forearm as he clumsily grabbed the radio mic to call Neilly.

Jim raced to the back outside corner of the hangar on the opposite side from Brush. He glanced behind him toward the gunfire on the tarmac. They both peered around the corner and the only thing they saw were each other's heads peering back from opposite sides of the hangar.

Jim motioned for Brush to move to the next hangar down. Jim turned again toward the front where the gunshots had now stopped. *Najma somewhere to the front and someone behind.* Assisting the SF was a priority. As he neared his broken helicopter he saw the three Special Forces on the ground and a Mexican running to the plane. He sighted, squeezed; Carlos flopped spread-eagle onto the tarmac.

Just as he fired the round killing Carlos, a small lead bullet punched its way into Jim's side. Najma had bided her time, waiting for Brush to disappear around a corner and then with her twenty-two shot Jim and then fired a hasty second shot creasing his head. If it had been a heavier caliber, she might have killed him, but the small twenty-two caliber bullet ricocheted off his skull.

Within seconds Brush began firing at Najma. She dropped in the ditch. Brush pulled out one of the grenades he had pocketed. He pulled the pin, counted to three and tossed it into the ditch where Najma had just fired from.

Najma almost had second sight in firefights and as was usual for her, did the unexpected. She had quickly crawled out of the ditch and behind a low rock, moving toward Brush not away from him. She was just beyond the grenade's killing range, even so the explosion threw her sideways. Blood trickled from her face and one ear. Slightly dazed, she peered over the edge. Brush was rushing straight at her old position. As he closed in, he realized she was no longer there. As he stopped, searching for her, Najma aimed carefully at his head and squeezed the trigger.

The black Suburban lifted slightly in the air as it came over the hill full throttle in front of the cabin. Shuskin had pulled Nusmen into the cabin with Nusmen yelling all the time for him to stop.

'You're hurting me, old man. Stop pulling at me. You are going to kill me!'

'You not going to die. Not bad enough wounded.'

'So you say, you crazy old fool. How do you know anyway?'

Glenda skidded the Suburban to a stop next to the cabin. Six heavily armed men and three women jumped out, hitting the ground and pointing rifles at the cabin. Four of the men faced in opposite directions protecting their flanks and rear. Gaston Reese motioned Marilyn and Jeff to the cabin, then yelled, 'Come outta there, hands up.'

Nusmen yelled back, 'I can't. I'm shot,' and then looked at Shuskin and added, 'And I'm dying.'

By the time Nusmen had responded, Marilyn Cutter and Jeff were on two sides of the cabin carefully peering in. 'It's an old man and the geekie guy that spread the bacteria,' said Marilyn.

Gaston stood holding his MP7 forward, walked to the cabin porch, looking in the door at the wounded Nusmen and the old transient. 'Jeff, get him patched up and stay here. Move out. Fleur, you cover our right flank and move up along the trees, then check for anyone needing attention. Joe, check out the barn and then come up on the high ground.'

Then he looked up the canyon toward the house and heard the

beat of the Black Hawk and the Gatling gun. 'The rest load up. Glenda, let's move it. Drop us out along the road below the house.'

The general surveyed the field and told the pilot, 'Put some rounds just over them.' The Gatling gun spun to life. Then he turned on the outside speaker and boomed. 'Put down your weapons and hands over your heads.' The loudspeaker on full volume, echoed back and forth across the canyon. 'You have to a count of two. One...' Most dropped their weapons and held their hands in the air before he got to two. Three chose to fire at the helicopter. Carter's men nearly instantly eliminated the three shooters before the chopper's pilot even knew they had been fired at.

Jim's dazed mind flashed through scenarios as he lay by the side of the hangar...

Get around the corner, Jim ordered himself. As he pulled his body under the mangled hangar door and drooping tail rotor, he evaluated the possibilities. He pulled himself backward toward the back of the hangar and got behind his red and silver oversized tool chest. Barely conscious, he strained to focus on the front of the hangar.

Gonzalo had trudged back up toward the Loup Loup ski area. Maybe some of his men would be behind him. He pushed the transmit button on his radio. No response. Then he tried calling Lazaro. Again no response. 'Any asshole out there!' he yelled. *What the fuck, I don't give a shit,* he said to himself. Fuck this loco operation.

Then his radio crackled to life and a voice said, 'Who's speaking?'

'Huh, ah Gonzalo. Who the fuck is this?'

'Where are you now, Gonzalo?' the voice said; he assumed it must be one of the men with Lazaro.

'Above the ranch,' he lied. 'Watching our men get killed is where I am.'

'Cool. A shame that, well, never mind, they deserve it.'

'Huh?'

'The least of your problems…ah, Gonzalo, is it? I now have a fix on your radio position. Oh, thanks for answering by the way. The US Army should be there soon to arrest you or maybe shoot you,' said Jason, five-knuckling Jake with a big grin. 'Cool, man. We hacked the famous hacker. The Wolf Pack is king of the digital mountain.'

The Wolf Pack not only managed to get back up and running but took over the communications from the Russian hacker, aka Griswald. They listened in for a minute and started calling the cartel members just for the fun of it.

Gonzalo couldn't believe what he heard and started to move up the trail as fast as he could, back to the cars. *Odio los americanos blancos,* he said over and over to himself. Smart-ass Americanos. He huffed and grumbled his way along the dusty trail. The air force had launched spotter planes at Sheilla's request. The Wenatchee National Guard had flown soldiers that were training close by to the ski area parking lot, the old wildlife house, and the lower ranch entrance.

'Computers and comms all back up and running, General,' said Sheilla. 'Wolf Pack fixed it. It seems our old friend in Mexico is also up and running and tried to shut us down. I haven't been able to contact Jim.'

'Things are about wrapped up here. Jim and Brush should have been here by now,' said the general sensing trouble.

The general looked down the canyon toward the cabin and saw the remains of a dust cloud drifting far off the road. 'Might be them here now.'

'General, Neilly. I've got nine others with me at the cabin. Jim and Brush were taking the helicopter. They should have been here a long time ago.'

Then a call came in from Techie Tom, 'Under attack, casualties.'

'Shit!' responded the general.

Lazaro peered into the hangar and seeing no one quickly walked across the front to the far side. Through blurry eyes, Jim forced his mind to focus and shot Lazaro in the head. The effort took its toll as his mind slipped further toward unconsciousness. From somewhere another round hit him. He barely felt it.

Najma had peered through a small hole in the metal and seen Jim lying on the floor. She could not see Lazaro but watched through the pinhole as Jim squeezed the trigger. She fired two shots through the hangar's side with her 9mm Glock. She could tell at least one of the shots hit its target as his body lurched.

Chapter 67

Najma, still slightly dazed and trickling blood, looked onto the tarmac and could only see bodies. She tried to focus on the inside of the hangar where her enemy lay perhaps dead. Just then a bullet tore through her shoulder and another passed close to her head. She turned toward the plane and fired her Glock at the man. Three shots in quick succession. Techie dropped back onto the tarmac. Barely able to lift his rifle. He had never been any good using his left hand, nevertheless he had tried to shoot using his left and his accuracy had been off.

Najma ducked under the crumpled metal that had been the Enstrom's tail and dropped onto one knee. Weak and dazed, she surveyed the hangar, noting Lazaro crumpled to her right. Her eyes flashed resolve, knowing Jim lay just a short distance away. As long as he died, she would win. No matter the cost. She stood, weaving slightly on unsteady legs and moved toward the tool chest, eyes staring, alert to any movement.

Najma rounded the red metal tool chest. Jim lay there, not moving, blood puddling on the glossy gray floor on both sides of his body. She felt a slight disappointment. She wanted him to know he had been defeated by her. She dropped to her knees next to him and then slumped to her side. Her face not more than two feet from his. She watched his face and saw a small movement. She pulled out her two-sided knife moving it to his throat. She willed him to open his eyes. She needed to look into the eyes of the one man that had bested her. The one man she could respect.

She moved the point of the blade to his cheek and caressed it with the tip. His eyelids fluttered and he opened his eyes. Both their minds were fuzzy and for a second they just looked into each other's eyes like lovers.

Jim could feel the tip of the blade. *Why had she hesitated?* he wondered. Why was she laying beside him? Why had she not shot him?

Najma had not seen his right hand under his side holding a small silver pistol. Jim had carried the small twenty-five automatic during and since Vietnam. He had never used it there or anywhere else. He squeezed the trigger once, then two more times before the light faded from his blue eyes.

Epilogue

Minutes later...

'Get your men to an LZ by the cabin, no delay. I'll pick you up,' ordered the general. 'Carter, wrap it up here.' The pilot dropped toward the ground and Carter jumped out just as the helicopter dipped its nose down the canyon toward Neilly.

Neilly called his technician, Tom Bryant, aka Techie, and got no response. Sheilla said his radio was working. Within minutes the Black Hawk crested a hill with the airport stretched out in front. The jet came into view. They did a fast pass over and saw bodies on the tarmac and several more around the hangars.

'No movement. Wait, one of the men on the ground has his arm up...it's Techie.'

Glenda couldn't get to the landing zone before the general left. She yelled at Jeff to stay at the cabin. She ran to the Suburban and got there about the same time as Marilyn, Gaston, and Joe. She floored the accelerator and they half flew, half bounded down the canyon road toward Beaver Creek Road. She raced straight across and up the hill, the shortest route to the airport, Balky Hill Road. Sliding her way around gravel corners and jamming on the brakes and pumping the accelerator, Glenda pushed the Suburban to the edge. Gaston looked at

Marilyn and raised his eyebrows. She responded with a look that said, *Isn't life exciting!*

'Set down here.' The general chose to set the helicopter down about a hundred yards up the hangar line. 'Sheilla, call the special response group at Fairchild.'

'Already done, sir.'

'Neilly, it's all yours. I'll take the door gun and give you support if you need it.'

They carefully moved to the bodies. Fleur started to work on Techie. Gaston entered the plane and found that the pilot was unhurt but unconscious. He had tried to drop to the floor when the shooting started, and apparently had knocked himself out.

Neilly moved cautiously around the hangars, checking for signs of life. Then Neilly and Mac entered Jim's hangar, stepping around the remains of the white Enstrom. A man was dead near the front. Then they saw another body near the back. As they rapidly moved closer, they could see it was Jim surrounded by blood.

'Shit. Get Fleur in here,' he shouted at Mac. 'General,' Neilly said as he moved toward Jim. He knelt by him and pulled out a small metal mirror. 'He's still breathing but has lost a lot of blood.'

Over the radio, 'Brush is behind the hangar. Not moving, we are almost to him.'

'Careful,' said Neilly. 'There's blood from someone else next to Jim.'

'We're clear, sir. Only two locals.'

The black Suburban slid to a stop just short of Techie. Glenda ran toward the hangar and then around the side and directly to Brush. She had been listening just as had Sheilla and Misa. All three women were speechless.

Glenda dropped to her knees. 'You dumb Canuck,' as she softly cradled him. He gurgled and some blood drooled down his chin. Without opening his eyes, Brush said, 'Not dumb enough to leave you.'

Hours later...

The army had a Sikorsky flown over for the general. 'You have the controls, Marilyn,' he said.

'Your new bird, General.'

'Not for long. I'll find another Huey.'

Weeks later...

Guillermo sat alone on the patio, drinking his third gin and tonic. Alva would meet an unpleasant death when he found him. But Guillermo did not know the Israeli assassin's body was undiscovered lying in the sagebrush near Wolf Canyon Ranch. At least what was left of him when the eagles and coyotes had had their fill. The remainder was quickly disappearing with all manner of crawling and flying insects.

It wasn't as if one piece of the plan fell apart at a time, causing it to fail. That he could have understood. But not one thing in Guillermo's carefully thought- out plan had worked. His enemies were alive. The Americans knew it was him behind the attack.

He had wasted millions and only made bigger enemies out of the US government, the CIA, and General Crystal. The United States president personally ordered the DEA and the Mexican government to target him and his cartel operations.

Months later...

An olive drab Huey sat in a small lush-green grass area below the house at Wolf Canyon Ranch. Inside the house, soft music from *Bridges of Madison County* played in the background, a fire glowed and danced red and orange in the oversized log fireplace.

Pedro sat on the floor with his arm draped over Rosie-O-Twisp. She had defended her family well and taken a bullet in her chest. For that Heather rewarded her with the run of the house.

It was a full house. Jim and Brush sat in chairs still wearing casts and bandages. They were both recovering, and for Jim's part, from the most serious wounds he had ever received. Brush had received his first wound, ending his long bullet-immune lucky streak. They were surrounded by Heather, Glenda, Misa, Sheilla, Vidya, Nusmen, Shuskin, and the general. Lola hovered about watching over Jim just as she would have done for her child.

'Anything on Najma?' asked Jim, knowing that Heather had a new attitude and he did not need to shelter her the same way anymore.

'Nothing other than they found the car she used off the Nighthawk Road.'

'Not surprising,' said Glenda. 'She killed the border guard at the Nighthawk crossing into Canada.'

'After that she disappeared over the border,' added Sheilla. 'After the killing the border guard, she didn't leave her usual bloody trail for me to follow.'

'We're not going to give up tracking her,' said Vidya. 'We'll recognize her brand of killing sooner or later. She will not be able to restrain herself from her ugly behavior for long.'

The general looked approvingly at Misa and Vidya. 'Anything you need, Sheilla will get it for you. I want you to be comfortable in your new home at BWC,' said General Will Crystal. All heads turned toward Misa and Vidya, and Jim said, 'Glad to have you with us.'

The general lifted his wineglass. 'Here's to life, health, and the pursuit of villains.'

Nusmen chimed in, 'And bacteria.'

Heather picked up the remote and changed the song to the Rolling Stones. 'Shuskin, you want to dance?'

Printed in Poland
by Amazon Fulfillment
Poland Sp. z o.o., Wrocław